CORRUPTS ABSOLUTELY

CORRUPTS ABSOLUTELY

ALEXA HUNT

A TOM DOHERTY ASSOCIATES BOOK

NEW YORK

This is a work of fiction. All the characters and events portrayed in this novel are either fictitious or are used fictitiously.

CORRUPTS ABSOLUTELY

Copyright © 2005 by Alexa Hunt

A Forge Book
Published by Tom Doherty Associates, LLC
175 Fifth Avenue
New York, NY 10010

www.tor.com

Forge® is a registered trademark of Tom Doherty Associates, LLC.

Library of Congress Cataloging-in-Publication Data

Hunt, Alexa.
    Corrupts absolutely / Alexa Hunt.—1st ed.
       p. cm.
    "A Tom Doherty Associates book."
    ISBN 0-765-31149-6 (alk. paper)
    EAN 978-0765-31149-8
     1. Government investigators—Crimes against—Fiction. 2. Drug traffic—
Fiction. 3. Journalists—Fiction. 4. Assassins—Fiction. I. Title.

PS3608.U57C67 2005
813'.6—dc22

                          2004057743

First Edition: April 2005

Printed in the United States of America

0 9 8 7 6 5 4 3 2 1

For Natalia Aponte,
an extraordinary editor who had the vision to believe in this book
and the skill to give me a key to unlock its highly complex backstory

ACKNOWLEDGMENTS

The idea for this story began back in 1998 when I envisioned a frightening alternative world in the near future and wrote a book. This was fiction, completed long before the tragedy of 9/11 and its aftermath cast a shadow across America. I never viewed *Corrupts Absolutely* as a cautionary tale, but perhaps it is.

Although most of the places in this book are real, the Iraqi War Memorial, Adair-Rawlfing, and "Little Lenny" are creations of my imagination. However, very recently a Fort Leonard Wood Annex, used for different purposes, has been constructed. The description of how the tactical nukes work is as accurate as I could make it, but there is sufficient controversy among civilian analysts to allow for literary license on my part. The same is true regarding the weapons, real and imagined, and their upgrades that the reader will encounter in this novel.

My husband, Jim, a former navy man and judo instructor, helped me choreograph the action sequences and did most of the prodigious military and technical research. Carol Reynard pulled a ton of material off the Internet for me, getting her computer shut down "for performing illegal acts" while trying to penetrate the labyrinth of government agencies.

My brother Roy C. Nehrt, who spent the last thirty-six years of his life immersed in politics inside the Beltway, provided invaluable insights and gave me guided tours of any site in the region I needed to see. He and his wife, Ginny, fed me wonderful meals after I spent my days walking the National Mall, visiting the Hoover Building and various war memorials, and riding the D.C. Metro to block out an underground shoot-out with drug dealers. I'll always miss you, Big Brother.

The Machias Bay Area Chamber of Commerce in Machias, Maine, went out of its way to provide me with maps and photos as well as answering dozens of questions about one of the few places in the story I was unable to visit. In Mazatlán, Mexico, everyone whom I interviewed was helpful, but I owe special thanks to my *pulmonia* driver Ramon for the wonderful guided tour on which I "found" Uncle Mac's house.

No manuscript sees the light of print before a great many people in New York contribute much time and effort. In addition to my wonderful editor, Natalia Aponte, I wish to thank Tom Doherty and all the folks at Tor Books. It has been a genuine pleasure working with you on *Corrupts Absolutely* and its forthcoming sequel. The same is true for my super agent, Nancy Yost, and the always gracious Julie Culver, who held down the fort when Nancy was out of town.

And speaking of gracious, I owe a huge debt of gratitude to many superstars who so generously took the time to read a newbie's book and offer words of praise: Sandra Brown, Stephen Coonts, Clive Cussler, Nelson DeMille, Eileen Dreyer, Tess Gerritsen, Tami Hoag, and Jon Land. I am honored to be working in the same genre with authors of such genius.

Power tends to corrupt and absolute power corrupts absolutely. There is no worse heresy than that the office sanctifies the holder of it . . .

—John Emerich Dalberg, Lord Acton

CORRUPTS ABSOLUTELY

CARTEL TARGETS FBI, DEA, JUDICIARY!

THOUSANDS MURDERED IN COORDINATED ASSASSINATIONS ACROSS NATION

August 9

WASHINGTON—The Hoover Bldg. came under siege midday when four armored-truckloads of Colombian Cartel assassins armed with assault rifles and rocket-propelled grenades broke through security, attacking FBI personnel in what appears to be a surgical strike. The agents targeted work on the special drug enforcement task force spearheading the arrest of key drug lords associated with Benito Zuloaga, strongman from Cali, Columbia. Zuloaga consolidated competing South American drug rings into a single cartel last year.

Civilians at the intersection of Ninth and Pennsylvania were also killed and injured as federal agents and terrorists exchanged fire in the uneven gun battle. No casualty figures are yet available, although nearby hospital emergency rooms report being inundated with wounded.

Federal judiciary and DEA officials have also been assassinated in similar attacks across the nation . . .

NATION'S JUSTICE SYSTEM IN DISARRAY

KEY INFORMATION CENTERS DESTROYED

August 9

WASHINGTON—In what appears to be an orchestrated military assault, four of the country's key centers directing the war on drugs were destroyed or severely damaged. Information Technology Centers in Butte, Mont., and Savannah, Ga., which provide data for FBI field investigations, were extensively damaged by truck bombs. The National Drug Intelligence Center in Johnstown, Pa., and the DEA's main operational center in El Paso, Tex., were virtually destroyed by similar explosions.

Reports of other attacks continue to pour in from across the country. At present, authorities are unable to determine the number of casualties, but early predictions range into the thousands . . .

A NATION UNDER ATTACK

August 9

NEW YORK—Today Manhattan erupted into a battlefield. At the Jacob K. Javits Federal Building a large group of armed men attempted to storm the lobby. In an intense gun battle they were driven back across Federal Plaza. At approximately the same time, the DEA field office on 10th Avenue was destroyed by gunmen wielding automatic weapons and lobbing hand grenades.

The firefights took place during lunch hour, with hundreds of panicked civilians on the streets caught in cross fires at both sites. "This was literally a 'Slaughter on 10th Avenue,'" said one injured bystander. Cars gridlocked and pedestrians ran for cover as bricks and debris from explosions rained down from the DEA office. The number of casualties involved has yet to be determined, although an NYPD source described the DEA raid as "a massacre."

These attacks are thought to be linked to other raids and assassinations across the nation. Mayor Sam Scapelli accused the Zuloaga Cartel. "They're responding to recent successes by local and federal authorities who have significantly curtailed Elevator sales," said the mayor. Elevator is the popular cocaine-Viagra combination that rushes to the brain with swift, often deadly results.

August 9

ST. LOUIS, MO.—The front steps of Thomas F. Eagleton Federal Building ran red with blood when three U.S. Circuit Court judges, two DEA agents and several U.S. marshals were gunned down. Men armed with automatic weapons opened fire, killing DEA agents Kenneth Seabold and Ernesto Ruiz, who were scheduled to testify in the well-publicized case against Colombian Cartel kingpin Alberto Sancho.

Also murdered were Judge Cybill Alvarez, trying Sancho's case, and Judges Thomas Kincaid and Albert Schnitzer, both active in the prosecution of Elevator operators in the bistate area. As yet unidentified courthouse workers and pedestrians on Broadway were also casualties . . .

August 9
DENVER, COL.—Fourth-grade students and their teacher on a field trip from Belmar Elementary School in Lakewood were caught in a hail of bullets as they approached the Denver Zoo. The class was walking along East 23rd Avenue when gunmen opened fire. The intended target was Judge Paul Hernandez of the 10th District Circuit Court, who was playing on the Municipal Golf Course directly across the street. Judge Hernandez, also killed along with two companions, has been labeled "Colorado's hanging judge for Elevator operators," to whom he's given maximum sentences.

Cartel assassins have been blamed for what a DPD source calls the "slaughter of the innocents." The names of children killed and injured has not been released pending notification of parents . . .

August 9
SAN FRANCISCO—"It's like Pearl Harbor all over again" was how a spokesman for Mayor May Reynolds characterized the wave of assassinations apparently carried out by the South American Cartel. Among the dead are Judges Alvin Wessel, Mortimer Kurtz, Juanita Estevez and Tom Dreyer, key players on the mayor's drug task force. Judge Dreyer's wife and two small children were also victims when a grenade was thrown into the family automobile by a Cartel operative.

An explosion destroying a local DEA field office has dealt a serious blow to city and state efforts to control drug "operators" peddling Elevator, the deadly cocaine-Viagra combination that's become the most widely used illegal narcotic across the U.S. Killed in that blast was Jules Denzer, the state's main witness against California "Elevator operator" Juan Rios. Three DEA agents, whose names are being withheld by the agency, also died in the explosion . . .

PRESIDENT DECLARES STATE OF EMERGENCY

CONVENES SPECIAL SESSION OF CONGRESS; CALLS FOR TROOPS TO RESTORE ORDER

August 10

WASHINGTON—President Lowrey has declared a state of national emergency and called out the National Guard and special antiterrorist units of the regular army to restore order as a panic-stricken nation demands protection from paramilitary gunmen roaming its streets. Congress will meet in special session as soon as there is a quorum in the Senate and House. Senators and representatives are having difficulty reaching the nation's capital since many airports have shut down because of fear of further Cartel activity.

They must deal with what the president describes as "the most heinous terrorist attack ever carried out on American soil." Lowrey went on to denounce Cartel boasts that they have crippled the U.S. government's ability to stop drug trafficking . . .

PRESIDENT, JOINT CHIEFS SAY STRIKE ON CARTEL WOULD INCITE WORSE RETALIATION

SOMMERVILLE, OTHERS IN PENTAGON, CONGRESS DISAGREE

August 11

WASHINGTON—Controversial three-star general Nathan Sommerville, backed by a small group within the Pentagon and numerous members of Congress, has proposed a surgical strike against the Colombian Cartel. President Lowrey and Gen. Howard McKinney, Chairman of the Joint Chiefs, rejected the option, citing hard intelligence that the newly consolidated Cartel possesses nuclear capabilities.

An anonymous CIA source confirmed that Cartel weaponry would enable them to decimate most of Central America and the U.S. Southwest. "Our missile defense systems might shield us and perhaps even Mexico and the rest of Central America," said McKinney. But the Chairman cited evidence that the U.S. and its allies to the south would still be vulnerable to Cartel PNDs (Portable Nuclear Devices), which are easily transported small nuclear bombs.

"I have been assured the mountainous terrain in Colombia would make conventional invasion an unacceptable risk," President Lowrey said, calling such a plan "Vietnam revisited."

Sommerville, nicknamed "Nuke 'Em Nate," has been under a cloud ever since he advocated using tactical nuclear weapons during the Second Iraqi War. Gen. John Kersch (Ret.) and Cols. Hoyt Brandies and Walter Bisset supported the idea of a nuclear strike against Cartel strongholds deep in the Andes. Congressional members from both parties who supported the plan . . .

SENATOR BLASTS CARTEL, ACCUSES ADMINISTRATION

August 11

DETROIT, MICH.—"They've underestimated us. Citizens won't stand by while Cartel thugs gun down children. We will fight back," said Sen. Wade Samson, D-Mich. En route to Washington, the senator has denounced President Lowrey's handling of the catastrophic attacks by Cartel forces that have left undetermined thousands of government agents and officials, as well as innocent civilians, dead or wounded. "How did this terrorist army assemble without being detected by the intelligence community? Someone was asleep at the switch and he resides in the White House."

Samson has long maintained that America is under siege by drug peddlers directed from Colombia. He has called this an "Elevator Epidemic," referring to the most common street drug used today . . .

SLAUGHTER! SAYS SAMSON

August 16

WASHINGTON—At a press conference on the steps of the Capitol, Sen. Wade Samson, D-Mich., called the Cartel's concerted attack on drug enforcement and judicial personnel across the nation "nothing less than a slaughter that demands a sweeping new approach to dealing with the war on drugs."

As the horrifying numbers come in from coast to coast, the term "Slaughter" is being used by media in reports of the thousands of federal judges, FBI and DEA agents who were assassinated in the massive strike, which inadvertently left as yet undetermined numbers of innocent bystanders dead and wounded, many of them women and children. The senator has long been an advocate of restructuring the federal government's antidrug operations . . .

CHAOS CONTINUES

URBAN CENTERS ACROSS NATION TERRORIZED BY CARTEL KILLERS

August 25

MIAMI, FLA.—The National Guard, even the use of highly trained special army forces, have had minimal effect on the reign of terror begun earlier this month. Here in Miami, five judges from the District Court for the Southern District of Florida were assassinated. Especially gruesome were the deaths of Judge Judith Moralez, her daughter Pilar and twelve other junior high students caught in the line of fire as she was returning the twelve-year-old to school after a dental appointment.

Cartel assassins have dealt crippling blows to drug enforcement operations across the nation, with appalling collateral damage to the civilian population. Elevator operator automatic weapons and explosives have brought the death toll of officials and bystanders to estimates ranging as high as five thousand dead and wounded. In response, ordinary citizens everywhere huddle behind locked doors, eyes glued to television as civil and military authorities plead for calm.

But there is no calm here in south Florida or elsewhere. With their armed escorts backing them, Elevator operators openly hawk their wares to desperate drug users. Estimates of Cartel profits since the Slaughter have ranged as high as a billion dollars a day . . .

DEA, ATF FOLDED INTO NEW SUPERAGENCY BY MARTIAL LAW ACT

BUREAU OF ILLEGAL SUBSTANCE CONTROL GIVEN WIDE POWERS; DRUG TRAFFICKING A CAPITAL CRIME UNDER NEW LEGISLATION

September 30

WASHINGTON—Weeks of public outcry against President Lowrey's inability to stop Cartel "Elevator operator" depredations has led Congress to pass the Martial Law Act, making any trafficking in illegal substances treason, punishable by death. Sens. Wade Samson, D-Mich., and Howard Fillmore, R-Idaho, shepherded the bill, which includes a new super drug enforcement agency, through a bitter floor fight in the Senate. The House has already passed the controversial measure. The Bureau of Illegal Substance Control, acronym BISC, will dispense justice directly to drug traffickers.

Sen. Adam Manchester, R-Maine, denounced the Martial Law Act as "the creation of a police state abolishing due process guaranteed by the Bill of Rights." His protests were largely ignored as the chamber passed the bill 73 to 27. President Lowrey is under heavy pressure to sign it into law immediately.

BISC will be led by a three-member Tribunal, composed of two elected federal officials and the third, a federal government administrator. The president will appoint Tribunal members to six-year terms. Their identity will be known only to him. With their ranks decimated by the Cartel on August 9, remnants of DEA and ATF personnel will be integrated into BISC. The FBI will maintain separate operations but will no longer focus on crimes related to drug trafficking.

Sen. Manchester's objections to the Martial Law Act and BISC are echoed by groups as diverse as the American Civil Liberties Union and the Cato Institute. Institute spokesman Ronald Wingate is outraged by the secrecy cloaking BISC. "Not only will the identities of Tribunal members be hidden, but their agents' identities as well. We are creating nothing less than a secret police."

Supporters of the Martial Law Act maintain such secrecy is essential to insure BISC's effectiveness. Sen. Samson pointed out that it was the very openness and high visibility of our judicial system and law enforcement agencies that made them "lambs for the Slaughter."

ACLU spokesman Ariel Stein countered with charges of "vigilantism." "BISC agents," she maintains, "will investigate an alleged criminal, weigh the evidence and carry out Tribunal death warrants. They'll literally be judge, jury and executioner."

1.

The '07 Civic Sun cruised slowly through the deserted parking deck, staying carefully within the chem-glow drive lines. Silently it rounded the corner and rolled down the ramp to the lowest level, then stopped in front of a new Corvette Electro-T, which was parked facing the wall.

The Sun's tinted windows concealed its occupants until the passenger side opened. A brief flash from the dome light revealed two figures, a man behind the wheel and a tall, slender woman, who slipped out and quickly closed the door. Without a word to her companion, she walked around the Corvette, checking the interior, then the license plates.

Satisfied, she signaled him to drive on. Over the barely perceptible hum of the electric engine, her footsteps echoed on the concrete as the small rental car moved toward the opposite end of the deck and parked. In a brisk, athletic stride, she approached the elevator a dozen yards distant and melded into the shadows to the left of the doors. She checked her watch and prepared to wait.

Minutes passed. She did not move. Her vigil was rewarded by the low growl of elevator cables. She shifted position ever so slightly onto the balls of her feet. The doors whooshed open, revealing a thickset man carrying an attaché case. He glanced left and right, then stepped hurriedly from the elevator.

She raised her weapon and took aim. He caught the motion from the corner of his eye and whirled, reaching inside his jacket. The only sound breaking the silence was a soft pop from her small automatic. A tiny hole no bigger than the tip of her little finger appeared in the middle of the man's forehead. His temples and eyeballs bulged grotesquely. Then, every bone in his body seemed to dissolve as he crumpled.

Glancing around the dimly lit deck, the woman walked over to her victim and knelt beside his body. When she rolled the corpse onto its back, a thin trickle of blood oozed from its ear, pooling on the concrete. Eyes stared blankly into space. Ignoring the slack face of death, she pulled the attaché case from beneath the body. The Sun approached noiselessly as she stood up. She tossed the case inside and slid into the passenger seat.

"You moved too soon. He caught you in peripheral," her companion said as he drove up the ramp.

"I know," she replied in a tight voice.

Glancing at her profile he grunted. "You okay?"

She sucked in a deep breath. "No." The car circled up the ramp three more levels. As he slowed to make the final turn, she swung her door open and was violently sick on the concrete floor. Raising her head immediately, she slammed the door and said, "Go!"

He anticipated the command, relieved to see a faint bit of color returning to her face. "The first one is always bad," he said.

Fishing a texture wipe from her pocket, she scrubbed at her mouth, then replied, "Yes."

"It'll get easier after a few more."

She forced aside the image of that perfectly centered red dot just above those dead eyes. "God, I hope not."

THREE YEARS LATER
2:12 A.M., EDT, TUESDAY, JUNE 16
ALEXANDRIA, VA.

He was running flat out, his chest on fire as if someone were tightening a piano wire around it. Sharp, stinging pain lanced through his lungs as he gulped enough air to yell, "Stop! FBI!" Without breaking stride, he closed the distance between himself and the two men he was chasing down the narrow street.

In the darkness, patches of light flashed between the buildings, black-and-white distortions, like images from an old twentieth-century cinema reel. The suspects' flight stopped abruptly when the car waiting for them at the curb peeled away before they reached it. As they turned, he tried to stop and level his weapon but was not quick enough.

They caught him limned in a sliver of dirty yellow light. The first slug spun him around, cutting a shallow furrow across his ribs as it slammed him against a rough brick wall. He gritted his teeth and raised his SIG-Sauer, squeezing off a shot, but the report was drowned out by the thunder of the second man's MACH10. He felt the solid thunk of metal ripping into his flesh. Chest. Thigh. Knee. The hits registered in his brain as he slid slowly down the wall. Someone screamed his name.

Sirens wailed in the distance. Everything faded to black but his knee still hurt like a bitch. If only the damn sirens would stop ringing. Ringing. He bolted upright into a sitting position. Drenched in sweat, he frantically ran his hands over his chest, down his left leg to stanch the bleeding. But there was no blood, only hot, sweaty flesh and the knotted lumps of healed scar tissue.

His knee still throbbed evilly as he swung his legs over the side of the bed and fumbled for the phone jangling on the nightstand. Running his fingers through his hair, he squinted at the clock. Two twenty-seven a.m. Taking a deep breath, he growled into the receiver, "Delgado. This better be good."

Elliott Delgado exited the 495 Beltway and turned west onto Braddock, glancing into his rearview vid screen at the nearly deserted highway behind him. *If I was still with the Bureau, I'd have a tail scanner tracking any car making three successive turns with me.* He consoled himself with the thought that he had been allowed to keep the Buick Electra-TE. The combination turbine-electrical engine had a specially designed third mode—a turboelectric flash drive allowing the Buick to go 190 kilometers per hour, small enough compensation for the titanium pins in his knee.

He rubbed the old injury as he pulled into the left-turn lane. Affluent suburban developments sprawled between dense stands of sugar pines. A few lights winked from distant windows, but at 3:15 a.m. the densely populated area adjacent to Accotink Park slumbered. The residents rested in the assurance that they were a safe thirty klics away from the urban war zone of central D.C.

Rival gangs of Elevator operators fought over the city. These El-Ops sold the street drug of choice, Elevator, a highly unstable combination of cocaine and the old nonspecific impotence drug sildenafil citrate, commonly known as Viagra, which sent the coke-laden blood surging up the carotid arteries to the brain with the speed of an elevator.

Del turned onto Danbury Forest and followed the winding road. What would he learn at this bizarre rendezvous? Cal Putnam had told him to take the back way into King's Park. His ex-boss knew he and Diana had lived in this old northern-Virginia development before their divorce.

Putnam had been the mentor who'd trained him, handpicked him for the most challenging assignments, and gone to the wall for him every time he'd been called on the carpet by punctilious politicians inside the Bureau. Diana had accused him of caring more for "that crotchety, foulmouthed old Okie" than he did for his own wife. She was probably right. God knew he'd spent more time with Cal than with her. By the time he was finished with hospitals, Putnam had been promoted to ADIC, assistant director in charge, and Delgado had climbed into a bottle.

Whiskey under the bridge as Cal would say, he thought with a laugh, recalling this stretch of road and the jogger's path across the bridge to the marina.

A good choice for cover. It would be nearly impossible for anyone to follow them here. A tail would stand out like a Vegas stripper in the National Cathedral. He pulled off the road and made a U-turn, then parked the Buick in the sheltering shadows of a big dogwood. After remaining in the car for several moments, watching for anyone who might follow him, he slipped out and climbed over the metal guardrail. The descent down the steep hillside was made more difficult by dense foliage and darkness, but he found the wide dirt pathway.

Tidewater in July was hot and fecund, infested with insects. Cicadas sang and mosquitoes hummed counterpoint between bites on his neck and arms. He'd remembered his .50-caliber Smith & Wesson but forgot to take a Buggone pill. A full moon silvered the treetops high overhead as he stopped to get his bearings. The gravel path was rutted, filled with joggers and cyclists during daylight hours, but now deserted. It twisted deep inside the park. Mentally he marked off the distance to the bridge.

Too damn far. The slight limp grew more pronounced with every kilometer. He remembered when he had run this course with ease every morning. But that was over seven years ago.

Getting out of shape, old man.

The sound of bubbling water grew louder as he neared the bridge over Accotink Creek. Then he saw a figure materialize out of the darkness on the other side of the rusty iron structure. He paused warily in the darkness until a familiar voice spoke.

"No need to play hide-'n'-seek. I been here for over half an hour. If I wasn't followed, you weren't."

Cal Putnam's nasal Oklahoma twang was unmistakable. Thinning gray hair and the leathery seams in his round face betrayed every one of his sixty-three years. He had shrewd blue eyes, a stubborn, pointed chin, and one hell of an attitude. Del had always liked working for a man who cut through the bureaucratic bullshit.

Delgado stood half a head taller than Putnam, whose slouched shoulders and paunch were the badge of a Washington bureaucrat chained to a desk. The old man was career FBI, working his way up to SAC in Oklahoma City before his thirtieth birthday. Now he was their number two man in Washington, the ADIC.

"What the hell's going on, Cal? I don't hear squat from you for five years, then this middle-of-the-night intrigue."

Putnam kicked a rock, then looked up at Delgado. "Don't piss in my hip pocket, Del. I'm not the only one up to my ass in alligators. You fly around more than Chuck Yeager ever did. But I hear you're one bitchin' reporter, ole son. Won a Pulitzer a couple of years back, didn't you?"

"You never ask a question you don't already know the answer to, Cal. And you didn't call me out here in the middle of the night to discuss my journalistic triumphs." Del leaned against the wooden rail of the bridge, taking the weight off his bum knee.

Putnam shrugged. "Nope on both counts. Mind if I indulge?" He pulled an antique meerschaum and a well-crumpled bag of tobacco from his jacket pocket.

"Fine by me. The stink will keep the insects away." Delgado knew the old man took his own sweet time getting to a point.

Putnam methodically tamped the shredded brown leaves into the bowl and lit the pipe, then took several experimental draws before nodding with satisfaction. He eyed Delgado's fingers massaging his bent knee and said, "Still dealin' you fits after three surgeries. Doctors could fuck up a rainstorm."

"I can walk. My pelvis rotates and I can even throw a softball for my kid again. Considering I got a full disability retirement from the Bureau five years ago, I'm not doing too bad."

"Damn shame those punks were able to do this to you. Maybe BISC has the right idea—no 'Stop, police,' no reading them their rights. Just a quick clean bullet in the brain."

"Judge, jury, and executioner all rolled up in the Bureau of Illegal Substance Control. I never liked it, Cal. Still don't."

"Hoped you'd still feel that way." Cal's chuckle was low and raspy.

"Does this have something to do with BISC—or the Bureau?"

"The Bureau, BISC, the Colombians, hell, ole son, the whole damn shootin' match. I lost two men in the last twenty-four hours. One in San Diego, one here in D.C. Both hit quick and clean. Both shot in the back of the head with a needle gun . . ." He puffed on his pipe, letting the words sink in.

"BISC isn't in the habit of losing those guns. Any rumor on the street about the bad guys finding a source for them?"

"I think the bad guys already have a source—some top-secret defense contractor, whoever the fuck supplies them to BISC."

"You're saying BISC terminated two FBI agents?" Delgado was stunned. "Why?"

"We've been hearing rumors on the street for months about BISC going after the boys from Bogotá. And to sweeten the pot, the Pentagon may be working with BISC."

Del whistled low. "The Cartel owns South America and most of Mexico. Attacking them would make the Second Iraqi War look like a lovers' spat."

"Yeah, if any of their nukes got through, California would really glow after dark," Cal agreed grimly. "Those agents were both investigating the situation. Then . . ." *Phitt.* The rasping scrape of his wooden match made the point as he relit his pipe. "They ended up dead. No one but the highest-ranking personnel in the Bureau knew what my men were doing. I assigned Nuñez and Crosby because they were the best."

Del remembered both agents, seasoned veterans. Not easy men to kill. "You think there's a leak in the Bureau?"

Cal nodded. "Both BISC and the brass asses have been nursing an itch to expand the war on drugs beyond our borders ever since the Slaughter. I think after years of BISC and the Bureau hating each other's guts, somebody in my command has gotten in bed with their fucking Tribunal and the Pentagon."

"You can't use normal channels to investigate for fear of tipping off a mole."

"Shit, it might be Drescher himself. Slippery bastard could hold his own in a pond full of eels." Cal hated the director, a political appointee with no experience in law enforcement.

"What about going directly to the president?"

"Wade Samson's a real hard-nosed son of a bitch. I haven't got the evidence to prove my suspicions—just a couple of dead agents killed by needle guns. I need more. Look, you won that Pulitzer for a story about an innocent man BISC canceled in Atlanta. You're a top-notch investigative reporter. You have due bills out all over."

"Hell, so do you, Cal."

"Yup. And I'm calling one in now, ole son."

On the drive back into Alexandria, Elliott Delgado thought about his conversation with Cal. Had he been crazy, agreeing to help? Sure thing. Maybe he'd never gotten over being an agent. He grinned as he turned into the underground parking facility of his Pitt Street condo. Maybe he just wanted another Pulitzer.

Either way, the rush of adrenaline was an addiction. Who needed Elevator to get high? He'd always had his work. That was both blessing and curse. Work sustained him when he was alone. But the reason he was alone was work. For the first couple of years of their marriage, Diana had tried to understand. But he had never been around when she or Mike needed him.

"It's over and done," he muttered to himself as he pulled the Buick into its slot and touched the sensor that set the security system for the custom automobile.

Del entered the elevator and fumbled for the coded ID card, which was the old building's pass at security. His apartment security was not much better than the building's, since he'd never bothered to have the door locks keyed into his computer, a small detail he kept meaning to accomplish but never had. Preoccupied by the information Cal had given him, he ignored the clutter in the living room and headed straight to the computer in his office. He fed the half-dollar-sized disc Cal had given him into the drive and gave his voice command to activate.

Data came up on the screen after a few twitches and a blip of protest. Another thing he kept intending to do was get a new machine. Pulling a cold Superior cerveza from the wall fridge, he zipped the plasti-tab and took a long pull as his eyes narrowed on the material. The text began with crime-scene photos of both terminations.

Poor devils never knew what hit them. He enlarged the screen to view Crosby's corpse. The barely visible point of entry was in the back of the head. The small, narrow missile from a needle gun penetrated only animal tissue, but once inside it vaporized, creating a wound the size of a golf ball, causing the eyeballs and even the skull to bulge out.

Instantaneous destruction. Surgical precision. There were no ricochets, no pass-throughs, no way for an innocent bystander to be hit unless the BISC shooter was a lousy shot, which never happened, or if the agent chose an innocent victim. Alarmingly, that occurred more often than politicians inside the Beltway would admit.

There was nothing more obscene than a body collapsed in death, boneless, vulnerable. Police photos revealed nothing of value to Del. Crosby was hit inside his own garage in a modest Maryland suburb. No one else was at home. Divorce. Delgado was certain it was an occupational hazard for Bureau members. Nuñez had been taken out in a shopping mall parking lot.

Del scrolled for the inventory of personal belongings. Both bodies had been picked clean as a pig carcass in a piranha tank. Not so much as a texture wipe was left in either man's clothing. If Crosby or Nuñez had been carrying any useful evidence, the BISC agents had removed it.

No witnesses to either termination. Sometimes there were. BISC agents liked anonymity but were occasionally forced to take out a drug dealer in front of bystanders. Since they were licensed to kill by act of Congress, the police had no jurisdiction.

"But these shoots weren't righteous," he muttered, taking another swallow of beer. Of course, he knew no rational being could finger a BISC agent even if one shot the pope. Hell, they had their fingerprints removed. They were shrouded in secrecy, feared. "What civilian would want to piss them off?"

Del scrolled through the day logs of the two men. Crosby had a scrawled "G. Goodacre, noon" under yesterday's date. The name was probably a code of some sort. Slim pickings but the only lead on Crosby he could glean from the disc. He instructed his computer program's search engines to locate any G. Goodacres.

Who the hell are you? He pulled another beer from the fridge and opened it. Since his bout with the bottle, beer and wine with dinner were all he allowed himself to drink. Two was his limit.

Shortly, the screen pinged, filled with a dozen entries. He scanned them. Mostly obscure, but then one caught his eye—Glenna Goodacre, an American sculptor, who's most famous work was the Women's Vietnam Memorial, completed in 1993.

As per Bureau procedure, he pulled the disc from the A drive and destroyed it.

A rendezvous site? Tomorrow he might find out.

2.

The smell of rotting garbage wafted from the graffiti-covered Dumpsters clustered on the corner of Cass Avenue. The summer heat hung miasmically over downtown St. Louis, intensified by an early-morning thunderstorm, which had left sour steam rising on the dead-calm air.

Bricks from an old church that had recently seen the wrecking ball lay scattered amid waist-high weeds where two teenage boys crouched, one black, the other white. They were shadowed by the vacant factory next door.

"Big say he be here a hour ago," the black kid whispered.

"He'll show or he's in deep shit," his companion replied.

The black kid sniggered.

Their argument was interrupted by the sharp click of a car door closing. The big turboelectric Lincoln looked out of place on the ancient brick street, as did the man who climbed out. He easily went 150 kilos, dressed in an Armani suit of funereal black. In spite of the sullen heat his chalk-pale face was sweat free, round and innocent-appearing except for the colorless eyes.

Two young black men carrying automatic weapons flanked him as he watched the boys emerge from the weeds. He motioned for them to lead the way through the open door of the abandoned factory standing directly on the street. One of his bodyguards preceded him into the dark interior; the other stood guard in the doorframe.

From her perch alongside the second-story window, Leah Berg-lund studied the layout below her. Their voices echoed in the cav-ernous space as the dealer and his youthful victims talked. Except for a few broken-down crates in the far corner, there was no cover for her quarry. She watched as the two boys scored a "bean bag" of Elevator caps, peanuts to a dealer like Big Frankie Dittmeier, merely a recruit-ing tool. After a few more such gifts, the whole Gateway Gang would be working for Big.

She'd climbed up the gutter alongside the window using an old paradise tree for additional support, not an easy feat. In fact, little about this assignment had been easy. The Elevator operator's guilt had been simple enough to verify. Terminating him was a lot harder. She'd been stalking Big for over two weeks, ever since her verdict had been upheld by Central. He and his guards seemed joined at the hip. Damn! She hated taking out an operator in front of witnesses.

Shit, why not nail the scumbag during a seventh-inning stretch at Busch Stadium?

Bracing herself with a foot against the gutter and her back against the trunk of the tree, Leah quietly shifted her "tool kit" and unfas-tened it. She removed the needle gun from her shoulder holster, slid the tubular shoulder stock from the kit bag, and quickly fitted the stock to the weapon. With practiced efficiency, she added the short extender barrel and clicked in place the laser scope.

Judgment day, Big. Leaning through the window, she sighted in on the guard in the doorway. A soft pop and he collapsed. As the second thug raised his Uzi, her shot penetrated his forehead. Big wasn't about to go anywhere fast. He lurched toward the door, his pallid complexion gone suddenly red with exertion and fear. She fired and Dittmeier crumpled onto the rough concrete in an ungainly lump. The two boys stood frozen in the center of the warehouse, too fright-ened to run.

"Don't move." She climbed inside the window and sat on the sill. The black kid was almost as pale as the white one now. They tried not to look at the Big's corpse. "You know what I am." It wasn't a question.

The white kid gulped audibly, his oversize Adam's apple working like a piston as he nodded. The black one stared at her perched in the window. With the dim light at her back, she was a spectral creature from one of his nightmares.

They both looked as if they were ready to soil themselves. Good. "Then you know I could terminate you, too," she said, staring at the bean bag the white youth clutched in his hand.

He dropped it as if it were a burning meteorite. "N-no," he choked out, backing up a step, ready to bolt.

"Try it and there won't be anything left of your leg below the knee. Can't play b-ball on a stump." Her tone was conversational, but it had the desired effect. He froze.

The other kid looked up at the dark figure with street-smart eyes. "Why you not do us, too?" His voice was a fraction steadier now, but he still avoided looking at the corpse by his feet.

"I don't like killing kids," she replied, implying that she had done it in the past. "For one thing it means extra paperwork, but if you try to score again, you'll die. You see now how it goes down. And trust me, it always goes down—BISC agents never miss. Take a good look at your Elevator operator . . . I said look at him!"

Against their wills, the boys complied, staring in horrified fascination at Dittmeier's body. She could see them shuddering. The white kid lost control of his bladder and the black one bent over and vomited on the bag of Elevator.

"I'm giving you a second chance. There won't be another. Go to St. Joe's on Tenth Street. They have a youth rehab program there."

The old church was only a couple of blocks away. They nodded, desperate to get away from the three dead men and the smell of their own humiliation. Before they could walk around Big's corpse, she said to the black kid, "Your name is Danny Taylor, age fourteen, known as Danny T on the street." Shifting to his companion, she said, "You're Rob Zigler, age fifteen. The guys in the gang call you Zig-Zag.

"If you don't stick with that program and quit the Gateways, we'll find you." They stared gape-mouthed, pure fear infused with amazement. "Move! Get the hell out of here!"

She watched them rush for the door, stumbling over the guard's body in their haste to escape. Maybe it would work. She knew the odds were at best even money, but sometimes . . .

Besides, the kid Zig-Zag reminded her of Kevin.

12 P.M., EDT, TUESDAY, JUNE 16
WASHINGTON, D.C.

Del wove his Buick silently across the Fourteenth Street Bridge, en route to West Potomac Park. The car cruised in the electric mode at sixty kilometers per hour. With a sky of brilliant azure and white cumulus clouds billowing on the eastern horizon, the air was so pristine he could smell the faint aroma of spirea blooming along the Tidal Basin.

Since the Fossil Fuels Prohibition Act, air quality had drastically improved. No auto could burn petroleum products in metro areas of the United States. In cities, electric vehicles, mostly two-seaters powered by rechargeable batteries, had replaced the polluting dinosaurs. EVs satisfied the American passion for private transport, even though consumers had to sacrifice speed. Seventy kph was as fast as an EV could go.

Del appreciated spirea as much as speed, so he didn't mind using the electric mode around town. Still, every so often he would take off south on I-95 and open up the TE's flash drive just to recapture that old adrenaline rush. Sometimes he really missed the Bureau, even after five years. His shrink told him he'd get over it.

"Haven't yet," he said to himself, drumming his fingers on the steering wheel. He turned onto Henry Bacon Drive and squeezed the large car into a small parking space. A few of his best *News-Time* stories had given him that old thrill—Miami *cubano* Hector Ruiz's first inaugural in Havana for instance, or finding out that BISC agent Gary McCallum had terminated an innocent man. Del enjoyed piecing together the puzzle; the game was worth more than the prize—even if the prize was a Pulitzer.

Hell, he still liked catching the bad guys.

Whistling through his teeth, he strolled into the park and took a look around. Because it was summer, a fair crowd of tourists did the requisite things, snapping photos of the Lincoln Memorial, making the emotional pilgrimage to the Vietnam, Korean, and Iraqi War memorials.

He neared the tree-shrouded circle where the Goodacre sculpture stood and fished the photo of Special Agent Crosby from his pocket. Spotting a park ranger, he flashed the picture and asked if the man had seen Crosby. No luck. By the time he'd talked with the fifteenth or sixteenth person, the blistering sun and tidewater humidity were taking their toll. He'd sweated enough to make middle-weight limit and worked up a fierce thirst. Unfortunately, the U.S. Park Service frowned on selling beer.

He settled for a water fountain. As he bent over to take a gulp, he saw the old woman beneath the low branches of a willow. She sat in the shadows, observing the passersby with the practiced eye of an artist, holding a sketch pad in one veiny hand and a charcoal pencil in the other. Her movements were quick, deft.

Delgado felt she was watching him as he approached, singling him out from the other tourists in the crowd. No one else noticed her and she seemed to like it that way. The willow branches rustled as he ducked under them.

"Afternoon, ma'am," he said with a smile, withdrawing the now well-thumbed photo from his pocket. "You ever see this fellow around the park?"

She studied the photo for a moment, her gaze practiced, assessing, then looked up at Del. Her eyes were shrewd, set in a sun-darkened face aged like a well-used chamois cloth. "I come here to sketch every day. I may have. Why?"

"Was he here yesterday?"

"I repeat, why do you want to know?" she countered without so much as a blink.

"This is a confidential FBI investigation, ma'am." He showed her his badge, which Putnam had allowed him to keep when he had retired. It had come in handy over the years. "The subject was murdered last night. We think this might be a matter of national security." He waited.

She waited. After considering a bit, she replied, "I like your face. It has character, Special Agent Delgado. That's a sadly lacking commodity these days. Yes, I saw him yesterday."

"Was he alone?"

"No. He met another man. They walked around the sculpture, then sat over there for a half hour or so." She pointed to the stone bench across the walk. "They must have been discussing something very important."

"They were engrossed in conversation?"

"Not so much engrossed as . . . secretive, always looking around surreptitiously, out of the corner of their eyes."

Del smiled. "I know the type you mean. Sometimes he stares back at me while I'm shaving in the morning." He smiled again. "Could you describe the other man?"

The woman returned the smile. "I'm not much good with words, but I did sketch them. They never noticed me here under the willow. I try not to draw attention to myself. It makes people self-conscious if they see me sketching them—or they want to pay me for a picture."

Her tone of voice indicated what she thought of that. Del's heartbeat sped up. "I'd really appreciate it if you could show me that sketch, ma'am."

She began flipping through the small pad. When she found the page, he recognized Crosby at once, engaged in some sort of argument with the other man. At least that was what it looked like judging from their body language. The detail on the faces was amazing, considering the distance she was from the bench.

When he asked her about that, she replied, "I saw them from three meters away as I walked by them earlier. I often choose my subjects that way. Something has to click. With them it was the way they acted . . . peculiarly . . . and the man you're trying to find, there was something about him. I sensed a great intensity . . . or perhaps it was fear."

7:45 P.M., EDT, TUESDAY, JUNE 16

Cuff Bedford was young, black, and had been fiercely ambitious. He'd graduated from West Point third in his class a week before his twenty-first birthday. A year later during the Second Iraqi War, all of his ambitions and a substantial portion of his body went up in smoke when he stepped on a land mine. He spent over six years in and out of Walter Reed while the army attempted to put back together what remained of his legs and his right arm. The surgeons managed to save his arm and right leg, but the left leg had to be amputated. They fitted him with a Pro-Lix. At least it didn't ache like the real one.

A grateful Uncle Sam rewarded him with a Bronze Star, a Purple Heart, a disability retirement, and a desk in the Pentagon. Bedford worked in Logistics as a requisitions specialist, or as he put it, an army MRE counter.

James Cuffington Bedford IV had been born into a family of career soldiers who had fought with distinction in every American conflict since the Civil War. A second lieutenant, Cuff was the first in three generations of Bedford men to retire below the rank of bird colonel. The family didn't take it well. Neither did Cuff.

Elliott Delgado and Cuff Bedford had met while Cuff was being fitted with his third prosthetic leg. Del was facing the second surgery on his damaged knee. During the weeks they spent in the hospital together, the son of a San Diego cop and the scion of a military dynasty had become friends. In spite of the differences in their backgrounds, they shared the nightmarish experience of repeated reconstructive surgeries and the loss of their careers.

While Del moved on to a different field, becoming a successful investigative reporter, Cuff remained buried in the bowels of the military bureaucracy, unable—or unwilling—to leave the army behind even after it had, in effect, left him. Bitterly, he watched bright young officers rise through the ranks. They walked through the Pentagon in straight, easy strides, while he limped in their shadows.

A little over a year ago when Del had mentioned that he was doing a story on fraud in government contracting, Cuff had volunteered some valuable inside information. He was out to get the military establishment that had used and discarded him. His tips always checked out.

Cuff said he'd meet Del at one of his usual haunts, the Iraqi War Memorial. Delgado had no idea what compulsion made Bedford revisit a monument commemorating the death of his dreams. Personally, he stayed as far away from the Hoover Building as he could.

Located in West Potomac Park, the memorial was a simple steel band spiraling twenty three meters high like the skeletal funnel of a tornado, symbolizing the Second Iraqi War's Operation Desert Whirlwind, the only American military victory since World War II. Del strolled around the white marble base of the structure until he spotted Bedford sitting in a Porta-Cart.

As Del approached, Cuff saw him and smiled. His tall, trim body still held hints of the grace and power it had possessed before the war. He resembled Tim Reed, a popular television star from the last century, strikingly handsome with chiseled, aristocratic features.

"How's it hanging, my man? It's been a damned long time." Cuff swung out of the cart, holding on to the roof with his good arm while he steadied himself.

Del made no attempt to assist him, remembering all too well what such solicitude did to a man's pride. "It's still there and it's hanging, Cuff. How about yourself?"

They walked slowly to the corner of the monument, making small talk, studying the names inscribed in neat brass letters. When conversation faded, Del handed Bedford the sketch. "You recognize this guy? He has career brass stamped all over him."

"Good reason for that, if it's who I think. Looks like Colonel Hoyt Brandies. A real young Turk. Rumor has it he would've gotten his first star before he turned forty."

"Would've?" Del echoed.

"He was killed early this morning in an Apache crash. Who's the guy with him?"

"A Bureau agent assigned to investigate a possible connection between BISC and the Pentagon. Funny thing. He's dead, too."

"This isn't just another story, is it, Del?" Bedford looked around nervously at the tourists strolling casually in the waning summer light.

"I need to know if you've heard any rumors about BISC agents working on a black op."

"The Bureau of Illegal Substance Control and the United States army are supposed to stay miles apart. You know the law."

"And I know how easy it is for a secret agency to break the law."

Cuff chuckled mirthlessly. "You always did have as much of a hard-on for BISC as I have for the army."

"We're a match made in heaven," Del said as Cuff bent his head to light a cigarette. "Those will kill you," he added drily.

"I know. And at twelve bucks a pack, I'll die poor." Cuff inhaled deeply, then looked at Delgado with cynical intensity. "You say an FBI guy was canceled?"

"Back of the head with a needle gun. And it wasn't just this one agent. There was another in San Diego, same MO. Both yesterday."

Cuff scrubbed his fingers through his hair. "Man, oh, man, that is one bitch of a coincidence."

"We both know better than that, Cuff."

Bedford paused, as if deep in thought for a moment, then sighed. "I've told you how easy it is to hide covert troop movements—assign them to the Balkans peacekeeping forces, then siphon some off to Afghanistan, Palestine, Taiwan, wherever the brass wants. But hardware, rations, medical supplies, they're a lot harder to hide . . ."

He took another drag on his cigarette, gathering his thoughts. "A month or so ago I overheard a couple of guys in my department brainstorming about moving Bradley AVs across rough mountain terrain. I doubt I would have remembered if they hadn't started talking about sending along Buggone, snake repellent, and jungle fatigues on the same operation. I dismissed it as another logistics fuckup. But maybe not, huh? Where's that kind of combo going? Sure as hell not Europe or the Middle East."

"I don't know the route, Cuff, but I know the final destination—Colombia."

"They're going to hit Benito Zuloaga's boys? They'll hole up in the mountains, make Iraq seem like a cakewalk by comparison. The Cartel's supposed to have nukes. Man, oh, man, what a cluster fuck that'd be!"

"World War Three," Del said grimly. "I need to know who the Pentagon insider is."

"You think Brandies?" Cuff asked dubiously.

"He was seen talking with Crosby only hours before both of them died."

"Dying in a copter crash is light-years away from being hit by a needle gun."

"The timing is one bitch of a coincidence, remember?"

"Let me put my ear to the ground and listen for a while. I'll be in touch," Bedford said as he climbed back into the cart.

"I appreciate it, Cuff," Del replied, gripping his friend's hand. As Bedford drove away, Del stared into the gathering darkness for several moments, then started to walk back to his car.

If only Gracie Kell was as easy to reach as Cuff, I might have a source hacking into BISC while he digs at the Pentagon. He sighed. All he could do was keep putting out cautious feelers for Gracie. He wanted to talk with Gary McCallum, too, but the disgraced BISC agent had vanished after Del's expose.

That one's a real long shot, Delgado.

3.

The camouflage netting overhead flapped in the wind as sand and fine yellow dust stung General Nathan Sommerville's face. The Sonoran wilderness was as harsh and unforgiving as Iraq, but the rugged isolation of this region afforded concealment essential to his assignment. The Globe Net satellites paid no attention to what was supposedly a Mexican military installation training forces for yet another strike against the Cartel in Yucatán.

The general stood peering across the brushy desolation of the desert floor at the distant horizon where jagged peaks of the Sierra Madre Occidental rose. Sommerville was tall with a craggy, uncompromising face. His rangy frame still showed traces of war-honed toughness, but he was well into middle years. A de Gaulle–like slouch to his shoulders indicated that he carried a heavy burden.

"Rafael Silva should arrive at thirteen hundred hours, General," Colonel Walt Bisset, Sommerville's executive officer, reported.

"At least that's something. Our esteemed Colombian president-in-exile's son has nerve enough to fight while his father swills champagne in Hollywood."

"Silva and his guerrillas say they're dedicated to destroying Zuloaga's Cartel."

Sommerville shrugged with a bitter resignation. "So did Hoyt Brandies."

"I'll never understand why the colonel betrayed us to the FBI." Bisset knew how hard the general had taken Brandies's defection.

"The closer we get to the countdown, the less we can afford leaks, Walt. The colonel and two FBI agents have been eliminated, but who knows if Hoyt talked to anyone else in the Pentagon—or if someone higher up in the FBI has been alerted? We're forced to trust our BISC wizards to find out." Sommerville detested the necessary evil of relying on a civilian organization, but in this instance, BISC was an essential component in the plan.

Bisset hadn't been out of the desert for the past six months. He knew little of the plot outside of his military objectives. "Can BISC keep the lid on, sir?"

"They'd damn well better." The general shifted focus to the mission he was tasked with accomplishing. "Our job is getting this rag-assed brigade ready to move. After the last exercises, I believe they're as good to go as they'll ever be."

"Colonel Obregón's Mexicans are solid, but Major Salazar's Colombians need more practice if they're going in with Silva to take Bogotá—"

"It's our assignment to knock out the Cartel," Sommerville interrupted impatiently. "This will be an American show, Colonel. Using foreign grunts, yes, but make no mistake, it's our technology, our brains, and our guts that will finally stop the flow of drugs that have turned American cities into war zones. If these Latin American playboys had kept control of their governments in the first place, the Slaughter would never have occurred."

The grinding noise of several Humvees pulling into the compound drew Sommerville's attention. Rafael Silva was punctual. "The shipment from Little Lenny is secured, is it not, Walt?"

Bisset nodded. "Yes, sir. Well out of sight. Even Obregón and Salazar think it's artillery ordnance. Salazar's champing at the bit to play with the Dragonflies."

"Let's let him. It'll prove an interesting diversion for young Silva."

"Then you're not going to tell him we're using tactical nukes, sir?"

"He's young, idealistic, believes he'll lead a great popular *revolución*. How do you imagine he'd take it if he learned of our plans?"

"Not well, sir. Not well at all," Bisset replied gravely.

"That is precisely why we will not allow him to find out until it's too late." Sommerville turned and left the pod, striding toward the newly arrived Humvees.

Rafael Silva was a compactly built man with the pale, chiseled features common among the Latin American ruling aristocracy. He wore camouflage fatigues with no insignia. Jumping agilely from the lead vehicle, he stood and saluted Sommerville.

The general returned the salute, taking note of the burly guards flanking Silva, their flat Indian faces expressionless, except for watchful black eyes that missed little.

"On behalf of the United States of America and the United States of Mexico, I welcome you as the representative of Colombia's rightful government," Sommerville said in Spanish.

The two men conversed in Silva's native tongue as the general guided his visitor on a brief tour of the facilities. Born with a natural affinity for languages, Sommerville had been assigned to Havana upon Hector Ruiz's election. There he had become fluent in Spanish. He also spoke Arabic, several Slavic dialects, and Chinese.

Wherever his country called him, Nathan Sommerville did his duty as he saw it.

**9 A.M., EDT, THURSDAY, JUNE 18
RESTON, VIRGINIA**

To the casual observer driving by, it looked like a country club. Lush green shrubbery and manicured lawns surrounded the elegant gated compound, which said simply Deep Woods. Situated in a modern bedroom community of affluent housing, it attracted no particular attention, which was precisely the way the Bureau of Illegal Substance Control wanted things.

The main building appeared to be a three-story Georgian residence, but appearances could deceive. The interior housed a massive computer complex where technicians meticulously collated and processed reports from across the nation, then referred them to appropriate division chiefs, whose jurisdictions were divided into geographical units stretching from Fairbanks, Alaska, to San Juan, Puerto Rico.

The enormous operation extended seven floors below ground. Most BISC personnel worked ten-hour days without ever seeing daylight. They arrived and departed in flex shifts via half a dozen well-guarded entrances into the densely wooded back acreage. Underground parking facilities concealed their EVs. Agents undergoing the rigorous training prior to field assignment were housed in dormitories and used classrooms disguised as barns, stables, and smaller clubhouses, all surrounded by the heavy woodland.

Tribunal chambers and private offices for the three Tribunal members were on the third floor of the mansion, affording the men an excellent view of the grounds. Nervously, an aide entered one member's office with a disc and a disturbing memo.

Jack Frankowski opted for the good news first, handing his boss the disc. "The Brandies cancellation has been ruled an accident, sir."

With a terse nod, Harmon Waterman inserted the report into his personal digital assistant and skimmed through it, picking out the important details. When he'd finished, he looked up, leaning back in his custom leather chair, massaging the bridge of his nose with small, bony fingers. "You have something more for me, Frankowski?"

The aide swallowed hard and handed the memo to his chief, then stepped back quickly. "Brandies appeared to work alone and contacted no one but Crosby, sir. We don't believe there's any link between the two of them and . . . this."

"Son of a bitch, who the hell's snooping around now?"

"We aren't certain yet what this means," Frankowski rushed on before the explosion could come. "You know we monitor all interagency contacts, especially those inside the Pentagon. We've assigned several of our best agents to the search."

"We're too close now for any more screwups, Frankowski. When Sommerville wanted to bring in Brandies, I knew it was a mistake. Now we have someone else inside the Pentagon snooping for a black op. This could blow everything sky-high even quicker than the Brandies fuckup. And you're telling me you haven't found this prick?"

"We will, but whoever it is, is damned clever, sir. His insertions have come from different locations, with a series of different user IDs and pass codes on old terminals to gain access to Data Central."

Waterman blanched. "Then this could be more than one person."

"I don't think so, sir. One person could move around this way if he was familiar with the system. An employee with a high security clearance would be given other workers' passwords so he could fill in for them while they were TDY. I don't think he knows we're onto him. It's only a matter of time until we check out all the access codes and uncover his identity."

"Time's running out! I want this stopped—cold, right now. Do I make myself clear, Mr. Frankowski?"

"Crystal, sir. I have agents on it round the clock."

"I want to know who this man's working for before he's canceled."

"It's probably the FBI again, but we'll know for sure soon."

"That could be particularly . . . delicate, as I'm certain you're aware."

"Yes, of course. Our source inside the Bureau is on it, too."

Down the hall in another Tribunal office a man studied a BISC vita. The black-and-white hologram projected from his PDA revealed little. He studied the eyes, always fancying that he could read anyone by their eyes. "What secrets are you hiding . . . ?" he murmured to himself, then began reading the personal history of Agent Leah Berglund.

Born in Minneapolis, well-to-do family. Father a cardiologist, mother from a prominent New England political dynasty. One sibling, a brother. The usual childhood. Honor student and superior athlete, graduated University of Minnesota Law School. Went to work in the Public Defender's Office, quit after a year and a half, switched to the Prosecutor's Office, where she earned distinction as a zealous assistant DA with the highest conviction rate in the department.

"Hmmm." The Tribunal member stroked his chin, chuckling. "An idealist, eh, Ms. Berglund? Always wanted to catch the bad guys." He continued reading: Four years ago Kevin Berglund, Leah's brother, died on an Elevator "ride." Within the year she joined BISC. Again an outstanding performance record, several commendations. Her kill record was perfect. Agent Berglund never missed a shot. As an assassin, she had few peers. But she was always a careful investigator and had cleared a number of wrongfully accused individuals.

"Yes, you'll do, honey. You'll do just fine." He requested an encrypted video link on his PDA.

12 P.M., EDT, FRIDAY, JUNE 19
WASHINGTON, D.C.

Alberto Santandar Jimenez, the Euro Union's ambassador to the United States, was dead. The elderly Spaniard had held the key post for the past seven years while slowly sautéing his liver in Scotch. The National Shrine of the Immaculate Conception swarmed with Secret Service agents as ranking dignitaries from around the world paid their last respects at the requiem mass, including President Wade Samson.

The crowd in the Great Upper Church had just begun to disperse when the regularly scheduled noon mass in the Crypt Church below began. Del genuflected woodenly and knelt in the back pew, uncomfortable with the trappings of a religion long ago forsaken. As the priest began his invocation, he wondered if Diana still took Mike to church. The kid never mentioned it.

His musing was interrupted when Cuff slipped into the pew and knelt beside him, grunting at his stiff leg. At least the artificial one bent without aching.

Nearly a hundred of the devout were scattered around the church, listening attentively, participating in the liturgy. Kneeling with heads bowed, hands clasped in fervent prayer, they were oblivious to the two men in the back.

"I have some leads," Cuff whispered. His voice was covered by the melodious chanting of the priest.

"Good. What gives?" Del asked as they stood for the gospel.

"Ever hear of Adair-Rawlfing?"

Del shook his head.

"It's a new army base in southern California just west of Yuma, smack on the Mexican border. There's been a whole shitload of very interesting material sent their way over the past year or so. Tons of light ordnance, including over a half million rounds of ammo for the old M16, not the current model 17, med supplies, bivouac gear, and enough MREs to feed a brigade-sized force for two to three weeks. First destination, bases from Seattle to Alabama. But everything ended up at Adair."

Cuff slipped Del a disc. "This is classified shit. Eat it if you're caught."

"Like it was a Dallas Cowboys cheerleader." Del slid it inside his jacket.

Bedford choked back a laugh. "Took some real gnarly digging to follow the trail, I want to tell you. Whoever's doing this is high up and damn smart."

Del flashed his friend a concerned look. "Any chance you could be traced?"

"I've been careful, but I can't tell you how I did it. Military secret," Cuff said with a grin. "Here's a really interesting thing. The last items sent were eight AAV7Cs, amphibs. Whoever these guys are, they're headed across water."

Del's mind whirled as they knelt once again with the rest of the congregation. "Near Yuma, you say . . ."

"Yeah, smack in the middle of the desert."

"The Baja-Sonora desert ends up on the ocean," Del reminded him.

"But I couldn't find anything in the way of seagoing transport. The amphibs are strictly short-range stuff."

"Short range, long range, what's the difference? Hell, you couldn't stage an amphibious assault with three thousand men and only eight goddamned amphibs." Del gripped the pew with white-knuckle frustration.

Cuff put his hand on Delgado's arm, "Easy, man, I don't have the battle plan, just a partial supply list. And a lot of that hardware makes no sense to me either . . . like those UAVs—"

Del cut in. "What's a UAV?"

"An unmanned aerial vehicle," Cuff explained. "They're using them in the Balkans. In 'Raq, our artillery used them to pinpoint long-range targets."

Delgado shook his head, unable to see where Bedford was leading him.

"Check the disc I gave you. Somebody's shipped a dozen Sikorsky Dragonflies—UAV choppers—to Adair-Rawlfing. Four meters long, a hundred two kilos, capable of two hundred fifty-two kph. And a flight time of sixty minutes. These little babies are an artillery guy's wet dream!"

"But?" Del coached.

"No artillery ordnance went with 'em," Cuff replied. "Now that wouldn't be so weird because Yuma Proving Ground is in the neighborhood and that's where they test artillery. But none of their ordnance has been shifted to Adair. I double-checked it."

Delgado cursed quietly. "Okay, none of this makes sense to us. So now we have to hunt for the guys who know what the plan is."

"I'd bet on a three-star general, at minimum. Lord knows there's a surfeit of them since the war." A trace of the old bitterness tinged Bedford's voice. "I'll find out who."

"Don't take chances, Cuff. At least three men that I know of are already dead."

"And there's more likely to be, my friend. But as my Alabama roommate at West Point used to say, 'My mama didn't raise no dumb children.'"

4.

The office of the vice president of the United States was located on the grounds of the Naval Observatory, on the edge of Normanstone Park just south of the National Cathedral. Vice President Harmon Waterman walked with a flat-footed but brisk stride from the helipad as the official chopper lifted off again after bringing him from Camp David and a special weekend meeting with Alexi Saminov, the Russian ambassador.

The press believed the meeting to be window dressing. After all, Waterman was only Wade Samson's comical running mate, the jug-eared little banty rooster who had missed out on both Iraqi wars because he was 4F, born with feet so flat that they never possessed arches to fall. Folks inside the Beltway might have sniggered over Samson's choice for vice president, but corporate America saw Harmon Waterman in a totally different light. He had begun with nothing but brains and guts, building a small EV recharger plant into a multibillion-dollar enterprise.

Waterman had been one of the first to recognize that the future lay with electrically powered vehicles, long before the prohibition of urban-use fossil fuels. By the time Detroit rolled the first small urban two-seater electric car off its assembly line, Waterman's people had the technology and the tools in place to build the squat fire-hydrant body rechargers for them, rechargers that now sat on the driveways of virtually every home in America.

Success in the business world did not automatically translate into respect in the glamour-oriented, media-fed arena of politics. But money did. And Harmon Waterman had made enough of that to guarantee himself second place on the handsome young senator's presidential ticket. Samson's press consultants put a spin on Waterman's looks and mannerisms, portraying him as a latter-day Ross Perot, filled with folk wisdom and reforming zeal.

The general population thought of Harmon Waterman as a benignly eccentric Horatio Alger. That cover masked an unflinching ruthlessness, which had crushed all his business competitors. Since his first assignment from the president was an appointment to the BISC Tribunal, his low media profile suited Waterman just fine. The Camp David weekend had been a real coup. He had in his possession the names of half a dozen Russians who were big players in the international network of drug traffic between South America and Europe.

Russian pseudodemocracy hung on by a thread while old-style Reds grew in numbers and bellicosity, eager to resurrect the Soviet empire. Only Yankee currency propped up the present government. In return for more cash, Waterman had just blackmailed the Russian ambassador.

Ignoring his aide's welcome, the vice president entered his office. "Get me a vid link to the president," he said, dismissing the man.

Samson always took his sweet time coming on-screen. While Waterman waited, he reviewed the disc Saminov had given him, savoring the faces of six people fated to die by needle gun before the end of the week. On impulse, the vice president decided to share his good news with someone else. He picked up an encrypted voice-only link that connected directly to BISC Central.

When his fellow Tribunal member's voice came over the line, Waterman began to speak. "As soon as I clear it with Samson, I'm sending you the disc. . . . Yep, old Alexi came through—did you doubt it? Get your agents in place. . . . CIA clearance? Are you shitting me? Hell, no, they can't slap their asses with both hands free, much less hog-tied the way they are. Personally, I'd put my money on the CIA director being in bed with the Russian mob. . . . Not after this, no. . . . Oh, by the way, have you been able to put that information in place? . . . Good. Our agent needs to locate it as soon as possible. That will neutralize them both. . . . Good work."

"President Samson on vid, sir," his aide's voice came through the audioport.

Waterman flicked on his vid screen. "Good afternoon, sir. We got more than we'd hoped for from that damned Russkie."

From the Oval Office, Wade Samson sat quietly observing his vice president and listening to his report. The president was the polar opposite of Waterman. Tall and strikingly handsome, he had thick, graying hair and patrician features that were perfectly balanced by an outgoing manner that made him seem like a friend to every voter. Presidential yet approachable, that was the image every winner had to cultivate.

He'd been swept in on a landslide in the last election. After all, he was the senator responsible for hammering through the Martial Law Act in the wake of the Slaughter. Poor old Harmon would never have a chance at succeeding him. Waterman just wasn't a people person, the president thought as he nodded to Harmon. Not to mention that he was as homely as one of the squat EV rechargers turned out by his factories. But he was always standing by with his checkbook, and the little son of a bitch got results. Take this matter with the Russian mob.

"Our esteemed ambassador could have danced around with Saminov for months to wring one of the names out of him. You got the six key operators in just three days. Outstanding work, Harmon," Samson said warmly.

"I do my damnedest, sir. I've alerted Central. They're ready to move with your okay."

Samson said nothing, drumming his fingers on the polished walnut desktop as he weighed his reply.

"Mr. President?" Waterman prompted impatiently.

"Just considering, Harmon, just considering. These people are foreign nationals, spread across Europe and the Middle East. I'm not certain if we want to involve BISC."

"Who else can do it? You know the situation inside the Company. We have to act fast and clean or else the mob will get word and send the targets underground."

Waterman's tone was reasonable, but Samson could sense the agitation of a corporate mogul used to quick decisions and instantaneous action. "I understand your point, Harmon, but, damn, it's risky, not to mention illegal."

Waterman laughed. "I guarantee results, Wade. Since you appointed me to the Tribunal, I've been monitoring their operations closely. BISC's better than the FBI, NIA, CIA, all the rest combined."

"But BISC is only authorized to act within U.S. borders." Samson played devil's advocate, turning the matter over in his mind. His comment elicited a snort from Waterman.

"Hell, the FBI is only supposed to operate within our borders, too. Ask Cal Putnam if they've always adhered to that."

Samson sighed, capitulating. Waterman was right. They desperately needed to stop an alliance between the Russian mob and the Colombians. "You win, Harmon. Let BISC cancel those six Russians."

The president could still feel Waterman gloating after they had switched off. It taxed him dearly to put up with the nasty little Electric King, or the Prince of Power as Waterman's foes on the Hill dubbed him. But, what the hell, the vice president was useful. And he'd never be elected dogcatcher without Wade Samson.

3:30 P.M., EDT, MONDAY, JUNE 22

"Hello. I'm Kasi Evans. Your new research assistant." The tall, blond woman stepped inside Elliott Delgado's office at *U.S. News-Time,* flashing him a professional smile.

Del looked up from the carton of fried meat that he'd been gulping as he worked. He leaned back and swallowed a greasy hunk of pork. A protesting creak sounded from the battered, old swivel chair he had refused to give up last year when the magazine's D.C. offices were remodeled. He studied her with slow, unsmiling deliberation. She was a long cool one, leggy and athletic-looking with short-cropped, white-blond hair and the pristine complexion of a Scandinavian. Yet, in spite of the apparent self-confidence, the wholesomeness of some Midwestern farm still clung to her. A year or two inside the Beltway should take care of that.

But not on his turf. "Hello, Kasi Evans."

"You are Mr. Delgado, aren't you?"

He nodded, taking another bite from the carton. "What's left of 'im."

"Ms. Carlyle in HR sent me. You did request a research assistant, didn't you?"

Months ago. When he was researching "BoBo" Johnson, he'd asked the officious Bettye Carlyle for someone to dig through the the El-Op's background. *Now* she finally responded. "Sorry, I don't need anyone at present, Ms. . . . Evans? I'm sure Ben will find some other reporter who can use you."

Ben Cohen was a misogynist, a cigar-chomping, obscenity-spewing dinosaur who remained, against all odds, the magazine's editor in chief. Ordinarily, he sent wholesome young professional women scurrying, but somehow Del didn't think the one facing him would wilt under fire. He watched carefully as her ice blue eyes flicked appraisingly across the room. She didn't miss much.

Piles of hand-scribbled notes, old magazines, and odd bits of paper littered every flat surface. A ketchup-stained Frank Lloyd Wright necktie and a rumpled raw-silk jacket were tossed over the back of the vid screen. An array of empty carryout cartons overflowed the waste can. His coffee mug was growing a rather spectacular subtropical mold that competed with the mummified shreds of a potted ficus for focal point of the office.

"You'd really hate working for a slob like me," he added genially.

Her eyes narrowed imperceptibly. "If you're the Elliott Delgado who won a Pulitzer for his articles about a mistaken BISC termination, I wouldn't care if you ate out of a trough."

Del chuckled. "I appreciate the compliment, but I don't need a researcher now."

"Look, Mr. Delgado, I really want the opportunity to learn from you. I've admired your work for a number of years. I have excellent credentials—Reuters in Europe. Over here, the *Minneapolis Star Tribune, Newsweek.*"

"I'm flattered, Ms. Evans, and I'm not questioning your qualifications. I simply have no work to give you." He shrugged and tossed the carton into the trash where it teetered precariously atop the heap.

"You're not going to give me a chance."

Delgato turned back to his computer and began typing. "Go see Ben Cohen. He'll reassign you," he said over his shoulder.

When she vanished without another word, Del breathed a sigh of relief. All he needed in the middle of a high-voltage investigation of BISC was some green wannabe dogging his footsteps. Hell, that could get her canceled. He grunted. It would probably get *him* canceled.

9 A.M., EDT, TUESDAY, JUNE 23

When Del walked into his office, the e-mail light on his PDA was flashing. He gave a voice command and the file opened to a message from Ben Cohen, commanding his presence in the war room. The "war room" was the staff's nickname for Cohen's private office. Many a reporter had emerged from it checking his body parts to see if they were still attached and functioning. Being a DEA man during the Slaughter would have been safer than being on the old man's shit list.

Del made his way down the long corridor to the door marked BENJAMIN Z. COHEN, EDITOR IN CHIEF. No one had ever found out what the *Z* stood for. No one asked. He knocked, then entered as the old man grunted.

Cohen resembled a constipated bulldog and behaved a lot less civilly. An unlit, well-chewed cigar jutted from the sagging wrinkles around his mouth. Gray beetle brows drooped, half-obscuring eyes that Del knew were the color of old gunmetal and twice as hard.

He fixed them on the reporter. "I thought you Chicano guys went for the Kasi Evans type," Cohen growled in thick Brooklynese. "Since when you turnin' away stacked blond lookers?"

"Since I don't need a research assistant."

"Funny. It says here you do." The old man shoved a crumpled memo at him.

"That was back in April."

"Oh, I ain't givin' you enough to do?" Cohen said in mock surprise, the shaggy eyebrows rising to mesh with the hair straggling over his forehead. "Good. You can take over Branson's assignment. Do that piece on Senator Chapman's park beautification legislation.

Or, how's about the publisher's idea—a story on a typical day in the first lady's life."

"What's this crap about, Ben? I don't want some hero-worshiping young journalism major tagging along behind me. And I have more than enough work."

"Kasi Evans is no kid. She's thirty-one."

That surprised Del. She'd looked not a day over twenty-three.

Cohen continued, "She knows her stuff. Seven years solid experience with some of the best outfits here and abroad. They don't come higher recommended."

"Then give her to Branson—or Miss Etherington." Carolyn Etherington was the publisher of *U.S. News-Time*.

"No can do. Evans wants to work with you. I think she deserves the chance."

"She talked you into this?" He was flummoxed when the old man shifted the cigar in his mouth as if stalling for time. Del would almost swear there was a faint pinkening of Cohen's broken-veined, beard-bristled face.

"Nobody fuckin' talks me into anything." Cohen's hamlike fist pounded his desk. "She's got guts and moxie. Came in here and laid everything out straight. No bullshit, no tears, and no threatening to file a sex discrimination suit. We just talked, goddammit. Anything wrong with that?" He glared at the reporter.

Del sighed inwardly and smothered a curse. "I requested her. I got her."

"That's what I like about you, Delgado. You're a goddamned quick study."

She didn't act smug, he'd give her that. He half-expected her to come strutting in that morning grinning like a Cheshire cat. Lots of people would have after pulling off the coup she had. But she was strictly professional.

"Look, Mr. Delgado. I know you resent having me jammed down your throat this way. If I didn't want this opportunity very much, I wouldn't have gone over your head. I'm honestly surprised Mr. Cohen agreed to give me a chance. I won't get in your way and I will work hard." She waited, gauging his reaction.

He nodded, beginning to see what Ben meant. The woman knew how to handle people. "Why are you so damned set on working for me in particular?" He perched on the edge of his cluttered desk, studying her through sharp, dark eyes. She remained standing in the doorway. In spite of some lingering hostility, he was genuinely curious.

She didn't miss a beat. "Because you're the best and I want to learn from the best. When I was in Minneapolis, I followed your work on the Ryan kidnapping. You weren't just after a story. You really identified with the boy's father. And there was the Hartheim case—what makes a cop turn bad? You followed the descent every rung down the ladder, not excusing what he did but understanding it, making sense of it for the reader.

"My favorite piece was the one on disabled veterans and the way our system has failed them, not just with medical care and financial aid, but with emotional support."

"You didn't mention the McCallum story," he said, surprised by several of the lower-profile pieces she'd chosen.

She shrugged. "It was brilliant. You won a Pulitzer. Everyone wants to know more about the supersecret BISC. However . . ." She eyed him with what he took to be a slight uneasiness. Then she cleared her throat. "I think you compromised your professional objectivity on that one. Your treatment of Agent McCallum was no harsher than he deserved for terminating an innocent man, but you seemed to be using him as a vehicle to get at the agency itself, to attack BISC."

Del nodded. "Not bad, Ms. Evans, not bad at all. You've got cojones as well as brains. Okay, I'll admit to a decided lack of objectivity toward BISC and the Martial Law Act."

"Pretty unpopular sentiments, Mr. Delgado." A smile was in her eyes.

"That's what reporters are born to be—iconoclasts," he said, returning her smile. It was hard not to like her. The trick would be finding ways to keep her occupied that would not insult her intelligence but would keep her from learning what he was working on. Still, he had a backlog of projects. What the hell.

He offered her a seat after clearing it of books and papers. Then they discussed how he usually worked with a researcher and the background he needed on the subjects he was currently considering for articles. Ever since the Pulitzer, Del had been given pretty wide latitude in picking and choosing what interested him.

Before Cal had complicated his life, he had been researching possible drug abuse in major league baseball. He gave her all of his files on that and other current projects. "This should give you quite a bit to do while I'm in Atlanta," he said. "The Monroe story is first priority. I want to know every detail about how baseball players train— their private workout schedules, diet, the medical monitoring their trainers do, especially—"

"What kinds of prescription drugs they take legally or under the table. If our MVP has ever taken an aspirin, I'll document it," Kasi replied, taking the discs, glancing at the labels.

"I'll check in with you in a day or two from Atlanta," he said. Cuff had not been back in touch, Del had still not reached Gracie Kell, and all his leads on Crosby had turned to dead ends. But his long shot had paid off. He was booked on the afternoon flight to meet Gary Mc-Callum.

"What are you working on there? Any background check I can do at this end?"

"Nope. Just a follow-up piece on McCallum. . . . I've already done all the background research on him that I'll need." Del had always believed that a partial truth was safer than an outright lie.

"I thought he dropped off the edge of the earth after he was dismissed from BISC," she said absently as she sorted through the stack of discs he had given her.

"He did. But Gary McCallum's a good ole boy from a wide place in the road down on the Chattahoochee River. I think he's run to ground there."

"And you can find him in that wilderness?" She looked up from her work, not bothering to hide her incredulity.

"I grew up tracking jaguars in the jungle during the summers I spent with my family in Mexico. If he's there, I'll find him."

"Good hunting, Natty Bumppo."

3 P.M., EDT, TUESDAY, JUNE 23
ATLANTA, GEORGIA

As the plane taxied after landing at Hartsfield, Del stared out the window at the flat, hot landscape of Atlanta. He stretched back in his seat and rubbed the bridge of his nose absently, thinking about the unexpected call from Gary McCallum that he'd received late last night. If anyone could guess about what might be going on in BISC, it was the former agent.

Gary McCallum had started out as a beer-drinking, drag-racing, tattoo-wearing member of a teen fraternity of Alabama farm boys reminiscent of the *Dukes of Hazzard.* The ancient TV show reruns were still popular while he was growing up in Tallapoosa County. The drug culture, such as it was in the isolation of southeastern Alabama, consisted primarily of whiskey stills and homegrown cannabis. The violence and disease of the illegal pharmaceutical industry had not touched his life.

But when he was caught in a youthful indiscretion with the county judge's daughter on the bed of his '95 Ford 150 XLT 4×4 he fled to Atlanta. A three-month stint of washing dishes in a Peachtree Street hangout for Georgia Tech students convinced him to obtain a GED and get a college education. After struggling his way through a degree in political science, he entered the law program at Emory University. Like so many other idealistic young attorneys, Gary wanted to catch the bad guys. BISC recruited him immediately after he was admitted to the bar.

His skills tracking drug dealers in the Southeastern coastal swamps were particularly useful for the agency. Coming from a rural culture of shotgun justice, he liked BISC's clear-cut approach to handling criminals. Gary spent his professional career in the wilderness until he was transferred to the Atlanta office. As he later confessed to Delgado in an Opelika roadhouse, "I should've stayed in the swamp where people had real names like Coy 'n' Elvis."

There he knew the guilty from the innocent and his quarry was easy to hunt. But life in the urban "swamp" was infinitely more complicated. During his first year as an agent in the city, Gary fell victim to an El-Op called Jazzy Harp. Wanting to throw BISC off his trail, the street-smart dealer had planted enough evidence for Gary to find

Samuel Irving Gould guilty of trafficking. BISC Central had concurred and McCallum terminated the insurance salesman.

Some hard digging by Elliott Delgado had uncovered that Sam Gould had no connection to the drug trade other than being in the right place at the wrong time. Del's series of *U.S. News-Time* articles damaged BISC credibility, but BISC Central was a Teflon entity.

Agent McCallum was not. The organization he had devoted his life to serving now considered him a liability. A clever prosecutor might have uncovered information during a trial that would further have compromised the agency's mission. Central arranged for Mc-Callum to vanish before the warrant for his arrest could be served by the Fulton County Prosecutor's Office. It was "witness protection" in reverse. Or so BISC said.

McCallum hadn't been so sure he trusted the guys at Central anymore. No agent had ever before been put in the public eye. He escaped from BISC custody and "lit out." After contacting Del to give his side of the story, he spent the following years drifting from one small town to another. Folks in the rural South protected their own and didn't much speak to strangers.

McCallum developed a fondness for cheap bourbon. The guilt over Sam Gould's death consumed him. His need for absolution grew in proportion to his drinking problem, and Elliott Delgado became his confessor of choice. Gary called him sporadically, "just to talk." As he trudged down the concourse, Del had to chuckle at the idea of himself as a priest. His aunt Serifina would love it. Uncle Mac's hearty belly laugh would rumble like thunder at the idea.

When he'd first begun his Pulitzer-winning story, Del had focused on revealing that Jazzy Harp was the real drug dealer, then on the innocent man's family and how his death had affected their lives. He'd been stunned when the missing BISC agent had contacted him. After he interviewed McCallum, the whole vision of the piece changed. McCallum had not blamed Delgado for uncovering the termination of an innocent man. Rather, he had seemed devastated by guilt, far more concerned with the wrongful death than with the destruction of his career.

Here had been a human face inside a faceless monolith, a man with human frailties caught in the net of an omnipotent agency. Mc-Callum was as frightened by the absolute power of BISC as was Delgado. But Gary was also frightened for his own life. He had granted Delgado only one interview. Even though McCallum's guilty verdict was upheld by BISC Central, he had steadfastly refused to discuss the agency. He did not want to compromise his former coworkers to the El-Ops.

Maybe now McCallum'll spill what he knows about BISC.

Del sure hoped so as he paid cash to rent a Ford turboelectric at the airport. Once he'd driven outside Atlanta, he checked it for monitoring devices and installed the tail scanner Putnam had given him. After spending several hours cruising down Highway 75 toward Macon, he was fairly certain BISC had no ground tracking on him. Late that night he parked the TE out behind an abandoned Missionary Baptist Church, removed the tail scanner, and walked up the road to a shack where he had seen an auto sale sign. He woke up the owner and bought an old Infinity ragwagon, again paying cash. By daybreak he intended to be thirty miles past Columbus, Georgia, headed to Opelika, Alabama. If BISC found Gary McCallum, it would not be because Del had led them to him.

5.

Delgado was a slob. A great reporter but a slob. She surveyed his refuse-strewn office and wrinkled her nose at the bitter aroma of day-old coffee still simmering on the warmer like a carafe of tarmac. "A wonder he hasn't burned the building down," she muttered, flipping off the switch.

How could a man stay so lean and rangy subsisting on junk food? she wondered, depositing the half-empty pizza carton on his desk in the wastebasket. Tomato paste and meat grease stained the desk blotter, which was scrawled with illegible memos. Pieces of paper, some handwritten, others printed, stuck out from beneath the blotter and were haphazardly strewn across the wide surface of the desk, along with books, newspapers, and computer discs.

Where to begin? She looked over her shoulder even though she knew the corridor behind her was deserted. Even the most die-hard magazine reporters didn't usually work at 3 a.m. The cleaning crews had left the building over an hour ago. Obviously they had strict instructions not to enter the great Elliott Delgado's lair.

Even if someone from the magazine staff found her in here and asked questions, she was Delgado's new researcher. That was excuse enough. She sat down at the desk and began a rapid systematic scan of all the materials on it, carefully returning each one to its exact original position. He might be one of those rare types who could discern order in chaos.

After finishing with the desktop and drawers, she moved to the file cabinets. Nothing was secured. Carelessness? Innocence? Or the old hide-it-in-plain-sight ploy? That would sure be a good bet in this kind of mess. She found background files on people, places, and events in the headlines along with pix consistent with the careful background research every good reporter did on his stories. Nothing here.

There'd been nothing in the apartment either. Earlier in the evening she'd sifted through it an inch at a time. Getting past the security in his condo had been pitifully simple. Using the newest BISC technology, she'd hacked into his computer with ease. She'd learned a lot about Elliott Delgado's personal life and background, but little that her briefing at Central had not already given her. And none of it was incriminating.

Oh, his great-uncle Francisco Mulcahey, mayor of the coastal city of Mazatlán, had ties to the largest Mexican cartel, headed by the legendary Inocensio Ramirez, who had graduated from roadside bandito to drug czar. BISC analysts had noted that Delgado still maintained a close relationship to the wily old Mulcahey. Elliott's father had died when he was nine and the youth had spent his summers with his uncle.

Francisco had become a father figure to the lonely kid. If there was any drug-dealing connection between Ramirez and Mulcahey, FBI agents working in Mexico had not been able to find it. As for the mayor's American nephew, he had also been found clean by the FBI, who screened him thoroughly when he applied to the Bureau. Delgado had a distinguished record with several commendations before the disastrous street shoot-out that had ended his career.

BISC Central's file on him had been compiled after his exposé articles on the agency. It had remained inactive until last month when a refitted old Boeing 727 favored by Mexican El-Ops for transporting drugs crashed in the mountains of southern California. One of Ramirez's planes. A survivor confessed in exchange for extradition home to Mexico. Among those implicated was Elliott Delgado, who had been in San Diego that week, ostensibly to visit his son, Michael.

In a procedure rare for the agency, she had been brought into Central five days ago, briefed, and given the file on Delgado's background. She had also been furnished with carefully falsified credentials as an experienced news researcher and taken a crash course in the workings of wire services and newsmagazines. Of course the ability to quickly absorb details and assume a cover identity was a prerequisite for every BISC agent.

Leah Berglund was the best.

That same week she had become Kasi Evans. With some assistance from Central her application for work as a researcher at *U.S. News-Time* had been moved to the top of the pile. She was hired and assigned to Delgado. His refusal to accept her only strengthened her suspicions about his possible complicity in the Ramirez drug ring.

But Leah was a scrupulously careful agent who never returned a guilty verdict without first conducting an exhaustive investigation. So far all she had was a deposition from an extradited drug trafficker.

"Come on, Delgado," she murmured to herself as she shoved the last file drawer closed and turned to his PDA base station. Odd that his home and office systems did not interface. Why was his system so primitive and inconvenient? Was he really that technologically challenged? Or was there a more ominous reason for the separation?

Leah set to work. Around 7 a.m. the first people began to trickle down the long, twisting corridor. She could hear the low hum of voices at the other end of the hall. Delgado must like his privacy. He had a secluded corner office. One of the perks of being a Pulitzer winner she supposed, but wasted on a man who didn't care if the mold growing in his trash can ate the drapes.

After four hours her eyes began to blur as she scrolled through seemingly endless files. Zilch. Then she noticed a file entry under the odd name bkhrs.doc. Weird. His dossier indicated Delgado was raised in the Roman Church but had not practiced since he was confirmation age. A book of hours, prescribed prayers and readings for the canonical hours, was something more likely used by a medieval scholar than an investigative reporter. She opened the file.

"Jackpot, Delgado," she muttered as the material came up on the screen. Names, places, dates, and dollar amounts, some of them quite substantial. The last entry was dated last month in San Diego, the day

Ramirez's 727 went down. A contact was given but no dollar amount. "A crash. No payoff. Too bad for you, mister."

She quickly copied the file, then erased all traces of her activity on the system and shut it down. The material she had to verify would keep her busy for several days. If the names and Delgado's contact with them checked out, he was a dead man.

A feeling of acute disappointment mixed with regret took her by surprise. Since joining BISC, Leah believed that she had gotten past emotional involvement with subjects. But Elliott Delgado's background had indicated that he was a man of principle who had put his life on the line in public service, then recovered from devastating injuries to pursue another outstanding career. In spite of their antagonistic first meeting, she admired the guy.

That was the trouble with this sort of undercover op. The agent was forced to interact with the suspect, see him as a person in everyday life. Far better to surveil a piece of slime like Big Frankie Dittmeier, observe the incontrovertible evidence, and follow through with the cancellation. Executing a human being was never easy for her, no matter how vicious the criminal. But at least there was distance.

She broke off the chain of thought angrily, forcing her attention back to the reporter's messy office. "If he can tell someone's gone over this heap, I'll volunteer for Dumpster-sorting duty behind the Euro embassy," she muttered, flipping off the lights. When she looked out into the hall, no one was there. Leah closed the office door and walked away. The small disc in her pocket seemed to weigh ten kilograms.

12 P.M., CDT, WEDNESDAY, JUNE 24
ALABAMA

Delgado pulled off the side of a narrow gravel road deep in the heart of the Tallapoosa River country. The air was sweltering and still, the only movement the flit of horseflies and an occasional bee. Dense stands of pine and post oak afforded precious shade from blistering sunlight. An overgrown trail, rutted deeply by spring rain, forked off the gravel road. Del pulled the Infinity under the conceal-ing branches of a big chestnut tree a short distance up the dirt trail and started walking.

Gary's directions had been a little vague. Del suspected it was de-liberate. When he'd thrashed through the underbrush long enough, McCallum would show himself. At least Del hoped he would. He stopped to take a thirsty pull on his water bottle and found it was empty. Frustrated, he wiped away the sweat stinging his eyes and squinted around the small rise he'd just crested.

A limestone formation jutted over grassland to the east, more woods to the west. "The hell with it, I'll stick to the shade," he mut-tered, and turned westward.

He hadn't moved more than thirty meters when a voice behind him called, "That's far enough, Newsman."

Delgado turned toward the rocks. The glint of a shotgun barrel was the only thing he could see. "You took your own sweet time, Mc-Callum."

Gary McCallum stood up slowly, holding a street sweeper in his big meaty hands as he scanned the area one final time. Satisfied, he placed the twelve-gauge Striker semiautomatic with its ten-round drum magazine in the crook of his arm with the easy comfort of a born woodsman and ambled toward Delgado. The ex–BISC agent was a bear of a man, half a head taller than the lean reporter.

Once McCallum had had the hardened body of a football player, but years of heavy drinking had taken their toll. His gut strained at the buttons of the frayed green plaid shirt he wore tucked into faded jeans. Dried yellow mud caked his military-surplus boots. In spite of their thick soles, he moved soundlessly across the rocky earth. Gary McCallum had serious freckles, big as dimes and quarters, spattered all over his arms and face. His neck was as red as a ripe tomato.

"Just makin' sure you weren't followed," he said, scrubbing a hank of pale reddish hair from his forehead.

"I was careful."

McCallum nodded, leading the way into a thicket of post oaks. "They're closing in like a pack of blue ticks around a treed coon. I made one in Dudleyville last week when I drove there to pick up some supplies. They use Southern boys so's not to raise suspicion, but when any stranger starts askin' questions, the locals know he's federal."

"You ought to move on if they're that close."

"To where? At least here I'm on my own turf. I have folks who protect me."

"You could leave the country."

"I'm through running, Newsman." McCallum ducked beneath the low branches of a hickory tree and gestured to the small cabin in a deeply wooded glen. A tall stand of sugar pines concealed it from overhead surveillance, and the rough, boggy woodlands guaranteed scant chance anyone afoot would stumble on it.

"Welcome to my humble abode," McCallum said wryly as he strode down the narrow ravine to the dilapidated shack. The gray wood was warped and weathered by decades of exposure to heat, humidity, and rain. Here and there narrow chinks of daylight filtered between the boards. The windows were screened but lacked glass. The roof sagged. The cabin looked like one good thunderstorm would wash it away.

"Where's the still?" Del asked, only half-facetiously.

"Used to be one, or so I was told. The hills around here are filled with deserted places like this. I've lived in more than my share the past years," McCallum said, stepping into the dim interior. He had to duck his head to get through the doorframe.

Del followed, blinking to accustom his eyes from the brilliant sunlight outdoors. With only two narrow windows, the place was dark. It smelled of rotted wood and spilled whiskey. A small, well-blackened Coleman stove sat on the table surrounded by cans of beans and corn, beef stew and other staples. Flies buzzed around the jagged lid of an open can of peaches. A half-empty bottle of bourbon sat on the edge of an orange crate beside the cot set up in a windowless corner. He could smell the faint sourness of the sweaty, unwashed sheets tangled over it.

How the hell does he live like this?

McCallum offered his guest one of the two chairs in the single room, noticing the direction of Del's gaze. "I don't sleep so good," he said as he tapped bottled water from a five-gallon carboy into a couple of none-too-clean glasses and offered one to Delgado.

"Thanks." Del downed the drink in several long swallows and took a refill.

"Not a night goes by I don't see Sam Gould's face in my nightmares," Gary said, taking a seat beside Del. "Hell, even worse, I see his kid's faces, kids growing up without a daddy because of my stupid mistake."

"We've gone over this before, Gary. You're only human. You made a mistake, yes, but no single individual should ever be judge, jury, and executioner—that's too much responsibility for anyone to handle without making mistakes. Do you honestly think you're the only agent who ever canceled an innocent person?"

"If the agent does his job right, it's supposed to be a fail-safe system. Central reviews each verdict, double-checks everything . . . or at least, they're supposed to," McCallum added with weary resignation. His shoulders slumped as he leaned back.

"Yeah, they're supposed to—but who knows if they do? That's my point. BISC is a secret organization accountable to no one."

"You want to bring them down, Delgado? God Almighty, I only wish I was sure it's the right thing." McCallum poured a generous slug of bourbon into his half-empty water glass. He offered the bottle to Del, who shook his head.

"If you don't think BISC should be destroyed, why did you contact me?" Del asked, watching Gary empty the glass in a few hard gulps.

McCallum set it on the table and stared at the reporter. "You know what the latest hit is on the street these days? Express Elevator. The sons of bitches add a combo of blood thinners and vessel expanders to the cocaine and Viagra for a rocket trip to the brain."

"I know. Did a story a few months back on it. The additives triple Viagra's effect. Often as not you get a corpse with a boner. Another street name's Double Stiff."

"It's not funny, Newsman."

Del sighed. "Dammit, I know it isn't."

"I've seen twelve-year-old kids who bled to death through their eyeballs. Brains like mush when the ME's autopsied them. I really liked my job, Delgado. I liked killing the animals who make and peddle that shit. I felt good about being that judge, jury, and executioner you bitch about. I was so damn sure I was right—and I *was* right . . . until Gould . . ." He rested his head in his big freckled hands, gathering his composure.

"Do you finally have doubts about more than your own culpability? You should, Gary. BISC is ultimately to blame—the agency and the leaders in our government responsible for the Martial Law Act—hell, even the voters who were in a frenzy after the Slaughter. But it has to stop sometime, somewhere. Now. With you. You wanted this meeting. Why, if you don't agree with me?"

"I've had a long time to think it through and it's still all garbled up inside of me, but I guess when they sent other agents to kill me . . . The first time was in Dothan two months ago. I knew the guy. Bill Garvey. We went through training together. God forgive me, I killed him. That made me think . . . realize. They call teams sent to take out rogue agents Sanitation Squads. But I'm not rogue. I never betrayed them. Maybe you're right, Newsman. Hell if I know. I'm fucked either way. But I gotta trust someone to figure this out and you're it. My time's running out.

"Like I said, they're closing in." McCallum looked around the squalid room, then stared at the empty tumbler in his hand. "I can't last much longer. Hell, who'd want to?"

Del waited as Gary poured another drink, this time without water. "I never gave you any deep background, only what pertained to Gould's case."

"No. You never gave me what I really needed." Del struggled to contain his elation. This was the payoff he'd waited for ever since he'd broken the Gould story. His heart beat like a trip-hammer as he listened to McCallum's voice.

"I still wanted to believe in the agency, in what they've done—and they *have* taken a lot of the scum off our streets. I couldn't let the hope for that go. Besides, I was so hung up on my own guilt that it was all I could think about. I just couldn't see betraying my coworkers, the men and women who served with me."

"Until they turned on you," Del prompted. "Look, I give you my word—and you know I've always been straight with you. Christ, I won't print a list of agents' names so the El-Ops can hit them. I want inside BISC—I want to expose the inherent corruption that always comes from the *top* of a secret bureaucracy."

McCallum nodded. "Yeah, you been straight with me, even if you are a Yankee," he added with a crooked grin.

"Where is BISC headquarters?" Del asked, taking a recorder from his pocket. He punched it on after McCallum nodded approval.

"Same place they train recruits. It's in Reston, a gated compound called Deep Woods." McCallum described the facilities and their location. "The recruits spend a full year in a training program that makes Quantico look like a Boy Scout camp."

"You ever been through Hogan's Alley?" Del asked, then conceded, "FBI agents only get sixteen weeks."

"I forgot you used to be a Fed, didn't you?" McCallum said, breaking the seal and opening a fresh bottle of Heaven Hill. "Hard to imagine an FBI agent becoming a reporter."

"Not so big a leap. The FBI's hardly a secret organization. Tell me about the training," he said, directing Gary back on track.

McCallum talked until the long shadows of twilight darkened the woods outside. He gave Delgado the names of other field agents he knew and his immediate superiors in the chain of command at Central. In spite of his prodigious consumption of rotgut whiskey, his hand was steady when he lit a match to the wick of an ancient kerosene lantern. He described recruitment techniques, the way the agency screened out high-risk applicants, and the rigorous training in unarmed combat and in advanced weaponry.

"BISC agents have to become experts with conventional long and short arms before learning how to use needle guns."

"Yeah. I've seen their leftovers," Del said bitterly.

Gary studied the reporter for a moment. "Get your facts straight, Newsman. The needle gun is the most responsible law enforcement weapon ever developed. Fires a .177 slug, a synthetic carbon missile really. Got a sensor in the tip. Hits meat or bone, bores in, then explodes. If it hits any other surface, it vaporizes. No collateral damage."

Del countered, "What if you lost your 'responsible law enforcement weapon'?"

McCallum raised his hands, palms up. "Electroencephalographic chips. Unique to each agent, implanted in his hands. The chips are married to a mate in the weapon. A needle gun can't be fired by anybody but its agent. And when the agent's brain dies, the chips die, the gun dies."

Del replaced the cartridge in the recorder, dropping the filled one into his pocket. "Any ideas who the Tribunal members might be?"

"Not much chance for field agents to find out. We usually work alone. Information is strictly need-to-know. Once training is over and an agent is in the field, he or she never returns to Central unless specially requested, and that's pretty rare. An agent knows his super and a handful of tech support people he can contact for help with transport, weaponry, that sort of thing. If the rank and file who work inside headquarters speculate about who the Big Three are, I wouldn't—"

Delgado tensed when McCallum suddenly reached over and doused the lantern. "What?"

"Quiet," he hissed, shoving Del to the ground and grabbing his shotgun, which was never out of reach. Crawling on all fours, he approached the window and cautiously peered outside.

Del barely breathed as he pocketed the recorder and eased silently to the other side of the window. "You heard something?"

"It's what I didn't hear. The chucks stopped whistlin'. Ain't natur'l for everythin' to go quiet less someone's out there."

Delgado noted the thickening of McCallum's drawl, something the best part of a bottle of bourbon had been unable to effect. But fear did. "I was so damn careful. How the hell did they follow me?" Del whispered, furious with himself.

"Don't be so sure it was you, Newsman. Central's getting smarter. Last time they sent a Cracker after me. Maybe this time it's a 'Bama boy. They combed the woods outside Dothan for weeks after I killed Garvey. They could've got lucky here."

"I wish like hell I'd been able to bring my Smith & Wesson through airport security. You have firepower besides that street sweeper around here?"

"There's an old AK-47, stockless, under the cot. Think I got two or three thirty-round clips in the box beside it." McCallum waited until

Del found the weapon and jammed the extra clips in his belt, then said, "Wait here while I get out the door and clear, then you hightail it for that big bush we passed coming in here. Lay low there and don't move."

The ex–FBI man had visions of the two of them shooting each other in the darkness. "Maybe we should stick together."

"I know this country, Yank. You don't. Just stay put once you get there. I'll know not to shoot you." His teeth gleamed white as he slid a wicked-looking knife into a sheath and strapped it onto his belt.

That done, he crept to the door and rolled out onto the grass in front of the cabin. For a big man as out of shape as McCallum obviously was, he moved with surprising grace and speed, vanishing silently into the darkness.

Del waited, peering through the open door, seeing and hearing nothing. He could sense them though. McCallum was right. The silence was unnatural. Del felt it in his bones and knew there was more than one of them. The instincts from a previous lifetime started to kick in. He had spent his summers growing up in Sinaloa and Nayarit. His uncle and cousins were all skilled outdoorsmen. He'd participated in more than a few night jaguar hunts as well as daylight forays for everything from jackrabbits to wild pigs.

Elliott Delgado could track and could shoot even if the deserts and jungles of Mexico were different from the woodlands of Alabama. And eight years as a FBI agent had schooled him well in hunting two-legged quarry.

He watched until the moon vanished behind a bank of clouds once more, then rolled out the door the way McCallum had. His injured knee and pelvis kept him from executing the maneuver as smoothly, but he was almost as quiet. Feeling for the ammo clips to be certain he hadn't lost them, Del made his way up the glen to the giant bayberry bush. He rolled underneath the sheltering branches and peered out as the moon reappeared, flooding the woodland with patches of silvery light that danced with the movement of the trees when a faint breeze picked up.

Not a sound but the soft sough of the wind through the leaves. McCallum must have made it into the deep woods undetected. If he could take the first one out with the knife, all the better. Delgado's knee ached like a bitch after a few moments in the crouched position. If he was not careful, it would lock up on him just when he needed to move fast. He checked the perimeter again, then sat flat on his ass and stretched his leg straight out in front of him, rubbing the joint.

A sharp burst of gunfire broke the night silence, bringing him bolt upright, frozen. The sound of a 9mm submachine gun was unmistakable. McCallum had a twelve-gauge shotgun! *Come on, Gary, dammit!* Del waited for return fire, while moving silently into position for a run. Thirty seconds passed, maybe a little more. Then a series of rumbling booms from the street sweeper echoed down the glen. They were in the timber on the other side of the cabin.

He rolled out from beneath the bayberry and took off in a fast lope, avoiding loose rock, trusting the mossy undergrowth to muffle his footsteps. Moonlight lanced through the canopy, its sharp silver shafts uncertainly lighting his course. After a couple of dozen meters, he stopped, knowing they were near, knowing how dangerous it was to be caught between friendly and enemy fire in the darkness.

From what Gary had told him, he expected the assassins to have the latest infrared equipment, maybe aerofoam body armor, even nitro cordite frag grenades. He knew they had automatic weapons, but so did he . . . if he could get in place to fire through the nearly impenetrable underbrush. How many of them were there? Two? Three? A miscalculation would be fatal.

Del flattened himself against the trunk of a big white oak, deep in shadows where the moonlight did not reach. He waited. After a few minutes that seemed like hours, the shotgun boomed again simultaneously with a short burst of 9mm fire.

He blinked stinging sweat from his eyes, not daring to raise his hand and wipe it away. The reports were close. His ears strained for any human sound and he thought he heard a soft moan . . . or was it the rustle of leaves on the breeze?

Then he heard the crunch of footfalls, unmistakably human. Two men? He could see two indistinct blurs converging in the underbrush. Neither one spoke. One was big. Gary? He couldn't see enough to tell, but intuition said that, even wounded, McCallum would never make this much noise. He held his position.

"McCallum's dead," a low voice whispered.

The second figure melted back into the darkness. "So's Brandon."

Damn, Gary. Delgado watched, scarcely daring to breathe. *Are these two fuckers all that's left?* Some primal instinct said no.

The two agents ignored their fallen comrade. One knelt and searched Gary's body. After a minute or two, they split up. One walked directly toward Delgado's hiding place, Colt submachine gun still held ready to fire. Del did not breathe as the agent passed within a meter of him. The man wore fatigues and a night-vision helmet, but in the steam bath of the swamp, he wore no body armor.

They're looking for the cabin. He knew when they searched it, they'd figure out Gary had had company—recent company. And then they'd come after him. He'd never be able to find his car in the dark. That left one option. He followed their voices until they found the cabin. A moment later a third member of the Sanitation Squad materialized from the far side of the glen and entered. An electric torch flared inside, illuminating the windows and sending thin slivers of light between the warped boards. One man lit the kerosene lantern.

Del moved closer to the open door so he could see inside. *Time to bake some BISCettes.* He checked the clip and spares on his belt and raised the AK-47 just as he heard a voice inside say, "Hey, there's two glasses here."

As the first agent reached the door with his weapon raised, Del sprayed a continuous burst of .30-caliber slugs across the shack, starting waist high, then lowering the barrel as he hosed it back and forth. The agent in the doorframe was thrown back inside. Splinters of wood sprayed out of the cabin wall as if they'd been processed through a chipper. The shredding boards began to wink with irregular but ever widening patches of light. Over the thunder of the AK-47 Delgado could not hear the men inside scream as a fusillade of lead smashed into their bodies. He could not even hear his own roar of primal rage.

He emptied the clip and jammed another into the weapon and resumed firing. By the time he'd started into the third clip, the kerosene had ignited and flames were licking through what little was left of the shack. Fragments of wood and wire flew up into a night sky from which the moon had fled.

The remnants of the cabin looked like a patchwork of fragile black lace backlit in brilliant orange. Then the roof crumbled inward with a sucking whoosh. Del stood watching the fire burn itself out. The ruins smoldered with three dead men inside.

He left them and went to get Gary's body. McCallum he would bury. Let the possums have the rest . . . if they'd eat scum that rotten.

6.

The San Diego leads checked out. So did the one in Vegas two months earlier and the one two months before that in Atlanta. Using BISC protocols, Leah had accessed the data banks of the three police departments. Each of the men on Delgado's list was a known trafficker seen in the company of an unidentified Caucasian male whose description—with slight variations in the three instances—fit Elliot Delgado. And the dates of these observations matched exactly the dates on Delgado's list.

His work was a natural cover for brokering drug deals. Delgado could hop from city to city "on assignment" and raise no flags at all. She started to close out the evidentiary file, but some impulse stilled her hand. "Damn you, Delgado, why would you be so arrogant as to think you could hide this from BISC? Or so stupid not to know it's your death warrant?"

She leaned back on the chair in her apartment and combed her fingers through her hair in frustration.

"Maybe I'll double-check the Atlanta deal, just for the hell of it." Leah knew she was stalling. What was it about Delgado? She didn't want him to be guilty even though she knew damn well he was. Hell, she didn't even like the guy . . . but she admired his work. He'd been in Atlanta doing a follow-up piece to the Sam Gould story in January. His list indicated he'd netted $25,000 for brokering a deal with an El-Op named Owen McGee on January 26. And now he was back there for another piece on Gould's killer. Delgado either had a lingering fascination with Gary McCallum or he was using the ex–BISC agent as cover for yet another deal.

Leah had a contact in Atlanta. BISC agents were not supposed to be able to access a field station without going through their own supervisors, but she had been teamed with Rhys Willis a couple of years ago and had saved his life. He had a strong feeling of gratitude and a low tolerance for red tape. On a hunch she pulled up his number and dialed. The vid screen was blacked out, but a disembodied voice said, "Willis here. You're on the clock. I'm a busy man and I hate night shift."

"Willie, my friend, I need a favor."

"Ah, Berglund, Sweet Thing, I'd recognize your mellifluous voice anytime."

In spite of what he said, she could hear the tiny blip of a voiceprint scan being run. As soon as it checked out, his vid screen came on and Rhys Willis's droopy-lidded, round face gave her a toothy grin. He looked like a lecherous elf.

"How's that delectable tush of yours these days? Tight as ever, I imagine, hmm?"

"I may have loosened up a millimeter or two, but you're still a cavernous asshole, Willie, a spelunker's dream," she replied conversationally.

He chortled. "I never disappoint. What can I do you for, Sweetums?"

She double-checked her encryptor to be sure they were scrambled, then gave Willis some details. "Subject's name is Elliott Delgado. On January twenty-sixth of this year he may have brokered a deal with an El-Op named Owen McGee. If you can find anything about McGee on or off record, I'll love ya forever, Willie."

"Let me spin the bottle and get back to you." The screen went blank.

Leah sat back and drummed short, carefully manicured nails on the desktop. She stood up and stretched, looking around the efficiency unit Kasi Evans called home. It was as bleak and empty as her life. The walls were freshly painted a neutral beige, the cheap carpet was off-white with cigarette burns in several places. The room's only window was decked out with miniblinds in lieu of draperies. An ancient green-and-beige-striped sofa sat under it flanked by two cheap lamps on Plexiglas end tables. The narrow bed was flush to the opposite wall. The wall facing the door held a sink, small electric stove, and particleboard cabinets.

The only thing in the sterile room that indicated occupancy was her communication kit, set up on one of the end tables. It was standard issue for all BISC agents, computer-base PDA vid screen with interfacing phone satellite uplink and scanner. The kit came equipped with several hidden compartments containing weapons and ammunition, passed on to her by a support tech when she had arrived in D.C. The entire complex was the size of an attaché case.

"This is your life, Leah Berglund," she said aloud, breaking the silence of four neutral walls, which seemed to be closing in on her.

Oh, Kevin, how did it happen? We planned our lives so differently. What would her kid brother think of her now? Bad enough that she'd become a lawyer, now an assassin. Leah swallowed hard, reminding herself that she was a federal agent, legally empowered, scrupulously careful, highly decorated . . . miserably unhappy.

A mad impulse to go out and buy herself something utterly frivolous like a lace Valenciaga blouse or a pair of Via Spiga stiletto heels flashed through her mind. She needed something that made her an individual, a woman, just Leah, not Agent Berglund. In the past three years she had lived nowhere longer than a month or two tops; usually it ran to days. Her assignments took her from Seattle to Sarasota, Manhattan to Memphis, with precious little R & R time.

Not that Leah requested much. She seldom saw her parents the past three years. Holidays without Kev were just too hard. The few days of leave she did take were spent with Adam. She poured herself a Scotch on the rocks and sipped, thinking of the grand old man. That's what former senator Adam Manchester was. A white-haired lion, the patriarch of the family. Her grandfather had retired from the Senate after the passage of the Martial Law Act.

A staunch conservative of the old Goldwater school, Manchester had been one of the few members of Congress who voted against what he considered the undermining of constitutional principles. When his last term expired, he declined to run for reelection.

The following year Kevin had died senselessly when a college party turned into a one-way Elevator ride to oblivion for him and two of his frat brothers. The whole family had been numbed with shock and grief, but expressed it in different ways.

With his inside sources high in government, Manchester learned that the Elevator operator who had sold death in a bean bag to naive freshmen had been hunted down and executed by a BISC agent within a month of the tragedy. That did not change Adam's politics, but it did change Leah.

When she joined BISC, she had feared he might disown her, but he did not.

"When this case is over, we're going sailing, Gramps." She finished the last swallow of Scotch just as her secured line rang.

"Sweet Thing, you owe me."

She switched on the vid screen and Willis's deceptively cherubic face came into focus. "What is it?" Dread tightened her throat suddenly. *Good-bye, Delgado.*

"The info is pretty self-evident," he replied. "Your El-Op Owen McGee is one dead puppy. No need to worry about canceling him."

"Good for him, Willie, but what about the meet with Delgado on the twenty-sixth?"

"McGee was moldering in his grave way before that. A legal termination on sixteen January."

"But that's ten days before—"

"That's what I like about you, Sweet Thing, you're quick. Good at math, not to mention the best-looking legs in the agency." He winked.

A sense of relief washed over her. *Maybe Delgado's clean.* But it was quickly replaced by apprehension. "Why would Atlanta PD records say McGee was operating when Delgado was there on the twenty-sixth if he was canceled on the sixteenth?"

Willis's face grew expressionless, all trace of levity erased. "I don't know, Berglund. Maybe somebody doesn't like Delgado. Wasn't he the one who wrote about McCallum? Central gets really testy when its dirty linens are aired in public. You have evidence from other sources saying Delgado's dirty, cancel him and don't look back."

And don't question Central.

The message was implicit. Leah forgot to breathe for a moment, then felt as if an anvil had been dropped on her. No. It simply could not be. No one in Central could manufacture evidence. There were too many safeguards to get around. "You're certain about McGee?"

"You can take it to the bank, Berglund, but don't take it to your supervisor. If you do . . . I'll have a sudden lapse of memory."

"I'd never compromise you, Willie," she said tightly.

"Good. Do the smart thing, Sweetums. Go with the evidence you got on Delgado and turn in a guilty verdict. Then it's out of your hands."

"The hell it is. I'm the one who'll have to terminate him."

"Your call, Sweet Thing, your call. Just remember we never talked." The screen went blank.

10:17 A.M., EDT, THURSDAY, JUNE 25
ATLANTA, GEORGIA

As his flight from Hartsfield to Washington National took off, Delgado reviewed the events of the past night. He had struggled to dig a suitably deep grave in the boggy Alabama clay for Gary McCallum's body, only hoping the bones of the BISC Sanitation Squad would be covered in kudzu by summer's end. He'd found their vehicle, a fancy Volvo TE and disabled the customized BISC GPS inside it, one of the tips Gary had given him. Then he had driven the vehicle into a muddy pond not far away from the cabin.

He used the Infinity to get back to Georgia. His rented Ford remained where he had left it. In a few minutes he switched the tail scanner from the Infinity back to the TE. With the Infinity's lights out, he eased it back onto the lot where he had purchased it the day before. He left the vehicle with keys in the ignition. The crafty old used-car shyster would probably have it resold in three days. Then he had fired up the Ford and headed toward Atlanta.

Thanks to Gary, he had a good idea about how BISC operated, even a few big names and the location of Central. He decided on a game plan. Now if only Gracie surfaced when he arrived in Washington.

Gracie Kell was the best computer hacker in the business. She had become an urban legend of sorts when she'd accessed the Euro's Economic Policy Planning records just after the union was formed nine years ago. Through an intermediary, she sold the information on world trade to the U.S. Department of Commerce for an "undisclosed" sum. Gracie Kell had been thirteen years old at the time.

A career in government or a Fortune 500 company might have been in her postdoctoral future if Gracie had fit the profile, but she didn't physically or psychologically. Nails chewed to the quick, spiked chartreuse hair, and studded biker's leathers with stiletto-heeled boots were not acceptable in Washington or on Wall Street. But even had the style fitted, her variety of paranoia wouldn't have. Gracie was a conspiracy theorist, certain that everyone from the Russian Mafia to extraterrestrials had hacked into the secret databases of the federal government and was using the information to subvert American life.

She was combination dominatrix and geek, who repeatedly tried to trade her hacker services to him for a weekend of his submission in her bedroom.

Delgado always paid her cash.

12 P.M., EDT, THURSDAY, JUNE 25
WASHINGTON, D.C.

When he reached his apartment, Gracie had left one of her bizarrely coded messages. Delgado was on a roll. They met at a small bar on North Capitol that afternoon. The neighborhood made him pat his .50-caliber Smith & Wesson every few minutes just for reassurance. Urban renewal wasn't a big priority in northeastern D.C. Even BISC stayed away from the drug-infested slums. Gracie had always been an idealist with a Georgetown liberal's sympathy for the poor. In her favor, Del admitted she put her money where her mouth was, not only living among them, but also giving away the fortune the Feds had paid her to welfare mothers, homeless veterans, even the members of teen street gangs. She earned what she needed to live on by hacking or, as she put it, by "interrogating" other people's computers.

The interior of the bar was dark and smelled like the inside of a trash Dumpster in the middle of a D.C. summer. If there was any air-conditioning, he was damned if he could feel it. The long bar with broken-down stools was virtually deserted. A man hunched over his beer while flipping channels on a remote aimed at a blurry television in one corner, while two others argued the pros and cons of a local boxer.

No one paid any attention to Del, least of all the listless bartender, who slouched on a stool paring his fingernails with a Swiss Army knife. The reporter scanned the high-backed wooden booths along the opposite wall until he spotted Gracie. She looked up from the holograph emanating from the PDA on the table and waved him over.

"You really picked a swell place this time, Gracie," he said, scooting his ass along the lumpy vinyl seat. "Remind me to burn these chinos after I leave here."

"This is where real people live, Delgado. No Feds would dare set foot in Dobbins Addition. Even the D.C. cops aren't on the pad up here." Her chartreuse hair looked almost silver-white in the dim light and she wore a tank top, displaying tattoos on both her matchstick-thin arms and shoulders. She chewed on the remnants of one nail, her eyes squinting at the holo in front of her. "What do you want?"

"If you don't stop biting your nails, you'll bleed all over your equipment."

She shrugged, then slumped against the bench and stared at him with thickly mascaraed brown eyes. "You didn't come here to talk about my manicure."

"No. I need information that only you can get for me."

Her eyes glittered. "Yeah?"

"It'll be dangerous, Gracie."

"What ain't these days." She flipped the protective cover closed and crossed her arms over her flat chest.

"Have you ever hacked into BISC Central?"

"How many times do I have to tell you, I'm not a hacker. I'm a computer interrogator. And, no, nobody's ever been crazy enough to ask me to fuck with BISC." She attacked another nail. "I might've played around with their system on my own . . . just for kicks." She grinned. "It's a bitch to get in. Set up in dedicated network hypercubes—called N-cubes—encoded by subject and security levels. The cube nodes communicate with each other using *multiple power encryption algorithms. Multiple!* That's the bitch."

Del tried to keep his eyes from glazing over. *Talking cubes? Algorithms?*

"Fuck, Delgado, if it don't have tits or a cork, you can't process it, can you?"

Del opened his mouth, then clamped it shut and shrugged.

Gracie beamed with condescension but her voice was gentle. "I like it when a guy can admit he's stupid. It's sexy." She leaned forward then, all serious once more, eyes darting around the room as if it suddenly weren't as secure as she'd indicated earlier. "You looking for anything in particular?"

Del took a copy of the disc he'd made based on McCallum's information. "Who the three Tribunal members are wouldn't be bad for starters."

She snorted and reached for her big sweating glass of Diet Coke, talking through sips on the straw. "I doubt Central has ever put those names into their system."

He conceded, "I imagine they might use code names, even on the inside. Okay. I'm looking for some pretty serious hanky-panky between the Pentagon and BISC."

"The brass and the terminators—I always thought they were in it together." Her eyes grew as round as her nose ring. "How'd *you* get in on the scoop?"

"I have a source in the Pentagon who's confirmed a black op centering around Adair-Rawlfing on the California-Baja border. They're going to hit the Cartel."

"They're going to eliminate the source—or take it over so they can sell direct themselves . . . yeah, that's the ticket! They'll set up labs on all the military bases and fly the raw coke in from Colombia. Then—"

"Let's focus, Gracie. All I want now is evidence that will link BISC to the Pentagon black op. Who are the rogue agents—or is the Tribunal itself involved?"

"Of course they are—all of 'em."

"Much as I mistrust BISC, I doubt the whole bureaucracy could be suborned," he said drily. It was a good thing Gracie's nuttiness didn't interfere with her computer genius. "Here are a few prompts to put you on the trail—some insider info from a former BISC agent."

Her hand froze on the disc as he handed it to her. "There isn't any such thing as a *former* spook. Nobody quits the Company. Nobody quits BISC either."

"They do when they're dead, canceled by a Sanitation Squad of BISC goons."

"Their version of an early-retirement incentive, huh? This one will cost you heavy coin, Delgado."

"No. No goddamned chains!"

"You don't know what you're missin'," Gracie purred. "But what I really had in mind this time was a story on the kids at the T Street homeless shelter."

"Gracie, I haven't got time to do another story right now. Look, I—"

"No story, no deal." She sat back and rubbed her nose ring with one ragged fingernail. "Those kids need help—the program's about to fold for lack of funding. You do know that homeless people are the primary victims of alien abductions, and kids—"

Del capitulated. "I don't know how in hell I'll get Cohen to run it, but I'll find an angle."

"Good. And I'll get started on BISC's inner sanctum tonight. Don't know how long it'll take. Check our dead drop every few days." She looked around the bar, gathering up the disc and her PDA and stashing them in a handbag that looked big enough to hold a couple of accordions. "I'm outta here. I'll get back to you."

10:15 P.M., EDT, THURSDAY, JUNE 25

Leah Berglund poured herself a double Scotch and took a good stiff belt, hoping it would calm her nerves. After Willis's bombshell she had spent the past twenty-four hours trying to figure out what she should do.

It was credible that a highly decorated former Fed could go bad. It was credible that an experienced investigator, through overconfidence or a lapse of sheer stupidity, would record a file of self-incriminating evidence. It was credible that a reporter noted for his accuracy could mistake the date of an important meeting. But it damned well was not credible that the same mistake would appear in the files of the Atlanta PD. The only explanation was that someone had set up Delgado.

Yeah, formerly FBI, presently investigative reporter . . . hell, the guy's enemies would be legion. But would any be powerful enough to salt the files of the police departments in a half dozen cities? She thought again of Willie's implication that BISC might be seeking revenge for the McCallum exposé. But Delgado had written that stuff over two years ago. Why wait?

She rubbed her eyes wearily, took another sip, and thought once again about the most disturbing possibility of all. Maybe the target for the setup was not the reporter but BISC itself.

"My God," she muttered softly, "if one of our own people thinks we'd kill an innocent man out of spite, what would the general public think?"

Damn, her head was throbbing. "But who would dare take on BISC?"

The empty room gave her no answers. Maybe Adam Manchester could. Or she could do what Willie had suggested—turn in the guilty verdict she'd first reached. Leah finished her drink, sat down at the computer, and began to type.

7.

Leah reported to work the following day after her third night in a row with only a few hours' sleep. Years of training and an iron will enabled her to conceal her feelings. Delgado was back from Atlanta. She could smell the acrid aroma of his coffeemaker blending with the greasy smell of a McDonald's sausage McMuffin.

"Don't you ever eat anything but junk?" she said from the doorway. Her empty stomach clenched uncomfortably, not from hunger.

"That's why they invented vitamins." He grinned and took another bite.

"McDonald's at eight in the morning. McDonald's anytime." She shuddered.

"I need grease and cheese to coat my stomach for the coffee. Help yourself to a cup . . . if you dare."

"No thanks. You said you'd keep in touch but you never called."

His dark eyes danced. "Why, Kasi, I'm flattered you missed me."

She ignored his remark and continued in her most professional voice, "I've been busy on the assignments you gave me." She handed him half a dozen discs.

Del waved the McMuffin, indicating she should place them on top of a pile of papers. "Good work. Did you complete the background on Jim Monroe?"

"A squeaky-clean all-star. Discounting the liniment his trainer uses to massage his shoulders after batting practice, he's never taken the simplest painkillers, much less anything that might illegally boost him for a game. Not so some of the other players, according to rumor. It's all here." She tapped her nail on one of the discs.

"Grab a seat. I get a crick in my neck looking up." He seemed oblivious to the fact that every chair in the office was piled with boxes and papers.

She cleaned the one directly in front of his desk and sat down. "How did it go in Atlanta? Did you locate McCallum?"

"Yeah. I found him." Her cool blue eyes seemed to look right through him. *Why is she asking about Gary?* He felt a prickle of unease.

The first thing he'd done after landing last night was to contact Cal and tell him what had happened. Putnam had assured him that he'd arranged to cover Del's back. Every day now he felt himself pulled in deeper. He'd escaped detection in Georgia, but sooner or later BISC would be on to him. If only Cuff and Gracie could come up with something. Maybe the meeting with Bedford tonight was adding to his case of nerves.

He convinced himself that Kasi's asking about the follow-up piece on Gary was natural. "I decided not to do another story on McCallum. He's hiding from BISC and I don't want to sic those boys on him or me. A fellow can end up dead that way."

She could feel the icy edge of goose bumps rise along her spine. "I believe McCallum is hiding from public censure, maybe even from some crank vigilante types who'd try to kill him because of his mistake—but BISC?"

A harsh, cynical smile curved his lips but his eyes were cold. "How long have you been in the news business—ten years, Cohen said? And you're still idealistic enough to believe any secret government agency won't kill one of its own to keep him from talking? You've got one hell of a lot to learn."

"Then teach me. I want to know if my government's abusing public trust."

"I think that's been pretty evident as far back as Watergate."

"You're accusing BISC, not President Samson's office," she persisted.

Stubborn, aren't you, Ms. Evans? The sausage sandwich sat like a lump of putty in his gut. He decided to melt it down with coffee, pouring a cup of the lethal black stuff, taking a gulp. "Samson appoints the Tribunal members. Maybe he's guilty, too." *Why the hell did I say that?* He could sense her reaction. *Dammit, I'm starting to sound like Gracie!*

"My God, you really do have a warped opinion of everybody in Washington."

"Occupational hazard." He shrugged. "Let me review these files and I'll get back to you." He read the disc labels. Two on Jim Monroe and the pro baseball prescription-drug industry, another on the murder trial of Grosse Pointe society debutante Sally Ford Wallas. "You must've worked day and night since I left. When's the last time you slept?" he asked, noticing the smudges beneath her eyes, the tired lines bracketing her mouth.

Between gathering evidence on Delgado's case and doing the research he'd assigned her, Leah hadn't slept more than six or seven hours in the past three days. "You don't exactly look like a satisfied Serta sleeper yourself."

His eyes were bloodshot and his hands unsteady. He drank from the coffee mug as if it were all that was keeping him awake. *Something happened with McCallum.* She knew it in her gut and felt a wildly irrational urge to tell him who she was and ask what he really knew about BISC. The thought rocked her. *Get a grip, Berglund. Don't blow everything.*

She squelched the devastating thought that BISC might be corrupt, that she had devoted her life to—and killed for—an organization with an agenda far removed from its charter. *Stick to what you have to do, dammit.*

"Take the day off, Kasi. You've earned the rest."

Delgado's words focused her. "What are you going to do?"

"The old man was lying in wait for me when I came in. It seems our esteemed publisher wants coverage of the opening of Bootstrap House, and whatever Carolyn Etherington wants, she gets."

"Bootstrap House—isn't that the new drug rehabilitation facility for children sponsored by Congressman Fuller?"

"Mr. Congeniality of the House himself. Yeah. This should raise his AR at least ten points in the polls."

"I've always admired Brian Fuller. He seems genuinely interested in kids."

"Yeah. Usually around election time."

"Do you detest all politicians?"

He managed a tired grin. "Only those who get reelected. Shows they've sold out."

"Let me go with you. I'm good with a camera."

"Maybe you didn't hear—I offered you a day off."

She shrugged. "Maybe I just want the chance to meet Brian Fuller in person."

"I thought a sharp cookie like you'd be above falling for a pretty face."

She looked him up and down appraisingly as he had done to her the first time they'd met. "Never underestimate the power of lust, Delgado."

Her frank perusal set off a sizzle that surprised him. He had intended to call Joe Baldo for pix. *What the hell.* "Get your camera."

Leah gathered up the Sony Mavica DC3 and the pixel discs she required and met Del at the metro station outside the *U.S. News-Time* building. They took the Green Line subway up to the U Street–Cardozo Station, then walked three blocks to where the new rehab facility was located. Grimy, litter-strewn streets, weed-infested vacant lots, and squat, ugly brick tenements baked in the midday heat.

They'd been wise to take public transport. Not an inch of curb within a ten-block radius was unoccupied as the crowd converged on a shiny, new three-story stone and synthetic-cedar building. The facility stood out like a freshwater lily floating on a cesspool.

"Very impressive," Del said as she snapped some distance shots of the crowd against the backdrop of Bootstrap House. "Easy to tell the guests from the locals."

Well-dressed politicians and civic leaders flashed their invitations and bypassed the police cordon. Behind it a teeming crowd of ragged local residents sweated in the stifling heat. Arthritic old people with seamed faces said little and watched stoically while edgy youths still energized with the anger of the dispossessed shoved and cursed at the cops. The only thing the generations had in common was soul-deep despair.

"They build a place to help kids beat the drug problem, then cordon them out of it so congressmen in stretch limos can get in without soiling their Armani suits."

"You are a cynic," she said, snapping a close-up shot of a Supreme Court justice. "But you're right. This is a media circus to benefit the politicos, not the kids."

"Let's go for that angle." Delgado motioned for her to follow as he approached a couple of preteen boys wearing baggy jeans and surly expressions.

Leah watched him work. He was a master interviewer of newsmakers and power brokers who could charm and disarm the ordinary citizen. In spite of his cynicism, the guy had a natural way with people, one that seemed to say, "No crap, I care."

She had not lied when she had told him that she admired his writing. Now she understood why the articles touched her. Why she had felt so hesitant to turn in a guilty verdict.

They worked the crowd for half an hour or so, then flashed their press passes and went inside, where Congressman Brian Fuller was holding court for a group of wealthy businessmen as TV news cameras whirred all around him.

"This program is the model for a nationwide campaign to save America's children from the ravages of drug addiction. With the generous support of civic-minded people of vision"—he paused to bestow a megawatt smile on a California aerospace tycoon and an Arizona real estate developer—"we will bring the private sector into partnership with the government for a drug-free America."

A smattering of applause followed as the California congressman made his way toward the dais set up in the huge foyer.

Leah had never seen Brian Fuller in person before, although she'd followed his meteoric rise from crusading L.A. district attorney to highly influential member of the House Ways and Means Committee. He was not as tall in person as he appeared on camera, but his sandy blond hair and earnest blue eyes highlighted a square-jawed face of movie-star handsomeness.

"Lots of the political pundits say he'll win the Democratic nomination for president after Samson," she said.

"God help both the party and the public if he ever does."

"I know he's slick, but what politician isn't? Why do you dislike him so?"

Del shook his head, muttering, "It's a long story." He moved closer to the dais.

She followed, intrigued even more after the ceremony and speeches when the floor was open to questions. While all the other dignitaries responded to Delgado's questions, Fuller pointedly ignored him.

The crowd thinned out while she took some last shots of the facilities and Del interviewed the new director. As they walked back to the Metro station, she asked about the mutual antipathy.

"Fuller's just another grasping, ambitious politician with charisma and an ego the size of Jupiter. They're all alike . . . until you get to know the guy behind the smile."

"And you do—know him personally?"

"I did." He kept on walking, hands in his pockets, staring straight ahead.

"Well, that's forthcoming," she said drily. " 'Shut up, Kasi, it's none of your business.' " They crossed the street in silence.

"He was my ex-wife's lawyer in the divorce."

"Ouch. I didn't know he ever handled domestic cases."

"He made an exception for me."

"Nice guy."

His expression lightened. "Him or me?"

She laughed. "Do I get to choose 'none of the above'?"

Their eyes met in a silent exchange. Delgado had deliberately deflected their conversation from the bitter topic, but not before he'd revealed his vulnerability. He knew that she was aware of it. She waited for him to frame a safe reply.

Suddenly the calm drone of traffic was shattered by a sharp crack of gunfire. As the bullet whizzed past them, Leah and Del dropped to the ground. More shots followed, ricocheting off cars, tearing into the heat-softened asphalt as they dived behind a beat-up yellow Volkswagen EV.

"Across the street, second-story window on the left. Stay down!" he yelled, pulling his .50-caliber Smith & Wesson out to squeeze off a return round. Another burst of fire erupted, this time from an automatic.

"That came from this side around the corner," she said.

"I make at least three shooters, one in the window and two down the block," Delgado replied, as much to himself as to her.

Leah rolled under the EV to use the tire for cover while unstrapping a small Ruger automatic from her left leg. While Del kept the boys down the street busy, she wiggled into position and stared intently at the window where the first shot had originated.

"Come on, you fucker," she whispered. An instant later she was rewarded when a face appeared above the sill with pistol raised. "Peekaboo." Her shot struck dead center, entering the bridge of his nose. His head pitched backward and vanished.

"Christ, nice shooting!" Del said with no time to wonder how a news researcher had wangled a gun permit in D.C. He was certain BISC had found him until he recognized the high-pitched laugh of BoBo Johnson. "Sorry I dragged you onto my own personal target range," Del said, crawling under the car beside her. "A goddamn O.K. Corral in the middle of U Street and not a cop responds."

"They're all busy guarding Fuller," she replied as one of the guys with some sort of automatic weapon repositioned himself. His pal opened up again with a long burst of fire from what sounded like a vintage Nam M16A1. Street-level El-Ops favored a chopped-down version of the weapon because it was cheap and fully automatic.

"Make a run for that old Lincoln while I cover you," Del ordered.

Leah grabbed the camera case, shimmied out behind the VW, and dived, rolling neatly beneath the much larger vehicle. She fired at the men whose trail of lead had buckled up hunks of tarmac close behind her. "Now, Delgado!"

He wasn't as agile as she was, but he knew how to zigzag. Street debris and loose rocks stung his legs as he ran, then jumped behind the

Lincoln, which was now riddled with bullets. The yellow VW looked like a block of Swiss cheese on four flat tires.

Up and down the block not one of the terrified people barricaded inside their doors would call the police. The overburdened cops would not respond in any case. This was the El-Ops' turf. Only BISC agents challenged their supremacy, and they did so in carefully planned, surgical strikes. No one was coming to save a couple of reporters.

"I don't know where you got the piece, but I'm damned happy you know how to use it. I only have one extra clip when this one's done."

Another burst of fire flattened the second tire on the Lincoln. She rattled the camera case. "I'm packing an ammo dump. But we'd better get the hell out of Dodge."

He nodded. "Our best bet is to use these parked cars as cover to reach the Metro station. Security there will radio for help in self-defense. If BoBo has more boys on the way, we'd better pray a train pulls in with our fucking name on it."

"I take it you know these guys?" she asked, diving for the next car without waiting for a reply.

He caught up to her, barely escaping a hail of lead. "Kasi, meet BoBo Johnson. His kisser ran on *U.S. News-Time*'s front page last month. I did the article."

Silently she cursed the news media for covering drug wars. All they did was run the key people into hiding, making the job that much tougher for BISC. "You'll pardon me if I don't offer to shake his hand. Cute laugh, though." She dived for the next car.

Within minutes that seemed like hours, they were within ten meters of the Metro entrance. The concrete shell over it would provide good cover, but the escalator going down would leave them easy targets from the top—if they rode it.

"Get to the entrance and cover me. I'll cover you while you ride down," Del said.

"What about you? They'll be on us before you can clear the escalator."

"I'll jump over the side."

She'd seen the CT scans of his injuries in the BISC file. "Bad plan. You're limping already. I'll cover you and make the jump."

"We do it my way." He shoved her out. "Now go!"

She didn't argue, just jammed another clip into her Ruger and took off. One of his shots must've nicked Johnson. She heard a keening, high-pitched string of curses after the last exchange, but when Delgado started after her, two M16A1s opened up again. "All you did was piss him off," she said when he landed beside her against the concrete wall.

He checked his clip. "We're damn lucky BoBo and his pal are lousy shots."

"Not lousy enough for you to take them both out with two rounds, Delgado."

"Okay, you weren't shitting about the ammo dump in the camera case. When you get down the escalator, just keep firing up while I jump."

"Cut the macho crap. I was an all-conference gymnast in college. I can do it. You'll only break a leg and get me killed dragging your sorry ass across the turnstile."

Her face was expressionless but her pale eyes glared like lasers. *She's right, dammit.* "Throw me your gun just before you jump."

Leah nodded, tossing him the camera case with the extra clips. He caught it and bolted down the moving risers. Bursts of automatic weapons fire came closer as he reached the bottom and swung behind the side of the escalator in a crouch. "Now, Kasi!"

She pulled off a series of rapid shots, then threw him the gun and climbed onto the narrow rubber railing as it moved downward. As soon as she saw the glint of a gun barrel appear over the top of the concrete wall above her, Leah dropped over the side of the rail. She held on long enough to gauge the drop to the ground, then let go when the zing of bullets ricocheted off the metal risers and walls around her. Delgado's fire held them at bay behind the concrete entry wall.

Leah landed hard, letting her bent knees absorb the worst of the shock the way she'd been taught. Nothing broken, but every bone screamed as she hugged the escalator wall, making her way toward Delgado's position.

"We can clear the turnstile and go below. They won't dare follow us down. The escalator's too exposed," she said as he returned the Ruger to her and pulled his Smith & Wesson from his belt.

Just then Junior Wilcox, BoBo's main man, leaned over to deliver another stream of fire. Del's eyes had never left the edge of the concrete wall above. He snapped a quick shot, catching Wilcox in the shoulder. The El-Op was slammed backward, dropping his assault rifle onto the escalator.

All Del had to do was wait for it to come to him while Kasi sent up a wall of fire to hold off Johnson. "Now we're cooking," he said as he scooped up the weapon. Most of a clip was still unspent. "Thoughtful of you to reload for me, Junie."

"We're outta here, Delgado." Leah took off for the turnstiles, vaulting across one, then crouching behind it to cover him.

Neither El-Op pursued them as they raced toward the stairs leading down to the train platform below. The ticket agent behind the heavy glass ducked to the floor of her booth when she saw two armed civilians running past. Their faces slack with terror, half a dozen people huddled behind station maps and support poles or crouched under benches. At the far end of the platform a lone security guard urged them to remain calm. The guard took one look at the assault rifle Delgado was carrying and dived behind a bench himself.

Seeing a link in the guard's hand, Del yelled, "Call the police!"

Leah checked for east- and westbound trains. No light in either tunnel. Suddenly more automatic weapons fire echoed deafeningly in the cavernous concrete vault. BoBo came down the stairs at the opposite end of the platform, sporting a bloody bandanna wrapped over the ear Del had nicked. Junior trailed behind him, his left arm hanging uselessly at his side, a pistol clutched in his right hand.

They opened fire amid the shrieks of the commuters. Del and Leah took cover behind a station map at their end of the platform. Their pursuers used the concrete wall of the stairs, much more substantial protection. The security guard never raised his head above the safety of his bench.

Leah whispered, "I'm out of ammo."

Del was afraid of cutting loose with the automatic for fear of hitting civilians. "Where the hell's the fucking train?" he grated.

"We can't get on it without risking the passengers already aboard," she said.

He knew she was right. BoBo and Junior would jump into another car, and the ensuing gun battle would trap even more innocent people between them. Del looked down the track. The rails were almost two meters below the platform and there were rungs for repairmen spaced at regular intervals along the tunnel.

"You think you can keep them pinned down with this thing?" he said, patting the M16A1.

Following his eyes down the track, she caught on to the idea. "Yeah, but I'm quicker. I should go over the side."

"No machismo intended, Kasi, but I bet you never played football. I've got one slug left in the Smith & Wesson. I'm going to have to drop BoBo and tackle Junior, who's no lightweight. I don't like it, but that's the way it's got to be."

She conceded. "Give me the 16."

"The biggest trick is to hold it steady and not . . ." He saw the look on her face and shut up, handing her the weapon.

Leah flipped the selector switch from auto to semiautomatic and peeked around the sign, noting the positions of the commuters. She'd have to be careful. Not only to keep them out of the line of fire but to watch for ricochets as much as possible. "On my mark, go for it."

She opened fire as Del snaked on his belly to the platform edge and vanished over the side. With any luck the El-Ops didn't see him.

Delgado crouched down, not daring to move too quickly even though every nerve in his body screamed for him to run. *If only I can keep from getting fried on these rails or hit by a train . . .* One false move and he'd be toast. The firing above him became sporadic. The two assault rifles answered one another, punctuated by an occasional taunt from BoBo. When Del reached the rungs to climb up behind the two dealers, he could feel the rumble of an approaching train. Time was running out.

Leah saw his head appear about ten meters behind where BoBo and Junior hid. She took a deep breath, set the selector switch on auto, and fired a long burst as a noisy diversion, all the while watching Delgado aim his Smith & Wesson.

Del squeezed the trigger with exquisite care and hit Johnson squarely between the shoulder blades. The big El-Op's body pitched forward. Blood loss had slowed Junior, but not stopped him, as he saw his enemy and raised his .45-caliber Glock. Delgado dived on him, clubbing the dealer's injured left shoulder as they hit the hard terrazzo floor.

Leah ran toward them, clutching the assault rifle. Delgado and the man he called Junior Wilcox rolled perilously close to the edge of the platform. The light from a train illuminated the curve in the tunnel ahead.

If they go over together, your problem is solved.

The thought flashed through her mind, appalling her. *No!* Whether or not Delgado was innocent, someone in BISC was falsifying evidence, and she could never live with that. Besides, her gut told her that the newsman was clean.

As the men rolled, she saw a chance and leveled the M16A1 for a shot, but the firing pin clicked on an empty chamber. *Jesus!* She dashed to BoBo's body, rolling him over and snatching up his assault rifle. She slid the bolt partially open. Pay dirt! She leveled the weapon just as Delgado smashed a fist into Wilcox's face and rolled free of the big man's grip. Junior tried to get up and lunge for Del, who was still on the floor, but the reporter landed a hard kick that catapulted Wilcox over the edge just as Leah's shot took him full in the chest. He was airborne for an instant before the train hit his body.

There wouldn't be enough of the corpse left for an autopsy.

8.

Del and Leah waited in one of the dingy gray cubicles the D.C. police used for witness interrogation. Their statements about the shootings had been corroborated by witnesses. All that remained was processing the paperwork. The deaths of two small-time drug dealers did not generate much excitement among D.C.'s finest.

"How the hell did you get the permit to carry that arsenal, Kasi?" *And how the hell did you learn to shoot better than most FBI agents?*

They had given their federal weapons permits to the squad of cops who'd arrived a safe ten minutes after Junior Wilcox had greased the rails at the U Street–Cardozo Metro station. As a former FBI agent, Delgado was exempt from the rigid gun-control laws that banned virtually all civilians from carrying.

Leah's cover story was well rehearsed. "My father worked for State. His last posting was to Belgrade."

Del's eyebrows raised. "I did a piece on American occupation forces in the Balkans a couple of years ago. Belgrade makes Beirut look like the Hamptons."

"It was hell. All diplomats and their families were given training in kidnap avoidance, unarmed combat, and shooting, but that didn't help my dad. He was killed by Pan-Slav terrorists when I was eighteen. I never wanted to look at another gun as long as I lived. After college, I did a stint for Reuters covering Euro politics, then came home and took a job with the *Star Tribune* in Minneapolis. The city streets in our fair land are just as dangerous as Belgrade or Zagreb. I got over my aversion to guns."

Del nodded. "You qualify to pack under some State Department rule . . . the Residual Target Policy, isn't it?"

"Yes. Prompted by Pan-Slav terrorist tactics. Killing an assassinated diplomat's surviving family is intended to demoralize our diplomatic corps," she said bitterly. "All 'residuals' are eligible for permits—if we qualify on a range. Upgrading my skills became an occupational necessity, but this is the first time I've killed someone." She shuddered, drawing on the revulsion of every termination etched in her memory. "Now that the adrenaline is wearing off, I'm feeling a little shaky."

"If it's any consolation, so am I." He reached across the table and squeezed her arm. "Look, I'm sorry about your father but damn glad you had that cannon and knew how to use it."

Leah met his shrewd dark eyes and could read nothing beside frank admiration, but Delgado was nobody's fool. He'd check out her story. BISC had every detail covered right down to the demise of both fictitious parents.

"You saved my life, Kasi."

And complicated my life no end. If he'd been killed by the El-Ops, she would've been off the hook with BISC. It had been so tempting, but Leah couldn't let Elliott Delgado die. She had to learn the truth, not only about him but about her own agency as well. The shiver of fear she'd let him see a moment ago was gut deep and very real. So was the anger. "You saved my life, too. I guess that makes us even."

"No one would've been shooting at you if you hadn't been with me," he said.

She looked at him, eyes narrowed. "You still trying to ditch me, Delgado?"

He shrugged. "I've made a lot of enemies over the years. I don't want you to get caught in the cross fire."

She stood up and paced on the grimy gray concrete. "I already was caught in the cross fire, remember? I can handle it."

He raised his hands in concession. "Point well taken. You're bad, you're suicidal, and you're still working with me."

"Good. Then we need to get out of this hole and file the story for *News-Time,* not to mention the piece Lady Carolyn wanted on Bootstrap House. What's taking the police so long?"

"The D.C. cops have never made law enforcement's top ten list. I imagine Cohen will spring us before shift change." *Or Cal will.* He'd phoned the secure line Putnam had given him before he'd called the editor.

While Del and Leah waited, they discussed how to handle a story about two reporters in a running gun battle with crazed El-Ops. In an era when civilian casualties during drug turf wars had grown commonplace in urban areas like D.C., even an attempt on the life of a high-profile reporter would not be all that unusual. But Leah knew he'd expect her to push for the story. She was relieved when he dismissed it.

"I think the general public is bored shitless with tales of slum violence. Cohen won't run it."

Thank God. Her photo on *U.S. News-Time*'s cover would mean plastic surgery, transfer to a desk job at Central, or other less palatable alternatives. "Okay. I'll take the photos from the open house to Layout while you write the copy."

"Jesus! You managed to hang on to your camera?"

She nodded. "I threw it in the shoulder satchel that held my ammo when the shooting started."

"You're really slick, Kasi Evans." He let his eyes travel from her face down her body, pausing perceptibly at her long legs, imagining for an instant how they'd feel wrapped around his hips.

His thought transmitted to her in a kinetic leap. Tension spiraled between them. Feeling her fair skin flush, Leah turned and paced but was trapped in the small cubicle. Nowhere to go. "All right, score one for Delgado. You just proved we both have hormones," she said, facing him head-on.

He grinned. "Sorry, just some of my vestigial Neanderthalism coming out. Shit, let's bust out of here." He walked over to the door and banged violently on it.

After a moment, footsteps sounded on the concrete floor outside and keys jingled in the lock. A big, burly uniform shoved the door open and scowled at them. "Keep your pecker in your pants, stud."

She let go a muffled chuckle at the irony as the cop went on, "You're not being charged. The lieutenant's signing off on the report even as we speak."

Before the officer could say anything else, Lieutenant Ralph Litzinger walked in, looking like a reincarnation of Groucho Marx sans cigar. "Good news, my friends of the Fourth Estate. Everything checked out. You're free to go with the blessings of the DCPD. Our only objection is the mess you made on the Metro rails. It'll take a hell of a lot longer to scrape Junior off the tracks than it did to clear you for putting him there."

4:05 P.M., EDT, FRIDAY, JUNE 26

"Berglund's stalling. She accessed the goods but hasn't submitted a report. In fact, she passed up a golden opportunity to take out Delgado and blame it on the two El-Ops we tipped this afternoon. They were added insurance and they couldn't kill the son of a bitch either. I don't like this, Harmon."

Harmon Waterman grimaced at the panicked voice on the other end of the line. Thank God it was a secured link inside BISC. The idiot never watched what he said unless he was in front of a television camera. "I have more than enough brush fires to douse without holding your hand," Waterman replied in a testy voice. "If Berglund doesn't perform soon, we'll eliminate her and assign a new agent to cancel Delgado."

"Don't underestimate him. We should have arranged an 'accident' for him just like Brandies."

"Brandies was a fucking Pentagon insider who lost his nerve and tried to turn us in. Delgado's hardly that level of risk." Waterman's voice grew even more impatient. "I'm a hell of a lot more concerned about who's trying to access our operation from inside the Pentagon."

"Frankowski hasn't come up with anything yet?"

"He's narrowed the parameters. Whoever this is, he's probably career military. Our people inside the Pentagon have to move very carefully while they're searching for him or they'll be detected."

"We don't have time for this, Harmon."

"No shit." Waterman ground his teeth in frustration. "General Sommerville's made tentative arrangements for a meeting with the president on the first."

"Once he sees our forces perform, he'll be behind us one hundred percent, I guarantee it. I watched them on maneuvers last week. Real impressive." Renewed enthusiasm fired his voice now.

"Yeah, but we damn well better find the fucking mole in the Pentagon before we begin putting on any shows for that arrogant pretty boy."

5:30 P.M., EDT, FRIDAY, JUNE 26

After leaving the police station, Leah decided to check back with her grandfather. Before she had phoned Adam Manchester last week with her disturbing request, she'd taken the precaution of purchasing a vid link with a personalized scrambler code. Using unregistered devices violated BISC regulations. Agents were required to communicate only on their government-issued PDA units, but she dared not involve the senator unless she took precautions.

Walking briskly to the Mall, she entered the National Gallery of Art and found a secluded alcove. Leah was careful to choose sites where tracing mechanisms would not work effectively. She pressed the number and waited while Manchester's unit in Maine processed. *Come on, Gramps, pick up.* Relief washed over her when he answered. As soon as he heard her voice, he flicked on his vid screen and his craggy, tanned face and heavy, snow-white hair came into focus.

"Sorry I wasn't able to get back to you sooner, Gramps."

"I was worried, Leah. I'll admit I've always worried since you took that job, but especially now."

The lines bracketing his mouth and creasing his brow seemed to have deepened in the past few days. *Lord, what have I gotten him into?* "What did you find out?"

"I've heard from some of my contacts on the Hill. I'm waiting on a couple of old friends who've retired but still have Washington connections. There is definitely something ugly going on. My sources report rumors that your Bureau of Illegal Substance Control is manufacturing evidence. Using their agents to terminate political targets. A Senate oversight committee was proposed to investigate, but as usual, Wade Samson quashed it, citing national security and hiding behind that thrice-damned Martial Law Act. Said he'd look into it on his own." The old man gave a snort of disgust.

"Then Elliott Delgado could have been framed?" Her voice nearly broke. How close she'd come to sending that guilty verdict!

"Given what you told me about him, I'd say it's quite possible."

"But why—because of the McCallum story he did? Why wait so long to retaliate?"

Adam shook his head. "I don't know . . . yet. But I did learn about several other cases—people with no previous drug histories whatsoever who were terminated because of the sudden urge to start Elevator riding. One was Paul Meers."

"I remember reading about him—the congressman who gave lavish parties at his Malibu estate. Supposedly he was offering Elevator to Hollywood celebrity types."

Adam nodded. "But what the media neglected to report was that Meers was one of the House members who caucused with Senate leaders proposing the BISC investigation."

"And his alleged drug activities were conveniently discovered before any sort of congressional investigation of BISC got under way." Leah felt numb, clutching the link in her sweaty fist as her mind whirled furiously. "You hate to say 'I told you so,' right?" Her smile wobbled.

"You know I wanted you to marry and have children, practice with a fine law firm, argue cases before the Supreme Court . . . but that's my dream, not yours, Leah-Pia."

The use of her childhood nickname brought the sting of tears to her eyes. "I always knew even though you hated my decision to join BISC, that you still loved me."

"I love you and I'm proud of you, honey, BISC or no BISC; and your dad and mom feel the same way."

"I know you're right about Mom and Dad, Gramps, but since Kev died . . . well, you're the only one I can talk to. Dad drinks and Mom survives on legals the doctor prescribes."

Manchester's voice was soft, thoughtful, "Yes . . . you're right, honey, but maybe losing a son is even harder than losing a brother . . .

maybe they're carrying a load of guilt you aren't. And one thing I know torments them—fear of losing you, too. Right now, I'm almost as afraid for you as Deborah and Erik are. You should resign from BISC. If that's not possible, I have influential friends. We'll hide you, get you out of the country—"

"No, Gramps. You know that won't stop this. And if we don't try, they'll keep killing innocent people." She swallowed down the unaccustomed lump in her throat. "I may have the blood of innocent people on my hands and I don't even know who. This is monstrous." Her voice grew steady but she shook with quiet rage. "I am going to find out why BISC has betrayed me and made me betray my country."

"Don't place the guilt of a society that abdicated its responsibilities on your shoulders, Leah."

"I was part of that collective outrage, that desire for quick justice, Gramps. I have to own my share of blame. You were right. Remember when you told me that the power given to BISC was absolute and absolute power corrupts absolutely?"

"I stole that from Lord Acton," he said drily. "Should be required reading for every citizen. So should John Locke and Thomas Jefferson, but that won't fix what's broken now. I can see there's no talking you out of this, so I'll just have to join you, won't I?"

"I could sure use the help, Gramps."

"I'm expecting to hear from a couple of other senators who wanted that investigation, and I have some discreet feelers out regarding the vice president."

"You think Waterman could be involved?"

"There were some rumors that he was a Tribunal member. Pretty much scotched in the past year or so, but it would make sense. He's Samson's moneyman and he'd love that sort of power. Never did like the ruthless old SOB—and it takes one to recognize another, believe me."

Leah grinned in spite of the horrific implication of presidential involvement. "Don't try to fool me. You're as guilty of tilting at windmills as I am."

"Just sit tight until I find out how deep this thing goes." His voice was gruff.

"What I'm going to do is stick like glue to Elliott Delgado until I can figure out where he fits into the puzzle. Leave a memo on this number when you need to reach me. Keep safe. I love you, Gramps."

"I love you, too, Leah-Pia."

When the senator signed off, Leah continued to hold the link tightly in both hands as an uncomfortable premonition slithered through her. Her academy instructors had said a good agent had a sixth sense. Hers had saved her life more than once.

10 P.M., EDT, FRIDAY, JUNE 26

The small, white marble monument to Washington, D.C.'s, World War I dead lay hidden in a thicket of pine and oak, deep inside West Potomac Park. A quarter moon glinted off the cupola. As Del climbed the steps, he could feel the neglected stone crumble beneath his feet. Wide columns shadowed the interior, but he could smell the faint aroma of cigarette smoke. As he stepped onto the floor, Cuff materialized out of the darkness.

"If you're going to do this cloak-and-dagger stuff, Bedford, you need to quit the cancer sticks. I could smell you thirty meters away."

"If you're going to do this cloak-and-dagger stuff, Delgado, you need to quit appearing on the nightly news. Any connection between those El-Ops shooting at you and what we're working on?"

"I doubt it. Damn, I was pissed when Channel 4 decided to do that story—a dozen drug-related shootings in D.C. this week and they pick me to put on camera."

"Nobody ever said you were Mr. Lucky, Delgado. Just don't start playing the ponies."

Delgado grunted an obscenity. "I'm heading for the West Coast to-morrow to check out Nuñez's investigation. Maybe he got wind of something going down at Adair or Yuma. Were you able to turn up anything more?"

"Mostly more weird shit that doesn't make sense. One item does—sort of. Brandies apparently had spent TDY somewhere in Sonora last month."

Del nodded. "That fits. If the brass is practicing for a coup against the Cartel, what better staging ground than northern Mexico?"

"Yeah. Right down the Gulf of California from Adair. I took a look at some maps. Only a few hundred klics over the border into really isolated wilderness."

"I have sources in Mexico. What else have you found?"

"Very mysterious. Some sort of delivery was logged in all hush-hush at Adair-Rawlfing on the fifteenth. No specs on what was shipped, but I did locate point of origin, which doesn't make sense either—Little Lenny."

"Little Lenny? That some sort of code?"

"Only to civilians. It's the Fort Leonard Wood Annex down on the Missouri-Arkansas line. The worst pesthole in the army. I'm surprised they didn't let the insects fly the cargo to Adair."

"No speculations on what that cargo might be?"

Bedford lit another smoke and took a long drag. "I'm still working on that. Oh, one piece of good news. I'm ninety-nine percent sure the Joint Chiefs aren't involved."

Delgado squinted at Cuff through the darkness. "Why?"

"Remember when I told you the Yuma Proving Ground tests all the newest toys—mechanized vehicles, tanks, artillery? Well, my department just completed a surprise inventory inspection there. The stats came across my desk yesterday, strictly routine. Didn't think much about it at first—everything was in perfect order. There's not one item unaccounted for.

"Then I got to mulling it over last night. The general in charge at Yuma, Mark Hailey, is a close friend and classmate of Howard Mc-Kinney."

"The chairman of the Joint Chiefs. So?" Del prompted.

"Yuma is spitting distance from Adair. If any of the big boys were involved in slipping hardware to Adair, the most logical place to take it from would be Yuma. Short trail, easy to hide."

"Not if they knew Yuma was going to be inspected."

"Doesn't work that way. Inspection sites are selected randomly by computer, and Yuma was done barely a year before. If McKinney or any of the Joint Chiefs were involved, Yuma is where they'd steal from. Hailey'd walk through exploding frag grenades if McKinney asked him. He'd never betray the chairman. And McKinney's known for keeping a really tight rein on the Chiefs."

"I suppose that's some consolation," Del said glumly.

"Yeah, but that leaves a barrelful of generals who could pull this off. The turkey commanding Adair is a prime example. Old 'Nuke 'Em Nate' Sommerville."

"That name has a familiar ring." Del snapped his fingers. "A field commander during the Second Iraqi War who wanted to use tactical nuclear devices against Saddam's Republican Guard."

"None other. He almost did. Thank God McKinney overruled the crazy mother or half the American forces downwind would still glow in the dark like bicycle reflectors, me included."

"Looks like I have a lot of snooping to do around Adair-Rawlfing."

"And I still have to figure out what could've been sent there from Little Lenny—and what the fuck they're going to do with eight amphibs in the middle of a desert and a dozen UAVs for target acquisition with no artillery to hit the targets."

8:20 A.M., EDT, SATURDAY, JUNE 27

Del stood by the gate, waiting for the attendant to announce first-class boarding as Kasi Evans appeared at the far end of the concourse with her camera bag slung over one shoulder. He watched her athletic stride eat up the distance. Her caramel-colored poly-silk jumpsuit emphasized her long legs. She moved with smooth, effortless grace.

There was more to the woman than met the eye, pleasing as that might be. It was crazy to take her with him to San Diego. Especially crazy after that sexually charged interlude in the interrogation room. One rule Delgado never broke was his prohibition on mixing his professional with his personal life.

Then why the hell did you call her at six a.m. and tell her to pack for an assignment in San Diego?

He'd rationalized that it was to keep her close until he was certain what was going on. Kasi Evans was not what she appeared to be, even though her story about her family background had checked out. Any

woman—or man—as cool and deadly under fire as she'd been yesterday almost had to be a professional. Could be FBI, CIA, even
BISC. But if she was working for the enemy, why hadn't she killed
him during the fight with the El-Ops?

She could be working for Cal. The old man had promised to cover
his back. She could be FBI. Whatever was going on, Delgado's gut
told him to trust her . . . up to a point. He was not about to divulge a
BISC-Pentagon conspiracy, but he did tell her he was investigating
weapons sales to Mexico by military personnel at Adair-Rawlfing.
She could do background research on personnel while he checked on
Nuñez's activities prior to his death.

"Hi. Sorry I'm late," she said breathlessly. "A tanker truck carrying
Pepsi syrup tipped over on the Fourteenth Street Bridge and I had to
use Memorial. Everybody else in D.C. had the same idea." *Did you
buy my story, Delgado? I know you checked it.* Leah met his hooded,
dark eyes, reporter's eyes that took in everything.

"They're not boarding yet," he said, handing her a ticket.

She glanced at it with appreciatively raised eyebrows. "First class.
I'm impressed. The perks of a Pulitzer?"

"I fly so much, it's an upgrade."

The attendant's voice announced boarding instructions. They
stowed their gear and settled in their seats. To forestall uncomfortable attempts at small talk while the other passengers filed past them,
he gave her a disc with pertinent details for the background research.
She could study it on her PDA en route. All business, she went to
work. Gratefully, Del set up his PDA and reviewed the Global Positioning System maps of the area surrounding Adair. This was going
to be a damn long flight.

10:30 A.M., EDT, SATURDAY, JUNE 27
MACHIAS, MAINE

Sheriff Daniel McLean didn't like surprises. Especially when they
involved high-profile people who had the aggravating temerity to
drown in his jurisdiction. Why the hell couldn't old Stephan Patrikas,
former ambassador to Greece and father of President Samson's chief

foreign policy adviser, have had the good grace to sail his damned sloop down to Bar Harbor before falling off and drowning?

Hell, his life was complicated enough being a North Carolina transplant in the Maine wilderness where innate Yankee reserve still vaguely mistrusted his soft drawl and laid-back methods. But they had elected him Washington County sheriff on the strength of his outstanding law enforcement background and his in-laws' five-generation history in Machias.

So far his first term in office had gone pretty well. Washington County was much larger than Rhode Island or even Delaware, but along the isolated coastline crime was usually limited to underage alcohol consumption and littering. In the rugged interior wilderness, the moose population outnumbered the human.

That was the way McLean liked it. The chief reason he'd moved here was to escape the congestion and violence of urban America. Although old Stephan Patrikas had certainly died violently, it might or might not be a crime, but McLean had a bad feeling about it. The body had washed in with the tide, discovered early that morning by a couple of rock hounds on Jasper Beach.

The Coast Guard located his sloop, adrift with blood and hair caked onto the boom, which had apparently whacked him in the skull, knocking him overboard. The sheriff was waiting lab confirmation that the samples matched up with those taken from Patrikas's body. Preliminary examination of the boat indicated that the old man had been drinking before the accident. This would hardly be the first time someone with a snootful had gone sailing and taken a fatal dunk. But something about this case just did not feel right.

Patrikas was local, born and bred a sailor. Yes, he'd been known to tip the gin bottle now and again, but never when sailing. In fact, according to everyone who knew him, and that comprised most of Machias Bay, he neither sailed alone nor drank alone. The autopsy was scheduled for that afternoon. Maybe Medical Examiner Silas Elworth would shed some light on the problem.

Lord knew he needed answers. Wade Samson's whiz kid had pressed him hard that morning, demanding to know how his father had died. Mark Patrikas's reaction to the news of his father's death had been just the right blend of grieving son and powerful politico, but something rang hollow. The kid was scared, McLean would swear to it. He'd have the chance to form a firsthand opinion when young "Mr. Mark" arrived to make funeral arrangements. That didn't give the sheriff much wiggle room.

He picked up his crumpled NBA Hornets ball cap and stuffed a sun-browned fist into it, then plunked it over curly red hair that stuck out over his ears like frizzled clumps of wire.

"Mattie, I'm goin' to amble down to Doc Elworth's lab. Just in case any more calls come in from the White House."

His secretary nodded a silent "ayup," her angular New England face as bland and businesslike as if Washington, D.C., phoned Washington, Maine, every day. "I'll transfer any calls from Mr. Mark, Sheriff."

Mr. Mark. Local boy makes good. Before moving to rural Maine, McLean had thought Mecklenburg County was clannish. Down east, they had refined the concept. Old man Patrikas hailed from a distinguished Maine dynasty that had made a modest fortune in the shipping trade after the patriarch, Socrates Patrikas, emigrated to Machias from Káristos, Greece, four generations ago.

When the sheriff reached Silas's lab, another local legend was pacing in the antiseptic hallway. McLean figured that former U.S. senator Adam Manchester looked as haggard as any man would after hearing that his best friend was dead.

Just then the ME opened the door and motioned both men inside his sanctum. The sheriff fished an antacid from his pocket and bit down hard on it.

9.

Delgado rented a Toyota TE at San Diego International and took the wheel, assigning Leah to navigate. She checked the GPS console on the Toyota's dash and programmed in Adair-Rawlfing Army Base.

"Three hours twenty minutes driving time," she said after scanning the data on the screen and issuing succinct directions.

He smirked. "This little honey can make it in two and a half."

"Boys and their toys." She sighed.

"And we never outgrow 'em." He grinned at her. "Fast cars, big guns, and beautiful women."

"Just remember, *junior*, any of the three can be more than a little fellow can handle."

Del could have sworn her cheeks pinkened ever so slightly. Perhaps he hadn't imagined the sudden sizzle between them in that D.C. interrogation cubicle. *This is crazy, Delgado.* "It was a bad idea to bring you out here," he blurted out. *Shit!*

She studied his harshly chiseled profile as he wove expertly up Pacific Highway in heavy traffic. "When I first walked into your office, you gave a masterful performance as a first-class asshole. You were trying to get rid of me then, too. Why?"

"To scare you off." Del held to his rule about sticking as close to the truth as possible.

"I don't scare so easily."

He grinned. "So I've noticed.

"Why did you want to get rid of me?" Her suspicions still remained.

"Truth? You reminded me of my ex." *Dumb thing to say.* "I mean, only superficially—you're both tall, Anglo blondes with great legs." *Even dumber.* He lapsed into silence, certain that he was now the one flushing slightly.

Leah suppressed a smile. "I gathered the divorce wasn't exactly amicable from what you said yesterday about Brian Fuller."

"No." He checked the rear vid and pulled out, flying past a double-tandem semi. "Diana wasn't cut out to be an FBI wife. Hell, who is? I just wasn't there for her . . . and then . . ."

"She found someone else?"

"Hugh Shrewsbury. Hollywood hotshot." He shrugged. "Our marriage was dead long before him. I guess he makes Diana happy. I know I didn't."

"No regrets, then?"

"Yeah. One big one. The divorce was hard for my son, Mike, especially after I was shot up and hit the sauce. By the time I got into rehab, the only guy who'd give me a job was Ben Cohen. He and Cal Putnam, my old FBI boss, were college roommates at Penn State. Cal talked him into taking a chance on an ex-agent and ex-drunk."

Leah was suddenly curious about Delgado-as-father. "Do you get to see your son often?"

"Like I said, one of this job's perks is frequent flying. I try to visit Mike every month, one way or the other. And we log a lot of vid time. But the bottom line is, I'm still not there for him."

Tense lines bracketed his mouth and drew it downward. *He really cares for his kid.* "So your ex moved to Hollywood with Shrewsbury and took Mike with her."

"No. We're both originally from San Diego. Diana hated my posting in Washington. She insisted on being near her family, so he commutes up to Tinsel Town."

"Obliging chap."

Not how he would describe Shrewsbury, but he let it pass. "Yeah. What about you, Kasi? Any exes, roommates, boyfriends, whatever?"

"I've never been married. Never had time for relationships. You know how the news business is."

He grinned now. "No anal retentiveness. I talked. Now it's your turn."

She knew he was affecting her in ways that violated every BISC regulation on the books. "What made you join the Bureau?" she asked, shifting the conversation back to him.

He shrugged. "My father was a San Diego police officer. Killed in the line of duty when I was a kid. He was my hero. My great-uncle sort of took over as a surrogate father, but he's in Mexico and my mother worried every time I went for a visit that banditos would nab me."

"She's not Latino, your mother?"

"Would she have stuck me with a moniker like Elliott if she was?"

Leah chuckled. "No, I guess not. So, you grew up as an amphibian of sorts."

"Summers in Mazatlán with my dad's people, the school year in San Diego with my mom. After she died when I was in college, I lost track of the Hastings side of the family. Uncle Mac and his brood have been all I ever needed."

"Mac? That's an odd name for a Mexican national."

"Not really. You'd be surprised how many O'Higgans and Muellers and Smiths there are south of the border. Nineteenth-century immigration. The Mulcahey clan started when an adventurous Irishman married into the Sonoran gentry in the 1830s."

"I'm impressed."

"Don't be. Our branch of the family didn't inherit the family fortune. They immigrated south to Sinaloa and went into politics." She chuckled, a deep husky laugh he found disarming and sexy at the same time.

"I thought you hated politicians."

"American politicians," he corrected as they sped along Interstate 8.

They discussed his big Mexican family and FBI career. Leah volunteered a bit about growing up in a depressingly homogenous Lutheran-Episcopal family in Minnesota and becoming an Olympic contender in gymnastics while in college. But she always deflected the conversation to other topics when talk strayed to her postcollege years.

On the isolated stretches of highway he floored the Toyota and they saw the first sign for Adair-Rawlfing in just under two and a half hours. She was glad he hadn't exaggerated about the driving time. Intimate conversation with Elliott Delgado was like walking through a minefield.

"Okay. What now? The brass on the base won't talk to you, much less let me take pictures." She peered at the tall wire fence studded with security lights and sensors.

"I hadn't planned on anything quite so obvious," he said drily. "We'll spend the night in Winterhaven, a wide place in the road just east of the base. Sometimes if you nose around the nearest army watering holes, you can pick up leads."

4 P.M., EDT, SATURDAY, JUNE 27
WASHINGTON, D.C.

Mark Patrikas mixed himself a double vodka martini and sat staring at the solid-walnut-paneled wall of his White House office. He'd made it so close to the top. *The fucking White House!* His father had been so proud. At first . . . before Mark had become embroiled in a conspiracy that was now spiraling wildly out of control.

As Wade Samson's chief adviser on foreign policy, he was the youngest member of the presidential staff. A Harvard whiz kid, Mark's short stature and slight build were saved from geekdom by a thick shock of curly black hair framing an arrestingly handsome face. He possessed a megawatt smile that had made him a media darling, but he wasn't smiling now. The wunderkind of Washington shuddered as the image of his father's boat with that bloody boom flashed into his mind. Unable to suppress the thought of Stephan Patrikas lying on that cold metal gurney, he gulped the vodka.

It was an accident.

But the sheriff in Machias didn't think so. Neither did old Senator Manchester. What if . . . ? Mark couldn't bear to finish the thought that had haunted him on the seemingly endless flight back from Maine.

He squeezed his eyes closed and polished off the double martini, then walked over to the liquor cabinet and mixed another. His hands were shaking worse than ever.

How had it all gone so wrong? It had begun as his brainchild. He'd written his doctoral dissertation on the political implications of Cartel dealings with the Euro Union and the Russian mob. He'd outlined the clear and present danger to U.S. interests if Zuloaga wasn't stopped. That was one of the chief reasons Samson had selected him.

Patrikas had used White House power to gather more information and design a plan to unite Colombian dissidents and Mexicans under American leadership. Of course, such a bold initiative had to be handled covertly. Only after the destruction of the Cartel could the American government take credit. Even if the chairman of the Joint Chiefs condemned his plan, a number of key people in the Pentagon had received it favorably. General Sommerville and Colonel Brandies had been behind him.

And Brandies died in an accident, too.

"If only those fuckers from BISC hadn't come in," he muttered to himself as he stared at the PDA on his desk. He had to know if they had murdered his father.

But if Stephan Patrikas's death was no more an accident than Hoyt Brandies's had been . . .

I'm a dead man.

He finished the second drink and requested an encrypted link on his PDA.

4 P.M., PDT, SATURDAY, JUNE 27
WINTERHAVEN, CALIFORNIA

Delgado had booked them into a motel that boasted in-room access to the World Net, still a big perk this far in the sticks. He set Kasi to work digging up everything she could find on Adair and its personnel. She might accidentally stumble on something useful. At least, she could find who had been posted there over the past couple of years.

He had asked for adjoining rooms and wondered if she was as dissatisfied with the sleeping arrangements as he was. If so, it didn't show. But then, Kasi Evans was a cipher if ever he'd met one. He'd talked about everything from his wrecked marriage to his aunt Seri's *frijoles con queso* and she'd revealed nothing about herself. Damn, she was slick and cool.

But, boy, was she hot.

"I've got to quit thinking with my dick and stick to business," he muttered to himself as he pulled up in front of the local sheriff's office. Although the town sat in the middle of the Quechan Indian Reservation, Imperial County maintained an outpost.

Del entered the small building, flashed his badge, and showed the guy Al Nuñez's picture. He explained that the agent had been killed while investigating something at Adair. In spite of the legendary hostility between local police and the Bureau, the deputy was cooperative. He remembered the dead agent, who had also paid a courtesy call. A sergeant from Adair had died in a car crash the same day as Nuñez. Funny coincidence.

Yeah. A real bitch of a coincidence.

There were no leads in Sergeant Frank Lester's death as far as the deputy knew. It might have been an accident but the sheriff's office had not been allowed to examine the crash site or the vehicle, which was impounded by the military police from Adair. They were handling the investigation so the deputy did not know what was going on. Del could tell the lawman resented being cut out of the loop by the MPs. He gave Del the names of several joints in town where Lester might have hung out.

After thanking the officer, Delgado drove to the seedy area filled with bars and strip joints that always sprang up around military bases. He pulled into the gravel parking lot in front of a place called Buckeroo's. Rusted-out pickup trucks sporting NRA bumper stickers seemed to be the vehicles of choice in the area.

Del was glad he'd dressed in worn jeans and a battered old leather jacket. He walked inside and ordered a beer.

He struck out at Buckeroo's and four other bars, then decided to try a strip joint. No one seemed to know anything about Sergeant Lester's friends. Finally, while he watched a decidedly overripe bottle redhead do the bump and grind wearing nothing more than a wink and a grimace, he got lucky.

Lester had a pal, an ex-sergeant named Buddy Spears, who had been busted out of the army after eighteen years, two years short of his twenty. Embittered over losing his pension, he'd kept pretty much to himself since the dishonorable discharge. Spears lived in an old trailer at the edge of town.

As Del pulled up in front of the decaying monstrosity, a horrible sense of déjà vu gripped him. *An aluminum version of McCallum's shack.* He wended his way past a set of worn tires piled next to a rusted-out air conditioner and an old washing machine. A few clumps of greasewood were the only vegetation around the place.

He knocked on the door, which clattered loosely against its sash as if ready to fall off. A tall, gaunt man with windburned skin and bloodshot eyes opened the door. His nose had been broken more than once, and the narrow white scar across his lower lip molded his mouth into a permanent sneer. His face looked as if it had caught more punches than a speed bag in a gym.

Delgado introduced himself but didn't flash the badge. This guy wouldn't feel any urge to cooperate with the authorities. "Could I talk with you a few minutes, Mr. Spears?"

"I ain't buyin' nothin'," Spears said in a thick Southern drawl, attempting to slam the door.

"Good. I'm not selling anything." The stench of dirty ashtrays, combined with his boozy breath, turned Delgado's gut.

"What the fuck ya want then?"

"I heard some talk at Muzzy's that you were given a raw deal by the army." Spears squinted at Delgado, who produced a bottle of Heaven Hill. "The bartender said it was your brand."

Spears shrugged and opened the door wider. "Fuck, it's the cheapest kind. That's always my brand."

He let Del enter his cramped quarters. There was an overabundance of cheap, dirty furniture, but otherwise the bleak desolation of the room reminded Del again of Gary's last refuge.

Spears took the bottle and broke the seal, then took a long, gurgling pull from it, making no pretense of sharing. He motioned for Del to sit on a sagging sofa while he slid into a big recliner. He studied Delgado warily. "What's the price for the booze?"

"Nothing much. You were stationed at Adair until—"

"Until the motherfuckin' army canned me. They had no damn right. Adelaide was my girl. That fuckin' red bastard diddlin' her while I was confined to quarters, it's enough to make a man puke."

Del had heard the tale in town. Enraged by Adelaide and the Navajo sergeant, Spears had climbed to the rooftop of the noncom's club overlooking the parade grounds, unzipped his fly, and shaken his cock at the couple while yelling obscenities. He was court-martialed for "sexual perversion" and dishonorably discharged.

"I didn't come to discuss your ex-girlfriend or her lover, but it was a crappy break, losing your pension and all," Del said with what he hoped was a straight face.

"Yeah. But what the fuck, over?" Spears took another long pull on the hooch.

"Sergeant Frank Lester was killed last week. I understand you knew him."

"What if I did?"

"The army may have screwed you both." That caught Spears's attention. "He may have talked to a friend of mine, guy named Nuñez. Funny thing is both of them died only a couple of days later. Nuñez was shot. Your friend Lester's crash might not have been an accident . . . but the army's not saying."

"You think Frank was murdered over spillin' somethin' to yer pal? 'N' the army's involved?"

"Any idea what the brass might be trying to cover up?"

Spears scratched his head and considered for a moment, studying Delgado out of bloodshot eyes. "Frank was bullshitin' at the sentry post when this here shipment come in. I was confined to quarters, but Frank told me 'bout it the next mornin'. Marked 'Top Secret.' That's army jabber for just about everythin', but this time they really meant it.

"Frank guessed it wasn't much over four hundred kilos from watchin' the men unload it. Just a couple of small crates, but they was made of some special metal alloy. With coded locks on 'em. Never seen the like, he says. Arrived round o two hundred. Not the usual time for an ordnance shipment—if that's what it was."

"Doesn't sound like the quartermaster requisitioned new cook pots, does it?" Del said. "What happened to those crates?" He already suspected the answer.

"They was gone next day. Fuckin' vanished like a carton of cigarettes layin' top of the vendin' machine at Muzzy's. Frank said they was no record it was ever shipped to Adair in the first place. Just like it never happened. He was a day-watch supervisor on the loading dock."

"This sort of abracadabra go on often at Adair?"

"Army's always playin' some secret war games. Lots of paper's shuffled, ordnance shifted round. Remember, we're on the Mex border 'n' Uncle Sam's been doin' his bit to help the greasers beat the Cartel."

If Spears connected the ethnic slur with Delgado's last name, he obviously didn't give a damn. Del ignored it as Spears rambled on. He'd polished off two-thirds of the bottle now and was warming to his topic.

"Old Nate, he always played it real close to the vest. Fucker's crazy."

"You mean General Sommerville?"

"Yeah. Old 'Nuke 'Em Nate,' our beloved commandant. Funny, I always heard he was a spit-'n'-polish, by-the-book motherfucker, but he's been letting shit slide a lot the past six months or so."

"How do you mean?"

"Always gone. Oh, not TDY. Just a few days here, a week there, but real regular, ya know."

"Did he leave the day those mysterious crates vanished?"

Spears grinned, revealing several missing front teeth. "Now ain'tcha the smart sombitch."

"Can you remember the date those crates and Sommerville disappeared?" Del asked, not holding much hope. Spears had pretty well pickled his brain in booze.

"Lemme see . . . it was the day they cut my discharge papers. Why's knowin' the day so important?"

"Humor me." Del pulled a fifty out of his wallet and Spears's eyes lit up. He climbed out of the recliner and crossed the room. After rooting through a pile of bills and junk mail, he finally located his discharge documents. "June fifteenth," he announced, seizing the money.

Leah slipped into her darkened room just minutes before Delgado got back and checked to be sure the adjoining door was locked. The tracking device she'd placed inside the glove compartment of the Toyota enabled her to follow him in the rental car she had arranged to have waiting for her on the motel parking lot. Knowing he had been a top FBI agent, she had been exceedingly cautious.

She had just about given up for the night after he'd stopped at the fifth sleazy hangout. Then he had emerged from the strip joint and purposefully driven to the trailer. What she overheard was not suspicious but required further verification. The dead men, Lester and Nuñez, could well have been involved in black market weapons sales in Mexico. But something about the conversation between Delgado and Spears just did not feel right to her. Leah's trust in her instincts had saved Delgado's life once. She prayed her intuition was going to do it again. She waited till the muffled noises from his room stopped and she was sure he'd gone to bed. Then she opened her PDA and accessed BISC protocols to run the two murdered men's names.

6 A.M., EDT, SUNDAY, JUNE 28
WASHINGTON, D.C.

After returning home near dawn, Cuff Bedford played Del's message about his conversation with Spears. No way could he sleep after that. He'd looked at his information from every angle, turning it over and over in his mind as he tossed restlessly in bed. Finally, he rose and cranked up the steam bath in an attempt to loosen his stiff, aching muscles while he continued to mull over the pieces of the puzzle.

The shipment mysteriously vanishing from Adair on the fifteenth matched the probable arrival time of the "package" from Little Lenny . . . and now he knew the deadly secret of the isolated pesthole. But connecting it to the rest was the bitch. If there *was* a connection.

He sat on the wooden bench in the thick swirling steam when suddenly it came to him. "The UAVs! The fucking UAVs. Of course, that's it!" He stood up so quickly he almost lost his balance, then reached for the small aluminum hand crutch resting against the wall.

Seizing it, he shoved the tempered-glass door of the steam room open and stepped out. He never felt the blow to the back of his head.

5 A.M., PDT, SUNDAY, JUNE 28
WINTERHAVEN, CALIFORNIA

Faint streaks of California sunrise filtered pale gold light through her motel room window when the soft ping of the PDA awakened Leah. She'd fallen asleep stretched crossways on the bed, fully clothed. Days without sleep had finally caught up to her.

Rubbing her eyes, she slipped over to the door adjoining Delgado's room. Not a sound. Good. She splashed cold water from the bathroom sink onto her face to clear the cobwebs, then sat down to scan the detailed reports on the screen.

After several minutes, she wasn't certain the cold water had helped. Frank Lester had indeed been a career army noncom who'd died on June 15 in a car crash, ruled accidental death by the military police at Adair-Rawlfing. But Alfonso Nuñez was FBI! Worse yet, he had been terminated by BISC in San Diego on the same day. The details in the summary were sketchy, but according to what she had, Nuñez was up to his eyebrows in Tijuana drug smuggling. Using trips to visit family in Rosarito as cover, he had brought back raw cocaine for processing at a lab in San Ysidro. His FBI credentials had exempted him from searches until BISC was tipped.

Just like the tip about Delgado. Or not. Leah sat back and massaged her aching temples with her fingertips. If Nuñez was so damn busy smuggling drugs from Baja, why the hell was he in Winterhaven talking to Sergeant Lester on the fifteenth only hours before he was terminated?

And why was Delgado so interested in either death?

She knew BISC sometimes used special teams to take out convicted traffickers by "accidental" means so as not to tip confederates. But Lester's accident occurred the same day as Nuñez's signature termination. It didn't make sense—unless the reason for covering up the sergeant's death was because of his connection to Adair.

From what she'd gleaned, Delgado believed there was something more going on at the base than simple black marketeering. A three-star general was involved.

And so was BISC. She typed another inquiry, attempting to get a fix on who else might be involved with Nuñez, asking for a lifetime dossier from FBI files and other sources. Now that she'd already located the man, the additional material on him came back to her quickly. Skimming rapidly from screen to screen, she almost missed it. A name: ADIC Calvin A. Putnam. Cal, Del's mentor, whom he had mentioned so fondly yesterday, the man who'd helped him get a job at *News-Time*. Was Delgado still working for the Bureau? Nuñez had been. And he, too, had been a protégé of Putnam's.

There had been a bitter rivalry between the FBI and BISC ever since the new superempowered agency was created. If Elliott Delgado and Alfonso Nuñez worked for Putnam . . . Delgado must be investigating BISC for the FBI! She suppressed a wild giggle of hysteria, recalling the impulse she'd had back in D.C. to confess her real identity and ask his help. Maybe it hadn't been such a crazy idea after all.

Apparently BISC was responsible for using honest agents like her to cancel anyone who got in the way. "But in the way of what?" Her voice broke. Had she devoted her life to a lie? How many of the people she'd terminated had been innocent? Leah wanted—needed desperately—to believe that her own investigations had been thorough enough to uncover the truth. But what if . . . what if she had fallen for manufactured evidence somewhere in the past?

"This is getting me nowhere." She forced herself to strip and jump into a scalding-hot shower, scrubbing until the tension screaming in every muscle had loosened and her skin was pink.

As she toweled dry, she still did not feel clean.

A light tap sounded on the door adjoining Delgado's room. "Morning, sunshine. Are you decent? If not, I'll be right in."

Leah opened the door to a smiling Del, who was holding a tray laden with coffeepot, cups, and glasses of orange juice. The aroma was heavenly.

"Room service?"

"I placed the order last night while you were slumbering deep," he said, noting the way her short hair curled when damp from the shower.

"Mmm. Resuscitation."

He watched over the rim of his cup as she laced hers with cream and took an experimental sip. There were still smudges under her eyes as if she hadn't had enough sleep. Yet he'd come in just past midnight, stopping to listen at her door. All had been quiet then, and he'd let her sleep until nearly nine.

Del had tried in vain to contact Cuff last night with what he'd learned about Sommerville and the mysterious shipment. That worried him. Still, when he'd awakened Cal Putnam with his concerns at 4 a.m., D.C. time, the crotchety old FBI man had been more upset with the hour than the issue.

"What single man with a workin' pecker sits home on a Saturday night?" he'd sputtered between curses. "Leave Bedford an encrypted message and get some sleep."

Putnam had been pleased with what Del had unraveled at Adair and agreed that Bedford was the best man to make sense of it. But when he'd called Cuff again an hour ago, his friend still did not answer.

Come on, Cuff, dammit!

Delgado studied Leah, who was staring at him. Realizing how preoccupied he seemed, he refocused and asked, "What did you come up with on Adair personnel? Anything interesting?"

She smiled and reached for a printout sitting beside her PDA. "I'm a pretty fair hacker. Getting in was easy, but I'm not sure what I found will make much sense."

He skimmed over the personnel records. "Lots of transfers in and out of Adair. It really spikes in the last six months."

"I noted that, too. What do you suppose it means?"

He shrugged, looking at their ranks and assignments. "Mostly grunts and noncoms assigned to MP duty, logistical support, people who might notice if any matériel went missing or wonder about odd middle-of-the-night deliveries and shipments."

"So they were transferred before they'd start thinking about it." She nodded. "The guy issuing most of the transfer orders is named Craig Willett, a captain. The base commander's acting adjutant."

"Sommerville has an acting adjutant? What happened to the regular one?"

"Colonel Walt Bisset. TDY to some Kosovo hellhole just outside Pristina."

"Conveniently untraceable." He took the sheets and headed back to his room. "I'm going to send this stuff to Cohen and see what our people there can dig up." *Please be home now, Cuff.*

"While I was slaving away in front of a vid screen, did you learn anything last night?" she asked, figuring he'd expect her to make the inquiry.

"Made a contact with a sergeant who saw some stuff come in and go out sans records. Maybe we'll put together a good exposé out of this."

He composed another report for Cuff, adding the details about personnel transfers Kasi had given him. The noose was tightening around Sommerville's neck. Now all they had to do was figure out where the general went when he left Adair and what he did when he got there!

I've been at this too long. He sat back after completing the encrypted transmission. Cal was right. He had to cut Cuff some slack and ease off. An idea flashed into his head. Before he could think better of it, he went back to the doorway and said to Kasi, "Our flight back isn't until tomorrow morning. I . . . uh, planned on seeing Mike today if things worked out on this end. You can have a day off to see the sights in San Diego if you want . . . or you could tag along with us. I planned to take him to the zoo."

"I love zoos and I'd love to meet Mike."

10.

Hugh and Diana Shrewsbury lived in what Delgado considered a megabucks "shack" of stone, glass, and stained cedar perched on the bluffs overlooking the ocean at La Jolla. He had called his ex yesterday to arrange an unscheduled visit with Mike. Somehow bringing Kasi Evans with him seemed the right thing to do. Whether Diana would agree remained to be seen.

Leah surveyed the ocean view, noting the midnight blue Jaguar sitting in the driveway at one side of the trilevel mansion. She whistled low. "Shrewsbury commutes to L.A. in style."

"That's Diana's car. He drives a Porsche TE with flash drive." Del's mouth was a harsh slash.

Leah watched as he rang the bell at the imposing front door. A moment later it swung open and a boy with curly, dark hair and blue eyes grinned at Del. He had his father's chiseled features, not yet harshened by life. His gangling preteen body showed promise of being tall and rangy like Del's.

"Dad! Mom said you might not make it, but I knew you would." His smile fairly beamed when his father hugged him with traditional Latino emotion.

Kev's smile. Leah's heart did a flip-flop. Then Mike noticed her standing behind Del and the grin vanished, replaced by wariness.

"Oh, Mike, meet Kasi Evans. She's working with me on a story. That's how I was able to sneak out here for an extra visit."

"Hi, Mike. I'm pleased to meet you," she said, smiling warmly but making no attempt at physical contact.

He nodded, half-shy, half-hostile. "Hi, Ms. Evans."

"Please call me Kasi." He nodded, still uncertain as they walked into a marble foyer. An Italian crystal chandelier as big as the national debt hung suspended from the thirty-foot ceiling, illuminating a curving staircase framed with intricate wrought iron.

"All right if Kasi tags along with us to the zoo? If we decide we don't like her, we can always feed her to the big cats at Tiger River."

"Yeah, I guess so—oh . . . I mean it's okay if you come with us."

He blushed, reminding Leah of Kev. Just then a tall, graceful woman wearing a turquoise silk caftan came floating down the stairs. Diana Shrewsbury was beautiful. *You're both tall, Anglo blondes with great legs.* Leah supposed she should take that as a compliment. She had agonized over what to wear for the outing, intuiting that his ex would be stunningly dressed. She'd settled on a simple combo of plum shorts with a white, boatneck top and flat-heeled sandals. Faced with the diaphanous Diana, Leah felt like a JCPenny clerk wandering through Neiman Marcus on her lunch hour.

"You're late, El," Diana said without rancor, giving him a light kiss on the cheek. "Hugh had to leave for his tennis date." Her hair was shoulder length, a pale honey shade that did not come from a bottle. As Del made introductions, she surveyed Leah with frank curiosity and offered her beautifully manicured hand.

"I'm Del's research assistant and photographer, Mrs. Shrewsbury," Leah said, although she could sense the other woman drawing her own conclusions.

"Mike should be back by seven o'clock, El. Tomorrow's a school day."

"Aw, Mom. It takes forever to get to the zoo 'n' it's almost noon now."

"Then we'd better get a move on. And don't tell your mother how fast we drive," Del added in a stage whisper.

Diana rolled her eyes. "Your father always drives too fast. Just be sure you buckle up," she instructed, giving her son a hug. Then she turned to Del with a worried expression. "There've been reports of gang shootings between Old Town and Balboa Park. Try to avoid 163."

He nodded. "I checked the advisories this morning."

Diana smiled at Leah and said, "A pleasure meeting you, Ms. Evans."

Leah replied in kind, deciding that she might actually like Diana Shrewsbury if they did not live in such different worlds.

"We'll see you at seven," Del said as they headed for the door.

Eschewing the convenience of moving sidewalks, the trio trudged up and down every kilometer of rubberized asphalt snaking like a labyrinth through the zoo. They devoured hot dogs and slurped snow cones in the heat. Leah and Mike rested for a moment on a bench while Del went around the side of the concession stand to get a drink from the water fountain. Just then a group of angry seniors approached. The loudest of them was a small grandmotherly woman with blue-white hair. She was shaking the zoo-specific GPS violently.

"Look at this piece of mechanical shit," her voice carried. "We been trying for two hours to find some big cats. This . . . this thing has told us twice we were lookin' at cats. I'm old, but I ain't stupid. The first bunch of those cats had horns, the second bumps." She slapped the GPS, but apparently without achieving the desired results. "Now look. This little turd says that concession stand over yonder is Tiger River."

"Sure," said a short man in a sombrero, "they're taking a hot dog break like everybody else."

The old woman burst into a frenzy of obscenities a Chicago cabby couldn't beat. "They must let the chimps play with these things when the tourists go home at night!"

"Naw, lady," a passing teenager chimed in, "chimpanzees are smart enough to take care of the equipment. They give 'em to the gorillas."

She yelled at the retreating kid, "You got it right, sonny," then shook the GPS again. "Why don't they bring back the paper maps? If they can print the directions that tell you how to operate this little turd, why not just print a map and cut out the middleman? If I could catch one of those smirking zoo guides, I'd ram this up his ass and see if it would lead him to the shitter!"

When Del rejoined Leah and Mike, they were laughing violently, clutching their sides, almost unable to stand. Leah choked out, "Did you ever hear an old woman talk like that before?"

Del chuckled, "Yeah, but at the time she was shooting at me. The old gal is right, though. We decided long ago the best way to navigate the zoo is to throw away those 'little turds' and just keep on going. After a few dozen trips, you finally get your bearings."

When both Leah and Mike had settled down, she said, "Sounds like you guys come here often."

"We do. Almost every month. I'm gonna be a zoologist—with a specialty in primatology," Mike said proudly.

"So that's why we passed the Gorilla Tropics three times. Here I thought we were just lost like everybody else." Leah grinned at Mike and he grinned back.

She didn't try to win his confidence. That would have made her feel soiled. She just listened to him. Even lying to him about her background bothered her more than lying to Del. But her easily offered friendship won the boy. She remembered Kevin at twelve, so precocious and bright, so filled with promise. He planned to be a psychologist. *I'm gonna be a zoologist . . .*

"Can we ride the aerial train, Dad?"

Del groaned. "You know how I feel about heights, Mike."

"Aw, Dad. You went last time."

"And you promised we wouldn't have to do it again next time," Del replied.

"I'll ride with you . . . if that's okay?" Leah ventured. "I love high places. You can see more."

"She's way cool, Dad. Okay if we go without you?"

"With my fondest blessings," Del said, handing the passes to them and waving them on their way. "I'll meet you at the main gate."

He watched Kasi and Mike laughing and talking animatedly as they climbed aboard the train. He was amazed at the way Mike had accepted her. On the only other occasion he'd brought a woman friend on an outing with his son, Mike had been jealous. Olivia had fawned over him and made matters even worse.

Kasi seemed to have a sense about kids. She knew to back off and give Mike space to get used to her, to show that she wasn't usurping his place with his father. Mike had never accepted Hugh's relationship with Diana, but then Del supposed that was natural. Divorce was hell on kids. Mike wanted his father to be there for him full-time.

I'm not much better than Shrewsbury. Mike was his own flesh and blood and yet he lived a continent away. Maybe when this investigation was over, he'd talk to Cohen about that West Coast assignment.

If he did that, would he ever see Kasi again? The thought bothered him far more than was reasonable. He'd only known the woman for a week. There was a strong sexual attraction between them, but it would be bad judgment to follow through on it.

Liar. You know you're going to screw her sooner or later.

Time to think of something else. He spotted a pay phone beside a concession stand and decided to give Cuff another ring. They couldn't talk on an unsecured line but at least he'd know his friend was okay.

Still no answer. Where the hell was Bedford? Del left no message, just disconnected, feeling a nasty clench deep in his gut. He called the airline and tried to arrange a return to D.C. on the red-eye, but they were booked solid. He could always try standby, the chirpy-voiced agent suggested. The thought of spending the night sleeping on airport furniture waiting for standby ranked right up there with covering trench warfare in the Balkans. He quickly dismissed that idea.

High above the zoo grounds, Leah and Mike enjoyed the stunning vista of Balboa Park. They talked about his school, hobbies, and friends. Suddenly he caught her off guard, asking, "Do you really like my dad?"

How the hell do you answer that one, Berglund? "I asked to be assigned as his researcher because I admire his work so much."

Kids can always spot equivocation even if they sometimes let it pass. This time Mike didn't. "Nah. I mean do you like him like a boyfriend?"

She could feel her cheeks flush. The Delgado men had the

damnedest effect on her. Leah couldn't remember when she'd blushed before meeting them. She looked into Mike's dark blue eyes, earnest yet watchful as Del's. "I'll be straight with you, Mike. I am attracted to your dad, but we just met, and after this assignment, I'll be gone. You, on the other hand, will have a relationship with him for the rest of your life. Nobody can take that away from you."

He surprised her with a crestfallen expression. "I sorta hoped you might stick around. I think Dad gets kinda lonesome sometimes."

Leah resisted the urge to hug him, swallowing hard to get herself under control. "Somewhere, someday, there'll be a woman for your dad, Mike." Her smile wobbled a bit. *But it won't be me.*

9:30 P.M., EDT, SUNDAY, JUNE 28
WASHINGTON, D.C.

Cal Putnam stared at his PDA, debating whether to contact Delgado. He had Del's hotel number in San Diego.

"Dammit, if this ain't piss down the well," he muttered, then opened his tobacco pouch. He sat back and tamped the shredded brown leaves into the meerschaum bowl and lit a match to it. The fragrant smoke cleared his mind and helped him to think.

Fuck the damned doctors. He'd quit when they planted him in the marble orchard.

Suddenly a red light on his console flashed, indicating the highest-security channel. He did not receive such calls often. Verifying encryption code as a matter of course, he opened the channel.

"Putnam here."

"Troubling news, Cal. Mark's unraveling. We won't be able to use him much longer, I'm afraid. His father's death really hit him hard."

"He suspects old Stephan didn't accidentally drown?"

"Yes, I'm sure he does."

Putnam sighed regretfully. "Our friends at BISC will arrange an accident for him."

"Not too soon I hope."

"Not much we can do about it." Drawing on the pipe, his mind whirled with possibilities. First Bedford, now Patrikas. He cursed silently.

"I don't know if this is connected, but old Senator Manchester placed a call to me this morning. Mark cut him off, but I checked his PDA and found the number. I've been trying to reach him but they're having a ballbuster of a storm in that godforsaken wilderness where he lives. Would you believe, half the Maine coast is without power?"

"Let me know as soon as you talk to him. This might be our big break."

After he signed off, Putnam smoked contemplatively for several moments, then decided against calling Delgado. Truman had said, get out of the kitchen if you can't take the heat. "Heat, my rabid ass," he muttered, "this is pure hellfire!"

"Mike's a great kid, Del." Leah toyed with her wineglass, then took a sip of the Syrah.

He grinned. "Yeah. He is, isn't he? Wish I could claim some credit for it, but I can't." He took a bite from his rare fillet, not really tasting it.

After taking Mike home, they'd agreed on dinner in the La Jolla Sheraton's restaurant so they could turn in early. Their seven-forty flight required a wake-up call at a horrendous hour.

Now they lingered in the dimly lit dining room overlooking the sea, drinking and talking as the excellent meal grew cold. "Diana raised him pretty much on her own," he said, thinking about his failed marriage.

"The old stereotype: you were married to the Bureau more than to her." Leah understood all too well.

"First the Bureau, then the bottle, then the magazine."

"Don't beat yourself up too much, Delgado. I had a long talk with Mike. He thinks he has one pretty terrific dad. I agree."

"When I'm around, I try. I've been thinking about requesting a transfer to our San Diego office."

She smiled. "Mike would love it. How would the Shrewsburys feel about it?"

He shrugged and finished the wine in his glass. "I think Diana would be happy. She wants Mike to have a father."

"I take it the stepfather thing hasn't worked out."

"He's away from Mike more than I was."

"And that doesn't bother Diana?"

"Money can be compensating . . . shit, that was a low blow. She doesn't deserve it. I think she's grateful for the security, and at least Hugh isn't likely to be cut down in an alley some night."

"There's more to the antagonism between you and Hugh than Mike's affection. He's the one who sicced Brian Fuller on you, not Diana."

"You don't miss much," he said, studying her with slumberous dark eyes. "Hugh and Brian were friends before Fuller entered politics. Fuller was an investor in Shrewsbury's film company when I headed an FBI task force investigating fraud in the movie industry. I was never able to pin bribery charges on them, but I'd bet my pension they were guilty. When Diana and I split, he was after blood. I bled. I bled plenty."

"I'm sorry." She started to reach for his hand, then stopped herself. *Crazy, Berglund.* She covered by picking up her wineglass and draining it.

He reached for his glass, too. It was empty and he realized he was violating two of his most stringent rules. *What the hell!* "Let's do it again, shall we?"

When she nodded, he signaled the waiter.

"Now, Kasi Evans, no more about me. I've spilled my guts about my family, my failed marriage, my midlife career change, the whole enchilada. I want to know everything about you. How does a single woman who's spent her life as career driven as I am connect so well with a kid like Mike?" He was remembering the scene as the three had pulled up in front of Mike's house.

After nervously clearing her throat, Leah had turned to the boy. "Mike, I'm not trying to run your business, but when you tell the story of those old people to your buds at school tomorrow, you might want to tone down the language." Then she had pitched her voice into an almost perfect imitation of the old woman's croaking screech. "Ya may be young; but ya ain't stupid."

All three had convulsed with laughter. Delgado smiled. Yeah, she knew her way around kids

Just then the waiter arrived with another bottle of Cline Cellars Syrah and opened it. Del shooed him away and refilled their glasses himself. Her mind whirled with images from long ago of two children giggling and squabbling in the way of siblings.

Suddenly she began speaking without thinking, without the guarded artifice that had caged her life for the past three years. "Mike reminds me of my kid brother, Kevin. The grin, the blue eyes, even the way he walks, but it's much more than that—it's the kind of person he is, bright, inquisitive, a little shy. Kev and I were closer growing up than most brothers and sisters. Our parents were good to us, just . . ."

"Busy?" he supplied. "I can imagine life in the diplomatic corps is pretty rough, and obviously dangerous."

She nodded at the fabrication and went on. "I was almost ten when he was born. It's kind of odd really. Mom and Dad were thrilled to have a son at last. I should've been jealous, but I wasn't. It's hard to explain . . ."

"If he's like Mike, I can understand, believe me," Del said gently.

"He *was* like Mike." She took a fortifying swallow of wine. "He died four years ago. He'd been an honor student all through school. His freshman year in college he pledged a fraternity. I remembered they'd had a pretty wild reputation for partying, but I figured it was just Kev's way of expressing the teen rebellion he never got out of his system during high school . . ."

The story poured out of her then, memories of their childhoods, things about Kevin and how he died, the horror of it and the disintegration of their family. Del's intuitive questioning and willingness to listen brought out things she'd never voiced aloud before, not to the BISC psychologist, not even to her beloved grandfather.

When she finally finished, they were the only two customers left in the dining room and the second bottle of wine was empty. Leah felt drained and yet exhilarated, as if she had purged some deeply buried demon. Somehow in the midst of the conversation he had reached across the table and taken her hands in his.

There was strength yet infinite gentleness in Delgado's hands. The thought and the sight became suddenly erotic when his thumbs began massaging soft circles on the pulses in her wrists. She looked up at him, revealing her desire when their eyes met.

"I want to make love to you, but—"

"No buts, Delgado. I want it, too." She raised his right hand to her mouth and pressed the palm against her lips, repeating the soft circles with her tongue.

His breath caught. "Kasi, you've just been through an emotional wringer. I don't want to—"

"Take advantage of me, Delgado?" she interrupted with a low, husky laugh. "Just which one of us is Little Red Riding Hood and which is the Wolf?" She pulled him up from the table so they stood face-to-face barely a foot apart. "Now, sign the bill and let's get the hell out of here."

They walked out of the restaurant without touching, feeling such intense desire arc between them that they dared not. Crossing the polished marble floor of the lobby to the elevator seemed like walking on ice, agonizingly slow when they wanted so desperately to run. They stood inside the elevator, two pair of eyes staring intently at the flashing green lights as it inched toward the fourth floor. Standing in the hallway, Del pressed the compucode in the door of his room with clumsy fingers, missed a key, and had to repeat it. *Damn! I feel like a high school kid getting laid for the first time.*

The moment they were inside, he shoved the door closed and she turned to face him, pressing his body against the door full length as she wrapped her arms around his neck, kissing him with voracious thoroughness. He could feel her breasts, hips, and thighs massaging him and feel his own body's instant response. His pelvis rocked into hers. When she reached down between them and pressed her palm against the bulge of his cock, he almost ripped the buttons at the neck of her charcoal silk dress.

Her other hand glided from his neck down to his shirtfront. Before he knew it, she had it open and peeled back, nuzzling the thick black hair on his chest. She nipped one flat, brown nipple with her teeth. He gasped, "You're better with buttons than I am."

"Then let me." She raised both arms up and reached behind her neck to unfasten the dress. The sheer gray silk slithered over the gentle thrust of her breasts. He cupped them in his hands, feeling their firm roundness. The pebbly points of her long, engorged nipples pressed against her lace bra. When he caught them between his thumbs and index fingers, she murmured a soft expletive of pleasure.

Leah stepped back and let the dress drop to the floor. She watched his eyes follow from her shoulders to her breasts, down to her navel, hips, and legs. She knew she had a good body, long, limber, muscular, but there was none of Diana's feminine softness. Would it matter?

"Fuck, you're even more hot than I'd imagined—and believe me, I have a damn good imagination." He ripped off his shirt and kicked off his shoes, never taking his eyes from hers. She wore only a gray lace bra and matching bikini briefs. Her breasts weren't big but they were high and large enough to swell gently against the top of the bra. Her legs went on forever. "I also imagined how your legs would feel wrapped around me."

"Shall we find out?" She slid off her pumps, then waited as he dropped his slacks and yanked off his socks. He was more heavily muscled than she would've thought, darker skinned even where the sun had not touched, except for the jagged white scars of his old injuries.

"Mmm, I love hairy men," she breathed, plowing her splayed fingers through the mat on his chest, then pulling him closer, locking her hands on his shoulders and clamping her thighs around his hips.

They fell against the wall with a thud, but neither noticed. They were too busy devouring each other's mouth. Her silk panties were moist, pressing against his hard penis. His bad knee started to buckle. They slid slowly down the wall, then rolled onto the plush carpet in the spacious sitting room.

"No fair. You still have clothes." He flicked the hook on her bra and she threw it across the floor, then rolled away long enough to shimmy out of the briefs, but he grabbed them before she could toss them and pressed the damp silk to his face. "Yeah, you're hot," he murmured, rolling over her and looking down into her flushed face.

She reached for his cock and stroked it, watching him grimace with ecstasy. "Don't you dare come yet, Delgado," she murmured when it started twitching in her hand.

Between gritted teeth, he said, "Then stop priming the pump, Ms. Evans."

With a low laugh, she rolled them over until she came up on top. "Let's spare your bad knee."

"Fuck my knee."

"I'm not that kinky."

He silenced her by taking her breasts in his hands and working her hardened nipples, alternately suckling one, then the other. His swarthy face pressed so intimately against her pale skin was the most erotic turn-on she'd ever imagined. She moaned, positioning her hips over the head of his penis, rubbing back and forth, lubricating it with her own wetness, then sinking down on it fast and hard.

Del thrust up, deep inside her, feeling her clench around him, slick and tight, then fought the overwhelming urge to do just what she'd commanded him not to do. His hands clamped around her hips. "Hold on, baby, let me last, God, let me last!"

She leaned down and began kissing his jawline and throat, nibbling and licking, while her lower body remained utterly still. Leah could feel herself growing as excited as he was. "It's been quite a while for me. I don't think you'll have to last all that long," she whispered against his ear.

He took a deep, shuddering breath and eased his grip on her hips.

They rode slow at first, kissing, caressing, exploring each other's body. She picked up the tempo. He let her.

He lasted.

After several moments, they peeled apart, sweat-sheened and a little dazed.

"This floor is goddamned uncomfortable," he muttered after a few moments.

She chuckled. "I didn't hear you complaining until now."

"Now we try the bed."

The 5 a.m. wake-up call buzzed nastily. Leah untangled herself from Del long enough to sit up, then flopped back on the mattress with a groan. Too much wine, way too much sex . . . scratch that, just too much wine and not nearly enough sleep. *Great way to begin the day, Berglund.* She turned her head and looked at Delgado. He was still asleep, the lout!

She studied his beard-bristled profile and watched the even rise and fall of his chest. The scar across his side cut upward, frighteningly near his heart. Another whitish mass encircled one hip, but the worst was the knee, knotted and lumpy after repeated surgeries. It was miraculous he'd lived, much less regained so much mobility.

He was a marvelous lover. Not that she'd had all that many, especially since joining BISC, which strongly discouraged agents from any intimacy that might compromise their work.

BISC. She was their agent, assigned to investigate this man. Instead she'd slept with him. Dear God, what was she thinking? With her hormones, not her brains, that was for sure. *But he's innocent.* Dare she turn in that verdict, knowing that someone had set him up to be canceled? To do what her grandfather had told her, the culprit or culprits would have to be high up in BISC, perhaps even on the Tribunal.

She sat up, oblivious of her nakedness, laying her head on her knees and hugging them, trying to clear her head and think. Difficult with the musky residue of sex hanging in the air. She slid out of bed and padded silently into her adjoining suite. Fishing a small case out of her toiletries bag, she removed a morning-after pill and swallowed it with a glass of tap water. According to the prescription date on the label, it was the first one she'd used in nearly two years.

No wonder I was horny. She turned on the shower and climbed inside, adjusting the temperature to cool, hoping to clear the cobwebs from her mind. The best thing was not to think of Delgado, not the sex, not anything else about him. She could not afford emotional involvement for both their sakes.

Del awakened to the sound of the shower. The door to the adjacent room stood open. He smiled and stretched languorously. Damn, he couldn't remember the last time he felt this good. Rolling over, he placed a call to room service, then got out of bed and headed toward the sound of spraying water. No sense dirtying two bathrooms.

8 A.M., EDT, MONDAY, JUNE 29
WASHINGTON COUNTY, MAINE

The storm's lashing fury had spent itself near dawn. Adam Manchester finished the handwritten entry in his heavy leather journal. His hand cramped as he laid down his Montblanc pen and looked out the window at the rugged isolation of his wilderness home. He'd been writing most of the night, copying the material from a printout that he would leave in a hidden file in his office. The same material was stored on his currently nonfunctioning computer. Since the power had gone out last night, he'd worked by candlelight, a nineteenth-century amenity he often enjoyed. There was so much to do, so little time.

He'd read in the Boston newspaper Geerson's boy had delivered to him this morning that Mark Patrikas had died in a car wreck on the capital beltway last night. BISC would be along to arrange an accident for him, too, but the storm would slow them down. There were still a few aces up his sleeve and he intended to play them. Maybe now he could get through to Samson, but before he contacted anyone, he had to guarantee that Leah would find everything she needed in case he failed.

The journal was a private way to store information, some would say the conceit of an old curmudgeon who'd had to be dragged into the twenty-first century. He smiled grimly, acknowledging that there was some truth to that. But he had a better reason for using the journal. They'd find the information in his files, of course, and with their fancy technology, gain access to his old-fashioned computer and erase it without a trace. Only Leah would know how to find the journal. Once he left the message for her.

11.

Seth Geerson walked into the Machias Post Office the minute Thelma Goodings unlocked the doors. She looked startled, and not much startled Thelma. But Clyde's boy had never mailed anything before. "Morning, Seth. What can I do for you?"

Seth presented the sealed and stamped envelope to her as reverently as if it were a winning lotto ticket. "Senator Adam, he told me to mail this. Said I warn't to give it to nobody but you, Miz Thelma." Seth was slow, but possessed the fierce loyalty often characteristic of the mentally disadvantaged. As the postmistress examined the letter, he watched intently, shuffling from foot to foot.

"He's marked this for Priority Same-Day. The rates just went up last week. I'll have to check that zone," she said as she turned and walked behind the counter. Seth stopped in front of the swinging gate and waited, his eyes never leaving the package as she punched in the code.

"Ayup. Just as I was afraid, Seth. It's a dollar ten shy. Senator Adam'll just have to come by later and pay the difference—or I can send it regular mail, two-day delivery."

Seth's expression shifted from fearfulness to outright alarm. "But Senator Adam said it had to go right now! It's terrible important, Miz Thelma. You gotta send it just like he said." His normally friendly face grew red with indignation.

"It's the law, Seth," she said in her most officious postmistress voice. "When the phone lines are open on the peninsula, I'll just call the senator and tell him to send the money."

Seth shook his head vehemently. "It's gotta go now. He said."

"You could give me the dollar ten. I'm sure the senator would pay you back."

"I ain't got it." The young man was practically in tears now. "After he finished drivin' me on my paper route, Pa went to work. He keeps my cash money."

Dan McLean walked in just in time to hear the last exchange. He'd never seen the Geerson boy so riled, but then Thelma Goodings was "tribulation enough to piss off the pope," as his daddy used to say. "What's the trouble, Thelma? Seth?"

"She won't send the senator's letter!"

"Insufficient postage," she said primly.

"Senator Manchester gave you a letter to mail?"

Seth blurted, "He flagged us down at his road on our return trip. He already read his Boston *Globe*. He thanked me for bringing it with the storm and all." The youth's face glowed with pride for a moment. "Then he give me that there letter and said it was real, real important and asked Pa to drive me here so I could give it to Miz Thelma. He said it hasta go *same day*." He enunciated the words emphatically.

The sheriff glanced at the letter Thelma held. He couldn't make out the address except for the letters D.C. The old man had been mightily upset at the ME's office Saturday, insisting Stephan Patrikas's death was no accident. Then the first thing that came in when power was restored to his office was the news that the old man's whiz kid son had died in a car crash last night.

"I'll pay the postage, Thelma. How much?"

"One dollar, ten cents, Sheriff."

He handed her a dime and a buck. "Reckon I'll take a drive out to visit the senator and collect what he owes me." He tipped his hat to Thelma and winked at Seth, then ambled out of the small office.

1:37 P.M., EDT, MONDAY, JUNE 29
WASHINGTON, D.C.

The lines at National were worse than usual as dark-suited business travelers waited nervously for airport security to scan them and their briefcases. The once shiny marble floors of the District's key airport were grimy and littered with debris and discarded food wrappers, the result of a chronic shortage of maintenance. Uniformed personnel, wearing full aerofoam body armor, carried the newest M17 laser-sighted assault rifles.

They performed the most dangerous job in the county—working where El-Ops or domestic or foreign terrorists might open fire with automatic weapons. Hijacking planes had become an art form before Congress finally appropriated sufficient funding to install technology and train guards to enforce weapons laws. Now and then the system still failed. The result was often severe "collateral damage" to airline passengers.

Del and Leah wended their way through the crowded maze to the security exit where their weapons were held. All civilians licensed to carry were required to surrender their hardware and show their permits before entering any airport. A young guard with old eyes inspected their ID and permits. He stamped their return tickets and handed them to a clerk in charge of the storage vault. As they waited, they talked.

"I have several things to check," Del said. "Sources who may've come up with some leads. I'll call you tonight at your place. Maybe we can have dinner."

"If you promise no carryout."

He grinned and raised his hand. "I promise, nary a cardboard carton in sight."

They hailed separate taxis, pausing awkwardly at the curb for an instant before reaching out for a quick embrace. Leah toyed with the idea of following him but dismissed it as too risky. Whatever he was doing, she'd have to find out some other way.

Gramps might be able to help. She'd heard about Stephan Patrikas's drowning death on the Saturday-night news and knew the senator would be saddened by losing his old friend. She could reach him on the personalized vid phone once she was inside the post office, an untraceable haven if not the safest place in town. The cab dropped her off by Union Station and she crossed the street to the monolithic structure.

Finding a relatively quiet corner, she dialed, then waited without a ring until a compuvoice came on the line, announcing in a nasal singsong that the number was out of operation due to local power failure. Leah sighed in frustration. The senator's isolated cabin on the eastern peninsula of Machias Bay was always the first to lose power and the last to have it restored. She often chided him about living alone in the wilderness so far from modern security. He always replied that he was a hell of a lot more secure in rural Maine than he'd ever been when he lived in the capital.

Her postal box was nearly bare. The names of BISC agents never appeared on junk-mail lists. One same-day letter lay inside. A nasty prickle of unease clenched deep in her gut as she reached for it and saw the return address.

Gramps.

She glanced around with seeming casualness and spotted no one suspicious. Nevertheless, she slid the letter in a compartment of her carry-on bag and strode out of the building with her hand resting on the butt of the Ruger concealed in her jacket pocket.

As soon as she hailed a cab for the short ride to her apartment, Leah retrieved the letter and tore it open, then froze when she read:

> *Pia,*
> *Go to the usual place and look for an unusual item.*
> *Gom*

If she'd been worried when she saw the envelope, she was terrified now. Gom stood for Grand Old Man, their nickname for Adam Manchester when she and Kevin had been children. Pia was half of the Leah-Pia endearment he'd called her by as a child and again the last time they'd talked. But what did the message mean? "Go to the usual place." What usual place? What unusual item? He was ordering her to do this, so it had to be important. The implications of the roundabout instructions were ominous.

Returning to her empty apartment, she tossed her luggage on the bed and sank onto the small sofa. As thoughts whirled around in her head, she automatically flicked on the TV news, a professional habit. The usual political peccadilloes were reported interspersed with El-Op street violence from metro areas around the nation.

Leah paid little attention until she heard her grandfather's name and immediately peered at the screen, listening intently. Her mouth was filled with the dry metallic taste of fear as the scene flashed to the Maine coast and the smoldering ruins of a house.

Adam's house.

"Former United States senator Adam Manchester may be dead. A body has been found in the charred rubble that was his house. Washington County sheriff Daniel McLean has refused to make any comment at this time, either to confirm the identity of the victim or the cause of the blaze, which occurred only hours after a severe summer storm soaked coastal Maine."

Leah sat frozen, hearing nothing as the chic blond newscaster moved on to a story about an earthquake on the Pacific Rim. *Gramps dead?*

"No." She mouthed the word like a silent scream, then killed the TV. Using her vid link in the apartment was chancy. She grabbed the unit and walked down the hall to the fire stairs, then called information. "Give me the number for the Washington County Sheriff's Office in Machias, Maine."

The encrypted message from Cal Putnam was waiting when Del reached his office. He walked to a bank of public vid links on the ground floor of the building and accessed Putnam's private number. Cal picked up on the first ring. They arranged an immediate meeting. Delgado didn't like the expression on Putnam's face.

A hazy sun presided over midsummer D.C., creating a sweltering steam bath. The air-conditioned dimness inside the Native American Museum embraced Del as he stepped through the door. Meeting in town during daylight was always dicey. His gut told him Putnam wouldn't have set this up without one hell of a good reason.

Once sure he had no tail, he strolled around the display of Chief Joseph and his Nez Percé until he saw Putnam sitting on a bench in an alcove. He made two men as FBI, standing watch at either end of the corridor. No one could spot him and Putnam without getting by them.

"What's happened, Cal?"

"Bedford's dead," he replied with characteristic bluntness.

"Cuff?" was all Del managed, feeling as if he'd just been sucker punched. "How?"

"DCPD's calling it an accident, but you 'n' me both know an idea would pop their skulls wide open. Happened Sunday morning in his condo. He'd been in the steam bath, had the artificial leg off and slipped, hit his head on the edge of the tub and drowned."

"Drowned? In the whirlpool bath?"

"That's what the ME's report says." Putnam's tone of voice indicated his skepticism.

"Cuff hated the damn thing. Said a one-legged man would have to be suicidal to hobble across that slick tile apron to climb into a deep marble tub. And Cuff Bedford wasn't suicidal."

"There was no indication of forced entry, but BISC would be careful of that."

"A Sanitation Squad specialty," Del replied, gritting his teeth as the fury washed over him. "I'm going to nail them, Cal. The whole bloody agency and every son of a bitch on their payroll."

"Just cool down. Having a farting spell ain't gonna help anything."

"Those motherfuckers wasted Cuff just like they did McCallum and Brandies."

"Don't forget Crosby and Nuñez and that sergeant at Adair, ole son. Bodies are piling up thicker 'n' fleas on a blue tick."

"I heard on the news about Samson's aide and his father both dying accidentally. Another odd coincidence. Any chance they're connected to what's going on?"

Cal shrugged. "Not the old man. He was out of the loop, but young Patrikas . . . he was a biggedy fucker. Always trying to fart higher 'n' his ass. He could've been. After you called Sunday, I got to thinking about that angle. Had a little tête-à-tête with that polecat Waterman." Putnam reached for his pipe, then cursed, realizing he couldn't fire up in the museum.

When Cal volunteered nothing more, Del let the reference to Waterman pass. Putnam would tell him what he needed to know, nothing more. "You called the police about Cuff?"

Cal nodded. "Something didn't smell right. After you rousted me out, I got to thinkin'. You said he was a loner, so I figured he might've gone out on the town, got laid on Saturday night. But when I called his place late Sunday morning, there was still no answer. DCPD found him. I had one of my men sit in on the investigation and put a burr under the ME's tail. But it's useless as warming up leftover snow to try 'n' prove Bedford was murdered."

"You know BISC killed him, Cal."

"Sure as shit stinks. And I know that if they've made your source, they've made you, ole son. Maybe it's time you went to ground. Go talk to those señoritas down Uncle Mac's way."

"Not before I check out one more thing here."

Gracie Kell chose a more scenic meeting site than the bar in Dobbins Addition, although Del wasn't certain if the tree-shrouded campus of Catholic University was any safer. He patted his Smith & Wesson for reassurance as he walked past a thin stream of students en route to classes.

Evening enrollment tended toward nontraditional students, mostly older with the usual smattering of ambitious blue-collar working stiffs and a fringe of the terminally weird, who frequented the campus of every urban commuter university. Gracie fit right in with the latter group.

He walked through the cafeteria line, purchasing a greasy batch of fries and a burger that looked as if it had been freeze-dried the year before he was born. He plunked the tray down on the table in the deserted area she had chosen and took a bite out of the indigestible meat without looking at her. "What have you got for me, Gracie?"

"I'm in, Delgado." She smacked her plum-black lips with barely concealed glee, draining dry the Diet Coke she was sucking through a straw. "Nothing on the Tribunal members identities but plenty of creepy shit. Your two Feds, Crosby and Nuñez? I read their termination reports. Ditto McCallum's and Colonel Brandies's and a bunch of other poor bastards your disc didn't mention. Those Sanitation Squad fuckers clean up guys who know too much. But here's the real kicker."

She shoved the empty soft-drink cup away and hunched forward, eyes narrowed, sweeping the half-empty student cafeteria. "The reports on your G-men were filed by regular BISC agents who reported them as righteous terminations."

"My source in the Bureau swears they're clean."

"Maybe. Probably were judging by what else I found, but the documentation in their guilty verdicts says they were dealing with big league El-Ops, one on each coast."

"Besides your normal paranoia, what else did you find to make you doubt they were guilty?"

"I found another file . . . on you."

By the time Delgado had pulled up in front of Leah Berglund's apartment, he was still fighting the killing rage that had consumed him . . . and losing. He tried to tell himself that she was being used, just like dozens of other BISC agents. *But it still bites like hell, doesn't it?*

He'd given Gracie more than enough cash to see her on the next jet to Havana. Once he'd explained about Cuff's death, she had been more than willing to go. Delgado sat in the car, hands clenched on the steering wheel, staring at nothing . . . remembering everything. How Kasi/Leah tasted and smelled and how she'd closed her eyes and bit her lip when she came. From the day she'd first walked into his office, the sexual currents between them had sure been real to him. Had it all been a sham to her?

Leah should have been alarmed by the expression on Del's face when she pressed the entry button to admit him to her apartment complex. But she was far too preoccupied by what Sheriff McLean had told her to notice. When the door opened, he stormed inside without a word and shoved it closed, then turned to her.

She had been crying. Her fair skin was blotched with red and her eyes were swollen, but he was too intent on his own anger to realize it. "Hello, Leah Berglund." Her eyes widened imperceptibly and she took a half step back as if bracing to defend herself. "Quite a surprise when a dumb sucker like me learns he's been sleeping with his executioner."

"How did you find out?" Her tone was flat, detached.

"Reporters have their sources—and sometimes they end up dead. But you wouldn't know anything about that, would you?"

"I don't."

"Cuff Bedford was more than a Pentagon insider—he was my friend and your Sanitation Squad goons arranged an accident for him."

"I don't know who—"

"You're BISC. You were assigned to investigate me on some trumped-up drug charge related to my uncle. Right? Tell me, did I earn a stay of execution because I was a good lay?"

Reflexively her fist balled up, knuckles tight, but she did not deliver the immobilizing thrust to his solar plexus. "You didn't wind up dead because I'm honest and thorough. I broke damned near every BISC procedure to save your ass."

"Frankly, I don't much give a shit about BISC procedure. I just want to know what you reported to the motherfuckers."

"You hypocritical bastard!" She turned and walked to the kitchen cabinet. Bracing her hips against the edge of the countertop, she glared at him. "You barge in here like a gored bull and accuse me of seducing you. Well, it takes two to tango, buster, and you wanted to dance. Yes, I lied to you. It was part of my job, but you lied to me, too, don't deny it. You're investigating BISC, not some black-market weapons scam. That's why you went to see McCallum."

"Who was conveniently canceled while I was there. They almost got me, too."

"You think I sicced a Sanitation Squad on you when I passed up a dozen golden opportunities to terminate you this past week?"

"I don't know what the fuck to think anymore." He turned away from her and paced in the small room, combing his fingers through his hair. "People I care about, former colleagues and old friends, are turning up dead and I know BISC's doing it."

"Tell me, Delgado, you're the hotshot Mr. Pulitzer, but do you ever watch the news? If you did, you might've heard Adam Manchester died in an *accident* this morning."

"Adam Manchester, the senator?"

"Adam Manchester, my grandfather, you son of a bitch!" She clamped her jaw closed, gritting her teeth with the pain.

"BISC? But why?"

"He was helping me . . ." The words dragged out of her.

"Helping with what, Ka—Leah?" His voice softened.

Hers didn't. "Call it an internal affairs matter. You were FBI. You ought to understand that."

"I understand they'll cancel anyone who gets in their way. If you've crossed them—"

"Like I said before, Delgado, I can take care of myself." Her tone was ice-cold. "Now take your wounded male ego and your FBI agenda and get the fuck out of my apartment!"

Del drove around aimlessly for half an hour as sultry twilight enshrouded D.C., then headed south on I-95, opening up the flash drive on his TE to 190 kph when he hit open countryside. He was more than halfway to Richmond when he finally turned around and headed home to Alexandria. The adrenaline rush of speed had not helped. Only two other remedies were in his repertoire.

He tried the bar first. Gatsby's Tavern was located just around the corner from his Pitt Street condo on Royal. He figured he could get as drunk as a skunk and still make it home. The antique bar traced its history back to 1770 and was famous for hosting the likes of George Washington and Thomas Jefferson. Five years ago Rufus Kale, another ex–FBI man, bought it.

"What can I do you for, buddy? You look like you could use a cerveza." Kale reached into the cooler behind the long cherrywood bar and pulled out a Montezuma Sol, popped the tab, and poured it into a frosted mug.

"Give me a shot on the side, will you, Rufe?"

"That bad, eh? Either your best friend died or it's woman troubles." "Both."

Del swallowed the whiskey in one burning gulp and chased it with half the bottle of beer while Kale watched silently. His face was black as a starless night and seamed by pain and experience. There wasn't much he hadn't heard. "You want to talk about it or just drink?"

"Both."

He shoved the shot glass back across the bar top for a refill. The place was almost deserted and it was past closing time. But he and Rufus went back a ways at the Bureau, even though they'd never partnered. Each had been retired for injuries sustained in the line of duty, Kale five years prior to Delgado. The barkeep had seen him through the whiskey haze after his physical rehab.

After Delgado quickly downed two more shots, Rufus said, "Drinking won't solve your problems, Del. You know that."

"No. But passing out will."

Del drank and talked and Rufe poured and listened until it became apparent to both of them that boilermakers really weren't going to solve anything. "Fuck, I can't even get drunk. Must be a mind-set," Del said at length.

"What you should do is switch on your PDA and start digging. You need answers that you can't get from the bottom of the bottle."

Delgado knew Kale was right. Thanking his friend, he walked home, letting the damp river air clear his head. The first voice command he gave the computer was "Background search on Senator Adam Manchester, cross-reference with Leah Berglund."

At least she hadn't lied about the old man or the kid brother, he'd give her that. When he finally tracked down Dan McLean, the sheriff was not a happy man. It was 2 a.m. His hair was shoved into curly red lumps and his eyes squinted against the light. He had just come off a twenty-six-hour shift and fallen asleep when the call from D.C. roused him. After verifying Del's FBI ID with Cal Putnam, McLean was willing to talk about the fire at Manchester's lodge and some other interesting items.

Del had just disconnected with Machias when he received a call from Havana—collect. Gracie Kell, too, was working overtime. When she relayed her info, he was glad he'd accepted the charges.

Leah awakened from a nightmare in which Delgado accused her of murdering her own grandfather while Adam stood behind him, a silent specter of reproach. She lay still, staring at the ceiling in the darkness, numb with anguish, unable to shed any more tears.

She'd learned when Kevin had died that tears did nothing to right the wrong. But she had tried anyway. "Tilting at windmills," she whispered in the silence. The walls were closing in on her. She had been so utterly spent that she'd taken her link off-line, poured a Scotch, and gone to bed.

Perhaps going to Gramps's place and walking over it might help her make sense of his last message. What was the "usual place"? Was it even in Maine? Or was it right here in Washington? No, she and Gom shared no "usual place" in D.C. Most of his congressional colleagues were retired from politics now. The others were unavailable. Although that was ominous, it only served to indicate that Adam would not have expected her to search in Washington.

In desperation, she had even tried her parents. When she'd called, her mother's ravaged face and baffled response was heartbreaking. Manchester knew his daughter. He would never have entrusted her with sensitive material.

He left it to me.

Leah was just about to throw off the covers and get up when she heard it. The sibilant snick of a compusecurity lock being overridden. She'd broken into enough high-tech places herself to recognize it instantly. And reach for the Ruger beneath her mattress. Suddenly the lights flashed on. The single-room efficiency left no place to hide even if she made it off the bed.

"Drop it." The emotionless command came from a horse-faced woman holding a gun in one red-knuckled fist.

Leah could see little but a tall silhouette through the pinpoints of light dancing in front of her eyes, but she knew the woman had her cold. She dropped the Ruger, careful to see that it landed on the mattress, and stood up. Her vision could not adjust as rapidly as her mind could work. The intruder had BISC written all over her, from her tall, athletic stance and close-cropped hair right down to the sturdy, flat-heeled shoes on her feet. The one thing not regulation was the weapon—not a needle gun but a Vektor 9mm with a silencer. Whatever the plan, this was not going to be a standard termination or she'd already be dead. *They want something first.*

A second figure, male, wider but not as tall, materialized behind the woman. When they entered the room, he closed the door.

"That's sensible, Agent Berglund," she said. "Now move away from the Ruger."

Leah backed off, stepping toward the kitchen cabinets until she felt the countertop pressing into her spine. Utterly oblivious to an attractive blonde clad in a thigh-length silk night slip, the man sat down on the sofa and picked up her PDA. He methodically unfolded the kit with the familiarity only another BISC agent would possess.

"You have something vital to national security, Agent Berglund, security which you've compromised by selling out to a Cartel mule," the woman said.

"Delgado's no mule. Let's cut the crap. What you really want is the evidence my grandfather gathered."

"Good. We won't play games then. Where is it?"

Leah's expression hardened. "Guess."

The woman's coarse features drooped like a basset hound on Valium. "I was hoping you'd be reasonable."

"Your fucking goons murdered my grandfather and you want reasonable? Fuck off, lady."

"Anything in the system?" the woman asked her companion.

"She was a busy girl. Lots of snooping into BISC internal matters. Illegal use of protocols to access information not on a need-to-know."

"But nothing on Manchester in there?"

"No, but we know she purchased an extralegal digital link. Probably called his old pals on the Hill with it. No way to tell what she's found out until—"

"You secure her, then get the medikit," she said.

Medikit! Leah knew they meant to use drugs to get her to talk. Very effective drugs. Her only consolation was that there was nothing she could tell them. She could feel the drawer handle pressing into her buttock. *How can I open it before she can shoot me?* Damn, she needed a diversion.

The man took a pair of nylon wrist restraints from his jacket and stepped forward, then halted at the sound of footsteps running up the hallway. Elliott Delgado pounded on the door, yelling her name. The woman turned her weapon on the door as he blasted the lock with that cannon of his. Leah had her diversion. She yanked open the drawer and reached for the .45-caliber derringer stashed inside, but the male agent was too close. He kicked the drawer closed, almost pinning her hand.

The female agent fired at Delgado when he crashed through the door, grazing him as he rolled to the right. Leah grappled with the male agent, who dropped the restraints and pulled out his needle gun. She swept her heel behind his knee but he was too stocky to buckle. They struggled over the deadly weapon. Quickly she applied an aikido wrist lock to his gun hand. Her thumbs pressed against the back of his hand, forcing it to bend inward, and with it, the barrel of his weapon. She could see the sweat beading his red face, smell his cheap cologne and pumping adrenaline as she slid her right-hand up to press the trigger over his own finger.

Del fired at the female agent while she leveled her Vektor. His .50-caliber slug plowed into her. Her shot veered wide. Knocked against the wall, she slid down into a sitting position, still clutching her automatic for another try.

Leah's opponent landed a clumsy elbow strike to her neck. The pressure she was exacting on his trigger finger eased, but the aikido grip kept the gun turned on him while she drove her knee upward, connecting with his testicles. She took advantage of his instantaneous weakening.

The soft pop of the needle gun was lost in the roar from Delgado's Smith & Wesson as he put a second slug into the horse-faced woman. This time she dropped the gun and sat very still, sightless eyes opened wide.

When the male agent crumpled to the carpet at Leah's feet, Delgado spun around, looking at them, puzzled. She stood weaponless. Then he saw the pinpoint of red centered just below the man's right eye and the needle gun lying on the floor.

"Are you okay?" he asked, wincing from the sting in his shoulder.

"Yeah." She looked at him warily. "You saved my ass a second time, Delgado. How did you know they were after me?"

He stopped short of embracing her and let his arms drop to his sides. She was dressed in a wisp of lavender silk that left damn little to the imagination. "A source of mine hacked inside the BISC system and read your termination order. I tried to call but your link's down."

"I shut it off. You're bleeding." She reached up to where the female agent's slug had sheared through his jacket and cut a furrow across the top of his shoulder muscle.

"That was a dumb thing to do. When I couldn't get through, I feared the worst. Used my flash drive right up 395 across the Fourteenth Street Bridge. Not a cop tried to stop me."

"Not a cop could catch you the way you drive." She pulled the torn fabric from the wound.

"Jesus!"

"This has to be cleaned out but I don't think it's deep."

"You going to play nurse?" He eyed her skimpy night slip.

"You may want to play doctor, but we don't have time now. All these shots fired in this neighborhood will eventually bring the cops, and I don't think we want to stick around for explanations."

"Lieutenant Litzinger won't be as understanding about the deaths of two federal agents as he was about BoBo and Junior."

"It will take a while to confirm their identities. They don't have fingerprints. Or DNA records. None of us do."

"I know. McCallum told me. How the hell were you able to fire his needle gun?"

"Let's just say I helped him shoot himself." She kicked at the syringe, which had fallen out of his pocket. "They were going to use meds to interrogate me."

"When I came busting in here, I wondered why they hadn't already canceled you—and why Ma Parker there wasn't packing a needle gun."

"How did you get past the security system downstairs?"

"I flashed my FBI badge at a tenant opening the door. He said he'd seen a man and a woman who didn't live here pass him, headed up to your unit." He resisted the urge to pull her against him. "We were lucky this time, Leah, but now they'll be after us like rats trailing a garbage truck."

She began gathering up her belongings with practiced efficiency:

toiletries, a few changes of clothes, her weapons. "I'm going to Maine, Delgado," she called over her shoulder as she walked into the small bathroom and closed the door to change.

"Oh, brilliant, just fucking brilliant! That's the first place they'll look."

"I don't care. I have to make arrangements for Gramps and—"

"Your grandfather may not even be dead!" She yanked the bathroom door open and peered around it.

"I talked to Sheriff McLean. Until he gets DNA tests back, he can't be sure it's Manchester who died in that fire."

"It was. There's no way in hell Gramps would do that to me. These Sani Squad apes were looking for evidence he passed on to me before they killed him." She emerged from the bathroom wearing a pink tank top and white stretch jeans. "I've got to find it."

"Dammit, woman, think! You can't help anyone if you're dead! Christ, are you gonna dishonor your grandpa by letting those bastards use him for bait?"

Del's last remark brought her to a halt. For a moment she stood very still, then slid into a pair of soft flats. "Why should I help you? Why should I even trust you?"

He sighed. "Because, like you just said, I saved your ass. Let's go back to my place so I can patch up this shoulder and get my gear. Then we'd better partner up for real, 'cause we're both A-list targets and we both want evens."

She looked skeptical, then glanced at the two dead BISC agents. Grabbing her suitcase, she headed for the door. "Okay, Delgado. I'll drive, you talk."

9:30 A.M., EDT, TUESDAY, JUNE 30
TYSONS CORNER MALL, NORTHERN VIRGINIA

"I don't like this, Delgado," Leah said as he pulled into the crowded parking lot. They were driving a Honda EV, an inconspicuous rental, which Cal had arranged.

As soon as they'd left Del's apartment, they'd found an all-night coffee shop where they'd talked for several hours. He laid out everything that had happened since that first night in Accotink Park with Cal Putnam up to Cuff Bedford's death. She explained that the investigation of him had led her and Adam to conclude BISC was terminating innocent people. Neither Del nor Leah knew who the conspirators were, only that they were probably subverting the highest levels of government and possibly the military to make a covert strike against the Cartel.

He slipped into a small parking space near the west entrance. "We can trust Putnam. He'll have tickets for us and weapons arranged when we land in San Diego."

"I still think I should've gone to Maine," she said as they got out of the cramped car and headed for the mall entrance. "I know Gramps left something vitally important or the Sani Squad wouldn't have waited to use meds on me."

"Go to Maine and do what? You admitted you can't figure out what he hid or where he hid it. If BISC wants it, they'll just wait for you and let you lead them to it."

"And they won't know you're heading straight for your son?"

He opened the mall door with a grim yank. "You're right. BISC doesn't know where Manchester's evidence is hidden, but they know where Mike lives. That's why I had Cal send his men to guard the house until I get there. I doubt BISC will believe we'd team up and share info."

"I can hardly believe it myself," she said, giving the crowds of morning shoppers a swift professional appraisal.

Del saw Putnam standing by the news kiosk holding a copy of *U.S. News-Time* in his hand. Del guided Leah to the stand and reached down for a hot-rod magazine. Dressed in faded jeans and boots, he hoped he looked the type. The attendant eyed Leah's cleavage as she thumbed through a *Vogue*. After it was apparent they were browsers, he turned to the other counter where a couple of kids were ready to purchase comic books.

"Ms. Berglund, I presume?" Putnam tipped his head, an old-fashioned mannerism.

She nodded, then continued to scan the mallscape.

"It's as safe as a saint in Sunday school. I have men posted I can trust." He turned to Del and handed him the airline tickets.

"Thanks, Cal." Del glanced at the itinerary. "We should have plenty of time to make it if there are no accidents on Dulles Access. What about the drop?"

"Being taken care of as we speak. Got me a pissin' buddy in El Cajon who has connections. He's filling your wish list. The agents I sent to watch the Shrewsbury residence should have everything waiting when you get there."

"The Smith & Wesson?"

"Twin to the one you're packing now. Ditto for the lady's Ruger automatic—.41 caliber I believe. Course I can't get her another needle gun."

Leah's head swiveled to meet his eyes. "I'll overlook that failure if you've gotten us some fully automatic accessories. If so, we'll make do."

Cal grinned crookedly, revealing tobacco-stained teeth. "I believe you will, Ms. Berglund, sure as shooting." He turned to Del and clasped his hand. "Take care of that boy of yours and watch your ass, ole son."

"From here on out, Cal, the only ones we can trust are each other."

12.

"So our investment in the FBI has finally paid off." Harmon Waterman watched the smiling face on the vid. *Just keep oozing that charm, my friend.* "You know they've tried to keep Drescher out of the loop, but this time I think we've hit the jackpot. Your backup may not be necessary."

"Fine with me. I'm sick of this dump," his associate said with loathing, looking at his surroundings. "I can be back in Washington by tonight if Delgado and the woman are neutralized."

"Don't rush your fences. Stay in place for now. The cleanup should take place within the hour. Watch the San Diego news tonight. There's going to be a most outrageous event on I-5. Just awful what a pack of crazed El-Ops with automatic weapons can do." His homely face split in a grin that did not reach his cold, pale eyes.

Del leaned on the bell, pressing until Leah was certain he'd short out the circuit. He'd raced up Highway 5 all the way from the airport to La Jolla at 190 kph. She figured if the police didn't stop them, the Lincoln TE's flash drive would explode. They made it without incident.

Leah surveyed the street where one of Putnam's men was staked out. *Why don't those FBI bozos just wear neon body armor?* she thought contemptuously. If BISC agents were that obvious, the El-Ops would run the country by now. She hoped Cal's "boys" were at least competent enough to have the weapons package ready for them.

"Come on, Diana, answer, dammit," he muttered, renewing his assault on the bell.

The door swung open and an older woman with steel gray hair and an affronted scowl said, "Good day. May I help you?" obviously meaning neither.

Del shoved past the maid, whose eyes widened with alarm. "Diana! Mike!"

Wearing an expression of incredulity, and hastily belting a soft terry bathrobe, Diana approached the second-floor balcony overlooking the foyer. "El, what on earth—"

His ex was a late riser, Leah thought smugly. She did not look nearly so daunting minus designer clothes and makeup. Her hair fell in damp strings around her shoulders as if she'd been interrupted in the shower.

"Sorry I didn't get the door sooner, missus. I was out at the pool," the flustered maid excused herself.

"Go back to work, Cici, I'll handle this," Diana said.

"Where's Mike?" Del demanded, climbing the stairs.

"What is going on, Elliott?" Diana stood her ground. Only her whitened knuckles clutching the thick terry robe closed revealed agitation.

"No time to chat. Mike could be in danger. I need to get him out of here."

"Tell me what's going on, El."

Sensing the personal confrontation brewing, Leah said, "I'll check with the Feds outside while you explain."

As soon as she was gone, Diana's expression shifted from exasperation to anxiety. "What Feds? What have you gotten mixed up in now?"

"I'll explain but first you tell me where my son is."

"In the mountains up north, camping with Hugh. Brian owns a fishing cabin in Oregon. His son Rob and Mike are school chums."

"Brian Fuller took Hugh and the two boys fishing?" he asked with patent disbelief. He knew the congressman and Shrewsbury were old pals, but he was utterly unable to imagine either of them baiting a hook.

"It's called father and son bonding, El, a concept with which you're not overly familiar." Fear lent an edge to her voice. "Why should Mike be in danger?"

Del took a deep breath and launched into a censored explanation.

After making a quick detour through the garage, Leah went out a side door. She spotted the second FBI agent, a black guy pretending to be a pool serviceman. *Shit, after he treats the water, Queen Diana's hair will probably turn green.* Whistling, she walked up to him and flashed her ID.

"We were told our man was working with one of you 'legal' vigilantes," he said, eyeing her as if she were a Pan-Serb terrorist.

"What are your orders when we leave?"

"I've got 'em on hard copy, right here in my pocket. Let me read 'em to you."

"Cute. Just phone home to verify that Mrs. Shrewsbury requires continued protection. You have the package?"

"My instructions are to hand it over to Special Agent Delgado." In spite of being zipped into striped coveralls, he looked as officious as if he were wearing a standard three-piece suit.

"Agent Delgado's busy inside. You know the drill. Turn over the goods."

He looked as if he were going to give her an argument, but the first agent approached, following the serpentine hedge around the side of the house. He was carrying a satchel. She reached for it while displaying her badge. Neither guy looked happy but he handed over the bag. She hoped everything on Del's wish list was inside.

Ignoring them both, she walked over to the pool house and knelt just inside the open door to examine the contents, then snapped the satchel closed and returned to where they stood waiting. "I'd like to say it's been a pleasure doing business with you, gentlemen, but some of your merchandise is crap." She headed back to the house.

When Delgado came down the back sidewalk alone, she asked, "Where's Mike?"

"I'll tell you on the way."

They left the high-rent district behind and cruised down the steel and concrete ribbon of expressway headed toward Tijuana. Del explained the situation. "So Mike and Hugh are up in the middle of nowhere—somewhere in southern Oregon with Brian Fuller and his son. They'll be gone for two weeks. Completely incommunicado according to Diana."

"A prominent politician like Fuller just takes two weeks off to be with his kid?" She was as skeptical as Del had been.

He shrugged, checking the rearview vid before changing lanes. "According to Diana, Fuller and Shrewsbury do this every year."

"A male bonding thing?"

"That's the term Diana used. I'd have figured both of them for two weeks at the Royal Hawaiian on Maui. Not a fishing lodge on the Rogue River."

"Funny," Leah said. "Why didn't Mike mention it when we were with him Sunday? A big adventure like that would really excite a twelve-year-old."

"Mike's a sharp kid. He knows there were some pretty hard feelings between me and his stepfather and Fuller. I've tried to explain that it's water under the bridge, that Hugh and I have buried the hatchet, but . . ." He changed lanes again.

"Have you—buried the hatchet?"

"I guess Shrewsbury tries but he's a jerk." Del seemed preoccupied, checked the rearvid again, and quickly cut across three lanes, nearing an exit. "Watch the tan Chevy two cars back." He slid the big Lincoln between a couple of imports and waited.

Sure enough, the Chevy switched lanes, too. "I think we have company," Leah said, turning in her seat to observe the Chevy. "Two people. They're closing, Delgado."

"Fuck! So's the Olds. I'd hoped he was just a driver on Elevator."

She dug into the satchel at her feet and extracted his Smith & Wesson and her Ruger. She checked the clips and jacked a round into each chamber, then put Del's piece on the seat by his right leg. Sliding her automatic into her waistband, Leah reached down again and pulled a Beretta machine pistol out of the satchel. She slammed the twenty-round extension clip in place, fastened the shoulder stock, and jacked a round into the chamber. "Look at this relic, for God's sake, and it's three-round burst-fire, not even fully auto! Where do your people buy their gear? Afghan flea markets?"

Del was too busy to give a damn about their equipment. He watched in the rearvid as the two cars behind them maneuvered into position, closing distance, cutting off other vehicles on the busy freeway as they neared the Highway 8 interchange.

Leah rooted through the bag on the floor, mumbling curses. Del's voice grew tight. "Damn it, woman. Stop digging in that shittin' bag. I need another pair of eyes up here. We're taking a detour." He cursed, swerving into an exit lane without signaling.

"Stay on 8 to 163 south. I have an idea." Leah dug into her handbag and pulled out the vid link she'd bought in D.C. She began punching in numbers as the two cars drew nearer. Del could only catch bits and snatches of her conversation as he dodged and swerved, trying to keep other cars between them and their pursuers. He heard the words "double stiff," "BISC," and "Washington," then some cursing, but by that time the guys in the Chevy pulled abreast of them and opened up with a cut-down Nam 16A1.

Del tromped the accelerator so the shooter took out their backseat window instead of them. Glass particles sprayed the back of their heads, catching in their hair, leaving tiny abrasions on their necks. Leah hunched down with the Beretta. The Olds caught up behind them and blasted out the rear window. Sparing only a glance to see that Del wasn't hit, she turned in her seat and took aim on the headrest. Her first burst of fire took out the front windshield. The second took off a major chunk of the triggerman's head.

Undaunted, the Olds driver bent low out of her line of fire and rammed into the back of their car. The Lincoln smashed into the side of a Volvo, whose driver spun his vehicle away, frantically trying to escape the mayhem. Del fought to regain control and swerved the

Lincoln into the Olds as it pulled alongside. It kissed the guardrail near the Washington Street exit.

"Exit here," Leah yelled. "Then head east. Run the lights!"

"No shit, Bobby Martin!" He went with his gut and trusted her, taking the ramp on two wheels with the Chevy and Olds in close pursuit. The assassins were firing in wild bursts. Leah returned the favor. They tore down the major thoroughfare, the now mangled Lincoln zigzagging around vehicles too slow to get out of the way, often veering through oncoming cars when Del crossed the median. The blare of their horns was drowned out by a blast from the Chevy. They were trying for the Lincoln's tires.

Their next shot connected. The explosion of rubber drowned in the roar of automatic weapons fire coming from the Chevy. Once again it pulled abreast, this time on Leah's side of the Lincoln. Del could feel himself losing control of the car as surely as he could smell burned rubber.

Leah crouched on her seat, firing short bursts with the Beretta at both cars. "Fuckers must have bulletproof heads," she snarled. The Chevy inched closer and Leah took a deadly chance. Leaning through her open window, she ignored the shooter as he was leveling his automatic at her and fired at the driver point-blank. The Chevy careened wildly out of control as the driver pitched against the shooter, who seized the wheel without letting go of his weapon. Not a bright idea. The Chevy crashed into a fire hydrant and overturned. The Olds dodged the flying debris and kept on coming.

Both cars limped to a standstill as she jammed the last clip into the Beretta. Del searched the rough industrial neighborhood for cover, wondering why Leah had chosen to exit here. "We'll have to make a run for that warehouse," he said, blinking away a thin trickle of blood from a superficial cut on his forehead.

"Don't look now but I think the cavalry's arrived, Delgado." Two carloads of shooters armed with fully automatic M16A1s and AK-47s barreled down the street from opposite directions, catching both cars in a cross fire.

"Let's bail," Del yelled, slamming the Lincoln smack against the corner of the three-story warehouse. Del grabbed the satchel and his

Smith & Wesson as they crawled out the passenger side, then ran down the narrow alley between two buildings. A gun battle ensued between the newcomers and the driver of the Olds, who must now have felt like George Armstrong Custer.

No one pursued them, but they kept running for several blocks. Leah could see that Del's knee was causing him considerable pain. In spite of the limp, he kept up with her until they reached a busy intersection. Ignoring passersby, who in turn studiously ignored her, Leah calmly disassembled the Beretta, returning it to the satchel. Then she and Del blended into the crowd.

"Let's get some coffee and lay low," she said, turning into a cheap diner after checking it to be sure it had a back door.

Once seated, he leaned forward, rubbing his knee, and asked, "You mind telling me who the hell you called?"

"The cavalry?" She grinned as a frazzled waitress approached, then ordered coffee. So did Delgado. After she was sure no one was listening she said, "I pulled an old BISC trick. The El-Ops monitor police frequencies all the time. We have an access protocol that duplicates it so we can send disinformation when we need it. I said an '08 Lincoln, plates TE-ZKH975, carrying a trunkload of confiscated express bean bags was being pursued by two cars of L.A. El-Ops."

"And some ambitious local boys decided to beat their rivals and the cops to the punch and heist the payload." He grinned back at her over the chipped rim of his cup.

"I'd read a recent report on heightened activity south of Old Town San Diego here in the warehouse district. I hoped a carload of 'double stiff' would tempt the locals. It was a chance . . ."

"But it paid off."

"You're bleeding again," she said, taking the paper napkin and dabbing the small cut on his forehead.

"And you've got sparkles in your hair." He brushed some tiny flecks of auto glass from her head.

They smiled at each other for a moment, their guards down. Then she turned serious. "Who do you think they were? BISC or the Bureau?"

"Not the Bureau," he responded quickly.

"They knew exactly where we were—no one else did."

"If they wanted us, they could've taken us out in La Jolla at the house. Why arm us first, even with Afghan rejects? Had to be BISC . . . or some military spooks."

"Or real El-Ops who were set up to take us out," she said.

"You thinking about BoBo and Junior?"

She nodded.

"Funny, I considered that, too. Especially after your little scam on the link. BISC could maneuver dealers into hitting us."

"So could that mole in the FBI," she insisted stubbornly.

"Hell, maybe so. All I know for sure is from here out we have to trust each other or we're toast." He studied her with shrewd dark eyes, waiting for her reaction.

"Agreed. Nobody loves us but us," she conceded. "Where do we go now?"

"First we pick up another car. Just something to get us over the border without a trace. Then I call Uncle Mac."

"I understand you wanted to take Mike to your family for safety, but what's in Mexico for us? We can't afford to lie low and do nothing."

"My source in the Pentagon as well as what I learned in Winterhaven indicate some major league funny stuff is going on in northwest Mexico. If anyone knows what it is, Inocensio Ramirez does."

"The drug lord linked to your family. Right."

"Don't be so cynical."

She grinned in spite of herself. "Look who's talking."

"Okay, okay. I'll fill you in on my uncle's career on the way." He stood up, tossing money on the table.

By midafternoon they were across the Arizona border nearing the Lukeville-Sonoita border crossing into Sonora. Their small Honda TE coughed and sputtered more than a smog ward full of L.A. lung patients, but it ran and the salesman had not been overly curious about ID once Del slicked him with an extra five hundred bucks.

"No one should expect us to cross the border this far east. Bonita will meet us in Lukeville with phony papers, and Raoul will have his

Cherokee Six waiting on the Sonoita airstrip. We'll be in Mazatlán by the time siesta is over."

"Who are Bonita and Raoul?"

"My cousins. Second cousins, really. Francisco Mulcahey is their grandfather. Bonita's an attorney in Hermosillo. She has connections. Raoul spent ten years with Mexican Special Forces, fighting in Yucatán against the Cartel. He'd just made lieutenant colonel when he learned his commanding officer was black-marketing with Zuloaga's boys. He reported it to the general, who had *him* put in the stockade."

"They framed him?"

Del nodded grimly. "Want to hear the real irony? The only way my uncle could save his neck was to ask an old enemy for help."

"Ramirez?"

"None other."

"What the hell am I getting myself into, Delgado? First I hook up with the FBI, then the Mexican Mafia!" She shook her head. "Guess things can't get much worse."

He chuckled. "Ever hear of Montezuma's revenge?"

4:45 P.M., PDT, TUESDAY, JUNE 30
SAN DIEGO, CALIFORNIA

Diana picked up the link on the first ring. Since she already had her makeup on and was ready to leave the house, she flicked on the vid image on her end. She was pleased when Marian Fuller came onscreen. Hugh and Brian had been close since college days at Berkeley, but her friendship with Marian had come about because their children now attended the same elite prep school.

"Good afternoon, Marian."

"Hi, Diana. I hate to bother you, but I just wanted to check on those tickets for the symphony next month."

Diana was an officer on the San Diego Symphony Society and had pulled some strings to get two adjoining loge boxes for a party of Washington VIPs the Fullers were hosting the end of July. As keeper of her husband's social-political itinerary, Marian was meticulous to the point of obsession.

"No problem at all. Center and right-center loges just as you wanted."

"Thanks a million. I owe you." Marian smiled impishly. "Just to the right of center. Think there's any political symbolism there?"

Her question was interrupted when two boys came barreling into the room.

"He won't share Martian Killers with me!"

"He just hogs it till he can mess up the sequence, Mom," the second boy wailed.

"Now, boys," a harried-looking woman remonstrated.

Diana recognized her as Marian's younger sister. She also recognized Rob Fuller.

"I thought I told you to keep them upstairs. You know never to disturb me in my office," Marian said crossly to her sister, who was half-dragging the two youngsters out of the room as they whined and sniped at each other. Turning back to the screen, Marian's gracious political smile beamed once more. "I'm so sorry for the interrupt—"

"What is Rob doing home? He's supposed to be camping with my son and their fathers."

Marian chuckled indulgently at Diana's alarm. "Oh, Diana, you know how overprotective we mothers can be. Rob came down with the sniffles yesterday. Dr. Lyons didn't want to risk possible pneumonia up in those mountains since Rob was already feverish. But Brian didn't want to disappoint Hugh and Mike—and neither did I." Marian beamed with female chauvinism. "Frankly I think the guys get a bigger kick out of playing mountain man than the sons do. Rob was heartbroken to miss it."

Rob had looked neither heartbroken nor the least bit ill to Diana. Still, children did bounce back quickly. But would a concerned mother then invite her own sister's child over and expose him to possible contagion? Marian signed off with more flustered assurances that Mike would have a wonderful time with Hugh and Brian.

Diana closed the link with a vague sense of foreboding, then re-opened it and requested a listing.

7 P.M., MDT, TUESDAY, JUNE 30
MAZATLÁN, MEXICO

Raoul Mulcahey set his Cherokee down at Rafael Buelna International Airport, where the grand old *patrón*, "Uncle Mac," waited to greet them.

Leah had read the background on Inocensio Ramirez and Delgado's family ties to the Mexican mobster. In spite of her reservations about Mulcahey, his grandson Raoul had won her over immediately. He looked like a latter-day incarnation of old Mexican film star Gilbert Roland, but his shrewd, cynical edginess reminded her of Del.

They had rendezvoused at a small airstrip just over the Arizona border. If transporting American fugitives from BISC was out of the ordinary to him, Raoul didn't show it. Between trading quips with Del, he gave her an aerial tour of the breathtaking beauty of northwestern Mexico from stark desert and jagged sierra to treacherous mangrove swamps and magnificent beaches.

As soon as they climbed out of the plane, Leah watched Uncle Mac approach. Francisco Geraldo Esteban Mulcahey was a tall, rawboned man whose craggy, square face and blunt features revealed more of his German ancestry than of his predominantly Hispanic and Irish bloodlines. He was handsome and vigorous in spite of his seventy-four years, with shrewd gray eyes and a heavy thatch of salt-and-pepper hair worn on the longish side. It added to his image as a man of the people, he liked to say. So did the cheap pigskin huaraches on his size thirteen feet and the unbleached coarse-cotton campesino shirts he wore bloused over frayed American blue jeans.

He played first base on the local senior-league baseball team, having narrowly missed out on a professional ball career as a youth. Since he could not make "the Show," he had turned to politics after spending several boring decades in his family's shipping business. His Honor the mayor of Mazatlán walked a tightrope maintaining the delicate balance between political autonomy and the powerful forces of the Mexican cartel.

To keep the violence and corruption of drug dealing out of his city, he maintained an open pipeline to Sinaloan kingpin Inocensio Ramirez. It was an uneasy alliance, but old Inocensio's protection made Mulcahey's beloved city a clean and safe island in a sea of drug-trafficking pirates.

"*El Tigre, cómo estás?*" He enveloped Del in a bear hug and the two men thumped each other with fierce Latino exuberance the same way Del and Raoul had back in Sonoita. *The same nickname, too. El Tigre. The Tiger,* she translated to herself as the men jabbered in Spanish too rapid for her to follow.

The old man turned to her with a smile just like Del's. "Please, a thousand pardons for my nephew's bad manners. You must be Señorita Berglund, the lady he spoke of when he called this morning. I am honored, señorita. Welcome to my city. It is yours." The mayor bowed over her hand with a courtly flourish that few men could carry off. He did.

"Thank you. Mazatlán is even more beautiful than I imagined. I only wish our reasons for coming here weren't so serious."

"After this sad business is over, you will return and enjoy at your leisure, no?" The old man spoke English fluently with a charming Spanish inflection as he opened the door of his pristine '79 Town Car. "My Serifina has prepared a fine feast for us."

As Leah slid onto the plush velour front passenger seat, she could see his eyes travel from her to Del and back. She fleetingly wondered if he sensed that theirs had become more than a professional relationship.

Mac revved up the powerful engine. There were no air pollution or fossil fuel laws in Mexico. The old Lincoln's body still retained its burgundy metallic paint job without a spec of rust. The plush interior was paneled in real mahogany with enough legroom for an entire squad of NBA starters.

From the backseat, Del asked, "Have you been able to contact Ramirez yet?"

"I sent word to Culiacán after we spoke this morning. Inocensio is out on the Gulf—on patrol, his *segundo* called it."

"He's primed for a face-off with Ochea," Raoul said. "The Colombians have moved into the Gulf of California in recent months."

"Inocensio wouldn't much care for that," Del replied.

"If he's upset with Cartel encroachments into his territory, might he support an American strike against them?" Leah asked.

"No way, Leah," Del said.

"You must understand how an, er, entrepreneur like Ramirez thinks, señorita," the old man explained. "Men like him . . . and me"—he gave an indifferent Latin shrug, lifting his hands from the wheel for a moment—"we value our independence. I've kept out American interests as well as drug lords. As long as Mazatlán is neutral, it belongs to its citizens.

"Inocensio understands this. He has risen to control the coastal drug trade and answers to no one—in Mexico or Washington or Bogotá. He is, as you *norteamericanos* say, a big frog in a small puddle."

"He views our Pentagon brass as just as much of a threat to his empire as he does Zuloaga's Cartel," Del said.

"Then he'll talk to us?" Leah asked.

"I believe he will do more than that," Old Francisco replied. "I put my ear to the ground, asking questions about your Bureau of Illegal Substance Control. The CIA would be amazed at what Mexican insiders know." He grinned, revealing strong, straight teeth stained faintly from tobacco.

"Anything about who the Tribunal members are?" Del ventured. Even Gracie had come up empty on that one.

"*Sí.* Although it is no great surprise. One is Samson's *segundo.*"

"Waterman—I knew it!" Del snapped his fingers remembering Cuff's speculation about the vice president and Cal's oblique mention of him.

Leah cursed silently. "I'm beginning to feel like a water-skier in a barge wake."

"I don't think Samson's involved. Putnam trusts him."

"And you trust Putnam," Leah replied, giving Del a dubious look.

———

The Mulcaheys lived in the old section of Mazatlán, far south of the tourist mecca Golden Zone at the upper end of the city. Far below, the seawalk, or *malecón*, stretched over seventeen kilometers along magnificent beaches. The family home perched high on the hillside of Paseo Centenario in a neighborhood of stucco houses from whose wrought-iron window grilles bougainvillea and lantana spilled out in fuchsia and golden splendor. Ornate fountains burbled inside the interior courtyards. The historic zone was situated on a rocky peninsula jutting out into the sparkling azure-green waters of the Pacific. To the south lay Stone Island's mangrove swamps and at the westernmost point of the city stood the tallest lighthouse in the western hemisphere.

Francisco eased his huge Town Car up the twisting, narrow street and pulled inside an arched gateway. The heavy steel doors were pushed closed behind him by two small boys, part of the assembled family who were eager to welcome their *americano* cousin. They crowded around him as he climbed out of the car, all speaking rapid-fire Spanish.

Leah sat in the car watching as he was mobbed with hugs, kisses, and questions. She heard the name Miguelito repeated often and knew they were disappointed that Del had been unable to bring his son. Quickly one older woman, plump yet daintily regal, joined old Francisco as he gallantly opened the door for Leah.

"Señorita Leah Berglund, may I present my wife, Serifina Maria Estrella de Mulcahey y Guzmán."

"Please, call me Aunt Seri. Everyone does," she said, enveloping Leah in a maternal embrace. *"Mi casa es su casa."*

"You're most kind," Leah replied, caught oddly off-balance by the realization that her own mother had never shown her such spontaneous warmth. "Please, call me Leah."

They consumed a sumptuous feast of smoked marlin, garlic-encrusted shrimp, and whole stuffed lobsters, all caught fresh that morning and prepared under Seri's watchful eyes. Leah felt as stuffed as the succulent crustaceans by the time she polished off a rich caramelized flan, all the while observing the boisterous interplay between Del and his family. Berglund Nordic reserve and Manchester

New England propriety had not prepared her for this sort of family free-for-all.

"Did anyone explain to you how our cousin received his nickname?" Raoul asked Leah with devilish laughter sparkling in his dark eyes.

Del groaned. "Please, not that threadbare old tale again."

"I wondered about it . . . Tiger," she replied, glancing quickly to Del, then back to his cousin as everyone at the table burst into laughter.

Raoul began with great relish, "We were boys. I was fourteen and he was twelve. *Abuelo* took us on a jaguar hunt."

"My first time," Del interjected.

"Yes. And almost your last. He was carrying an old Winchester twelve-gauge, the same as I. Somehow in the dark he managed to get separated from the rest of us. Then we heard this incredible growling. Everyone came running, calling, 'Elliott, where are you?' We could hear the cat and the boy, but no one could see them. We turned on our electric torches. Then I stumbled on something—his shotgun. The jaguar had treed him and backed him out on a limb."

"But he was *muy feroz*—as ferocious as the cat itself," Uncle Mac said fondly. "When he was unable to hold on to the Winchester—"

"I dropped it in pure panic," Del confessed.

"He pulled out a small Swiss Army knife his papa had given him," Francisco continued.

"He and the jaguar were perched out on that limb swiping at each other and snarling back and forth like two tigers," Raoul finished.

"Uncle Mac shot the cat and I got tagged with the moniker *El Tigre*."

"But you never dropped your weapon again," Raoul said.

It was apparent to Leah that his family took exceptional pride in Del. The only one in her family who'd ever praised her work was Gramps.

And now he was dead because of it.

A huge full moon hung low like a diamond-dusted ball suspended on the horizon, casting its glow on the courtyard. The soft murmur of the fountain soothed, as much as Leah could be soothed. She paced around the old limestone courtyard, inhaling the fragrance of jasmine and frangipani, then took a seat.

She had been unable to sleep, even after the late-night strategy season she, Del, Francisco, and Raoul had held. All the aunts, uncles, and scores of cousins young and old had departed for their homes or retired to their beds in this big old house. It was quiet now and she would have to be up at dawn. But sleep would not come. She'd risen and rechecked the familiar Mavica, then dressed in a loose cotton shift and sandals, a gift from Aunt Seri, and come down to the courtyard.

"I was just thinking of an old song. Moonlight does become you."

Leah turned and looked up at Del, who stood on the balcony directly above. He, too, was dressed and his eyes glowed restlessly in the silvery light. She looked at the moon. "Maybe if it wasn't so bright, I could get some sleep."

"I couldn't sleep either," he said as he walked down the stairs. "Too keyed up about tomorrow. If Ramirez's sources are accurate, we should have a very busy day." She nodded, chewing on her lip. He sensed there was more to her agitation than the promise of tomorrow's danger. "Since we can't sleep, let's take advantage of the light and I'll give you a tour of the *malecón*, the waterfront boulevard. But I warn you, the climb back up is a lot harder than going down."

"I'll manage."

He chuckled. "I may not, but we can always hire a *pulmonia* to take us home."

"One of those cute little open air cabs? I'd like that."

Del grinned and offered his hand. "Deal."

They slipped through the gate like two fugitive lovers, which in an all too real sense they were. Hand in hand, they strolled down the steep streets, deserted at this late hour, but within a half dozen blocks the hum of automobiles and beat of distant music began to blend with the lapping of the ocean waves on the beach.

"I've always wondered what it would've been like to live here early in the last century, before the tourists came, when this was just a quiet old fishing village."

"It's breathtaking," she said as they walked along the seawall overlooking the ocean. Clubs and restaurants glittered in the distance as they gazed across the bay. But the true brilliance lay beyond, shimmering on the waves. "Moondust," she murmured watching the lunar reflection on the water.

"So tell me about Leah," he said.

"I wasn't making up the story about Kevin," she began.

"I didn't think you had. But there's more," he prompted, waiting patiently.

"My family is the antithesis of yours. Oh, they're devoutly religious, Lutheran—Episcopal . . . but staid. Reserved Norwegian and English stock. Stiff upper and all that."

He smiled at her. "Knowing you, I believe it."

"Except for Kev, the only one I was really close to was Gramps. He encouraged me to study for the law when my parents wanted another doctor in the family. After all, we were only spitting distance from the Mayo Clinic."

"But you wanted the law."

She nodded. "Always. I started out as a public defender, then switched to the prosecutor's office."

"I wanted to catch the bad guys, too. That's why I joined the Bureau."

"Yeah. But you just caught them. You didn't have to execute them."

"I've had to kill in the line of duty, Leah. It's never easy."

"People who were shooting back. It's different with BISC."

He couldn't argue with that. "Now you doubt everything you once believed in."

She stopped walking abruptly and shivered in spite of the warm ocean air. "I suppose I always had a kernel of doubt about it . . . deep down. No matter how evil the dealer, how blatant his crimes, I had to pull the switch alone. Each time I lost a little of my humanity, I think . . . but vengeance for Kev kept me going . . . until now. I may have killed innocent people, Del—"

"Shhh . . ." He took her in his arms. She was coiled tight as a spring, ready to snap. "Maybe, but I doubt it. Knowing you as I'm coming to, I imagine you've always been meticulous and dogged on investigations."

"But Gramps found out how BISC set people up—planted evidence—"

"They tried with me. You didn't fall for it, did you?"

"What if there were others? What if—"

"What if you stop the penitential frenzy and let me kiss you?" He stroked her face with his fingertips, staring into her eyes.

"Kiss it and make it well? I don't think it'll work this time, Delgado." But she let him do it anyway.

They hailed one of the small open taxis to take them up the steep hill to the Mulcahey house. The trip was much faster than their stroll down the *malecón*. When they slipped into the courtyard, he secured the gate. Then she turned into his arms with feverish intensity, kissing his neck, nuzzling the hair springing from the top of his open shirt.

"*El Tigre,* I intend to make you purr very loudly."

"Then we'd best go to your room. Mine is too close to Aunt Seri's," he replied with a wicked chuckle, leading her up the stairs.

7 A.M., MDT, WEDNESDAY, JULY 1
SONORAN DESERT

"We're ready to roll, sir." Colonel Walt Bisset saluted smartly. He was in full dress uniform. Already the heat shimmered like a blast furnace. God, how he hated these command performances.

"I've just confirmed their chopper will be landing at o nine hundred hours. Apparently they enjoyed sleeping in this morning," Sommerville groused.

"We have time for a last-minute review of the operation if you wish, General. Major Salazar is champing at the bit to show off his Colombians."

"That man is depriving a village somewhere of an idiot," Sommerville said testily as they walked out of the headquarters pod.

"Rafael Silva has been working with him, sir. I think you'll be pleasantly surprised at the improvement he's made the past week."

Sommerville sighed as yellow dust mixed with sand swirled evilly in the scorching breeze. "Let us by all means keep Don Rafael happy."

"The Dragonfly UAVs are working out splendidly, General," Bisset said as they walked across the open area designated as a parade ground. "Actually deploying them for aerial surveillance was a brilliant strategy. All the men have gained invaluable experience learning to run them. General Silva's men have been especially effective."

General Silva. Fast-track promotions when your father is a head of state—even in exile, Sommerville thought with a sour grimace. He looked across the field to where Silva, still in fatigues, observed as the Mexican and Colombian officers waited to pounce on the American leader like Christmas puppies. Sommerville disliked not being able to read young Silva. The man would fight well, but what might happen when their plans for taking back his country unfolded? Silva could be dangerous.

The Mexican colonel, Manuel Obregón, was a short, austere man with a heavy mustache that made him look a bit Hitlerish. He stepped forward and saluted first, followed by the Colombian, Major Rios Salazar, a thickset, muscular man with flat *indio* features. Both were decked out in full dress uniforms and weighed down with enough ribbons and medals on their chests to bring less sturdy men to their knees. The general returned their salutes.

Since Obregón was the ranking officer of the "host nation," Sommerville exchanged brief pleasantries with him, then turned to Salazar. "I understand your men, under General Silva's direction, have been deploying the UAVs with good results."

"We have used them to detect a number of farmers and shepherds, General. Stupid men who have blundered near but pose no threat."

"We verified that they were local before releasing them," Obregón added, unwilling to let the Colombian take full credit. "My men put the fear of God in them."

Sommerville nodded, well able to imagine the brutish colonel putting the fear of God in the devil himself. "With the president and all the other dignitaries scheduled to arrive this morning, the last thing we need are civilian observers."

13.

Raoul brought the Cherokee in for a landing at Caborca's dusty airport. Primarily an agricultural center, the city was a small stop-off on the railroad linking Tijuana to Hermosillo. Brushy mountains dotted the barren landscape to the east. Like giant garter snakes, green stripes of river valley threaded their way over the thirsty desert floor.

"Rough country. I've scarcely seen so much as a gravel road since we left the coast," Leah said.

"What better place to hide a secret training facility?" Del asked.

"All they've got watching them are a few sheep and cattle," Raoul said as he brought the Cherokee to a surprisingly smooth landing considering the condition of the airport's one small runway. Then he taxied toward a tin-roofed hangar whose bay stood open so that he could conceal the plane. Inside, a beat-up old Jeep Wrangler waited for them. Francisco had made the arrangements last night through the same contacts who had supplied information about the covert training facility.

"Why wouldn't the Globe Net pick up that kind of unauthorized military activity and report it to the NRO?" Leah asked as they climbed out of the plane.

Del looked at his cousin. "As a former member of Mexican Special Forces, you answer that one."

"Ever since the Cartel took the Yucatán Peninsula, we've deployed against them. We push them out of Veracruz, they retake Oaxaca. We don't control our own country anymore. It's an ongoing military chess game. Check. Checkmate."

"Since the Samson administration initiated its 'lend-lease' opera-tion to supply Mexico with American hardware, it's not likely that this would raise any flags," Del added. "At least anything the Penta-gon couldn't cover up." He eyed the old Jeep skeptically. "You sure this heap will take us into the back of nowhere *and* get us out?"

"Hernan Cabril stands behind it," Raoul said with a slashing white grin. He raised the hood and checked the engine. "There should be carboys of gas and a gallon or two of oil somewhere in the hanger. Just in case."

Del and Leah located the supplies. When he hefted one of the plas-tic carboys onto his shoulder, she started to do the same. "Take the oil. I'll get these," he gritted.

She swung the carboy up smoothly. "I can pull my own weight, Delgado."

She was coolly remote once again, as if last night had never hap-pened. He watched her carry the heavy container. Her ragged print skirt swished around her ankles, and clumsy leather sandals slapped on the hard-packed hangar floor. They were all dressed as poor campesinos, but Raoul and Del's swarthy Hispanic coloring made their disguises considerably more authentic. Aunt Seri had given her some walnut dye for her pale Nordic skin and she wore a black wig. From a distance she could pass, but up close there would be trouble. She couldn't begin to speak Spanish fluently enough, much less mimic the uneducated dialect of the locals.

She's used to taking risks worse than this, Del reminded himself.

Within a few minutes they were under way. As the sun climbed high, so did the temperature. This was high desert country, and once they moved away from the irrigation around Caborca, the vegetation was greasewood, creosote bush, and smoke tree. Within a couple of hours they reached a ridge overlooking an endless undulating gray-green. Low hills dissected the arid expanse. No roads did.

"Where the hell to now?" Del asked as Raoul consulted his Global Positioning System, cross-checking it with a hand-drawn map from Hernan Cabril.

"This is where we leave the road behind. Now things get rough." Raoul grinned.

"*Now* it gets rough," Leah echoed. "I wouldn't call what we've been riding on a road any more than I'd call this rattletrap modern ground transpo." Sweat trickled from beneath her wig, plastering it to her neck. The thin cotton blouse offered little protection from the merciless sun.

"You look as overheated as the radiator," Del said, noting her reddening skin.

She swore. "I forgot my sunblock tabs. The skin dye won't help with UV and I'm really susceptible."

Del exchanged a look with Raoul, who went back to his navigation after saying, "There's enough water to spare for the mud."

"Mud?" she said.

"Some of our family on the Santandar side are fair-skinned. We loved using this concoction on our cousins." He enjoyed her incredulous apprehension as he set about pouring enough water into a tire rut to create a stiff, pasty mud from the hard-packed clay.

"I think the heat's gotten to both of you. Mud pies?"

Del only grinned at her before he slid beneath the Jeep. He emerged with a handful of icky black goop scraped off the engine block and began blending it with the mud. "Come here."

"Oh, no. You're not—I won't—" She backed away.

"Just how bad do you burn?" he asked, drawing near with the ichor.

"Why can't you use the clean oil?" she asked, reaching for one of the plastic jugs.

"Won't adhere—too thin. It'll just dissolve the mud paste," he said reasonably.

Leah muttered a string of obscenities at her carelessness, then capitulated. "Okay. Get it over with."

He began smearing it on one arm, then gave her a handful to apply to her face. "Be careful. Don't get it in your eyes. God only knows what leaks out of that engine."

"Great." She felt his hands move deftly up her other arm, then glide across her chest above the blouse's neckline. "You're enjoying this, you bastard."

His fingers traced the outline of her collarbone with intimate familiarity. "Can't deny that. Sit down and let me get your feet. Nothing'll slow you down like ankles swollen by sunburn."

She did as he asked, embarrassed by the way Raoul studiously avoided looking at them. Did the whole family know they were lovers? Did they think she was a cheap American slut? *Why the hell should I give a damn?*

"If Cabril's recon is accurate, we should reach the base in another hour," Raoul said as Del washed the mess from his hands.

"Cuff never was able to figure how they were transporting material from Adair with only short-range amphibs," Del said as they bounced down the slope into the trackless wilderness. "They could get down the new Colorado channel with the AAVs, but then what? This is over three hundred klics from the top of the Gulf, not to mention transport inland once they landed."

"Samson's lend-lease again. Old U.S. transport and supply vessels, Tig," Raoul said. "Six, maybe seven of them have been deployed around the Horn into Pacific waters. I got that straight from an old compadre still in Special. The politicos in Mexico City say they'll be used for amphib operations into Oaxaca."

"That makes sense," Del reasoned. "They could rendezvous with the AAVs from Adair at the mouth of the Colorado. Then send a fleet of deuce-and-a-half trucks to meet the transport ships, probably above Cabo Lobos."

"Good guess. I'll make a few calls to my compadre when we get back."

"Things are beginning to fall in place." Del took a swallow from the canteen Leah handed him.

"Now all we have to do is see what they've gone to all the trouble to hide in the middle of all this scenic grandeur," Leah muttered, looking at the arid waste.

They followed a boulder-strewn arroyo to their destination. When they heard a copter in the distance, Raoul swerved beneath the cover of some stunted cottonwoods, then killed the engine.

Leah focused her monocular on the horizon through the leafy cover of branches. "There—over that rise to the left," she hissed.

Raoul swung his old army-issue binoculars to where she indicated, then cursed.

"What is it?" Del asked, taking the binoculars from Raoul. "Sikorsky Dragonfly. I'll be a son of a bitch."

"When the hell did you learn to identify UAVs?" Raoul asked as he followed the drone aircraft's flight pattern.

"My friend Cuff gave me discs with specs and photos. We couldn't figure how they were going to use them in an invasion since there was no artillery ordnance coming out of Adair."

"Watchdogs," Leah said, scratching her forehead with the monocular.

"*Sí*, the Sikorsky comes with some very sophisticated surveillance gear from what I've heard. None of those *muchachas* are on lend-lease from Washington, you can bet."

"Well, from what Cuff was able to learn, they have twelve of them."

"That's too many just to patrol the perimeters of a base like this."

"That's what he thought, too."

"*Es enigmático, verdad?*" Raoul murmured, watching the craft arc to the east. "Whatever they're concealing, it lies beyond there." He pointed to a low cluster of hills across the valley floor.

"How the hell do we get closer with those things scanning the area?" Leah itched so horribly from the grease and mud coating her skin she could scarcely think straight.

Del watched her rub her arms in misery. "Desert survival skills weren't in the BISC training manual. Don't beat yourself up for forgetting the med."

"I should have known better. I screwed up. Okay?" She knew her voice was testy but was too wretched to give a damn.

Raoul, still concentrating on their objective, announced, "From here on, we walk. See the way this arroyo zigzags from here to the base of the hills?"

"That's one hell of a walk, *Primo*."

"Let's do it," Leah said, slinging a canteen over one shoulder, her camera gear over the other.

They made their way across the open plain, one clump of scrub vegetation to the next, following the irregular, rocky channel. Regularly every quarter hour the drone made a sweep of the area. Then they hit the dirt, lying on the hot, muddy ground beneath prickly smokethorn bushes that tore at their clothing.

"If we were stopped, we'd sure as hell look the part," Del said at one point as he lay beside Leah beneath a bush. His clothes were filthy and torn, his skin scratched and smeared with mud.

"Only if we ditch our gear," she said, tapping her pixel-disc camera case and long-range monocular. She looked at the Israeli TAR-21 assault rifles Del and Raoul carried.

"*Los hombres del norte* always carried the best firepower," Raoul said.

"The men of the north?" she translated, confused.

"What my cousin means is Sonora has a long and colorful history— since the late nineteenth century—of bandito strongmen, Pancho Villa, Emiliano Zapata, Alvaro Obregón. No matter how ragtag poor, they always went well armed." He patted the TAR, equipped with a red-dot target-acquisition system.

"You think we could pass for local banditos—and they'd let us go?" *Toto, this definitely ain't Kansas.*

Raoul shrugged fatalistically, but Del said, "I don't plan on letting them catch us."

"Nor I. *Vámonos.*" The drone was gone. Raoul slipped out of the smokethorn thicket with effortless ease.

Leah did the same in spite of her screaming skin, but she could see Del's bad knee was giving him trouble. Suggesting a break was pointless. She'd detected an undercurrent of rivalry between the two men as soon as she'd met Del's cousin.

Raoul Mulcahey had joined the elite Mexican Special Forces around the same time Del went to Quantico. Like Del, he'd been forced out of his first career, but his body remained whole. He was happily married, with three adoring daughters. She intuited that Del both loved and envied his cousin. He'd never show weakness in front of Raoul.

They crossed the plain without further incident, then considered how to reach the ridge over which the Sikorsky made its sweeps. Several deep, narrow crevices snaked down the incline. They selected the one closest to their cover, then ran for it just after the copter made its latest patrol.

They reached the rocky cover and sank to the ground panting and sweat-soaked. Del grimaced, rubbing his knee, which he stretched straight out in front of him, then said, "I can hear gunfire—howitzers?"

Raoul listened. "*Sí*—105s firing in regular cadence."

"A twenty-one-gun salute?" Leah speculated.

"We may have stumbled onto a special show. Let's not be late." Delgado doggedly started climbing with Leah and Raoul close behind.

Shortly, the firing stopped. The faintest echo of what sounded like a bugle floated down to them. They quickened their struggle up the steep slope. When they reached the top, they could see the valley below, cleared of virtually all vegetation and now worn smooth by the weight of truck tires, tank treads, and human boots.

They observed some sort of ceremony. An honor guard stood rigidly at attention as a group of dignitaries filed past them and took their seats on a reviewing stand over which flew American, Mexican, and Colombian flags.

Leah busily snapped pictures of the individual VIPs. Then she lowered the camera and sighted in with her monocular. "I think I recognize the one in the center. You'd know better." She handed the lens to Raoul.

He murmured a low Spanish oath. "His Excellency Ernesto Portillo-Ortiz himself."

"The president of Mexico," Leah said.

"*Sí*. And the one sitting beside him wearing general's stars—that is Rafael Silva, son of the dictator the Americans tried to keep in power in Colombia."

"After Zuloaga and his boys drove his old man into exile, Carillo became a puppet president," Del said, using the monocular to scan the reviewers. "Silva's presence explains the old-style Colombian flag. Rumor has it Rafael's been given covert U.S. support to liberate the homeland."

"He has a badass group here," Raoul replied.

"Who's the American general?" Leah asked.

"Son of a bitch, Cuff, you were right. Old 'Nuke 'Em Nate' Sommerville himself," Del murmured.

When he handed her back the monocular, Leah grinned. "Gotcha both." They quickly exchanged glances, then grinned wryly. A ring of motor-mud circled the right eye of each man.

"That'll teach you two bastards to laugh at *gringa blanca*." She went back to snapping pictures while the men discussed the tripartite strike force's overall size.

Leah zeroed in on a sea of camouflage netting and modular pods grouped at one end of the parade ground, then swung her camera to the opposite end where a complex of boxlike structures lined up in rows, two to three stories tall in places, open-sided single stories in others. She snapped several light armored vehicles modified with TOW missile mounts and a row of Humvees positioned in front of the complex.

"I think we're going to have an exercise of house-to-house guerrilla fighting techniques," she surmised.

"Shit, they've only got around three thousand men. They're either counting on a massive popular uprising when they hit the beaches in Colombia or else a lot more U.S. and Mexican backing, 'cause one lousy brigade ain't gonna cut it."

"My country cannot give it. Portillo-Ortiz is barely holding out against Cartel encroachments now."

"How are they going to get the United States to back them?" Del asked.

"Harmon Waterman is BISC Tribunal and vice president—" Leah stopped short.

"I don't buy Samson being in on this," Del said.

"Why not? Because Cal Putnam vouches for him?" Her tone was cynical.

The demonstration commenced then, drowning out their argument as the U.S. Special Forces team led the joint assault on the mock-up of a Colombian city street. She took a series of shots of their hardware, including the Sikorsky Dragonflies and modified LAV 25s.

"We'd be smart to use this racket as cover and get the hell out of here," Del said over the boom of exploding shells.

"Tigre is right. *Vámonos.*"

Leah carefully replaced her camera gear in its heavy leather case, then followed Raoul back down the narrow, twisting ravine. As the weapons fire died away, all they could hear was their own harsh panting and the crack of loose rock beneath their feet.

Del kept up but he was damned if he knew how. After the first few bone-jarring leaps down the ravine, he was certain the cartilage would peel from the bones in his knee. The only way he could tolerate the hellish pain was by focusing on Raoul and Leah.

He watched his cousin move with pantherish grace. Raoul had stayed in shape after he was cashiered from Special Forces. His father had left him the family cattle ranch, a small but profitable outfit on the Sonora-Sinaloa border. Working the stock kept him fit. He'd never gone off the deep end like Del.

Fuck it, I can last.

He gritted his teeth and kept on until they reached the Jeep. Raoul fired it up as soon as the Sikorsky made its next sweep. They played hide-and-seek until they reached the other side of the hills and began the ascent back to the road. Just as they were congratulating themselves on being in the clear, they spotted another vehicle cutting across their path at full speed.

Del used the monocular to check it out. "A jeep. Looks like Mexican army," he said, handing Raoul the lens.

"*Sí*, and they don't look friendly."

"All the patrols weren't aerial," Del said.

"Or they spotted us from the air and this is their cleanup squad." Leah reached down for her own TAR.

"Chill out, Ma Parker. Let's see if we can bluff our way out first. Act like a demure Mexican wife. Let us do the talking."

"You want me to walk three paces behind the Jeep?"

"Just keep those sweet baby blues down so they don't make you as a *gringa*."

Both men placed their weapons out of sight but in easy reach. The jeep contained three enlisteds and one lieutenant. All wore regular Mexican army uniforms.

"What is the trouble, Lieutenant?" Raoul asked in Spanish.

The three enlisted men, clutching American M17s, eyed them

speculatively, while their officer spoke. "Why are you out here? There is no road for kilometers. This is no place to bring a woman."

"We're looking for Pozos de Cerna. Is this not the shortcut?" Raoul replied artlessly.

The lieutenant got out of the jeep, signaling for two of his men to do the same as he approached them. "This is a restricted military area. No civilians allowed. Who are you? Let me see some identification."

Leah watched the two soldiers spread out to either side of them so they could catch the interlopers in a cross fire. "We may have to shoot our way out."

"I have the left. You take the right, if it comes to that," Del whispered.

The lieutenant eyed her closely as he approached. Grease and mud ran in rivulets down her face. "What's wrong with you? You're not Mexican!" he accused, reaching for his sidearm as he signaled his men. They raised their automatic weapons.

Raoul's first burst took the officer full in the chest. Then he swung the TAR at the jeep driver who dived below the dash. Simultaneously, Leah's fire cut down the soldier on her right while Del took out the one to the left. The one in the jeep fired short bursts at their vehicle, but didn't raise his head to aim.

Leah had taken cover behind their Jeep. From there she fired a long burst that tore apart the front of the other vehicle. The driver panicked and tried to jump clear. Raoul nailed him before he landed.

"Shit, what now?" Del said when all was quiet.

"I vote we get the hell out of here," Leah replied.

"Not before we hide the evidence." Del walked over to the lieutenant and searched his body. "If we leave them here, Sommerville will know his security's been breached."

"Tig's right." Raoul scanned the terrain. "We are some distance from their encampment. It could take days for search patrols to cover this much territory. If we hide our mess well, maybe weeks."

"Men have been known to go AWOL," Del added.

"There's a deep arroyo with some heavy brush over there." Leah pointed to a drop-off about a hundred meters away.

They covered the soldiers with stones beneath a thicket of smokethorn, then pushed the disabled jeep to the edge of the precipice and watched it tumble into the chaparral below.

"No one from the air or any distance at ground level should spot it," Del said as they observed their last hour's backbreaking labor.

"Now can we get the hell out of Dodge?" Leah asked impatiently. "I've got a case full of pixel discs to put on the computer and I need a bath."

"I want that talk with Inocensio Ramirez Uncle Mac promised," Del said.

9:30 P.M., MDT, WEDNESDAY, JULY 1
CULIACÁN, MEXICO

Inocensio Jesus Emanuelo Ramon Ramirez sat behind his custom-made mahogany desk inlaid with rosewood. No papers were on the glossy surface. His line of work didn't require them. But he enjoyed the intimidation factor when Cartel representatives had to sit on the other side of the desk in low-backed chairs. Reclining on his butter-soft leather throne, he surveyed the room, inhaling a Cohiba Triángulo. The cigar ash burned evenly, its smoke sweet and potent. Nothing but the best for the most powerful drug lord on the Pacific coast.

He'd let Mulcahey's nephew and the woman cool their heels long enough. Any more and Francisco would be pissed. But he had to be certain he made his point. While this situation was volatile, it presented unique opportunities for an individual bold enough to seize them. No one had ever accused Inocensio Ramirez of being a slug-abed. He flicked the intercom on his desk.

Ramirez's "receptionist," an unshaven thug with a Browning 9mm sticking out of his designer jeans and an MP5 submachine gun slung over his shoulder, squinted at Del and Leah through bloodshot eyes. *El jefe* had time to see them. He escorted them from the bare warehouse bench where they'd spent the better part of an hour waiting.

Leah seethed as they followed the greasy-haired El-Op across the dirty concrete floor. He'd had way too much fun frisking her for weapons. She ached to reposition his testicles between his sternum

CORRUPTS ABSOLUTELY | 187

and his tonsils. But Del cautioned her that his uncle had gone to considerable trouble setting up the meeting. The information they might get from Ramirez was worth the aggravation.

"Ramirez owns the governor, mayor, and every man, woman, and child in Culiacán. He's not going to let anyone armed inside his turf," Del said.

"A pretty sleazy layout for the biggest drug trafficker on the coast."

They approached a heavy door leading into an adjoining building at the rear of the warehouse. Leah spotted the remote vid sweepers, one on each side of the door. Then the slow hum of an electronic lock sounded and the door swung open.

The Frito Bandito stood with his brawny arms crossed, smiling as the two gringos stepped into another world. Leah ignored him as her feet sank into plush carpet. The walls were paneled in solid walnut, but were saved from being too dark by a pair of Italian cut-crystal chandeliers suspended on either side of Ramirez's immense desk. Two deeply cushioned Paoli chairs sat in front of it like kneelers positioned before an altar.

She took in the lavish room, realizing everything was expensive. The decor had only one real effect—intimidation. She speculated whether the big man behind the desk intended it that way or simply had egregiously bad taste.

Ramirez was going to fat around the gut, a fault that his tropical print shirt did nothing to conceal. Around his thick neck he wore a gold chain that looked heavy enough to hoist the anchor on her grandfather's thirty-foot sloop. Diamonds and rubies the size of medium hailstones winked on his meaty fingers as he extended one hairy paw to Del. His face was round with a big nose and bushy eyebrows set over crafty, heavy-lidded dark eyes. His teeth, those not gold, were stained from cigar smoking. When he smiled, Leah felt no reassurance.

"Welcome to my humble workplace, Señor Delgado, Señorita Berglund," he said in heavily accented English as they shook hands. "*Mi casa es su casa.* May I offer you refreshment? Some fine old sherry perhaps?"

The traditional hospitality didn't seem the same as when Francisco Mulcahey offered it. She and Del declined with thanks and took the proffered seats across from Inocensio, who sat Buddha-like with his garishly jeweled hands crossed on his belly, one holding a huge cigar.

"I trust my cigar does not offend you, señorita? It is Cuban. The finest. Forty-five dollars *Yanqui*." When Leah indicated no offense, he asked Del, "Would you care for one? No? Well, then, down to business—and I *am* a man of business, never forget it." He set aside the cigar and leaned forward, thick paws pressed on the desktop.

The maid probably doesn't have to oil the furniture. Leah returned her gaze to his face, which had lost all traces of affability.

"I have been prevailed upon by my old compadre Francisco—did you know he and I worked on his papa's shrimp boats as boys? *No importa,*" he interrupted, waving his hand. "Cisco and I, we grew up together in Mazatlán. When he asks for my help, I give it . . . but what I tell you, it is *muy peligroso,* very dangerous. If anyone was to find out your source, I would be placed in a bad position . . ."

"A good reporter never reveals his sources, Señor Ramirez, and I *am* a good reporter, never forget it."

Ramirez's lazy eyelids raised a fraction. "Then you understand what would happen if a mistake were made." His gaze moved pointedly from Del to Leah, then back. "You have a very fine big family in Mazatlán. I would not like to see them in jeopardy."

"But you'd place them there if we give you away." How dare this bastard threaten decent people like the Mulcaheys! "I get the message Señor Ramirez," Leah said evenly.

"So do I. If you believe I'd risk my family, you'd be dealing with a fool. And you do not suffer fools. So why the threat?" Delgado's tone was carefully measured.

Ramirez studied him. "You are no fool, señor. You have much to lose in Mexico." His eyes shifted to Leah. "She does not."

"You know who I am. BISC has betrayed me. I intend to put them out of business. Not you. That would be good for your business, no?"

Innocensio threw back his head and laughed, gold teeth glowing in the brilliant light. "A woman with cojones—they do not exaggerate about female BISC agents. *Sí,* you are right. BISC gone would be very good for my business. But you must understand, I walk a line.

On one side is the Cartel, always trying to gobble up my trade, especially with the Pacific Rim Union. I want Señor Zuloaga otherwise occupied."

"On the other side of your line are the Americans," Del interjected. "As long as they're focused on the Cartel, the heat's off you. And if the Mexican government is busy fighting Cartel forces in the south, you operate in the north with impunity."

Ramirez steepled his big, blunt fingers together and stared over them at Del, nodding. "Your *tío*, he has schooled you well in our politics."

"He's been caught in a three-way squeeze all his life. He understands."

"I stay out of Mazatlán. He stays out of Culiacán."

For the hundredth time Del wondered what his uncle had on the old bandit that kept him out of Mulcahey's city. "*Tío* said you know what's going on in Sonora. We saw Portillo-Ortiz and Sommerville in bed with Rafael Silva."

"*Sí*. It is loco, what your government and mine plan. I have sources in my Federal District and a few in yours, as well. Portillo-Ortiz wants to reclaim all of Mexico from Zuloaga. Most Mexicans support him. Your Pentagon has long wished to see Alejandro Silva back in power and the Cartel crushed, but to accomplish this they must have full American backing."

"That's where BISC comes in?" Del asked.

Ramirez nodded. "At least one Tribunal member is involved. There will be an international incident in the next few days."

Del leaned forward. "What sort of incident? Where? When?"

"All I know is that some military *jefes* and BISC hope this will unite the American people for a full-scale war in Colombia. The small force playing child's games to the north of us, it is only a means to that end."

"You don't want the Cartel completely destroyed. That would mean your president could turn his attention to you next," Leah said.

"True, señorita. But I am not without some small bit of patriotism. I do not believe this loco scheme can succeed. And my country sits between North and South America, does it not? We would be caught in the middle of this war."

"Why couldn't they pull it off?" Del played devil's advocate just to see where Ramirez was going.

"Because the Cartel knows of this plan. They have a—*¿cómo se dice en inglés?*—a man inside in Washington."

"A mole." Del cursed under his breath. "You don't know who it is?"

"*Lo siento,* I do not."

"And all of this is going down in two or three days? If we take these pictures to the wrong person . . ." Leah's voice faded.

"We don't have much time—or much to go on," Del said.

"There is one thing more . . . something you must know before you return to Washington. Your Vice President Waterman is one of the Tribunal members." Ramirez paused, sensing that they already knew. "The other two are a congressman from California, Brian Fuller, and the *segundo* of the FBI, Calvin Putnam."

11: 30 P.M., EDT, WEDNESDAY, JULY 1
WASHINGTON, D.C.

"I've been trying to reach you all day. I've lost four men and a jeep on patrol. Lieutenant Martinez was a good officer, quite astute. He wouldn't have been an easy target, but someone has taken him out."

"I see, General. That is troublesome." Harmon Waterman nodded, although he and Nathan Sommerville were on an encrypted link with no screen access. He could hear the agitation in the other man's voice, also the arrogance.

"I've had aerial sweeps and ground patrols scouring the area. These men did not go AWOL. Our operation has been compromised. I have to move up the launch."

Waterman bristled. "Let me remind you, General, that decision isn't yours to make." Then in a more conciliatory tone, he added, "You just sit tight for a few hours."

"Precisely what is going to occur in a few hours?"

Waterman said coldly, "The intruder snooping on your turf will be terminated. He has connections to Cartel scum on the Mexican coast. He's slipped through the cracks a couple of times but we'll nail him today."

"How can you be so certain if he's eluded my forces as well as yours so successfully?"

"We're holding his son," the vice president said smugly.

14.

Del drove 190 kph down Highway 20 from Culiacán. En route Leah said little. She knew Putnam's betrayal had to be a horrible blow, but the terror twisting Del's guts came from knowing that his son was in Fuller's hands. They sped through the quiet streets of Mazatlán and pulled up to his uncle's house with screeching tires. All the lights were already blazing in the house, an evil omen.

Francisco Mulcahey stood at the top of the stairs, his smooth olive complexion leached as gray as his hair. "This was delivered just over an hour ago. The message with it said it concerned Miguelito and that I must give it to no one but you," he said, handing Del a disc.

As they walked upstairs, Del told Francisco what they had learned from Ramirez, then sat down at the PDA in his uncle's office and inserted the disc. When he gave a copy command, the computer refused. "Fuller's covered himself, the bastard," he muttered, then stiffened when Mike's face appeared on-screen. The boy was standing in a large, open room backed by a stone fireplace. Fuller's cabin. His expression was not frightened, just uncertain.

"Uh, hi, Dad. Hugh said I should tell you we got here and that we're safe. I—"

The screen blipped, now switching to Brian Fuller's smiling face. Leah could feel Del recoil after seeing his son, then Fuller. Del sat utterly still, gripping the PDA table with white knuckles.

"So glad I located you, Elliott. We haven't spoken in ages. This is a great location for a getaway. I hope you'll accept an invitation to be my guest."

The words were delivered in smooth political style as if he were inviting an acquaintance to a fund-raiser, but Leah could sense the venom behind the oily facade. Then the screen blipped again and a printed message appeared:

"Directions will arrive by courier within the hour. Come alone. Don't try for another Pulitzer. Bury what you've learned and Mike goes free. Fail to comply with our wishes and he dies. You have twenty hours as of 22:00 PDT."

Del gave a replay command but the computer responded, "Unable to comply. Disc nonfunctional." He pulled it out and cursed. "Self-destruct."

"It wouldn't matter anyway. The way he staged the three-part scenario, any court in the country would throw it out. Because of the three distinct segments, they'd say you spliced it together," Leah said, placing her hand on his shoulder. She could feel the unbearable tension radiating from his body.

"He plans to kill Mike no matter what I do," Del said bleakly. "The son of a bitch wants to do it right in front of me. I could smell it on him."

"Then you will not walk into his trap. I will begin arrangements," Francisco said. He picked up the portalink on his desk and walked out of the room, speaking rapidly in Spanish.

"He'll rally the whole family—and pull in every due bill he has with Ramirez to boot." Del leaned his elbows on his knees and cupped his hands over his bowed head, trying to think.

How can he keep from losing it? If this were Kev, Leah was certain she'd be a basket case by now. "I'm going with you," she said.

He looked up at her face for a moment, then replied, "Thank you, Leah. God knows I need you."

"What are we going to do?"

"Raoul has a brother who's still in Special Forces. We have less than twenty hours to assemble our own SWAT team and go in. And I'll tell you now, Leah, Fuller isn't walking away from this alive."

———

As the disc had promised, Del received directions to a rendezvous, in the Rogue River country on the California-Oregon border. The courier service didn't know who had sent the directions, any more than they knew who had sent the disc earlier.

Raoul filed no flight plan for the night run up the coast. He checked out the Beech King Air B200 that Ramirez had provided for the long flight. Raoul's brother Ernesto and another commando from Special Forces met with Hernan Cabril, Ramirez's *segundo*, who worked out of Durango. He furnished aerofoam body armor, nitro-cordite putty, frag grenades, and TAR-21s without a blink. Del wondered again about the relationship between his uncle and the drug lord.

Hoping against hope that Diana knew more about the location of Fuller's cabin than she'd told them, Del called her house. When the maid finally answered at 3 a.m., she informed them that Mrs. Shrewsbury had left on a trip late Tuesday night. She had not said where she was going. Del was afraid he had a pretty fair idea.

"Damn, for all we know, they could have her by now, especially if Putnam's in on the conspiracy. Some trusted agents he had watching her, the son of a bitch!"

"But why help us get safely out of D.C. just to set us up now? That doesn't track." Leah was trying to assure herself as much as Del. "I do know one thing—if we get within fifty klics of her car, we should be able to find it." He looked at her curiously. "While you were talking to her on Tuesday morning, I planted a homing dot on the windshield registration of that fancy blue Jaguar." Leah shrugged. "Old habits."

"Agent Berglund, you're a beaut! If they're keeping her and Mike in one place, which I strongly suspect, we'll find them."

"You think they'll expect you to bring help?" she asked.

"Fuller's never been one to leave anything to chance. He'll be prepared."

Just then Uncle Mac returned looking a little less strained since they had a plan under way to rescue Mike. "You will have an element of surprise. They will expect you to travel by commercial airlines, which would take far longer. Seri is arranging passage for your cousin Fernando, booked in your name."

"Nando looks enough like me to pass. We'll need a woman who resembles Leah, too."

Francisco looked at her and nodded. "You are very brave, señorita." He studied her face, then added, "On the Santandar side of our family there are some blondes. None with hair so short, but that will be easily remedied. Esperanza I think . . . or perhaps Josefina."

"Whoever agrees to impersonate us will be under BISC surveillance," Del said. "You must make them understand how dangerous this will be."

"They understand family," the old man replied as if that settled everything. His shrewd gray eyes measured Leah with approval.

Within an hour they rendezvoused at the airport just south of the city where Raoul waited by the Beech King. He did not seem surprised to see Leah with Del as he introduced his brother Ernesto and another Mexican Special Forces officer named Joaquin Schmitt. Schmitt was married to Ernesto's sister-in-law. Leah was pleased to note that both men looked like dangerous professionals. So did the normally genial Raoul. All three wore camouflage fatigues and grim expressions. They were armed like Israeli commandos.

Del and Leah had changed into battle gear before leaving the house. They examined the arsenal Ramirez's men had given them. "BISC doesn't have better gear than this," she said, checking the action on a Steyr M9 pistol.

"The Bureau didn't have as good," Del replied grimly. "And nobody in the U.S. gets their hands on the Israeli TAR-21s. A coalition of U.S. arms manufacturers got Congress to ban their import. Too much competition for the new M17s."

"Well, your Congress does not dictate to Inocensio. With the money that old bandit makes, he can afford the best," Raoul said as he loaded coils of climber's rope and mountain survival gear into the plane. "I plan to come in low off the Oregon coast. If these maps are accurate, I can sit us down within a mile of a small resort town where Joaquin will requisition a vehicle for us."

"You mean steal one," Del said, studying the GPS.

A flash of the old white smile touched Raoul's face. "*Sí*. We will find Miguelito and his mother, Tig. I swear it."

"I'm grateful, Cousin," Del said in Spanish.

As they climbed aboard the airplane and finished storing gear, Leah considered the incredible power of family loyalty. And realized how much she missed Adam. *We'll stop them, Gramps. I swear it.*

6 A.M., PDT, THURSDAY, JULY 2
THE OREGON COAST

They skimmed above the rough breakers crashing along the rock-covered bay. The fog was lifting and a pale gold ball of sun rose above the eastern mountains. Raoul admitted relief that in the absence of an airstrip he would not have to attempt an instrument landing.

They'd had several brushes with patrol boats off the California coast, but no one had spotted them, a tribute to Ramirez's system. Leah now had a whole new appreciation of how efficiently drug smugglers could slip past U.S. coastal defenses if the pilots were desperate and skilled enough to take the risks that Raoul had—and possessed detailed information regarding Globe Net surveillance and U.S. Coast Guard patrol schedules.

Raoul made an inspection pass of the grassy meadow he'd chosen for a landing. "It should work. There is enough room to maneuver and it is level. The only thing which is troublesome is what the vegetation may conceal, but . . ." He shrugged carelessly. "I have set down in far worse places and walked away."

Leah, never a happy flier, was not reassured by his Latin fatalism, but kept her disquiet to herself. During the flight they had reviewed all the maps and information on the small seaside town of Wind Harbor and had outfitted themselves with the new super-lightweight body armor that could stop practically any slug smaller than one from a cannon the size of Del's Smith & Wesson.

"If we crash, at least we're more shock absorbent," she muttered to herself, then looked over at Delgado.

He had spent much of the flight thinking about Mike and his ex-wife, praying for the first time in many years for divine intervention to keep them safe, worrying that Fuller might have used the boy to vent his spleen against the man. Del's preoccupation had been obvious to the others, but there was so much to prepare for the mission, there had been no time to talk about it.

Now as they strapped themselves in for landing, Leah took the seat beside him and reached for his hand. "We're going to get Mike out okay, Del."

"Fuller hates my guts. God only knows what he might do to my son."

"You said Hugh Shrewsbury had tried to be a decent stepfather—"

"He's Fuller's friend and business associate. For all we know, he could be part of the conspiracy."

"I don't think so. And he'd try to protect Mike for Diana's sake. Even a bastard will do a lot for love," Leah argued with more conviction than she felt.

He looked at her in the uncertain light filtering in the window, dark circles under her eyes intensifying her pallor. His fingers grazed her cheek. "Still the idealist even after BISC," he murmured, then started to say something else just as they hit the ground.

They all braced themselves as the plane began to bounce wildly over the tall grass and clumps of vinegar weed. The craft bucked and rocked from side to side. Raoul worked the controls with cool precision as the right wing clipped a small buckthorn tree, uprooting it. The metal groaned with stress but held as the plane continued, veering to the right, slowing. Finally, he cut the engines and leaned back, rubbing his neck. "I have landed here. Now I only pray I can take off again."

"One thing at a time. Next item on the agenda is securing transport to the coordinates," Del said calmly, all business now that they were ready to move.

Leah watched with relief as he unstrapped himself and began working his GPS to determine distances.

"I make Wind Harbor to be two miles southwest," he said. "You should have enough time to make any necessary repairs to the plane while we check out the gear."

"What are we sitting around for, hombres?" Ernesto stood up and began opening the carefully packed containers holding the nitrocordite putty and frag grenades. His specialty was explosives.

Leah pulled the TARs and extra clips of ammo from their cases, issuing everyone their equipment as Del ticked off the itinerary. "We have less than an hour to get to town and steal a car before the locals are up and about. Joaquin will make the selection and Leah will be his cover. Everyone ready to move out?"

The swarthy Mexican's English was thickly accented, liable to raise questions if they were challenged. Leah's blond, all-American looks would hopefully serve to allay suspicion. Their cover story was that they were on exercises from the Smith River Army Training Center just over the California border. They hoped they wouldn't have to use it.

8:20 A.M., PDT, THURSDAY, JULY 2

Diana Shrewsbury looked like hell and felt worse. What was left of her smeared makeup was thirty-six hours old, and her hair hung in straight, oily clumps. Dark circles ringed her burning, red eyes, the result of twenty hours on the road. Once she had located Fuller's old friend from the district attorney's office, Ed Koller had been able to draw her a rough map of the route to the hideaway where Hugh and Brian had taken Mike. That had been Tuesday evening. By that time her imagination had conjured up all manner of dire scenarios, which she forced herself to rationally dismiss.

Whatever their quarrel with Elliott Delgado, Brian and Hugh were not going to involve her son in it. Diana could not imagine what was going on, but she damn sure intended to confront her husband and his friend and find out, then take Mike home.

Please, let Mike be all right. She had repeated the mantra over and over as she drove straight through from San Diego north across the Oregon border into the rugged Rogue River country. The highways had long since dissolved into switchback gravel roads barely wide enough to accommodate a single vehicle—where there was road at all that had not been washed out by spring rain.

Twice she'd lost precious time doubling back when a county road proved impassable. If she'd had the faintest idea how isolated and wild this region was, she would never have allowed Mike to go in the first place. Who would ever have thought that a busy man like Brian, a United States congressman and potential presidential candidate, would have the time or inclination to retreat into this hell?

"I'll kill them for bringing Mike here," she muttered savagely as her Jaguar hit yet another giant rut in the road, spraying gravel and mud on her already ruined paint job. Stopping in Medford to rent a four-wheel-drive vehicle would have been a sensible idea—if it hadn't been the middle of the night when she'd reached there.

Some instinct made her push on without stopping. The same instinct had kept her from calling the police. Something was not right. El had not explained what he was working on that might jeopardize Mike's life, but she had never seen him so upset in all the years they'd been married. He'd given no indication that Hugh and Brian were involved and seemed satisfied that Mike was safe with them.

Why then had Marian Fuller lied to her? Diana was certain Rob had not been ill. Marian's response had set off warning bells in her head. Something was going on, perhaps the reopening of the old FBI investigation into corruption in the film industry. That might wipe out Hugh financially and destroy Brian's political career.

Disheveled and exhausted, Diana did not at the moment give a damn if both men were ruined, just as long as her son was safe. She slowed at the narrow road ahead and studied the contours of the area, noting the landmarks Ed Koller had described—a red rock formation at the entrance and in the distance, looming ominously over the pristine beauty of the wilderness, a jagged peak shaped like a bear's paw with claws flexed.

She turned and continued on to a sharp curve, passing a rusted-out van abandoned on the side of the road. Diana hadn't seen a car for over seventy miles. It should have struck her as odd to see a junker there, but it didn't. She had her mind on other matters. When the road forked, she veered left. As she approached Brian Fuller's cabin, she glanced nervously at the glove compartment, then opened it and pulled out the .32-caliber Colt automatic and slid it into her blazer pocket.

The leader of the BISC Sanitation Squad, Paul Mathiason, stood next to the congressman, watching the car skid to a halt in front of the cabin. "Just like the outposts reported—a blue Jaguar with one female occupant. I assume you know her, sir?"

"I know her. What the fucking hell is she doing here?" Brian Fuller stared at the battered, mud-encrusted remains of Diana Shrewsbury's once gleaming sports car.

"Who is she?" The tall, angular BISC agent repeated his question, signaling the two men with him to retreat into the side room to guard their prisoner.

"Goddamn trouble," Fuller snarled. "Shrewsbury's wife."

"The kid's mother." The agent's voice was emotionless. Mathiason much preferred the hard-nosed calculation of the vice president to the mercurial arrogance of the pretty-boy congressman. Fuller unconsciously smoothed a lock of sandy brown hair back into his $200 haircut. So far out in the country they'd have to walk toward town to go squirrel hunting and the son of a bitch was worried about how he looked! Agent Mathiason smothered his disgust and asked, "Should I take care of her?"

"Wait. Maybe I can get rid of her. Or maybe we can use her, too." Fuller chewed his lip, vacillating for a moment. "Go in the side room with the boy. Put a cork in that kid and don't let him even twitch." He opened the screen and stepped out onto the porch as Diana climbed the stairs. Her normally sleekly groomed hair was stringy and her face blotchy and pale. "Diana, darling, what on earth are you doing here? You look ghastly," he said with what sounded like genuine concern.

"I want to see my son and my husband, Brian," she said, making no attempt to return his brotherly hug. "Where are they?"

"Hugh took the boys out on the boat, Diana. They'll be gone all—"

"Don't give me that crap, Brian. I saw Rob at home with Marian. Why are you lying to me?"

He laughed affably, flashing vid-friendly perfect white teeth. "So that's what brought this on. Hugh said you'd be upset if Mike came without Rob. That's why I convinced him not to tell you. Calm down, darling. They're fine."

"Then where the hell *are* they, Brian?"

"I told you, out on the river for the day."

"Why didn't you go with them?"

He sighed. "You're overwrought, Diana. My God, did you drive all the way from San Diego?" He looked at her ruined Jaguar, damning Marian for not letting him know she'd made such a monumental screwup. "You need to lie down and—"

"No." Diana pushed past him and entered the large room. Noting the door on the right standing ajar, she quickly jerked it open, revealing a large bathroom/shower area. She turned to the door on the left, which she assumed led out onto the glassed-in sleeping area visible from the road.

"I wouldn't go in there, Diana," Fuller said, all attempts at conciliation vanished as he clamped his hand on her shoulder, whirling her around.

He stepped back, raising his hands when she pulled the automatic from her pocket and leveled it at him. "Where are Mike and Hugh?"

"Easy, darling, easy. We wouldn't want a tragic accident here, would we?"

"If I shoot you, it won't be an accident, Brian. I've practiced at the target range ever since Hugh had me take gun-safety classes. This has something to do with my former husband, doesn't it? He was frightened for Mike. Fool that I was, I trusted you and Hugh more."

"I confess to an intense personal loathing for Elliott Delgado, but that has no bearing at all on how I feel about Mike. He's like my own son."

"Who isn't here. And now neither are Mike or Hugh."

"Ah, but they are, my dear," he said with a placid smile as Mathiason grabbed her from behind, knocking the gun from her hand with one expert chop. A second agent seized her in a choke hold, which immobilized her instantly. "And now, you'll join Mike. Like your son, you are a bargaining chip. Alas, poor Hugh proved only a liability."

He motioned for the BISC agent to take her now unconscious body into the side room and secure her.

The Mercury Mountaineer Joaquin had "requisitioned" bounced up the rough, narrow road with ground-devouring swiftness. Within twenty minutes of leaving Wind Harbor, they were off the state highway. The vehicle's mud-covered exterior, which had once been black, was scratched and pocked from their swift drive through the wilderness.

Joaquin drove while Del, sitting in the front seat beside him, watched for the landmarks in their instructions. In the rear of the SUV, Raoul and Ernesto double-checked their gear and went over possible search-and-rescue scenarios. Leah worked with the tracking device, looking for the homing dot she'd planted on Diana's Jaguar.

Nothing was registering yet. She frowned in concentration, saying, "If only we knew for sure she drove. For all we know the Jaguar could be sitting on some airport parking lot in southern California."

Del turned back to her and said, "Maybe, but if I know Diana—and when it comes to Mike, at least, I think I do—she would've barreled up the highway nonstop and probably packing heat."

Leah looked over at him, startled. "Armed?"

"Yeah, you have one more thing in common. Although I doubt she's the dead shot you are. When the carjacking incidents by druggies got bad on the San Diego freeways, Hugh wanted them to have some protection, so they both enrolled in one of those survivalist shooting classes."

"They're illegal."

"Once a federal agent, always a federal agent," Del said with as near a grin as he'd managed since they'd left Inocensio Ramirez in Culiacán. "Illegal but going on in every urban center in North America."

"Then she might blunder into Fuller and create a bigger mess." Leah swore under her breath. *Brilliant remark, Berglund.* Delgado's face was drawn and hard as granite once more. She turned back to the tracer in her hand.

Del heard her gasp and jerked his head around. "What? Talk to me, Leah. You got something?"

"It's her car. Son of a bitch, it's her car!" She fiddled with the GPS on the tracker, then gave him the coordinates.

"That's not twenty klics away."

"What is the absolute earliest time they might expect us with optimum commercial air connections?" Raoul asked, checking his watch.

"According to Aunt Seri, not until early afternoon," Del replied.

"*Bueno*. We have about three hours to form a plan and execute it. We will need every minute, especially if Miguelito isn't being held where they want us to go. And I fear they will not be so obliging as to allow that."

"My gut tells me he's up here somewhere close," Del said.

"Our best lead is Diana's car—assuming she either knew something or learned something we didn't," Leah said. "I think if we go after her, we'll find Mike."

"Then let's head for her and see if these directions match," Del replied grimly.

They did. Joaquin pulled the Mountaineer off the narrow country road onto a trail marked only by an odd formation of red rocks. Dense conifers canopied the start of the gravel road, which twisted and turned as it wound gradually uphill. Scattered meadows opened up a vista periodically before they plunged once again into the trees. The area was utterly deserted.

"We just crossed the creek. There's a sharp curve in the road ahead. Good place to stop for recon," Del said, looking at Raoul, who nodded. Joaquin pulled over and killed the engine.

"We're within three kilometers of the car," Leah said as they quietly picked up their weapons and slipped out of the van.

As Raoul, Ernesto, and Joaquin split up and slipped off both sides of the road into the woods, Del said to Leah, "Stick with me."

"Like cheese on pizza. Remember, I'm an urban cowgirl." They walked up the side of the road, cautiously approaching the bend, using the brush for cover. "Bingo," she breathed quietly.

"The first lookout post . . . we hope," he said, eyeing the rusted-out old van hanging onto the edge of the road by two flat tires.

"Could it be a junker someone left?" she whispered.

"Yeah, and his chauffeur followed to pick up the driver after he abandoned it."

They crouched out of range of the van's rear vid, which was incongruously clean and new looking. Del caught a faint motion through the trees and waved to Raoul, then whispered to Leah, "Raoul will wait a bit and see if the guy in the truck makes regular reports before he moves on him."

"I may not be Special Forces or a G-man, Delgado, but I know that drill," she snapped, then instantly regretted it. "Sorry. I didn't mean to be a bitch."

"Forgiven."

Time dragged with tortoise slowness. Minutes became hours, or so it seemed. Then the absolute stillness was broken by a soft pop. Leah was up and running, followed by Del, who was slowed by a leg cramp. Before they had covered half the distance to the van, they saw Ernesto slip across the road and dash to the front of the vehicle.

Leah, careful not to be obvious, slowed slightly so she and Del arrived together. Their companions huddled, conversing in Spanish. Raoul looked up with a grin. "The door is open, compadres. Ernesto found another lookout at the fork in the logging trail about one hundred and fifty meters off this road. Neutralized. As is the one in the van. Joaquin and Ernesto have not uncovered any others."

"You tell how often these guys were reporting in to base camp?" Del asked.

Raoul shook his head. "*Lo siento,* Tig. They do not seem to be calling in. We dare not wait any longer. In a couple of hours the flight our cousins are on will be setting down in Medford. After that their BISC tail will realize they have been suckered."

Leah nodded. "He's right, Del. Let's get it done."

The five of them hurried across the road and up the gravel logging trail until they came to the fork. "Diana's car is about two kilometers up this left road," Leah said.

"And Fuller's instructions said to take the right," Del replied.

"Then by all means we must see what lies to the right first," Raoul said grimly. He nodded to Joaquin and Ernesto. "Hombres, you sweep the area here and perhaps a klic up the left trail for any additional sentries. Del, Leah, care to join me?" Without waiting for a response, he headed silently up the right path. Leah and Del followed.

After several minutes he raised his hand and they halted. Up ahead they could barely make out what looked through the brushy cover to be several tents and two Humvee/truck conversions. Raoul motioned for them to remain while he moved ahead.

Del shook his head. "Well, this is our welcoming party. If there's going to be the risk of any fireworks here, I'll make book on Fuller's cowardly ass being safely away from it. He'll keep Mike and Diana with him to use as shields if something goes sour."

"You know the guy." Hell, it made sense to her.

When Raoul returned, he reported that about a dozen men were encamped in the compound. There was no sign of Miguelito, Diana, or Fuller.

"Now, we'll see if my hunch and Leah's GPS readings are right," Del said.

Hurriedly, they made their way back down the trail. Ernesto and Joaquin were waiting. Raoul explained what they had found up the right fork of the road, then instructed Ernesto, "Lay your mines there, *mano*, and be ready."

"*Sí*. When they hear you attack, I will have a surprise for them," his brother replied. Ernesto's shrewd black eyes scanned the target. He could already see the best places to sink his putty for maximum effect. Raoul gestured to the others and they began to make their way up the left fork of the road.

"And there it is," Leah whispered, spotting Diana's Jaguar sitting in front of the big log structure jutting out over the steep ravine that divided it from the military camp on the other road.

They split up and began recon of the dense woods surrounding their target. Raoul and Joaquin climbed the tall pines to look inside the windows along the right side of the house—after Raoul efficiently garroted another lookout in the woods. Leah and Del made their way to the opposite side where a glassed-in room extended out over the steep hillside. It was held up by several heavy cedar support poles.

"Here's where I earn another all-conference gymnastics medal," she said.

Del stood guard as she shimmied up a pole. He watched and waited, terrified of what she might see inside. *Please let them be alive.* If they survived this, he swore to hell with Pulitzers, to hell with Cohen and the whole damn D.C. beat. He was going to spend the rest of his life with his son. It seemed to take forever for her to climb back down. He held his breath as she turned to face him.

"They're in there. Bound, lying on a couple of beds. One guard glued to a vid screen at the entrance of the room, playing solitaire."

"Lying down. Are they unconscious . . . or—"

"I said they were tied up, Del. If they weren't healthy and alert, why bother?"

His breath whistled out. Then he reminded himself that they were only halfway home. "Let's see what the others have found," he whispered. "God, I hope Fuller's inside. I want that motherfucker dead."

"Count on it," Leah assured him. "The penalty for treason is death."

15.

The team reassembled in the thick copse of fir to the south of the house. "Mike and Diana are tied up in the addition. One guard playing vid games. His back's to them," Leah reported.

"Three men with the congressman in the big room," Joaquin said. "They are armed with Colt submachine guns, but they're sitting around a table playing cards. I think we can take them out before they can do any harm. Fuller is by the fireplace watching CNN."

Raoul stroked his mustache, considering. "We must be certain we've secured Miguelito and the señora before we hit them."

Leah reached for a coil of soft nylon rope lying with their cache of weapons and equipment. "See the curve of the roof from the cabin to the addition? We toss this over and secure it. No one will hear it through those heavy cedar shingles. I climb up and wait, then swing in." She pointed at one of the big windows in the addition.

Raoul nodded. "*Sí*. We must take out the three armed men in front precisely as you break through the glass."

"I'll have the 'hostile' in the side room before he can turn around," Leah said coolly. She could feel Del's eyes on her as they talked. He was grateful for her professional skill. Was he also repelled by it? The disturbing thought passed as they finalized the plan.

Exact timing was crucial. When all were certain of what they had to do, they split up. Leah turned toward the cabin to wait for Joaquin to throw the rope over the roof. When Del called her name, she stopped. Raoul and Joaquin had moved out. They were alone.

"I just wanted to . . . hell . . . be careful going in." He reached out and enveloped her in a powerful hug.

They simply held on to each other in a fierce affirmation of life, and the shared hope that they could save Mike. As they parted, she whispered, "Don't go getting shot up, Delgado. You only have one good leg left."

"I sorta hoped you were interested in more than my legs, Leah."

She understood what he meant, just as he understood what she had said. She turned and walked away.

The rope came slithering over the roof. It fell soundlessly against the heavy shingles and dangled a few meters from where Leah waited. She checked her watch, counted off the time agreed upon for Joaquin to secure the other side and take his position at the front of the house. Then she began to climb.

Once she was in action, muscles straining, she focused on the mission. But this was unlike her BISC field assignments. Then she had simply terminated strangers, criminals. This involved people she cared for. That complicated matters. *Do the damned job, Berglund.*

The thin nylon bit into her hands even through gloves. She pulled herself up, careful not to bump the side of the house and alert the guards inside. Sweat burned her eyes and trickled down her neck. She ignored it, concentrating on reaching her position on the roof kitty-corner from her targeted window. Even though the body armor was lightweight and flexible, getting onto the overhang was difficult. The heel of one soft-rubber-soled boot caught on the edge with a slight scrape, then slipped off. Cursing, she stopped her dangling swing by placing a hand on the siding and tried again. This time she caught, then carefully levered herself up and slid silently onto the overhang. After gathering the rope in her hands, she rechecked her TAR and adjusted the sling so the weapon was across her chest. Then she sat up, perching on the edge of the roof, waiting.

Raoul and Del worked their way under the deck and crouched behind the stairs leading up to the front door. Shit! Del counted twelve steps. He rubbed his knee.

Joaquin had already shinnied up one of the deck's support beams, slipped over the rail, and made his way to the front door on his belly.

The cousins below waited as their comrade quietly plastered a small glob of nitro cordite and a detonator to the door. Then came a soft, short rapping noise—like one made by a woodpecker—at the corner of the deck. Joaquin was ready.

Del looked at Raoul. "Let's do it."

They were on the second step when Joaquin blew the door. Shards of screen wire and wood flew everywhere as the two charged up the stairway.

Leah heard the nitro-cordite blast. Tautening the rope, she swung down, feet braced to go through the glass. The hot, wretchedly uncomfortable body armor had better work or she'd be bleeding like a steer in a slaughterhouse.

Across the ravine, Ernesto heard the sound of the blast followed by weapons fire. He crouched in a thicket of fir thirty meters from the road to the soldier's encampment, detonator in hand, waiting.

Del and Raoul reached the hole that had been a front door just as the crash of breaking glass sounded to their left. Joaquin came in behind them. Two of the BISC agents sat on a pair of sofas facing each other, playing cards on a coffee table between them. The third man was in the kitchen. Both cardplayers dived for their submachine guns on the floor beside them. One guard never got off a shot. The .223 slugs from Raoul's TAR tore into him. The other rolled behind the end of the sofa, firing short bursts as the three attackers dived for cover. The man in the kitchen used an open refrigerator door as a shield, firing a Vektor 9mm he tore from his shoulder holster.

Leah crashed through the glass and landed lightly on her feet, her knees bent. The guard jumped out of his chair when the explosion rocked the building. Reaching for his Colt, he whirled at the sound of shattering glass. She raised her TAR and fired a single burst dead center into his chest. All hell broke loose in the main room of the cabin as she moved toward the door.

Ernesto listened to the gunfire echoing across the ravine. A dozen heavily armed troops in two Humvees responded with amazing speed, bouncing down the narrow, rocky road. He let them pass until both vehicles were within the minefield he had laid, then blew the second Humvee sky-high.

As pieces of steel and men flew into the air, the first Humvee's driver slammed on his brakes. The heavy carrier halted, but before the men could jump clear, the thick white smoke from the first blast enveloped them.

Nitro cordite left a stringent stench when it exploded. Ernesto pressed the detonator quickly several more times. Only one wounded "SS" man got clear. Mulcahey finished him with his TAR-21, then started running toward the firefight.

Brian Fuller had been sitting by his vid screen on the opposite side of the room, watching a Washington news report, when the front door blew. The noise and concussion from the blast had stunned him for an instant. Then he dived behind the big leather recliner. The deafening rattle of automatic weapons fire blended with the crash of shattering glass. He was surrounded!

Terror tripled his heartbeat. He hunkered down. The squad at the base camp should be here in minutes. Then he heard a series of explosions and gunfire from that direction. This was a full-scale strike! Who the hell were these guys? When he heard Delgado's voice, the rage lent him courage.

Fuller lunged across the open space between the chair and his big oak desk in the front corner of the room and clawed at the handle. He yanked so hard the drawer came off its casters and flew out of his hand. He flung it away and grabbed the .380-caliber Colt, which had fallen from the drawer onto the braided rug.

Ignoring the congressman, Joaquin focused on the BISC guard behind the couch, while Raoul tended to the man in the kitchen. When the barrel of a Colt submachine gun appeared over the end of the sofa, Joaquin disassembled that end of the furniture with a long burst from his TAR-21. The Colt clattered to the floor. The guard trapped in the kitchen fared no better. The refrigerator door proved to be poor armor against .223-caliber rounds. Several short bursts from Raoul's assault rifle perforated it and the man who crouched behind it.

Del saw Fuller dive to the desk, but was unable to get a clear shot. While Raoul and Joaquin finished their work, Del heard the click of a round being jacked into a chamber during a brief instant of silence. Fuller was armed now. Del rolled to the front of the desk. "Come on,

Brian. Time to show 'n' tell. You got a gun, motherfucker, use it!" He could hear Fuller's frantic, ragged breathing.

"You're a dead man, Delgado, a walking corpse and so's your kid!" Fuller yelled back. His voice cracked with fear as he cursed his old enemy.

Sudden death. If they both poked their heads over the desk, whoever got lucky would kill the other man. With his son in the next room, Del did not want to die this way. Damn, he didn't!

At least he could control his fear. In the eerie stillness after his men were down, Fuller sounded like an asthmatic in a flour mill. Silently, Raoul motioned for Del to move away as he and Joaquin leveled their weapons on the desk, ready to cut loose. Before he could comply, the door from the bedroom behind him opened and Leah peered through the crack. Fuller heard the sound. Thinking it was Delgado, he lunged out, Colt automatic firing wildly.

All four of them hit him at once. Congressman Brian Fuller was reduced to a lifeless, bloody pulp.

Del jumped to his feet and rushed toward Leah. "Where's Mike?"

She turned and walked through the large bedroom behind her to the open door leading to the addition. Del knelt beside Mike's bed and grabbed his son with a sob, rocking back and forth. Leah leaned over Diana and used the razor-sharp combat knife on her belt to cut the restraints from the other woman's wrists and ankles. Then she began carefully peeling the adhesive sealing Diana's mouth.

Mike squirmed against his father, mumbling incoherently from behind the flex tape covering his mouth until Del realized what he was doing. As Leah spoke softly to Diana, he released the boy and removed his gag and bonds.

"Dad! I knew you'd come!" The boy threw himself into his father's arms as the words tumbled out. "I told Hugh, but . . . I don't think he believed me."

Diana, still numb from the restraints, hobbled over to father and son and put her arms around her child to reassure herself that he was unharmed. Mike turned into her arms and hugged her. "Mom, I was so scared when they brought you in all tied up. Yesterday Hugh said to be quiet and let him take care of everything. But he never came back, 'n' when I tried to go looking for him, those guys tied me up."

Del and Diana exchanged a look over the boy's head. Her face was ashen. He reached over and gripped her shoulder in reassurance. "I'll see if I can find out what happened."

Turning to his son, he said, "Take care of your mother, okay, Tiger?"

Leah watched the intimate family tableau, then stepped back so Del could pass. She had already used a bedspread to cover the bloody body of the agent she'd killed. This moment was for mother and child. She had no right to be here, but then Mike saw her.

"Kasi! You were keen! You 'n' Dad saved me!" He launched himself across the room with the resilient energy of childhood and hugged her.

Automatically she hugged him back and felt something that had been frozen deep inside since Kevin's death begin to thaw. As he chatted excitedly, she tried to deflect his questions about the "secret agents" who had come with them and were now disposing of the dead men in the front room. When she explained that her name was Leah Berglund, not Kasi Evans, and she worked for the government, his eyes got even larger. *We're just "action heroes" from vid games to him.* Perhaps it was better that way.

"What's going to happen now?" Diana asked her quietly.

She's terrified for her husband. "We'll have to get you somewhere safe where Fuller's friends can't use you again."

"Why did Mr. Fuller have those guys tie us up?" Mike asked.

"He was involved in something illegal with other people high up in the government," Leah replied.

"And it's not over," Diana said quietly.

"I'm afraid not."

"Was . . . was Hugh involved in whatever Brian was doing?"

"I don't know for sure, Diana, but I don't think so." But Leah was gut certain that Shrewsbury was dead. She sensed that Diana intuited it, too. When the carnage in the great room had been cleaned up, Leah escorted her charges out of the house.

Del had already decided where to take his family for their protection. If Fuller could use Mike, so could Harmon Waterman . . . or Cal Putnam. Del met them on the front steps. His expression was grim when he asked Mike to remain with Leah while he and Diana spoke privately. Leah and the boy could see what Del told Diana was bad, although she quickly regained her composure as they continued to talk.

"Hugh's dead, isn't he?" Mike asked, near tears himself but fighting them.

Leah gathered the boy in her arms and settled him down beside her on the steps. "I'm afraid so, Mike. Your mom will need you to be brave . . . and patient. Think you can do that, Tiger?" she asked, using the childhood nickname that Del had transferred to his son.

"Yeah. I'll take care of Mom," he replied, swallowing a lump in his throat. The neat action adventure wasn't fun anymore.

3 P.M., EDT, THURSDAY, JULY 2
RESTON, VIRGINIA

"I don't like this, Frankowski. I don't like it at all!" Harmon Waterman's pinched face reddened. Even his protuberant ears turned crimson. "What the fuck is going on? Last night Sommerville called me on a rampage about a compromise of our Sonoran base. Probably Delgado and Berglund. The general raised such a stink I moved up the timetable for the strike. Now the agents with Fuller haven't checked in and you can't raise them."

"I doubt it's Delgado and Berglund, sir. Our reports indicate they boarded a Mexicana flight in Mazatlán bound for San Francisco, then took a hop from SFI to Medford, Oregon. We had visual sightings in both airports. They should be on the ground"—Frankowski consulted his watch—"within half an hour, sir."

"Let me see the visuals of them in Mazatlán and San Francisco."

"Yes, sir." Frankowski returned a few moments later with a disc that Waterman inserted in his PDA.

The resemblance between the men was astonishingly close. He might not have caught it, glancing from the file holo of Delgado to the vid from the airport. But the woman was off. Brown eyes, hair just a shade too dark blond. Waterman began to curse. The tendons in his scrawny neck stood out and his Adam's apple bobbed like a cork. "These are ringers. Goddamned fucking ringers, not Delgado and Berglund!" he shrieked. "Whatever blind bastard let this get by him—" Waterman choked. "I will personally rip off his balls!"

Frankowski was a stickler when it came to detail. "Ah, sir, it's not a *him*. Agent Angela Burkhardt is responsible for the . . . ah, oversight."

Waterman slammed his fist on his desktop. "Bitch! I'll rip off her tits!"

Frankowski simply nodded, then asked, "Should I send a team to Oregon, sir?"

"At once. And for God's sake, not a fucking word of this to any of our people at the Pentagon—or the FBI."

4 P.M., EDT, THURSDAY, JULY 2
MACHIAS, MAINE

"Sheriff McLean, Special Agent Brad Walters, FBI."

The tall man standing in the doorway of his office held up a badge for McLean's scrutiny, then slid it smoothly back inside his suit jacket as he extended his hand.

McLean returned the handshake, sizing up the agent. Pin-striped, buttoned-down, from the top of his crew cut to the tip of his spit-shined shoes, Walters looked like a J. Edgar Hoover poster boy. "What can I do you for?" McLean asked with a folksy grin, offering the agent a chair across from his cluttered desk.

"I'm here regarding the death of former senator Manchester. Whenever a United States senator dies violently, we need to make certain the death is accidental."

"Even a retired senator?"

"Adam Manchester was still a highly influential man in Washington, Sheriff."

McLean shrugged. "Not much to report, Special Agent Walters. There was a fire out at his place on the peninsula after the storm. House burned clean to the ground. Too bad the old man was inside. Probably sleepin'." McLean let the lazy syllables of Carolina roll in his speech, a habit he'd picked up after moving North. Yankees tended to take good ole boys less seriously and let down their guard.

"To the best of your knowledge, who was the last person to see the senator alive?"

"Can't rightly say. Probably Seth Geerson. Boy's a little slow. He delivered a newspaper to Manchester early Monday mornin'. Far's I know, no one else saw him before the fire, which started a few hours later."

"I thought you said he was asleep when the fire broke out?" The agent shifted slightly in his chair.

"I said 'probably.' Old Adam was an early riser but he sometimes napped midday. 'Sides, after the bodacious storm we had, he was probably up all night. I sure as hell was."

"I appreciate your help, Sheriff. Now, if you could give me Seth Geerson's address, I'd be grateful. Just following up leads, you understand."

"Yep, I surely do, Special Agent Walters." McLean obliged the man with directions to the Geerson place.

After Walters left, McLean sat massaging the bridge of his nose, deep in thought. Patrikas's and Manchester's accidental deaths so close together had never added up for him. Again he cursed his rotten luck that old Abel Forrester had waylaid him en route to Manchester's house the morning of the fire. By the time he'd helped Abel pull his truck from a muddy ditch, it had been past 11 a.m. The house out on the peninsula was still burning when he arrived, but too far gone to get anyone out.

Manchester had been adamant in his opinion that Stephan Patrikas's death was no accident. Although McLean could prove nothing, he'd been inclined to agree.

Funny that the FBI agent never asked about the DNA tests on the body recovered from the fire. Walters just assumed Manchester was the dead man. A careless assumption.

Not the Bureau's standard operating procedure . . . unless they already knew it was Manchester. But how could they?

He'd just received the fax from Bangor an hour ago confirming the DNA match. He flipped through the phone file on his PDA and started to enter the law enforcement hotline number to the Bureau in Washington, then stopped and selected another number in Winston-Salem instead.

"Special Agent Eustis Carver, please. . . . Hey, Eustis. . . . Yep, it's

Dan. I need a favor. Can you run a check on one of your colleagues for me? I didn't get the badge number, but the name's Walters, Brad Walters. . . . Yeah, I'll wait."

"Curiouser and curiouser," the sheriff muttered to himself as he left the Geerson place. Brad Walters was FBI, all right, but the man who'd been in his office that afternoon was not Brad Walters. After McLean had learned from Eustis that the real Walters was a sixty-three-year-old man on permanent desk assignment in Omaha, he'd called the D.C. hotline . . . which confirmed that Brad Walters, age thirty-six, was on a field assignment out of Bangor. Little ole young "Brad" had big connections inside the Bureau.

That didn't make McLean happy.

The Geersons hadn't been much help to the impostor agent. The sheriff had called them as soon as he'd gotten off-link with Eustis and told them not to divulge that Manchester had given Seth a letter to mail. Old Mr. Geerson had done the talking after sending Seth to his aunt's place down the street. The boy would never have been able to tell a believable lie.

Old man Geerson was country smart. Since he'd been driving the truck when Seth delivered the newspaper, he said that was the last they had seen the senator before he died. The impostor had asked only a few simple questions, seeming to accept the story, but when he left, he headed south on Highway 191 away from town.

As if he knew exactly where the Manchester place was located. But as far as McLean had been able to ascertain, no one had given him directions to the senator's isolated coastal property.

The sheriff decided to take a little drive down to the peninsula himself.

4 P.M., PDT, THURSDAY, JULY 2
THE OREGON COAST

Del and Leah watched the Beech King take off with Raoul at the controls. Mike waved at them from a passenger window. He and Diana would be hidden in the mountains of Durango by nightfall, safe with Del's family. It had been difficult for him to part from his son. When the plane became a speck in the Pacific sky, they walked to the Toyota TE with flash drive that Joaquin had "requisitioned" for them. They quickly changed back into the street clothes they had brought with them on the plane.

"The way you drive, we'll be in Portland with time to spare. You'll make that redeye to D.C.," Leah said as they drove off.

"I don't want you going to Maine alone, Leah. It's suicide."

"Del, we've been over this ground. You're going to catch a flight to D.C. and I'm booking a flight to Bangor."

"I don't like you going to Maine without me," he persisted with almost childlike stubbornness. "BISC will be waiting for you to show up. For all you know, that sheriff could be working for them."

"And what you're doing will be perfectly safe, of course. Walking right into a Tribunal member's lair."

"I have to face him, Leah. You were right when you said it didn't make sense that he'd help us get out of D.C. and then bait a trap with Mike to kill us on the West Coast."

"Don't trust him, Del. Don't trust anyone in Washington."

"I won't, but I wish you'd gone with Raoul to Mexico. Then you'd be safe." He rushed on, "Yeah, I know, old-fashioned idea. Stupid."

"Correct on both counts." She watched him as he negotiated the twisting country road to the highway.

After a few moments of silence, Del said, "You're an enigma, you know that?"

"Me?" She looked surprised, then laughed. "I've told you about myself."

"As much as you've let anyone on the outside in, I guess. But that's not what I meant. You're a woman who can kill when she has to, but you're also a sucker for kids and causes."

Leah studied him for a moment, then sighed. "Delgado, that vestigial streak of male chauvinism sometimes turns your mind to mush. What you just said about me fits most of the cops in this country. Fits you. Fits Raoul, for christsake! What's he have? Three daughters?" Del nodded. "And I'll bet," Leah continued, "that daughters and wife have their doting male wrapped around their collective little finger. Right?"

Del laughed fondly. "God, you got that straight."

"Yet Raoul Mulcahey is one of the most deadly and merciless fighters I've ever worked with. Is he an enigma to you, Del?" she asked softly.

He digested that for a moment. "All right, counselor. Oink, oink! I confess. Damn, a logical woman is a pain in the ass."

Leah let out a spontaneous burst of laughter, but then her mood turned pensive. "Does it bother you that I've killed . . . criminals . . . people . . . I—I sensed something back at the cabin . . . anger? . . . Resentment maybe?" She felt her chest tighten with sudden dread. *What have I laid myself open for?*

"You're a dangerous woman, Leah Berglund. Not only logical but intuitive."

He was smiling as he spoke, so she let out the breath she'd been holding.

"Yeah, I was resentful. Shit! I am resentful . . . that you could climb up on that roof and swing through that window to protect my son and I couldn't. I was also resentful because I knew that Raoul would be through that blown front door before I could get there." He rubbed his leg. "Hell, I know. Self-pity again, but I get points because I resented without regard to gender or nationality! By God—like in the old days—an equal opportunity resenter!"

Leah's laughter was cathartic. When it subsided, she noticed that Del was smiling. He almost looked smug.

"Resentment isn't what this conversation is really about, is it, Leah?"

She didn't like his tone of voice or the direction of the conversation. Instead of rising to the bait, she turned and stared out at the ruggedly beautiful scenery.

Del wouldn't let it drop. "You think you're not the sort of woman a guy takes home to meet the family—but I took you home. You met my family. And they liked what they saw."

"Yes, what they saw. Not what I am. They don't know about me."

"Hell, Raoul knew before we went into the desert or you wouldn't have been with us. Ernesto and Joaquin just saw you in action. Trust me, they approved. And Uncle Mac? He knows everything, about everyone involved with his family, and he tells Aunt Seri. She's the one who really counts and she's accepted you like a daughter."

Leah sighed and shrugged. "All right, I wanted your folks to like me, but I was afraid of what they might think. I've never been around a family like yours . . . so close-knit . . . so big and yet so willing to do anything for each other. It makes me . . . I guess, kind of uneasy. My parents were distant. Adam Manchester was the only one . . ."

"I'm so sorry about him, Leah. I know how I'd feel if someone killed Uncle Mac. We'll get the bastards."

"We owe them for your friend, too."

"Yeah. Cuff. We went back a ways . . ." He told her about his years of rehab and explained the peculiar bond he'd shared with Cuff Bedford.

She talked about losing Adam and trying to unlock the puzzle of his last message.

"An unusual item in the usual place," he repeated, drumming his fingers on the steering wheel as they flew up Highway 5 nearing Portland. "I don't think it's the item that's unusual, only that it doesn't fit wherever it's been placed."

Leah snapped her fingers. "The journals! He kept journals ever since he was a boy."

"You mean like writing with a pen—on paper?" Del asked, a bit bemused by the notion. "I thought I was the only dinosaur alive who actually took notes on scraps of paper. He went me one better."

"Now all I have to do is figure out where he could've hidden a journal."

"You can damn betcha that's why BISC burned his house—to make sure nothing was hidden in some secret compartment or wall safe."

"I want them, Del. . . . I've never wanted to kill anyone before— not when the actual time for a termination came. But this time . . ."

"I know."

A companionable silence of shared grief lasted as they neared the exit to Portland International. Del parked the stolen Toyota in a long-term deck, wiped it clean of his prints, and left the hazard lights on.

Airport security would have it back to its owner little the worse for wear, just as the SUV had been returned to its owner in Wind Harbor. That one they would have to replace.

"We shouldn't go into the terminal together," she said, her cool professional demeanor once again in place.

"You're right, although I doubt they'll make you on the monitors in that getup." He touched the long brunette wig she'd purchased in Medford. "Damn, I wish I didn't have to worry about you while I'm in D.C."

"Hey, it's mutual, mister." She reached up and cupped his unshaven face between her hands, then kissed him.

"Keep that link handy. I'll call you from Washington," he said. "As soon as I know the score on Putnam, I'll be on the next flight to Bangor."

"I'll be in Machias." She hesitated, then reached out the same time he did for another kiss. As she turned to walk away, she called over her shoulder, "That's a great ass, Delgado. Take care of it for me, would you?"

1 A.M., EDT, FRIDAY, JULY 3
WASHINGTON, D.C.

The narrow Georgetown street was quiet at this hour, still distant enough from the violence to the east. The dim echo of gunshots broke the stillness infrequently. That was as good as it got anywhere in D.C. Del had paid the airport cabby and walked six blocks to Putnam's place, just as a precaution. The old man was cagey enough to have agents planted in a wide ring around his house. Delgado wanted the element of surprise when he confronted his old friend. He'd been a guest in Cal's home several times in years past. The security system was top-drawer.

That's why Del had called Gracie in Havana for help. The transaction she'd arranged nearly wiped out his savings account, but her contacts sold nothing but state-of-the-art BISC gadgetry. Gary McCallum had described its breaking-and-entering technology and this was it. Del had also purchased another Smith & Wesson .50 caliber.

The house was situated on a deep double lot in an old neighborhood that hadn't fallen victim to "redevelopment," code for replacing elegant single dwellings with row houses that packed people together like chickens on a poultry farm.

Two big magnolias cast their leafy shadows on the brick patio outside the French doors accessing the living room. His target. He'd made his way up the alley behind the house and climbed over an iron gate after disabling the motion sensor on the brick wall. He slipped through the yard, grateful for the overgrown shrubbery that Putnam never got around to pruning. Operating the variably sequenced data card on the house's security system was substantially more complicated. By the time the door finally snicked open with all systems disabled, he was sweating like a hog in a slaughterhouse.

Easing the door wider, Del slipped inside and closed it. Bright moonlight streamed in the big windows as he made his way through the house to the library. His eyes grew accustomed to the dark interior of the book-lined room. Cal's Buick TE had not been in the detached garage out back. Putnam often didn't return home until the wee hours, but Del's encrypted link to his office indicated that Cal was in town. Delgado knew his nighttime ritual. Sooner or late he would stop for a shot of bourbon from the liquor cabinet in his library before retiring.

Delgado sank into a big leather chair and waited.

Cal's Buick, a slightly newer version of Del's own TE, pulled into the garage. The old-fashioned wooden garage door's rumbling descent awakened Delgado. He touched the Smith & Wesson, praying he wouldn't have to use it, wondering if he could.

True to form, Putnam entered the house via the kitchen and made his way to the library. When he flicked on the light, seeing Delgado seated behind his desk didn't alter his expression. He nodded wearily and headed for the booze.

"Wondered when you'd show up. Name yer poison." He pulled out the bourbon bottle and set it on top of the cabinet, then paused, waiting until Del replied.

"I'll have what you're having."

Putnam nodded. "You usta drink Scotch while you were on the

hard stuff." He poured two shots of bourbon neat, keeping the bottle and glasses in Del's view all the while, then handed one to Del. "You finally figger out everyone who goes round in the dark ain't Santy Claus, huh?"

"I found out you're a Tribunal member, along with Waterman and Fuller. Why'd you play me this way, Cal?"

"If I told you I was on the Tribunal, would you have worked for me?" He downed the whiskey in one swift gulp and poured another.

"You have a point. But you lied to me, Cal. Why the hell would you join BISC in the first place? You said you hated the bastards, they were—what were your words?—'foxes in a henhouse.'"

"I may be a fox in the henhouse, but I ain't eyein' the chickens. I'm watching the other two foxes."

Delgado looked skeptical. "If you and your men are watching the other chickens, you've been doing a piss-poor job of it. Fuller tricked Hugh Shrewsbury into bringing my son to Oregon to bait a trap for me. The agents you had watching his house were gone when Diana tore out after Mike."

Now Putnam's expression did shift. He muttered an inventive curse. "I didn't pull them, Del, but I'd bet my ass I know who did."

"Drescher?"

Cal nodded. "Your boy and Diana all right?" He was reasonably certain if they weren't, Delgado wouldn't be giving him this chance to explain.

"We got them out. Fuller's dead."

"I can see how you know he was a Tribunal member, but how'd you find out about ole Harmon and me?"

Ignoring the question, Del took a sip of the whiskey. "I'm not sharing jack shit with you until you level with me."

"Fair enough," Putnam conceded.

"You said you were investigating Waterman. What have you found out about him?"

"Son of a bitch'd steal flies from a blind spider. He's running the whole shebang. We're pretty certain about that."

"We?"

"Wade Samson 'n' me. It's a long story."

"I have all night."

Pouring himself another shot of bourbon, Putnam said, "I thought you would." He walked over to the bookshelves lining the outside wall and took down one fat volume of statutes, then pressed his palm against the surface behind it. A small safe on the opposite wall appeared. It required a retinal scan to open. He grinned when Del reached for his Smith & Wesson, then slowly removed a disc from inside the safe and handed it to him. "Play it." While Delgado did so, Putnam fired up his meerschaum and plopped down in the big leather chair in front of the desk.

Del inserted it into the PDA. It was audio only, rehearsal for a speech to be given before a joint session of Congress. The dictation was fragmented and repetitive in places, jumping around with lots of asides about proper theatrical gestures, facial expressions, and other choreography to enhance dramatic effect. But the overall message was crystal clear: a plea for unlimited war powers to be given to the president of the United States.

It was Brian Fuller's voice.

When the disc was finished, Del looked at Putnam. "I don't get it. Just because Sommerville takes a little jaunt into Colombia, why would Congress cave in and endorse an all-out war in South America? Why would Samson be crazy enough to ask for a full-scale war?"

"Fuller's sayin' the *president* wants a declaration of war. He isn't sayin' *which* president. Either you haven't been getting enough sleep, or your roof ain't nailed on tight, ole son."

"Waterman." Del came bolt upright in the chair. "Of course, Waterman. They're planning to kill Samson and put Waterman in the White House!"

"What better way to whip up a public frenzy for war?"

"If you blame it on the Cartel," Del interjected. His mind whirled as he considered the implications. "How the hell did you get this?"

"Remember back in the seventies—nah, you weren't even born then, but you must've read about Watergate and the reporter's source, a fellow they called Deep Throat."

"If you have an insider feeding you information on the conspiracy, why not break it wide open—use the Bureau to investigate—arrest Drescher, Waterman, Sommerville, and Fuller?"

"We didn't have enough hard evidence. Only the tape Fuller made. Can you believe how fucking dumb that was! 'N' ole Brian fancied himself a leader." Putnam scoffed and tossed back another shot. "Damn fool couldn't lead fat people to biscuits.

"I hadn't been able to dig up anything tangible inside the Pentagon—and Wade and I didn't know how deep the conspiracy ran, who all was involved—including people high up in the Bureau. Appointing Drescher as director was a payback to a powerful bunch of fat cats in Congress. Wade couldn't say no, but he'll can the bastard if he finds proof Drescher's dirty. I knew Waterman and Fuller were using BISC. My source was privy to some things, not others."

"Who is this source?"

"Was. Mark Patrikas."

"Samson's brilliant international policy strategist. Always sounding Klaxons about the Cartel." Del nodded. It made sense in a perverse way. "If he was part of it, why'd he turn to you?"

"Boy got caught tryin' to fart higher 'n' his ass. Waterman and Fuller convinced him they had an inside track in the Pentagon—that the Joint Chiefs were behind them 'n' all they needed to do was nudge Samson with a popular uprising in Bogotá led by Rafael Silva. Backed with U.S. military support, of course."

"Yeah, I imagine Patrikas would go for that—but he owed his whole political future to Samson. He wouldn't want to see Waterman succeed to the presidency."

Cal nodded. "You *are* smart enough to see through hog wire after all. Young Patrikas came to me when he found out Waterman and Fuller were planning to assassinate his president. They'd assured him Wade would support a war against the Cartel once the Colombians were in revolt. Damn young fool thought they could manipulate Wade Samson."

"And when Patrikas figured out it would never work . . ." Del put the pieces together.

"Yup. By that time he was in too deep. He wanted to stop the assassination but that meant stopping the whole shooting match." Put-nam struck a match and relit his pipe, then took a deep draw. "He got all feather-legged and started trying to feed me information anony-mously so I'd stop it and he'd keep his skirts clean."

"But you learned his identity."

"For someone that book smart, the boy was so dense light bent around him." Cal shook his head regretfully. "Wade Samson and I used him, milked what we could, but Waterman's slick as snot. Other than stealing that disc, Patrikas couldn't give us much of any-thing on them that'd hold up in court. And we couldn't trust anyone on the inside, especially in BISC. We needed information on the military operation, but Waterman kept Patrikas in the dark about that. I needed a man with connections to the Pentagon—and Mex-ico."

"And I fit the bill perfectly. I assume Waterman found out Patrikas had betrayed him and had a Sanitation Squad arrange his crash."

Putnam's eyebrows raised. "Not many outsiders know about our very own SS. Yep. That's our guess. Wade could see Mark going to pieces. Sure as shit stinks, Waterman could, too. I wanted to bring him in but that would've created more problems than it solved."

"So you fed him to the wolves . . . just like Adam Manchester." Del studied Putnam's face. It revealed nothing.

He scratched another match and relit his pipe, carelessly tossing the wooden match toward an ashtray, then said flatly, "Wade tried to reach Manchester but Patrikas blocked him. By the time Wade found out, it was too late."

Thinking of Leah's desolation, Del exploded, "How many people have to die before you fucking do something!"

Putnam sat forward in his chair and put his pipe in the ashtray. "Look, ole son, the political implications of this are a hell of a lot big-ger than you, me, or any one person—up to and including Wade Samson. We're talking international here.

"We got the Euros on one side and the Pacific Rim on the other, squeezing us like a six-teated bitch with a seven-pup litter. Then throw in the Russian Mafia peddling secondhand nukes just to make things interesting. What do you think the repercussions would be if the fucking upper echelons of the Pentagon, Congress, and the Bureau—not to mention BISC—are exposed as leaders of a coup to take over the White House!

"We have to stop this thing, but you don't try to kill the snakes before you get a hoe in your hand. We need to know who's involved in every branch of the government, then move quick and quiet to squash 'em. Now, you ready to tell me what you got?"

Del leaned back in the big desk chair and rubbed his eyes. Putnam was right about one thing. He was too tired to think straight.

When Delgado hesitated, Putnam played his ace. "Reason you're so pissed you still don't trust me isn't because of Manchester—it's because of Manchester's granddaughter, isn't it?"

Del looked up, startled.

"Who the hell do you think arranged for Agent Berglund to get your case? I kept tabs on Central's investigations ever since I figured out Waterman was using BISC to terminate people who got in his way. When your file popped up, it was a way to cover your back and keep Waterman off mine."

"But I was set up so she'd kill me."

"But she didn't, did she?"

"You knew she'd see through the frame—or at least you hoped she would."

"Best I could do for you, ole son, best I could do . . . Now, I've talked enough to drive a mad dog off a meat wagon. It's your turn."

Del pulled out copies of Leah's pictures of Sommerville and the Mexican president and began.

16.

"The shit's hit the fan, Wade."

Wade Samson somehow managed to look presidential even when awakened at 3 a.m. His silvery hair was slightly mussed and he squinted into the vid screen, but his manner was calm as he replied, "The timing for this scatological explosion couldn't be worse, Cal. I have a nightmare weekend coming up. The Euro premier tomorrow, not to mention all the other heads of state here for the big hoopla on the Fourth. I assume you've heard from Delgado in Mexico."

"He's not in Mexico. Right now he's on his way to Maine."

Samson leaned forward in his chair. "Has he found out something about Manchester?"

"So far, only that the BISC agent I sent to cover him is Manchester's granddaughter." Putnam waited to see if the president would swing at his curveball.

"You never mentioned this granddaughter before." He blinked but said nothing more.

"No reason to until now. Seems as if the wily ole coyote left her some sort of a journal with enough in it to get him killed."

"Should we send backup for Delgado and this woman?"

"They've been able to take care of themselves until now. Best not to start choppin' till we've treed the coon. Let them search for whatever it is Manchester's found while we deal with the evidence in hand."

"What did Delgado find?"

"Our guess about your pissin' buddy Portillo-Ortiz was right on the money. We got him by the short 'n' curlies, right along with

Rafael Silva and ole Nuke 'Em Nate Sommerville. Delgado watched their 'joint liberation force' put on quite a fireworks display."

"In Mexico?"

Putnam nodded. "I've got a disc full of close-ups and the GPS co-ordinates for their site."

"Excellent." Samson smiled now. "A call to my colleague in Mexico City will be on the agenda, but do we know who's involved inside the Pentagon? My instincts tell me to trust the chairman of the Joint Chiefs."

Cal nodded. "I'd call General McKinney, Wade. Once he sees what's on this disc, he'll put Sommerville's nuts in a vise to find out who else is involved."

"Nate always had dreams of glory," Samson said with statesman-like regret.

Putnam muttered an expletive. "Biggedy sucker wouldn't go to a funeral 'less he could be the corpse. This'll make sure he ends up one. Take Colombia's president in exile and his son down a peg, too. That old playboy may be living high on the hog in Hollywood, but you can damn betcha he knows what his son's up to."

"You've learned nothing more about Fuller and Waterman's assassination plans?"

Although the president tried to hide it, Cal could detect a faint strain around his mouth now. "Unfortunately, nothing on the coup, but Fuller's dead as a carp at a fish fry." Putnam explained how Mike Delgado and his mother had been rescued and the congressman and his men dispatched in Oregon.

"This means Waterman's going to be isolated once McKinney brings in Sommerville and I lay down my cards for the Mexican president and the Colombians."

"I think his fangs will be pulled . . . but there is one more thing to consider, Wade."

Something in Putnam's voice tightened Samson's guts. "And that is, Cal?"

"Delgado tells me the Cartel has a mole in Washington. They know about the planned attack and they're ready to retaliate."

"Good God, man, the CIA says they have nuclear weapons! If they even suspect an attack, Zuloaga might just be crazy enough to attempt a preemptive strike."

"If I were you, Wade, I wouldn't wait till sunup to call *el presidente* or the Joint Chiefs."

7:05 A.M., EDT, FRIDAY, JULY 3
THE MAINE COAST

Leah drove east on Highway 1, following its twisting zigzag with practiced ease. No matter how many times she visited the rugged coast of northeastern Maine, she would always be awed by its beauty. Her flight from the West Coast to Bangor had been wearying. After landing, she'd paid cash for a rental car using a phony ID. The clerk behind the Avis counter hadn't spared more than a glance at it or her before turning over the keys to a Hyundai TE. Since her limited cash reserves didn't allow for a flash-drive model, she settled in for a leisurely trip. It was only a bit over 160 kilometers to Machias.

Alone in the car, she had time to think. And to grieve. Here in his home county she felt so close to Adam it was almost impossible to believe he was dead. "We'll get them, Gramps, I promise," she said, swallowing the tears she refused to shed. Leah didn't know just when she'd started thinking of herself and Delgado as "we." It seemed they'd worked together for months, not mere days.

He'd called her link while she was in the airport, not a secure place to talk. Her relief that he was still alive was palpable, but she worried about the reliability of Putnam. She waited desperately to clear the terminal. Once out on the open road, she'd contacted him, eager to learn how the meeting with his old boss had gone. He'd explained everything, then adamantly demanded that she wait for him in Bangor.

She'd refused. The next scheduled flight from D.C. was not until ten-thirty. By then she could drive straight to Machias, talk to Sheriff McLean, and decide on a plan. She gave him the address of the small motel in Machiasport where she'd reserved a room as Lollie Whittaker. When he reached town, they could proceed with the investigation.

But proceed how? Where outside of the sprawling old house could

Adam have hidden the journal? *The usual place.* Obviously it was not a location where books and papers fit. She let her mind drift back to childhood days, lazy summer afternoons on the bay. She and Kevin loved sailing on the *Deborah M,* Adam's small sloop. Under his instruction they'd learned to handle it with considerable expertise. Was the boat still in the marina? Surely BISC had searched it from stem to stern, but it was a place to start.

It isn't the usual place, a voice kept insisting. Besides, since the sloop had a chart desk crammed with maps and navigation books, a journal wouldn't be terribly unusual in that setting, only easy to find. It was like groping through the heavy fog banks sitting off Machias Bay. Swirling. Impenetrable.

Leah rubbed her aching head and concentrated on driving. She had already passed Ellsworth. Nearly 100 kilometers to go.

Sheriff Dan McLean stared at the pile of files strewn helter-skelter across the top of his already cluttered desk. "Thank God it's Friday," he muttered, taking a sip from the mug of ink and spar varnish that Mattie called coffee, trying to remind himself again of why he'd moved to Maine and run for sheriff.

"Peace and fishing, my ass!" The phone was buzzing out at Mattie's desk. For him, no doubt.

"It's Hank Pullium from Cathance Lake Variety. More vandalism last night. He's sure it was the Barlow kids again," Mattie sang out.

He sighed and picked up. After promising yet another drive up to "give Henry Barlow a good talking to about them boys," McLean hung up just as a striking blonde with an unsmiling face strode into Mattie's office. He studied her through the doorway. Her long-limbed, athletic frame had a coiled energy. She was dressed in dark slacks and a striped tank top with flat-heeled shoes. He gauged her height to be almost equal to his own. A formidable woman.

After a brief exchange with Mattie, she turned toward his door. Extending her hand she said, "Good morning, Sheriff McLean. I'm Leah Berglund. We spoke on Monday."

"The senator's granddaughter, yes. My sincere condolences, Ms.

Berglund," he replied, shaking her hand as he ushered her in and pulled up a chair for her. She swallowed and he could sense rather than see that she was fighting back tears.

"You've confirmed his death, then?"

"The DNA report came through yesterday. I'm sorry."

She settled onto the chair, deflated by the loss of that last tiny breath of hope. Then, summoning up purpose, she leaned forward. Her pale blue eyes were intense, focused, and hard. Cop's eyes, he suddenly realized as she asked, "Have you been able to find out anything about how my grandfather died?"

"According to the ME's report, he died of smoke inhalation," he said cautiously.

"Was there any evidence of foul play?"

Her voice was steady and her eyes like lasers. This sure was no magnolia blossom. "I'm afraid there wasn't enough left after the fire to make a determination. The ME ruled accidental."

"What about the fire? Was it an accident, too? Just after a drenching rainstorm?"

"You have a point, but as you know, his place is right isolated. From what the fire marshal could find, it looks as if the propane furnace blew up. It was old and hadn't been inspected for a number of years . . ." His voice trailed off, wanting to see what she'd ask next. He wondered about her reasons for believing her grandfather had been murdered.

"When we spoke Monday, you seemed skeptical about two deaths so close together. Stephan Patrikas died only last week."

"Well, your granddaddy sure believed his friend had been murdered, but he wouldn't say why. Why do you think the senator's death was murder?"

Leah studied the big, lanky lawman. His Southern graciousness masked a shrewd intelligence. She'd seen enough good ole boy acts during her stints in Atlanta and Newport News. She was uncertain whether to trust him. When in doubt, best not to. "I have no evidence that my grandfather was murdered, Sheriff, other than the fact he was—as you said—adamant that Stephan hadn't been sailing while drunk."

"You spoke with him about Patrikas's death?"

She hadn't, in fact. There'd been no time. "Yes. They were old friends. Close friends. I think it's a very strange coincidence that two such hale and hearty men die 'accidentally' in less than a week."

"Point taken, ma'am," he conceded. "I recall you said when we talked that you were a reporter. Would your granddaddy have been helping you with any kind of insider story—background on something political, anything like that?"

A very shrewd good ole boy indeed. "You know more than you're revealing, Sheriff."

"So do you, ma'am. Looks like we've done reached an impasse." He leaned back until his antiquated swivel chair creaked in protest.

"Not if you tell me what's set off your radar first."

He studied her with hooded eyes, then tossed the pencil he'd been fiddling with onto his desk and leaned forward. "Yesterday afternoon an FBI feller came in, said the Bureau was investigating the senator's death." He could sense her subtle stiffening but her expression revealed nothing. "Funny thing was, when I checked his ID, he wasn't FBI. Now what do you make of that, ma'am?"

"He was probably BISC." Leah made a gut-level judgment, just as McLean had probably done. Neither one of them would share everything, but limited cooperation might prove useful . . . very useful. She and Delgado would need all the help they could get since BISC was lying in wait for them.

Delgado's flight into Bangor arrived early. He picked up a rental car and met with his FBI contact to pick up the weapons Cal had authorized. He made it to the motel in Machias just after noon. Leah was talking on her link when she opened the door for him. She waved him into a creaky chair flanking a small table veneered with plasti-oak.

"Classy digs," he murmured, looking around the dingy room. The only thing to recommend it was the single large bed against the back wall.

Her eyes followed his as she hung up from the call. "Don't go getting any ideas, Delgado. We don't have time."

"What ideas?" He shrugged innocently and grinned at her. "You've got a dirty mind, Agent Berglund."

"This was the only room they had left—they told me it had two beds when I—" She stopped in midsentence with an oath. "Why the hell am I justifying anything to you, dammit!"

"To borrow a phrase from Cal, you're strung tight as hog wire," he said, rubbing her arms in what he hoped she'd construe as a brotherly fashion. She didn't pull away. "I assume you verified that it was your grandfather who died in the fire."

Leah nodded, unable to speak for a moment. "Just got off the phone with the ME. He insisted he has to talk to me in person. I told him I'd get back to him. I think the guy's a flake. Sounded weird. Now, I want to know what went down between you and Putnam."

Del released her and started pacing as he explained what had transpired at Putnam's place the preceding night. She interrupted now and again with questions.

"He handpicked me to investigate you?" Leah didn't know whether to be flattered or chagrined. She knew damn well she was pissed off. "He used me—gambled with me—with your goddamned life! What if I hadn't made that call to Atlanta?" She felt the sickening burn of bile rise in her throat. "I almost didn't . . . what if—"

"But you did. And he was right to trust you. Any other agent Fuller and Waterman sent would've killed me. Better you than them, Leah." He willed her to look at him, knowing instinctively that it would be unwise to touch her just now.

At length, she sighed and capitulated grudgingly. "Now that it's over and I didn't fall for their setup . . . there's no use second-guessing anything."

After he told her the rest of what he'd learned from Cal, she asked, "Do you think he's told you everything?"

"Hell, no. You were a spook. You know the drill. But I do think he's on the level. He wants to stop Waterman and put an end to BISC." By this time they'd both taken seats at the wobbly table and were sipping from styro cups of incredibly bad coffee.

"So Wade Samson's been aware of the conspiracy from the get-go. Do you trust him?"

"That's a more difficult call," Del replied cautiously. "As the driving force behind the Martial Law Act, he has to bear a lot of responsibility for the inevitable abuse of power. But Putnam trusts him and I trust Putnam. Hell, if he was part of Waterman's scheme, he'd have had Cal eliminated the first time he called the White House. Don't forget, Samson's the one Fuller and Waterman plan to assassinate, according to Mark Patrikas."

"That makes sense," Leah said, "but something about it still doesn't feel right."

"Hell, nothing about this feels right. I only wish we had a line on when or how they plan to assassinate Samson. Have you been able to dredge up any more ideas about where your grandfather may have put that journal?"

"I searched the *Deborah M,* Gramps's sloop. Nothing. No surprise."

"Yeah, as sharp as the senator was, he'd expect BISC to look there."

"I did have a useful talk with the local constabulary. I think we can trust McLean."

"McLean's the sheriff?"

"Yeah. A Carolina transplant and one smart son of a bitch. I would've driven out to Gramps's place and looked around if he hadn't told me what happened yesterday."

After she explained about the BISC agent's visit to McLean, the coffee in Delgado's gut rumbled ominously. "You say he's surveilled the guy impersonating Agent Walters?"

"We're pretty sure he's BISC Sanitation. He's staying at the only other motel in town. Doesn't want to miss anything. I'm sure he made me the minute I walked in the courthouse. He was just waiting for you to get here. Now he'll try to take us both out together."

"Probably. The key is, who else is in his squad? There were four sons of bitches in Alabama for one man. And remember the small army in Oregon when they were waiting for the two of us."

"They expected us both to show up here." She no longer considered proceeding without Delgado. After this was over—if they survived—she'd think about the implications of that disturbing fact.

"I'd guess at least a half dozen BISC goons. Waterman's got to be running scared by now. How much help do you think this sheriff can give us?"

"Hard to say. He's no hick, although he likes to play it that way. Apparently Walters, whoever he was, bought into the act. That may help us out. McLean's got a plainclothes deputy watching the entrance to Gramps's property. I warned him about how a Sanitation Squad works. He says the deputy has good cover—running a tractor in a field across the road."

"Let's put our heads in the lion's mouth and case the arson scene."

"First let me make a call to McLean."

2 P.M., EDT, FRIDAY, JULY 3
WASHINGTON, D.C.

"We are in a world of hurt, Cal." President Samson's expression was grim as he ushered Putnam into the office in his private quarters on the second floor of the White House. The ADIC had been brought with the highest secrecy with no prior notification. Putnam didn't like it.

"Your talk with President Portillo-Ortiz go okay?" Samson paced, combing his fingers through his hair until the silvery strands stood up at spiky angles. Not the slick image the president normally projected. Putnam didn't like this one little bit, no siree.

Samson dismissed the question with a flick of his hand. "Yes. My compadre in Mexico City practically shit himself backing down when I explained that both the Cartel and I were aware of his involvement in a plot to attack Colombia. But old Alejandro Silva's gone to ground, and his son and their little cadre of 'liberators' are sticking with Sommerville and his American contingent."

"Sommerville and young Silva may be crazy, but they can't do squat without Mexican support."

"They still have some Mexican support. They went aboard the Mexican ocean transport Portillo-Ortiz had thoughtfully provided for them at Guaymas. Near as we can figure, they sailed sometime late Wednesday—one LPH, an amphibious assault vessel, plus five

LSDs providing cargo room and loading docks for all that hardware they've slipped through Adair. The whole damned flotilla is presently nearing the Gulf of Chiriquí, ready to make a run straight for the Colombian coast."

"Closest I ever came to a ship was a tug ride round the Statue of Liberty, but I didn't think those big ole transports could move that fast. How the hell did Sommerville get down there so quick?"

"According to the chief of naval operations, those old babies have retrofitted turbine engines and can do twenty-eight knots if they push it." At Cal's still baffled expression at the naval terminology, Samson just said, "Bottom line, before sunup Sunday they can be landed and rolling into the Colombian interior."

"Only if we don't send some F-22s and blow them the hell out of the water."

Samson resumed pacing and digging at his scalp again. "That's a dicey option, Cal. When I shared Delgado's information about the black op with the Joint Chiefs, McKinney went fucking nuts about that mysterious shipment from Little Lennie . . ." Samson turned and faced Putnam. "The Cartel isn't the only player with nuclear weapons. The Fort Leonard Wood Annex, it seems, stores some pretty fancy tactical nukes, a fact the Chiefs had neglected to share with me. And those Sikorsky Dragonflies Bedford couldn't figure into the equation—they can deliver payloads big enough to knock chunks off the Andes! Everything Bedford dug out for Delgado fits."

Now even Putnam blanched. "We're trying to knock down a hornets' nest with a short stick here, Wade." He cursed creatively as he fumbled with his pipe, finally getting it lighted as his thoughts spun.

"I have intermediaries making attempts to talk with Zuloaga's people, but it'll be touch and go if we can't stop that damned flotilla from reaching the Colombian coast."

"Looks as if ole Nate's fixing to have himself a real Mexican stand-off. Given his past history, you can damn betcha he'd press the button."

"That's the best guess of the Joint Chiefs. McKinney and Kensington both wanted him quietly cashiered after Iraq . . . but I thought it was expedient to keep him since he was a war hero."

Not dismissing Sommerville had been a political calculation that had now backfired catastrophically on the president, but Putnam let it pass. "The general's counting on Waterman to clear a path for him. The players are all in motion because the assassination is scheduled sometime soon. You oughta stay under wraps."

Samson's face was the color of bleached putty now and no amount of makeup could disguise the bags and grooves marring its surface. "The Fourth will be the first speech by a sitting president in our nation's capital since the Slaughter. I'm booked solid the entire weekend, starting tomorrow through Sunday night. Do you have any idea of the international repercussions if I suddenly canceled everything?"

"How about a sudden case of 'pendicitis?"

"No. The safest thing I can do is to stick like glue to Harmon Waterman. He's not supposed to be with me for the kickoff speech at the Washington Monument, but I'll insist he alter his schedule."

"I'll have a couple of my best agents strap the fucker to your back if need be. You can damn betcha the cowardly little shit won't want to be near the line of fire," Cal said grimly.

"We'll double security and pray Zuloaga can be assured of our good faith because we've gotten the Mexican government to withdraw from the invasion."

Putnam, who'd been without sleep for three nights running, had taken a seat on a Chippendale sofa while his chief continued to pace. He fiddled with his pipe, relighting it and taking a deep draw. The kick of tobacco allowed him to think clearer. "You know, Wade, I find it hard to swallow that a self-serving son of a bitch like Alejandro Silva would go along with a bunch of gringos turning his country into a nuclear junkyard. No matter how much he wants to destroy the Cartel, he needs somethin' left that doesn't glow in the dark when Colombia's 'liberated.'"

"The Joint Chiefs speculated about whether or not President Silva and his son are aware of the extent to which Waterman and Sommerville are willing to go," Samson replied consideringly. "The consensus was that they weren't. The Mexicans sure as hell weren't either." He stopped to look at Putnam, liking the direction in which the crafty old man was heading.

"Let me put my best men to lookin' for ole Silva. Knowin' him, I'd bet a Lincoln TE with flash drive to a Ford EV that we'll find him quicker 'n' a fox can get inside a henhouse. Then we reunite him with his soldier son aboard Sommerville's little armada. Once they know the plan, I'd just bet they'll pry ole Nate's finger off the button."

"The Mexican government has more than a passing interest in helping us since ground zero is right off their coastline. I'll place a call to Portillo-Ortiz right now. You just get me Silva's ass."

Putnam nodded, thinking. "We'll need some special help to slip the old man aboard whichever of those ships holds Sommerville and his nukes. Let me make a few phone calls . . ."

2 P.M., EDT, FRIDAY, JULY 3
WASHINGTON COUNTY, MAINE

"Great country if you're a mountain sheep or a Pilgrim," Del said, eyeing the jagged hunks of granite strewn along the bay coastline. "Picturesque, but I'd hate to spend a winter here."

"It takes hearty stock to survive a Maine winter. Your blood's too thin, Delgado."

"Only because of all that Latino heat." He flashed her a glance and winked before returning his attention to the rear vid. "Still no tail. They're laying for us. You sure the cavalry will ride in when we call McLean?"

"He has a copter waiting across the bay. Only five minutes away. What choice do we have either way?"

" 'All in the valley of death rode the six hundred' . . . Shit! I'd bet we're outnumbered worse."

Silas Elworth had been the medical examiner for Washington County for nearly thirty years, and this was the goddamnedest mess he'd ever been in. He sat at the PDA in his office and tried the link again.

"Damn fool said he'd stay close. Where the hell is he?" the old man muttered, shoving a wisp of salt-and-pepper hair out of his eyes. He combed it across the ever widening expanse of his scalp for protection from the sun. Silas knew folks laughed about the affectation, but to hell with them. It was his goddamned scalp.

Just as he was about to break the link connection, a voice answered. "Yes, it's Silas. Who the hell else you think it'd be?" he replied sourly. "Yes . . . we're encrypted. Of course. . . . She arrived first thing this morning. I *tried* to get her to come straight over but she put me off. Said she'd be here tonight. . . . You're probably right. She's headed your way. I know it's dangerous. . . . Okay, I'll call him. That's what you should've done in the first place! Now what—"

The ME was talking into a dead link. He cursed and reconnected, then placed another call.

When Del and Leah pulled up the narrow, winding driveway, stands of jack pine and rosebay in full bloom brushed against the sides of the car. They'd seen the deputy churning up a good crop of rocks and dust at the entrance to Manchester's property, but the isolation of the place filled Del's gut with distinct unease.

They crested a rise a few hundred meters up, and the blackened ruins of what had once been a sprawling log house lay directly in front of them. Leah had seen the newscasts, but a video did nothing to prepare her for the wrenching gut kick she felt at the sight of charred timbers and bare piles of scorched stones. She sucked in a breath, then swore, gripping the wheel with white knuckles as she pulled up in front and killed the engine.

Delgado looked at her but she quickly shook her head. "I'm okay."

They got out of the car and walked the perimeter of the house. There weren't two stones left standing together. The lovely old home must have gone up like a volcanic eruption. She walked over to where the propane storage units had been.

"Outdoors. Easy to tamper with," Del murmured.

She nodded. "He never had a chance. I wonder what happened to Hezekiah?" At his puzzled look, she explained, "He was a sort of handyman, jack-of-all-trades around the place, when he wasn't off on a bender. According to Gramps, that was more often than not in the last few years. He drifts in and out like the tide, but not nearly so regular."

"Anyone question him since the fire? He might have seen something."

"According to McLean, he hasn't turned up yet." She stood surveying the surrounding land, heavily forested to the east, open meadowlands sloping upward toward the bluffs overlooking the bay.

"Any ideas about 'the usual place' coming to you?"

"I've played and replayed childhood memories . . . they're tricky, especially after . . . after losing Gramps."

"I know. I lost a whole year after my father was killed. I was nine. After that, Uncle Mac became surrogate father as well as grandfather."

"Gramps had to do that, too—when his son, my uncle Rafe, was killed. I was only ten myself . . . Rafe's son, Paul, was a couple years older. I was horribly jealous of him until Gramps explained that he'd lost his father and I needed to—" She stopped abruptly as thoughts began to tumble in place. "I think I know where the usual place is!"

He scanned their surroundings and felt the Smith & Wesson hidden beneath the light jacket he wore as protection from the brisk bay wind. They were both packing weapons, again courtesy of arrangements made by Cal. "Where is it?" he asked.

"The cave—a wind-hollowed-out hole in the cliffs overlooking the bay. I was focusing so much on Gramps that I forgot about my cousin Paul. He's an engineer now working for some big Pacific Rim multinational in Hong Kong. He spent the summer after his father's death up here with us. We found the cave even though Gramps had forbidden us to climb up on those cliffs by ourselves."

"Dangerous?"

"Very. But you know kids," she said, heading toward the meadow.

Del followed, watching for any signs of BISC agents as she explained.

"We sneaked out all sorts of camping gear—food, blankets, flashlights, even matches. Made a regular hideaway. We'd send each other notes saying 'meet me at the usual place.' Then we'd slip out at night climbing down the trellis at the hall window after everyone else was asleep. Sometimes we'd build a fire and roast marshmallows.

"Then one night Gramps found one of the notes in my empty

room and followed us. Boy, did we both get a tongue-lashing! The grand old man could really be fierce. Just like an Old Testament prophet."

"No more climbing down the side of a cliff over the water, I take it."

She nodded. "I can't believe I forgot . . . but that winter Kev was born and then Paul's mother remarried and they moved to Seattle. Anyway, I think I blocked it because it's the only time I can remember that Gramps was really angry with me."

"Let's not go directly to the cave," he said, meandering over toward a stand of tamarack.

"You're right. We're probably being surveilled."

They meandered around the rocky outcrop and the cluster of trees surrounding it. Generations ago some hardy, or perhaps foolhardy, farmer had struggled to eke out a crop from the thin, stony soil. Now all that remained of his labor were fields hewn clear of trees except those protected by the boulders.

Once inside the concealment, Del pulled out a monocular and swept their surroundings. "No way to slip up on us."

"But we've got to get from here to the edge of the cliffs." She pointed to a slight rise a good sixty meters away.

"When we reach the edge, how fast can we get down the side and disappear in this cave?"

"It's not a hard climb as I recall, but only if I can find the exact spot where we used to go over. It's been more than twenty years. Hell, Delgado, wind erosion may have changed it so much we can't even use the pathway."

"Would Adam have found it if you couldn't?"

"You have a point. Let's just wander along the edge as if we're still deciding what to do."

They left the cover of the trees and headed in the general direction of the water, then skirted along the jagged, rocky ledge overlooking the bay below, much too far below for Delgado's peace of mind. The sun had dipped behind a bank of billowing gray clouds and the temperature must've dropped ten degrees since they'd left Machias. He felt the sweat on his neck and under his armpits in spite of the chilly wind.

"How much farther?" he asked Leah as she stepped to the edge of the drop-off.

She turned to him and noticed the sheen of perspiration, the pallor on his face. Then she remembered that day with Mike at the zoo. "Shit, I forgot you're afraid of heights."

"I'll get over it, or my pants are going to be a mess," he said through clenched teeth. "That link of yours had better be working. Once we're down, we'll be trapped there by the BISC goons."

"Now's the time to find out." She grabbed his hand and put one foot over the edge of the cliff.

He muttered one of Aunt Seri's prayers that he never even knew he remembered and followed her.

17.

Del did not dare look down even though he could hear the angry roar of the ocean below. It seemed louder since he'd climbed over the edge of the cliff. The path was no more than a narrow zigzag down the steep slope. A few scraggly pines braved the salt air and harsh winds, allowing for an occasional handhold, but mostly they had to rely on shuffling sideways along the narrow ledge and scrambling over outcroppings of granite.

"Damn, this better be worth it," he muttered when his knee hitched painfully.

"Just a few meters more," Leah said.

"You're not even breathing hard or sweating. I could hate you for that," he grunted as he scanned the top of the cliff. "So far, no one peering over the abyss. We'd be sitting ducks if they opened up right now."

"Inside quick," she hissed from an opening obscured by overhanging rocks and reed grass.

Del followed her into the cave, which extended a good dozen meters in depth. He blinked at the darkness before she flicked on a small electric torch. The remains of long-ago campfires blackened the floor. That was the only sign of human habitation. He leaned against the cold stone wall and massaged his knee as she began searching the rear of the cave.

"There any back door to this joint?"

"Nope." Her whispered voice echoed. "Watch the front for visitors while I look."

He drew the Smith & Wesson from its shoulder harness and stood guard at the concealed opening. If those SS bastards climbed down after them, they'd be the ones who were sitting ducks now. Of course if they took the smart way and went around the end of the small inlet, they could come back along the water's edge with plenty of cover, searching the face of the cliff above for the hiding place of their quarry. "Anything?" he whispered into the darkness.

Leah knelt and lay down the torch beside the sealed package, her heart pounding louder than the ocean. "Bingo," she breathed, then began to tear open the plastic protecting the heavy volume from salt air. At once she recognized Adam Manchester's bold, slashing penmanship and blinked back tears. The normally flowing script was jagged, as if he had been writing in a great hurry, under extreme duress.

She quickly scanned the pages, gasping at what they revealed. Del kept watch at the opening of the cave. "What's in it?"

"It's worse than we thought . . . much worse. Sommerville has tactical nuclear weapons with him. The strike force intends to take out Cali and Medellín completely and besiege Bogotá so they can hold it until Congress officially votes a declaration of war."

"Let me guess—that'll be after Samson is assassinated and Waterman's in the catbird seat," Del said.

"Stephan Patrikas's death wasn't an accident. Mark was beside himself when he found out Waterman intended to kill Wade Samson. He confessed everything he knew to his father."

"It was probably old Stephan who convinced him to contact Cal."

"Stephan was afraid for his son. He asked Gramps to help . . . just before he died. Gramps knew he didn't sail drunk . . ." She continued reading. "We've got to contact Washington, Del! Now!"

"What is it?" Her voice had a hysterical edge, not like Leah at all.

"Gramps's last entry before he tried to escape and do it himself. He found out more about the assassination. It'll be at the Washington Monument!"

"Samson's scheduled to speak there on the Fourth! No president's gone public in D.C. since the Slaughter." News reports had made a big deal of it for weeks.

"Gramps doesn't have any details—just a reference Mark heard about 'extra' fireworks on the Fourth, which led him to believe it would be a bomb of some sort—possibly a suicide mission if they use Silva's Colombians disguised as Cartel."

"Yeah. In their own minds they'd be martyrs for Colombian liberation. Silva wouldn't have a hard time finding volunteers. After Samson's killed by supposed Cartel crazies, President Waterman can crack the whip of public outrage, force Congress into declaring war. With Sommerville and Zuloaga packing atomic arsenals, we'll have a nuclear holocaust in the Western Hemisphere. Not even old man Silva would want that. They must have convinced him we'll liberate his country with conventional warfare."

"Silva's not important now, Del! President Samson is. Putnam has to convince him of the danger." Leah closed the journal and tucked it into her jacket, then stood up. When she turned to him, he raised his hand for silence, his body tense as a coiled spring. Then she could hear it, the stealthy, scuffling sounds of footsteps.

"Make that call," he whispered, but he could already hear her pressing in the number, waiting a beat, then speaking hurriedly in a low voice.

The sounds stopped suddenly. Well, they weren't as smart as he thought. They should have come up from the beach. Del crouched in the opening, using a large rock for cover as he watched the pathway from above. A shot zinged out and he felt a sharp pull on his jacket sleeve. He rolled back into the cave, cursing.

A long rip crossed the sleeve of the Windbreaker, its blackened edge torn by a bullet. The slug had come from the beach. They were attacking from both directions! He tried to peek over the edge to the water below. Another shot pinged above his head. "They're lousy shots."

"BISC agents are never lousy shots. They're just trying to drive us deeper into the cave."

"It's working," he muttered as another shot sheared off the wall, raining splinters of granite on their hair and clothing.

"If we're pinned in here, whoever is above us can toss in a canister of gas."

Cuff had told Del horror stories about the high-tech gases the military used—crap that could induce everything from nerve paralysis to instantaneous death. He didn't like any of the possibilities. "Those sons of bitches come prepared for every contingency, don't they?"

"It's useful when you trap an El-Op in a building."

"I'll bet," he replied. "How long till the cavalry comes?"

"Five minutes—or less, if that deputy on the tractor is still alive and able to reach us." Leah cursed. In five minutes they would be unconscious, paralyzed . . . or dead.

A sharp clink of metal hitting rock sounded at Del's feet—a canister. He reached down to pick it up and throw it out, but Leah knocked him away. "Don't touch it!" she hissed, using her foot to kick the metallic sphere neatly over the lip of the cave. A faint trail of grayish smoke followed it, dissolving in the brisk wind that whipped it out to sea.

"If you touch a 'smoker' with your bare hand, your skin will absorb the agent. Thank God the wind's in our favor . . . for the moment. It shifts quickly," she added.

"We've got to get the hell out of—" He heard the rap of another canister landing, farther inside this time. Leah intercepted it with the side of her boot and smashed it back outside.

"You ever consider pro soccer?" he asked between coughs.

Leah hissed, "Don't talk, don't breathe until the wind dissipates that stuff. It's synapse-spasm gas. If it was one of the more lethal agents, we'd be meat by now."

He tried to spot the thrower's position. "I make him down between those two rocks." Was it his imagination or did his tongue feel thick, his arm numb as he pointed?

She nodded. "We gotta move fast. Wind's shifting. Cover me." With that she jumped out of the cave and rolled toward the sharp edge of rock just below. A shot whistled down from the path above them. Del swung around and caught the shooter's face in his sights, exposing himself to the men below when he fired. Bull's-eye.

But another burst of fire sprayed the mouth of the cave. He dived back in as Leah returned the fire from her position. The pitching ace on the beach below warmed up with another canister, but an instant before he could lob it, the sharp crack of a rifle crumpled him. The gas was released from the canister when he fell.

Two figures dived away from the circle of gray fog spiraling in the wind. Leah took one out. Their mysterious ally hit the other. Del took advantage of the distraction to bound out of the cave and over to her cover.

"Any idea who our pal is?" he asked, ducking behind the rock as the person above nipped off several rounds at their attackers below.

"Too soon for McLean. Probably his tractor jockey. How many left?" She wasted no time on speculation, just glad of the help.

"None left above, I'd guess. I nailed one up there and now our sharpshooting Samaritan is above us, so that must be clear." Another burst of fire sent them both crouching lower in the rocks. This time the attack came from an outcrop about ninety to one hundred meters to their left, slightly higher on the steep slope than the boulder they were hiding behind. "Shit, we're still in a cross fire."

"Yeah, well, you don't live in one very long," she said, blinking away the minute fragments of rock stinging her eyes. "If we can make it to the beach, there's more cover and we can fan out."

He eyed the steep incline of jagged rock and knew there was no way in hell he could scramble down to sea level. "I'll cover you."

"I'm not leaving—"

"Go, goddammit!" He ducked as another burst of fire from below pinned them.

As soon as it was over, he shoved her out, then kept his eyes glued to the shooter's position on his left, praying their friend with the rifle was still in the game. He was. When the barrel of a Colt 9mm machine gun appeared over the edge of the rocks, Del trained his weapon on it, waiting for the human target to appear. Their ally didn't have to wait. From his angle at the top of the cliff he had a clear shot and took it. The Colt clattered down the rocks.

Leah reached the scrub brush and rocks at beach's edge just as the distant whir of a chopper carried across the bay. With any luck there was only one SS left uninjured.

She spotted a blur of movement between two boulders about forty meters away and sighted in on his hiding place.

"Come to mama, you mother," she murmured, trying to focus in spite of the stinging pain in her eyes. A head appeared at one side of the rock barely discernible through the cover of a small chokecherry.

She took aim and squeezed. The Ruger's sharp echo covered the crunch of metal smashing into bone and soft brain tissue. "And then there were none," she murmured to herself as the chopper came sweeping across the bay, hovering just above the edge of the shore.

Dan McLean and a deputy jumped down, and McLean signaled the pilot to land. The SS guns were silent. Cautiously Leah and Delgado both stood up as the deputy, a tall, gangly man of middle years, said, "Looks like a Balkan combat zone."

Two bodies lay half-submerged in the icy, lapping water of the bay. Another was crumpled behind the rock twenty meters or so away. The one Leah had just killed hung over a chokecherry bush like a rag doll with its stuffing ripped out. She watched Del climb painfully to where the shooter above them had been hidden. He signaled all clear, then began a painfully cautious climb down to the waterline.

"Looks as if you folks are the Injuns and these fellers are the Seventh Cavalry," McLean said.

"We had some help." Del grunted, still breathing hard from the exertion of getting down the cliff. Solid, flat ground had never felt so good.

As he gave the sheriff and his deputy a brief rundown on what had happened, Leah stood clutching the journal tightly to her chest, staring intently at the tall figure walking slowly down the beach toward them. He carried an old .270 Winchester bolt-action deer rifle mounted with scope.

The three men stopped talking as soon as they noticed his approach. Everyone was stunned. Their "sharpshooting Samaritan" was Adam Manchester.

2:30 P.M., EDT, FRIDAY, JULY 3
RESTON, VIRGINIA

"We should have eliminated Putnam. I told you that weeks ago," the director of the FBI said. He was a big man, gone to fat but tall enough to conceal the worst of it. He wore an expensive hairpiece and the unctuous smile of a career politician.

Harmon Waterman sat behind his desk in the BISC command center, a dozen other considerations turning in his mind as he pretended to pay attention to Martin Drescher. The man had been useful, even though he was venial and stupid. Especially because he was venial and stupid. "Now, Marty, think this through. I have an SS team in Maine to take out Delgado and Berglund. Without them, Putnam's got nothing."

"What about Manchester! Your Sanitation Squads haven't been able to dispose of one seventy-five-year-old man alone in the wilderness, for chrissake!"

"We plugged the leaks on this end," Waterman snapped. "The objective is to make certain that Manchester can't get to Putnam. And if Delgado and Berglund escape my team in Maine, they'll just head straight here looking for Putnam. We can eliminate them before they reach him. With less than twenty hours to go, no one can stop us."

"I still don't see why you don't kill Putnam now."

A dull red color stained Waterman's face. Putnam had been enough of a plague without having an officious bureaucrat like Drescher hound him about the difficulties. "In case you haven't been paying attention, Putnam is the key to this whole fucking mess! If we had him killed, Samson would go underground and Delgado and Berglund would go to the newspapers with everything they have!"

"But if they do reach Putnam, he'll stop Samson from speaking tomorrow." Drescher, too, was getting irate, his oily veneer peeled back a fraction.

"Then we see to it Cal's inaccessible by link. Why do you think I had you break procedure and come to Central, Marty? It's time for you to flex your muscles as director of the FBI." Waterman savored Drescher's jacklighted expression. *Like a rat caught crawling out of a garbage can.* "You're Putnam's boss. For national security reasons, his link will be monitored . . . by you."

Waterman produced a court order from the top drawer of his desk and handed it to Drescher, who was sweating beneath his toupee now. *The cowardly son of a bitch's finally going to earn his keep,* the vice president thought with nasty relish.

The director's eyes, slightly protuberant anyway, nearly popped from his head when he looked at the document. It was signed by

Cleve Mallory, the federal judge who had just been nominated to fill a vacancy on the Supreme Court.

"You screen all Putnam's calls—personally. Don't trust anyone else to do it for you. If Delgado tries to contact him, he's unavailable. Same thing if Putnam tries to reach Delgado. All we have to do is keep Samson and Putnam isolated until tomorrow. Got that?"

Drescher nodded, trying to keep his hands from trembling, failing miserably.

"By the time Putnam realizes what's going on, it'll be too late. Samson will be dead, the Cartel under siege, and I'll be sworn in as president of the United States."

The FBI director clutched the court order so tightly it crumpled in his fist as he said, "I'll have this implemented immediately . . . Mr. President."

12:30 P.M., MDT, FRIDAY, JULY 3
MAZATLÁN, MEXICO

"Yes, Mr. President, a million thanks for all that you have done to make our attempt possible. . . . Let us all pray for success. The alternative is unthinkable. . . . Yes, long live Mexico." Francisco Mulcahey disconnected the link and turned to his grandson, who had just entered the office.

"I take it that was our illustrious head of state," Raoul said drily.

"Yes, Colonel Mulcahey, it was." The old man waited a moment for the words to sink in, then watched the sudden blaze of joy in Raoul's eyes.

"A promotion above and beyond reinstatement. Grandfather, you are truly an amazing man. How the hell did you get General Rojas to admit he was wrong about me?"

"His commander in chief called him and told him he must 'correct the gross clerical error' which had led to the unwarranted charges against you. That was immediately after President Portillo-Ortiz received a call from President Samson strongly suggesting that your Special Forces unit would handle this mission better than anyone else—but only if you were once more in command."

"And all of this because of the conversation you had with Tiger's old boss at the FBI. Incredible!" Raoul felt suddenly euphoric. The cloud that had hung over him, besmirching his family honor for the past two years, had at last been lifted, wiped away by presidential fiat. Colonel Raoul Francisco Mariano Mulcahey was back in the army!

His expression turned serious. "Ernesto and Joaquin are en route to Culiacán. When I explained to Inocensio what we would need, he never questioned anything, even offered me several of his best men as guides around the Gulf."

"Take them," Raoul's grandfather said without hesitation. "You'll be on their ships in waters they are most familiar with."

Raoul grinned. "I already told him we would. Did the president indicate how soon the men I requested will reach Culiacán?"

"You're men are airborne now. By the time you reach there they'll be landing."

"Then all we must do is wait until the Americans send Alejandro Silva."

"Mr. Putnam indicated his agents have located him in California. I imagine they will brief him, then fly him directly to Culiacán. It should not be long."

Francisco stood up and embraced his grandson. "Go with God. Your grandmother prays for you."

"Then we are assured of success." Raoul left his grandfather with a familiar swagger back in his step.

The old man smiled.

3 P.M., EDT, FRIDAY, JULY 3
WASHINGTON COUNTY, MAINE

The journal tumbled from Leah's numb fingers and fell to the rock-strewn sand as she sprinted toward her grandfather. She could see now that he was limping and extremely pale. "G-Gramps . . . it is really you," she said, reaching out to him as he laid down his rifle and took her in his arms.

"Leah-Pia. I knew you'd do something foolhardy and dangerous, not listen to Silas."

"Doc Elworth? But what . . . who . . . ?" She couldn't think or speak at that moment.

He held her and soothed her by gently running his hand over her hair. "Silas reached me by link when you didn't go straight to his office as I wanted you to."

"For a feller supposedly incinerated, you don't look too bad, Senator," Dan McLean said drily as he strolled up. "Silas finesse that DNA test?"

The old man nodded. "It was Hezekiah Carroll who died when BISC burned my house. He was sleeping off a drunk in the den. He did that sometimes."

Leah held on to her grandfather, still not quite certain this wasn't a dream. "I was so sure you were dead."

"I wanted to contact you more than anything, Leah, but I was trapped in the woods with those BISC agents after me. I'd taken to carrying that"—he motioned to the rifle lying at his feet—"and an ammunition belt everywhere I went since this mess started. I kept them occupied with false trails. I know these woods. They didn't, and they weren't well trained or equipped for tracking. That bought me some time, but I had no way to reach you. When I finally led them far enough away from Machias, I headed back, straight to Silas."

Manchester looked uneasily at McLean, who said nothing. "I should've come to you, Sheriff, but given the scope of this, the high-ranking members of government involved, I made what I thought was the best choice. It was a mistake," the old man conceded.

The sheriff nodded. "I already figured you were holding back at Stephan Patrikas's autopsy. How'd you get away from these guys in the first place? I thought they were sure you were dead, but it was just the opposite. They knew you *weren't* dead." McLean nudged the body of the one who had posed as an FBI agent.

"I was watching when my house blew. Saw two of them tampering with the propane tank, but something must've gone wrong. It went off with Hezekiah inside before I could do more than nail one of them."

McLean nodded, remembering local stories about the old senator's marksmanship and distinguished military record during the Vietnam War. "Then they lit out after you."

"You eluded a BISC SS team for four days," Leah said incredulously.

"I may be old but I'm not totally feeble, Leah," the senator replied testily.

Delgado coughed to suppress a chuckle.

"There were only three of them sent to take care of me, but after I killed one, they called in reinforcements. When I reached Silas, he tried to throw them off the trail with the false DNA report. If they believed I was dead and the rifleman was someone else, I hoped it would put them off your trail, Leah. Other than falsifying the DNA evidence, I kept Silas in the dark. By then Waterman had put even more agents in the field, watching everywhere in Machias. I couldn't raise anyone I trusted in Washington. You were the only hope I had, so I tried to clear the field here by leading them away. It didn't work . . . although there were three less BISC agents in Maine before you arrived."

"I wanted to come here directly when I received your note, Gramps, but Delgado convinced me that we'd work better as a team. I was in Mexico with him." When Manchester's hard gaze fastened on the reporter, she said, "I think we'd better pool what we've learned, then devise a safe way to get all this information to Wade Samson."

"I take it the president and BISC are in a pissin' contest," McLean drawled.

"Harmon Waterman plans to have Samson assassinated tomorrow at the Fourth of July celebration at the Washington Monument," Manchester replied grimly.

"It isn't going to be easy getting to Samson with Waterman's people circling the White House like vultures," Leah said, looking at Del.

"Cal Putnam will get through to him. I can access his encrypted link."

"It's no use. He's not responding." Del cut the link and stared around McLean's cluttered office. They'd been trying to reach the ADIC for over an hour without success. It was as if Cal Putnam had dropped off the edge of the earth.

"What do you think's happened to him?" Leah asked. "He knew where we went—that we might find vital information up here."

"Could Waterman be monitoring Putnam's private link?" McLean asked.

Del rubbed his eyes, reddened and bleary from lack of sleep. "I don't see how. Cal has his own special security team inside the Bureau . . . unless—"

"Drescher's the director, the only one who could override him," Leah cut in. "You said Cal didn't trust Drescher. If he's part of this, he might be able to keep us from getting through, at least for the short term."

Del nodded. "We always wondered if Drescher was the mole inside the Bureau. It would explain a lot of things, starting back with Nuñez's and Crosby's deaths. No telling how many other agents he's suborned or fooled into believing I'm the enemy."

"Yeah, and you're in bed with BISC." The minute Leah said it, she regretted the unfortunate metaphor. McLean didn't notice but Delgado did. A faint grin etched his beard-stubbled face in spite of everything.

The three of them were cloistered in the sheriff's office. McLean's deputy had escorted a badly weakened and exhausted Adam Manchester to Silas Elworth's house under protest. The elderly senator needed medical treatment and rest.

"What do we do now?" McLean asked.

"Assuming Cal's still in the picture, we get to him in person—if we can't, then we go for Samson."

The sheriff looked at Delgado. "Easy as all that, huh?"

"We've made it this far." Leah checked her watch. "We have less than twenty hours to stop Waterman. The clock is ticking, gentlemen."

"That chopper of yours available, Sheriff?" Del asked.

"The voters of Washington County may take a dim view of risking their expensive equipment, but I reckon I'll risk my reelection for national security. If Waterman and his pals get their way, the copter could end up requisitioned for fighting in Bogotá. I imagine the taxpayers of Washington County would cotton to that a lot less. Besides, my department owes those BISC bastards for blastin' Bucky White off that tractor at Manchester's. I'll have Kerry gas 'er up and meet you at the helipad in Machiasport."

"How the hell are we going to keep BISC from shooting us out of the sky before we get there?" Leah asked. "If they make us on Globe Net, BISC will take us like a duck flying over a hunter's blind."

McLean winced, envisioning pieces of his new helicopter bobbing on the Atlantic like mallard feathers.

"All we can do is try to sneak through," Delgado replied grimly.

They were airborne in Washington County's new Bell 507 Jet Patrol copter within an hour, estimated arrival in D.C. around eight that evening, plenty of time to reach Cal Putnam and stop Waterman's assassins—if they could stay in the air. There was not much conversation over the loud whir of the blades. Everyone was tense.

Leah scanned the open waters around them with her high-powered monocular. Deputy Kerry Frost kept his eyes fixed on the horizon as he piloted the helicopter. The sun was dipping westward and the ocean reflected golden reddish light against the slate sky of the North Atlantic. "Station at Cutler reports a front moving in," he said after listening to a forecast on his headphones.

McLean nervously kept tabs on the ship's radar vid. "Great. Even Mother Nature's gonna have a piece of our tails."

"Does it mean we'll be forced to land?" Leah asked. She had spent enough summers on the Maine coast to know how fierce and swift summer storms could be.

"Hard to say." Kerry Frost was a taciturn New England youth with a butter-yellow buzz cut and pink-rimmed eyes. He blushed every time Leah, or any woman under sixty, spoke to him.

Delgado sat beside her, mulling over contingency plans. The weather was only one factor, and a minor one at that. "I don't like the silence from Cal. He has to know by now that someone's messing with his link."

"We can't take a chance trying to contact him while we're in the air. BISC has to be searching for us with every tool in their arsenal." They all knew how familiar Leah was with that arsenal. "Once we're on the ground tonight, we can try again. My digital link is hard to trace. It could buy us some time, once we're in range to call him."

"We may not have to worry about the weather or getting into D.C." McLean's laid-back drawl had a pronounced strain to it, even over the noise of the blades. "Two blips on the screen, coming in fast." He turned to Kerry. "What do you make of them?"

"Two copters, judging by the speed and low altitude," the pilot replied, punching in the readout on his screen for more detailed information.

"What are the odds that two copters flying in formation like that would be approaching our flight path unless they were searching for us?" Del asked.

"Not good," replied McLean. "Can you get a configuration display at this distance, Kerry?"

"Trying, sir . . ." A 3-D diagram suddenly rotated on the vid.

"They've found us," Leah said tightly.

"Apache Longbows, AH-64Ds," the pilot whispered in awe.

Del studied the screens for a moment, then cursed. "Kerry, get us the hell off this ocean and land this crate anywhere there's cover!"

The young pilot's Adam's apple bobbed as he nodded, already veering the ship in a steep dive for the coastline. Del scanned the terrain, praying for enough clearance to land and enough cover for them to hide in before the gunships could open fire.

"How did they catch our scent so quick?" McLean asked, bracing himself in the copilot's seat as the Bell 507 tipped nearly on its side.

"My guess would be that there was one agent left in Machias watching for us. There's an army base in upstate New York that Waterman could've used," Leah replied, her eyes never leaving the rapidly approaching gunships.

"We have to set down!" Del yelled.

"I have to reach land first," the young pilot replied.

"Here they come." Leah raised the MP5 she'd kept by her seat.

Del, too, raised his weapon, the submachine guns a pitiful defense against the power of an attack helicopter. A flash of flame glinted over the water and the sharp bursts of 30mm cannon fire erupted directly beneath their descending craft. Kerry swerved sharply as another burst rocked them just off the starboard side.

"Son of a bitches are trying to drive us further out over the water so they can finish us off without a trace!" Delgado continued scanning the dimly lit shore, which was still too far away for comfort. They dipped and danced crazily in midair like a puppet with strings tangled, avoiding incoming fire. "Over there, a beach with the timberline close by," he yelled to Kerry.

"I'll try." Frost didn't sound optimistic.

McLean squinted at one of the gunships. "Anything in particular we can aim for that might disable them?" he asked Kerry.

"Maybe the cockpit window. Rest is armored."

"Damned small target," Del groused, trying to take aim from the crazily veering copter as another round of cannon fire came whistling past the fuselage, missing by a coat of paint. He fired at one attacker while Leah aimed at the other.

"Bastards are not only bulletproof, they're fast as lightning," she muttered.

"Maybe this will help even the odds," McLean replied, pulling a stubby shoulder arm from a rack fastened to the patrol chopper's bulkhead.

"Is this what I think it is?" Leah asked, seizing the weapon.

"Grenade launcher, tear-gas and stun grenades. Whole ball of wax. Be my guest. Both varieties in the locker under the rack."

Leah unlatched the ammo locker and plucked out a stun grenade, broke open the launcher, slid the grenade into the chamber, and snapped it closed.

The lead gunship was closing head-on now. Just as it opened up with another burst to their starboard side, she fired the launcher. "Lucky shot," she breathed as bright orange flames suddenly exploded skyward from the cockpit of the Apache. It tilted to one side for an instant before the blades began sputtering erratically. Then it dropped like a stone. The waves below enveloped it, fire and all.

"Bulletproof but not grenade-proof. Thank you, Jesus!" Del said as they sheared away from the remaining ship, which had fallen back when the first one was hit.

Frost brought their copter down, almost skimming the water.

Then he pulled a lever releasing the sliding doors on either side. "If I can't make it to land, jump clear when you hear the splash." It was the longest speech the young deputy had made since they'd met.

Now the remaining gunship closed on them, firing freely, desperate to destroy them even if that meant it would be picked up on local police scans. A burst of fire tore into the rear of the patrol copter and it began to saw back and forth raggedly, out of control, bouncing like a flat stone skipped across water by a kid. A mercifully sandy stretch of beach lay ahead of them about eighty meters. The gunship fired again and the rear of the copter exploded into flame.

"Everybody, bail!" Leah yelled, yanking the door on her side wide open as the fire cast the ship's interior in deadly orange light.

The copter slapped into the ocean as if the water were a concrete slab, tossing Leah out like a rag doll before she could see if the others were behind her. The sheriff and Del remained inside the cockpit as the ship began to sink, frantically working to free the deputy. She swam around the flaming wreckage bobbing on the red and black waves to see what was wrong. Then she heard the pulsing roar of the Apache overhead as Del and McLean lowered the injured pilot into the water.

"Go under!" she yelled as the ship above them came down for the kill. Another burst of cannon fire exploded the remains of the Bell 507 just as they dived.

A civilian aircraft, probably on hailing frequency, approached from the north and the Apache took off, circling in an arc, no doubt planning to return and make certain there were no survivors when the coast was clear. It bought them a little time.

Leah came up coughing, shaking her head to clear it as she frantically scanned the flaming wreckage for her companions. "Over here," Del yelled as soon as her silvery hair broke the surface.

"What happened?" she asked.

"Frost was pinned. Looks like he may have a broken leg."

"We'll all have worse if we don't get the hell out of this water," she said, scanning the shore.

They took turns with the deputy until they reached the shallows, but by that time they could hear the slapping hum of helicopter blades in the distance once again. Even if the interloping airplane radioed for help, it would arrive too late.

"You reckon . . . they'll think we went down with the copter . . . if we can make it to the trees before they spot us?" McLean asked between gulps of air.

"I doubt it, but let's give it a go," Del replied. They ran toward a tall stand of white pine a dozen meters from the incoming tide.

A short burst of fire kicked up sand like a white tornado, whirling it across the beach, stinging the backs of their legs. Frost tried to hop on one foot as the men half-dragged him. They hit the trees, vanishing into the dim interior, as wood splinters and small tree limbs flew behind them. Then the gunship veered away.

"Think they're giving up?" McLean asked.

"Not a chance. They're coming in for a landing," Leah replied as they laid Frost down behind a huge decaying log.

"Leave me," the deputy gasped.

"Not a chance," Delgado echoed. "You still have that digital phone on you?" he asked Leah.

She was already punching in 911. "If that civvy plane hasn't alerted them already, we'll have this area crawling with cops and EMTs. But we don't have time to answer questions."

"Looks as if we're just outside Kittery. I can handle the authorities and wait with Kerry—if those boys in the gunship don't beat my fellow officers here," McLean said.

"Maybe we can create a little diversion," Leah offered.

Del watched her remove a couple of flares from her belt. She had pulled them from the ammo locker just before their wipeout. "It's been good working with you, Sheriff, Deputy. Take care." Del followed her toward the edge of the trees, trying desperately to keep up with her fast sprint. His knee already ached like crazy from the icy water. "Give me one of those," he said.

She slowed and turned to hand him a flare. "As soon as you hear the chopper, set that baby off in the brush." With that she took off in a hard, fast run.

He loped along the edge of the beach for about thirty or forty meters before the whir of rotor blades grew louder again. Ducking into the scrubby brush and trees, he worked quickly setting a flare, lighting it. The brilliant orange light shot skyward like the beacon it was intended to be. Up about another hundred meters or so, he saw the second flare go up.

The chopper landed between them on the beach. Del watched as two men in army camouflage jumped out of the gunship, M17s ready to fire. *We'd better make every shot count.*

As if echoing his thoughts, Leah took out the first one with a clean shot to the head. *She must've run back down through the brush to get close enough,* he thought with admiration. He drew a bead on the second man, who'd thrown himself to the ground and lay down a withering burst of fire across the brush from where the kill shot originated.

Del wasn't as good as Leah. His bullet tore into the soldier's back, hitting aerofoam armor. The .50-caliber packed enough wallop to slow him, but not take him out. He rolled to his feet and dived into the brush. Cursing silently, Del fired again and the target stumbled. Maybe he'd gotten lucky. Time to go see.

The danger was shooting each other in a cross fire. Leah knew it. She also knew the long, ugly furrow across her thigh was bleeding like an El-Op with a shiv in his guts. No time for first aid until that last man was out of the game. Delgado had hit him, maybe even broken a rib or two with the body shot, but she knew the drill. She'd been trained the same way. When you were in the zone, pain just didn't count. Doggedly she worked her way closer, listening for Del . . . and for her prey.

18.

Delgado could hear the sirens in the distance. They had to get the hell out of Dodge. McLean would field the questions while he and Leah hit the road for D.C. But how to get safely away while that lone gunman was lying for them? Only one way. He crawled toward the spot where the shooter had gone to ground.

In Cal's vernacular the son of a bitch was tough as a boiled owl. Del followed his trail in the dim twilight, noting that his quarry was dragging one leg. With his fingertips he could feel the slight furrow in the soft earth and it was wet . . . blood. He went slowly, stalking like the experienced hunter he was. Where the hell was Leah? Unconsciously he'd kept track of her shots. Six so far. Jesus, he couldn't remember how many clips of ammo she had. Suddenly a dense stand of pines directly ahead of him erupted with the sound of automatic gunfire.

He heard her return fire mixed with the bursts from an M17. His blood ran cold as he followed the injured man's sign. A big tacamahac tree with a trunk nearly a meter wide provided cover for the soldier, who exchanged shots with Leah. Her cover, what there was of it, couldn't keep her alive for much longer. She fired again. Then came a click. She was out of ammo.

"Hey, handsome!" he yelled, crouching for a shot that had to count. The shooter spun on his good foot and raised the assault rifle. He never squeezed the trigger. The force of the .50-caliber slug smashing into his face almost tore off his head.

"Leah!" Del ran forward. When she stood up and stepped over the rotted log, his knees felt weak with relief. "Damn, woman, you scared crap out of me!" He started toward her, needing to reassure himself that she was indeed alive, but she brushed by him and stared at the corpse.

"Thanks, Delgado. That shot was a beaut. Couldn't have done better myself."

"Yeah, you could've. You'd have made the shot before he wounded your partner," he replied quietly, noticing her limp. "How bad?" He touched the bloody rip in her fatigues.

"We should've kept the damned body armor. This is an inconvenience I don't have time for," she muttered.

Del sighed in resignation. "You're the only person I could imagine who'd refer to a gunshot wound as an 'inconvenience.'"

"It missed bone, artery, and tendon," she said dismissively as she pulled some flexi-wrap bandaging from a pocket in her fatigues and wound it around her leg.

"Look, I know you're bad, mad, and tough as a polecat, but at least let me help." He took the bandaging from her hands and finished the job, wincing at the amount of blood she must've already lost.

"Hear those sirens? We don't know how long McLean can stall the locals—or how soon before Waterman sends another reception committee our way."

"Can you walk if I help you?"

"I can make it by myself, thanks," she replied, still all cool business as she began walking through the brush toward the highway sounds in the distance.

"At least this makes us even. With a bullet in you I'll be able to keep up," he quipped, waiting to see how she'd respond.

"Remind me to shoot myself anytime you're having trouble with your knee."

Still distant. "I'm always having trouble with my knee, Leah, but that's not what's bothering me."

Leah could hear the fear in his voice, fear for her. "Look, Delgado . . . Del . . ." She slowed a bit, biting her lip. "This is the way I am . . . the way I've been trained." She could not look at him. That would finish her for sure.

Then he understood. Her face looked like bleached bone in the twilight. He fought his Neanderthal urge to pick her up and carry her. He'd have to sucker punch her first. Instead, he changed the subject. "I have an idea about how to reach Cal."

"Yeah, I'm listening."

He explained as they made their way across Highway 1 to the row of outlet malls on the other side.

8:53 P.M., EDT, FRIDAY, JULY 3
KITTERY, MAINE

The Olde Harbour Motel room was small and dingy with fake walnut paneling darkening its walls. Cheap pine disinfectant vied with stale cigarette smoke in the closed-in space, but it was near enough to the ocean to hear the soothing lap of the tide coming in. Leah lay on the bed watching the door, her Ruger clutched in her hand, ready to roll onto the floor if someone besides Delgado entered.

She hoped like hell she wouldn't have to do that. The staples the young emergency-room doctor had put in her thigh throbbed like a bitch. She'd given false ID at the walk-in clinic and Del had paid cash. Because it was obviously a gunshot wound, the doc had tried to hold her, even offering the bribe of Percodan for her pain. She'd refused the drug and Del had shoved their way out of the place before the authorities arrived.

Of course, that meant as soon as they got away from the clinic they'd had to ditch the old Pontiac he'd hot-wired on the outlet mall parking lot. She grinned in spite of the throbbing down her leg. Damn, Delgado was as good at boosting cars as an eleven-year-old kid in the D.C. slums. Right now he was out "requisitioning" another vehicle.

And checking on Gracie.

Before she agreed to go to the clinic, Leah had insisted they locate a small cybercafe on the highway. She'd waited in the Pontiac while he'd used a terminal to contact Gracie Kell in Havana. If anyone could get them in touch with Cal Putnam, it was the "interrogator." By now she'd had several hours to work on the problem.

Time was running out. In less than seventeen hours Harmon Waterman would be president of the United States and World War III would be under way. They had to reach Putnam. She checked the clock sitting on the wobbly plastic nightstand beside the bed. Where the hell was Delgado?

She knew she'd blown it with him after the shooting on the beach. *He wanted to hold me. Why couldn't I let him?* The man had saved her life and all she had given him in return was terse sarcasm. But Del's world was no longer hers, had never really been hers. His was one of large, close-knit families and deep, abiding belief in love and permanence. How could she even presume to fit in with the Mulcaheys? Hell, she'd been blessed to hang on to Gramps, her one and only anchor in this treacherous life.

Her depressing reverie was interrupted by footsteps nearing the door. She tensed, rolling onto her side, gun aimed at the door. Although the room was dark, BISC agents could burst in with night-vision goggles and take her out in a heartbeat. Then she heard Delgado's voice and a sigh of relief whistled through her as she answered.

"Give me a couple, I'm not moving any faster than I have to right now." She crossed the room and unfastened the dead bolt and chain. Both precautions were pitiful because of the flimsy construction of the motel door, but every second of delay helped.

He slipped inside and closed the door, then turned on the ugly Lucite lamp. "You look like hell. Get any sleep?" he asked, depositing a small parcel on the table.

"Yeah, sweet dreams of mushroom clouds floating over Phoenix." She found herself lapsing back into the sarcasm, holding him at a distance. Sighing, she combed her fingers through her hair and asked, "Did you hear from Gracie?"

"Yes. She's still working on getting through to Cal. Seems he's out of BISC Central's loop. Not at the Bureau either. My guess is he's holed up with Samson at the White House."

"Can she break in to him there?"

He shrugged. "If she got into BISC, I think so. Just a matter of time."

"Time we haven't got."

He opened the package on the table and pulled out two greasy cartons. "We'll need energy for the long drive. Moo shu pork and shrimp lo mein."

She grimaced. "Looking at that stuff just put an inch on my thighs."

"Eat. You can use an inch to make up for what those BISC goons shot away." He shoved a carton at her, then dug into the other, still standing as he shoveled in hunks of fried meat and bean sprouts. "I got another car. An '09 Caddie with flash drive. According to a neighbor I chatted up, the owners are visiting their grandchildren in California. Won't miss it for another week at least."

She grinned. "Jeez, Delgado, you're getting to be a badass felon."

"Don't remind me." He shuddered. "My palms were sweating when I slipped into the garage and backed it down the driveway."

"We need to conserve what little cash we have to buy gas along the road. Speaking of which, I think it's time to hit it."

He studied her ravaged face. "You sure you're ready? And don't bite my head off for asking, Woman of Steel."

"About earlier . . . at the beach . . . shit." She turned away and rubbed her hand over her face in frustration. When she felt his hands gently cupping her shoulders, she turned to him and they embraced, just holding each other for a moment as he soothed her, rubbing her back as if she were Miguelito in need of assurance. *Some Woman of Steel,* she thought as she burrowed her head into the curve of his neck and hung on for dear life.

"It's okay to be human, Leah," he murmured into her hair.

"All too human. I've killed innocent people—I—"

"Bullshit! You don't know that, and I don't believe it. You're too careful, too concerned with due process. God, look at you—the only time you can get into the cold-professional-killer mode is when *you're* the one bleeding! Forget about BISC, what they told you, how they trained you. Just be Leah. Leah is more than good enough . . . believe me?" He tipped her face up to his, cupping it in his hand, willing her to meet his eyes.

She couldn't speak for a moment, then swallowed and looked at him. "I think I'm falling for you, Delgado. Does that scare you?"

A faint smile curved his lips. "Not one bit, Berglund. Female Clint Eastwood impersonators turn me on."

9 P.M., EDT, FRIDAY, JULY 3
GULF OF CHIRIQUÍ OFF THE COAST OF PANAMA

Nothing occurred on the Pacific coast from British Columbia to Tierra del Fuego without Inocensio Ramirez knowing it. His spies were everywhere. One of the easiest venues to infiltrate had been the Mexican military. Since enlarging his drug trade with the Pacific Rim, Ramirez had most particularly become interested in having men aboard Mexican naval vessels.

Innocensio believed the best spies were those with the lowest profiles and the greatest mobility. With a covered tray in hand, a cook or cook's helper could roam through a ship, into "officer country," the armory, the communications shack, even the pilothouse. On long, boring watches, sailors always welcomed someone from the galley bearing snacks. Additionally, the ship's reefers, or refrigeration units, provided excellent concealment for drug shipments.

Serving mostly as cooks or galley help, a small cadre of seamen monitored the Mexican government's coastal patrols. They remained in contact with their boss using specially designed palm-size digital units. Messages were picked up and relayed to Culiacán via Ramirez's own private "satellite," an old Gulfstream corporate jet outfitted with digital communication equipment. The signals were disguised as "overload" satellite communications clutter.

ChiChi Bernal was one of Ramirez's best men, fluent in American English and Mexican Spanish. Presently Bernal was aboard the lend-lease amphibious assault ship *Okinawa*, recommissioned the *Lázaro Cárdenas*. Sommerville's American Special Forces soldiers spoke freely around him, having no idea that he understood every nuance. Three other Mexican sailors working for Ramirez were also aboard.

Raoul Mulcahey's Learjet, on loan from the drug lord, shadowed Innocensio's Gulfstream as it made a sweep along the coastal waters of the narrowing isthmus. As the two planes drew near the Osa

Peninsula of Costa Rica, the Gulfstream relayed "satellite communications" from the *Cárdenas* to Raoul.

"Do you have the package?" Bernal asked.

Glancing across the cockpit to where Alejandro Silva sat unhappily, Raoul replied, "Affirmative. What's your status?"

"We've been hiding in the heavy shipping-lane traffic through the Middle America Trench headed to the Canal. Orders are to slow to five knots now that we're in Chiriquí waters. There are clusters of small, uninhabited islands in the gulf where we can lay low and wait until nightfall."

"Then make a quick run to the Colombian coast under cover of darkness," Raoul speculated. It made sense. Sommerville could strike Medellín and Cali by dawn, maybe reach Bogotá by midday.

"We're scheduled to hit the beach at o three hundred hours," Bernal said. "Get this. An added bonus. All the brass are assembling aboard the *Cárdenas*. Last-minute strategy session in the captain's mess."

"Give me the coordinates."

As Raoul recorded them, Inocensio's man Pablo Sanchez read them over his shoulder. "Not all those islands are as uninhabited as our naval officers believe. I can have a dozen of our 'fishing vessels' in the area to provide cover as we slip alongside the *Cárdenas*." His teeth gleamed white in a swarthy, narrow face.

Raoul unrolled a map and began outlining a plan for two dozen men to commandeer an amphibious assault vessel holding two thousand soldiers. If all went well, the Colombian and Mexican forces would stand down once President Silva explained the Americans' plans to unleash nuclear war in Latin America.

"The key thing is to separate the Americans from their nukes before we all start glowing in the dark." Mulcahey asked Bernal pertinent questions regarding the layout of the *Cárdenas* as he and Sanchez studied diagrams of the old *LPH*.

"I will be on the sponson at twenty-two hundred hours. It's just forward of the Sea Sparrow launcher on the starboard side," Bernal said.

"Speak Spanish, man. They're Mexican Special Forces, not goddamned gringo SEALs," Sanchez growled into the speaker.

But Raoul figured it out, pointing to a catwalk platform on the diagram, sticking out from the right side of the ship in front of the missile emplacement. "Be waiting to bring us up, Bernal. Mulcahey out." He turned to the decidedly pale and haggard Colombian president, who looked in desperate need of a drink. "If all goes well, Excellency, we can clean out Captain Escobido's wine cellar shortly." Raoul grinned wickedly.

Silva's smile seemed forced. "I shall look forward, Colonel."

9:40 P.M., EDT, FRIDAY, JULY 3

Aboard the *Cárdenas,* General Nathan Sommerville was most unhappy. In spite of his request for a communications blackout, the vice president had risked breaking it. Something was seriously amiss. The general could feel it in his gut as soon as the messenger entered Captain Escobido's quarters. Making their excuses, he and Colonel Walt Bisset headed for the com "shack."

Harmon Waterman's voice was tight with fury. "I can't reach that fucking greaser president. Samson and Putnam must've got to him. Frankowski received a garbled message from Drescher earlier this evening. The cowardly prick was panicked, ready to go crawling to Samson, I'd bet on it."

"Your BISC people have prevented that, I trust," Sommerville said coldly.

"Of course, but it may mean your operation is compromised. I wanted Drescher interrogated, but the damn fool bolted. Crashed his car into a concrete wall in the parking basement of the Hoover Building trying to get away from my men. He's in a coma now. We have to assume Portillo-Ortiz has given Samson particulars about your LPH and convoy of LSDs."

Sommerville stiffened. "My aide will arm the weapons immediately." He nodded to Bisset, whose gray complexion indicated that he understood. The colonel left the com shack to carry out his orders as his chief continued speaking to Waterman. "Samson doesn't have the nerve to risk a nuclear incident this close to land."

Waterman cursed. "Then we have us a standoff, don't we, General?"

"Perhaps . . . but we only need hold them at bay until tomorrow noon. I assume you've learned nothing regarding Samson's plans to thwart us."

"In case you hadn't noticed, General, Wade Samson hasn't exactly taken me into his confidence here lately," Waterman snapped. "Fuller's been taken out and I've pushed up the whole timetable on your operation to satisfy you. When the fireworks start here in Washington, I want you in place to hit Zuloaga and hit him hard!"

ChiChi Bernal watched the seemingly disorganized cluster of shrimp boats bob in the path of the *Cárdenas*. Their presence had forced the big LPH to slow to five knots since bringing the officers from the LSDs aboard. As Inocensio's fishermen pulled in their nets and shook their fists, the distraction enabled Pablo Sanchez's five men and the Special Forces commandos under Raoul Mulcahey to slip onto the ship. They brought with them the terrified Colombian president.

Bernal watched as they climbed the netting he'd dropped from the catwalk. First to reach him were Mulcahey and Sanchez. Wasting no time, their team spread out across the ship, each man with his assigned task. When everything was secured, they'd put President Silva on-screen to all the ships in the convoy. He'd explain to the Mexican and Colombian forces how they'd been duped.

"Joaquin, you and your men keep the president under wraps until my signal," Raoul commanded, then turned to Bernal. "Take us to the nukes." Ernesto and another explosives expert were with Mulcahey to disarm the weapons if they'd been armed.

Bernal grinned and picked up a tray sitting on the railing. "This way."

He walked across the deck and led them below. In the twisting labyrinth of passageways, they heard footsteps ahead. Raoul motioned his men to stop. He closed the distance to Bernal. The cook ambled around the corner, whistling casually.

Walt Bisset approached him. ChiChi knew there was only one reason Sommerville's adjutant would be coming from the ship's reefers. The same reason he and Mulcahey were headed there. "Motherfucker's already armed the nukes," Bernal whispered in English to Raoul.

They carried on a banal conversation in rapid Spanish, hoping to slip by the American. Sommerville's aide looked grimly preoccupied and paid no attention until he noted the insignia on Raoul's collar.

He turned and started to speak as Bernal reached beneath the napkin on the tray, still grinning guilelessly. The Mexican's .25-caliber Colt, equipped with silencer, made a soft pop. The colonel's eyes widened a fraction of a second before the small hole appeared in his forehead. He dropped to the metal deck with a thud.

"Stash him in storage," Bernal said with no more concern than another would have after swatting a mosquito. He yanked open a narrow door a few meters down the passageway just as Ernesto and a second commando came charging around the corner after hearing the shot.

"Dispose of him, then cover our backs," Raoul ordered the commando. He and Ernesto followed Bernal to the reefers.

When they reached the food cooler, the cook spoke to the American sentry in broken English. "I take from *el capitán*'s dinner, *especialmente* for you." He presented the tray with a flourish, then reached under the napkin once again.

General Sommerville left the com shack with a grimly familiar feeling gnawing at his gut, the same one he'd had that night in Iraq when Saddam's Republican Guard had broken through his line. *By damn, I was willing to use nuclear force then. I won't hesitate to use it now.*

Being familiar with Sommerville's history, that lily-livered Samson would know the general was not bluffing. Then, he'd been thwarted by little men without vision, men who failed to see what was at stake. Nothing had changed. Except now he would act in his country's best interest and none of the goddamned political pygmies could stop him.

Samson's own indecisiveness would defeat him. The man was a weakling, unworthy of the high office he held. Unfortunately Harmon Waterman was little better. Politicians were never trustworthy.

Once Zuloaga and his cohorts were destroyed, General Nathan Sommerville would be hailed as a national hero. He'd always believed military men made the best presidents. Perhaps he, too, would be granted that opportunity to serve his country.

The general entertained no thought of failure as he returned to Captain Escobido's mess. To hell with dinner. They were sailing immediately, full speed for the Colombian coast. The nuclear warheads aboard the *Cárdenas* were armed.

Ernesto Mulcahey stood in the chill of the ship's reefer, blowing on his hands to warm them. Outside, ChiChi and the commando stood watch. Bernal had dragged the body of the guard inside and nonchalantly hung it on a meat hook behind a side of beef.

"I have a creepy feeling old ChiChi would as soon cook up that stiff as one of those sides of beef," Raoul said.

Ernesto grunted agreement, focused on a dozen nuclear devices laid out in front of him, arranged in three rows of four each in the center of the huge steel cooler vault. Each device was about the size of a suitcase.

"Well, what's going on? Was Bernal right—are they armed?" Raoul asked.

Ernesto knelt in front of one of the cases and opened the lid. "Yes, they are armed," he replied calmly. "The arming devices are digital receiver relay switches. Each one's about the diameter of a cigarette and half as long." He studied the problem. "They were inside this container." He pointed to an empty black box. "They're inserted into here." He pointed to a receiver mounted on one of the nukes, tapping it with his finger.

"Mother of God, don't do that!" Raoul hissed.

"Not to worry, big brother. They're not that sensitive. See, they're screwed into place so they make contact with the sensor probe that leads to the detonator housed inside the bomb."

Raoul asked, "How does the generalissimo set them off then?"

"Two ways. It could be done by setting the timing." He pointed to a tiny digital readout above a keyboard. "But for the general to do the deed whenever he wants, he'll use a transmitter. He can send the precise digital signal to the switch, which then relays the message via the probe to the detonator. Boom."

"I really don't care for that boom part."

"All the relays must be set to operate on the same digital impulse—one very big bang."

"What if you're wrong?"

The younger brother shrugged with Latin fatalism. "Boom? The key to disarming them is to remove the detonation couplers."

"How the hell can you do that? Do you need any special tools?"

Ernesto looked up and grinned a big, toothy smile, tapping his thumb and index finger together. He reached down to a small projecting cylinder tip on one of the devices and screwed it out of its socket, then moved to the next one.

"Ernesto, if we get out of this alive, I'm going to beat you like a piñata!"

When he finished disarming the nukes, they left the commando locked inside the reefer with the devices. The Special Forces soldier understood his orders. He'd been left with enough nitro cordite to sink the ship before the enemy could gain entry and rearm the devices. That way they would all go to the bottom without exploding the nukes.

As they left the reefers, the small link on Bernal's belt vibrated silently. He removed it and spoke. "Yes." He listened for a moment, then closed the link. "Your commandos have the Colombian president hidden outside the com shack. They're ready to take it."

As they approached the com shack, Raoul asked ChiChi, "How many men inside?"

"Usually only two . . . sometimes a kibitzer drops by . . . like me." He grinned wolfishly.

A wonder he doesn't have a blood ring around his lips. "You guard Silva. I'll take care of securing the station."

General Sommerville paced back and forth in the narrow quarters he'd appropriated from Captain Escobido when he came aboard in Guaymas as commander of the joint expedition. Although all LPHs were spartan by design, the Mexican naval officer had appointed the place with every available comfort, including a mahogany wet bar fully stocked, a climate-controlled "wine cellar," and even a suspension mat. What the hell the fool needed with a water bed when he was already afloat eluded Sommerville.

He checked his watch again. Damn, Bisset was taking too long. "Why the hell doesn't he return?"

The general had dismissed the Mexican and Colombian officers and sent them back to their ships without informing them their flotilla was carrying a dozen armed nuclear devices. He stared at the small, black rectangle in his hand, innocuous-looking as a vid remote. Just a few simple numerical sequences, then press the send key and the fleet would vanish from the face of the earth.

The general did not mind dying for his country, had always believed that he might do so. What he did not expect was to end up as a footnote in the history books, or far worse, to be branded a traitor and buried in infamy. His mind refused to consider such a possibility. He sat down behind the obscenely large walnut desk and gave a voice command activating the vid screen. Where was Bisset!

Expecting the bland, sallow face of Sergeant Waverly to appear on the screen, he was stunned to see old Alejandro Silva instead. "What the hell's going on!" Sommerville roared. All channels were jammed on his link. He took a few seconds to catch the gist of Silva's prepared speech—the cowardly traitor was telling the Mexican and Colombian forces that the Americans planned a nuclear strike that would endanger the western coast of Mexico and destroy Colombia.

Sommerville knew what he had to do. Wasting not a moment, he programmed in the series of numbers graven in his memory for the past year, then headed for the door with the detonator clutched securely in his right hand. At the moment it was worth more than all the guns aboard the ship. "Sergeant!" he roared.

"Your sergeant has been detained, General," Raoul said, entering Sommerville's quarters.

The two men stood facing each other, Sommerville rigidly alert, Mulcahey deceptively indolent.

"You're Mexican Special Forces, Colonel. I assume you realize what I hold in my hand." He was careful to remain well out of the younger man's reach as he raised the detonator. "It's programmed."

"I never doubted you'd do it. That's why we had to kill innocent soldiers, men only doing what they were told was their duty."

"It is their duty to destroy this cancer threatening the Western Hemisphere."

"We see duty differently. What I see in you, General, is a self-aggrandizing, egomaniacal old man attempting an act of treason."

"My cause won't die with me, Colonel." Sommerville held up the detonator and pressed the small red button.

Mulcahey made no attempt to stop him. "It's been disarmed, General," Raoul said after a moment of stunned silence from Sommerville.

The old man seemed to crumple, then regained control. "It would appear, Colonel, that I am your prisoner."

"Appearances can be deceiving. My government wants no part of you, General. Alas, neither does your own. You have become. . . . an embarrassment to Washington." Raoul pulled a single sheet of paper from inside his uniform and extended it to Sommerville.

Slowly, almost loath to touch it, the older man stepped forward and took it. He began to unfold the paper, then paused and looked up at Mulcahey. "If I might be left alone for a moment, Colonel?"

Raoul nodded in understanding. He had read the message for Sommerville sent by President Samson as it printed out aboard Ramirez's Learjet.

He waited outside the door to the general's quarters for several moments. Then he heard the single shot.

19.

Del eased the big maroon Caddie into the crowded parking lot and searched for a vacancy near the cybercafe as Leah studied the GPS on the console, searching for the fastest route through the next leg of their desperate drive to D.C.

"According to Roadmaster, there's construction on I-95 if we drop south," she said. "I vote for staying on 84 until Scranton, then going down 81 through Harrisburg. Best to avoid the congestion around New York and Philly anyway."

"We've been lucky with highway patrol and local cops so far. Let's hope it keeps up," he replied as he got out of the car.

"Lucky because I've kept your lead foot from hitting the floorboard a couple of times already."

"Yes, mother. Let's hope Gracie has been able to patch through to Cal by now. If so, she's probably chewing her cuticles bloody waiting for me to contact her."

Leah sighed wearily. The sharp pain in her thigh had settled into a dull throb, but she dared not use meds because they might slow her reflexes. The pain and lack of sleep were telling on her. "I sure wouldn't mind turning this one over to the Bureau and Secret Service."

"The key is Cal. Wish me luck." He studied her pale face in the dim light of the Caddie's interior. "Try to catch a few z's while I'm gone."

"Sure thing," she replied drily, "nothing to it with the fate of the Western Hemisphere hanging in the balance. I think I'd be better off keeping my eyes wide open. Watch your ass, Delgado. I'll have the Caddie ready to rock 'n' roll when you walk out of that joint." She slid across the seat to the driver's side, ignoring the pain in her thigh.

"I still think it's a lousy idea for you to be driving with that bad leg," he groused, knowing it would do absolutely no good to argue with her. Besides, it was always better to have your partner ready to make a quick getaway in a situation as touchy as this.

Just as he disappeared into the neon glitter of the cybercafe, a helicopter whirred overhead. Leah used the car's rear vid to check it. TV news. Better safe than sorry. She'd never feel the same about copters droning in the sky again after the air battle that evening. *At least they can't locate us in this car . . . I hope.*

Still, they could be certain Waterman must have BISC monitoring Globe Net for a trace of them on every conceivable route to Washington. There was also the possibility of roadblocks set up as cover with BISC infiltrators watching for them while local cops were checking for completely legitimate offenders. She had argued for splitting up since BISC would be expecting a man and a woman, but Del had been adamant. Their best bet was to stick together and work as a team, playing to each other's strengths.

She checked the clock on the console. With luck they could be talking to Cal Putnam before sunup. Rubbing her eyes, she leaned back, and the seat of the luxury auto adjusted to a reclining position. God, how she longed to dump this whole mess in Putnam's lap and be done with it.

Hearing footsteps nearing the car, Leah picked up her Ruger and held it hidden against the side of the door, watching a beefy man with stringy hair lumber toward the Caddie. The bill of his ball cap hid his eyes, but something about the way he moved set her nerves tingling. It was pure gut instinct, but she went with it. She swung the door open and smashed it into him. He went down hard but came up with a needle gun in his hand, trying to sight in on her as she slammed the door and gunned the engine to life, laying down a smear of rubber across the asphalt.

He fired twice but the projectiles vaporized harmlessly off the window. A stupid mistake. Always have a backup weapon that penetrates when you're chasing a subject in a car. She cornered the big boat sharply and came around the lot headed straight back at him. He ran toward another man, also in a ball cap and jeans. Like the first turkey, this one also wore black dress shoes, not exactly a common accessory for a blue-collar Joe.

As they sighted in on her, she could see that the second agent was smart enough to have a Vektor 9mm. He leveled it at the front windshield of the Caddie and fired. Glass shattered, raining pellets across her head and shoulders as she ducked low and kept coming fast.

She leaned out the window and fired a quick shot at the first agent, who had ducked behind a parked car. The Ruger penetrated the side windows of the small EV and went straight through to his gut. The shooter with the Vektor stood a dozen meters away, directly in her path. He blasted away but sheer momentum kept the heavy car moving. By the time he realized that she was going to hit him, it was too late. His last shot went straight up into the air as the Caddie's hood connected with his body, plowing into it like a combine through a field of ripe wheat.

He flew several feet in the air and landed hard on the pavement to her left. He wasn't getting up. She checked the rear vid. Neither was his partner, who lay crumpled beside the Volkswagen. All the shots had been fired with silencers, but the sounds of glass shattering and her car skidding across the lot had drawn more than enough attention. She whipped the badly damaged Caddie up in front of the café and laid on the horn.

Delgado appeared at the door, shouldering his way through the crowd and jumping into the backseat. "Go!" he yelled before the door was even closed. She peeled out of the parking lot and took off down a side street, then turned several times, backtracking in case some of the witnesses were lucid enough to tell police the direction they'd headed.

"Damn, Berglund, can't I leave you alone for ten minutes without trouble?"

"BISC's found us. How the hell did they do it?"

"We'll puzzle that one after we ditch this car. A bright maroon Caddie is loud enough. A maroon Caddie with a shattered front windshield shrieks." He scanned a deserted industrial complex up

278 | ALEXA HUNT

ahead and tapped her on the shoulder. "Pull in there. We can ditch this baby in that warehouse on the right."

She pulled in, then slowed as he hopped out of the car and ran over to an entry bay that was secured with a rusty old padlock. "Not exactly state-of-the-art. Nobody's been using this joint for years," he muttered as he blasted the chain apart, then struggled to raise the bay door.

Leah pulled the wrecked car inside and killed the engine, then got out and walked over to where he stood in the darkness. "Did you get through to Gracie?"

"No problem there. She reached Cal at the White House. I gave him bare bones about what we have. One good piece of news—Sommerville's been taken down, courtesy of my family."

"Thank heaven for *big* favors," she muttered.

"Yeah, but you're not going to like the rest. Before we could arrange a pickup site, I heard the commotion in the parking lot and had to take off."

"At least Putnam will be able to keep the president from that bomb tomorrow."

"Afraid not. It seems Samson's determined the show must go on. They're going to 'invite' Waterman to the party though, just as a precaution. Samson is sure if the bastard is sitting next to him, there won't be any bomb."

Leah cursed, unconsciously touching the staples on her aching thigh as she paced. "What if they change plans and bring in a shooter with a scope?"

"I mentioned that," he replied drily. "But we didn't have time to argue the point. We need access to the Net so Gracie can link us to Cal again."

"Just a wild hunch, but I'd say cybercafes aren't where we try. Now that they've made us in this area, they'll be watching every public access site. How about a link in a private residence?"

He raised one eyebrow. "You mean breaking and entering, I assume?"

She grinned. "Well, Delgado, it's damn late to be getting religion after you've committed GTA twice in the past twenty-four hours."

He shrugged. "Speaking of which, I'd better boost another set of wheels pronto. We need to put some distance between us and Hart-ford before we try for a rendezvous with Cal. You wait here. Give me until . . ." He checked his watch. "Midnight. If I'm not back by then, figure I've turned into a pumpkin. You're on your own with that." He gestured to Adam Manchester's journal, which she carried in a pack strapped to her waist. Then he reached out and drew her into his arms for a swift, hard kiss.

When he started to release her, she held tightly to him and their eyes met, glowing like coals in the dim moonlight filtering through a grimy window. "Delgado, get this straight—I am not Cinderella and you are not going to turn into a pumpkin. Got it?"

"Got it, fairy godmother," he muttered, lowering his head for an-other kiss before he took off into the dark outside.

12:20 A.M., EDT, SATURDAY, JULY 4
RESTON, VIRGINIA

Harmon Waterman was not a happy man. The fiasco off the Panama coast had cost him his entire American strike force. The double-dealing Mexican government had captured all the painstakingly assembled matériel, including the nuclear devices. The highly trained men set to lead the mission were prisoners, held by their former Mexican and Colombian allies. Nathan Sommerville was dead by his own hand.

He tossed the report on his desk and scowled. "Well, at least there's some justice in that," he muttered to himself as Jack Frankowski stood nervously in the doorway. When his aide cleared his throat, Waterman looked up. "What now?"

"Benson and Fulkerman are dead. Looks as if Agent Berglund took them out herself on the parking lot of a cybercafe near Hartford. Del-gado must've been inside. The report says a white male matching his description fled with a woman driving."

"They're only nuisance value now, but we still need to tie up loose ends. Send out another Sanitation Squad. Make sure they get it right this time." Waterman paused then, considering. "We have to assume they've reestablished contact with Putnam. But that will work in our favor."

"Er, how so, sir?" Frankowski dared the question. He had started to sweat when Fuller died. Nothing had gone right since, as far as he could tell. And all because of Delgado and Berglund.

Waterman's already florid face grew redder. Normally his subordinates never questioned him, especially Jack. Was his key administrative assistant losing his nerve? The vice president relied too much on Frankowski to drive him away now. Reining in his temper, he explained, "Probably all Delgado and Berglund know is that we planned to use explosives to kill Samson. I was afraid after all that's happened that Samson might not let me join him on the podium today. Not an hour ago, dear gutless Wade made a personal call to me, insisting I do just that."

For the first time in several days, Jack Frankowski actually smiled.

1:00 A.M., EDT, SATURDAY, JULY 4
NEWBURGH, NEW YORK

They cruised a narrow gravel road not too far off the highway, about a mile from an affluent suburban area. The lane was shadowed by the branches of old oak and maple trees. Somewhere in the distance a dog barked at a passing car.

"There. The pseudo-Tara with white columns," Leah said, pointing to a big house all dark inside, almost hidden by overgrown shrubbery. The grass was high, uncut for several weeks. "It might be deserted."

"It might be for sale and empty inside, too."

"No Realtor's sign," she countered. "Let's give it a try. Won't cost us anything if you're right."

He turned the small, black Taurus into the driveway, killing the lights and inching his way up the curving gravel path until a big weeping willow concealed the car from the street and the house. "Wait here while I see what's up."

"Think, Del. This is my sort of game, remember? BISC trains us damn well in the fine art of breaking and entering."

They both got out of the car and made their way silently to the house, which sat in Gothic decay, guarded by a thicket of pyracantha bushes whose sharp, thorny branches tore at their skin and clothing as they checked windows for an alarm system. It was a primitive one, easily disarmed, but when Leah followed Del inside, she heard his barely discernible curse.

"What?"

"There's someone here—a light down the hall."

"Why couldn't we see it from the outside? We checked the whole perimeter."

"In a barn this size, I'd guess an interior room without windows," Del replied. "Probably where the computer is."

"We haven't got time to waste. You'll have to con them with your badge. I think a civilian would sooner trust a Bureau man than a BISC agent."

"Let's see if the computer's in that room before we try talking our way into anything."

They made their way down the hall, wincing as the ancient floorboards creaked, but whoever was at the other end did not respond. Del prayed they had not phoned the police. Then Leah tugged on his arm.

"There." She pointed through the doorway directly across from them. It housed a roomful of computer hardware.

Del slipped inside and flashed his electric torch around. "This should work. You keep an eye on whoever's in the room down the hall. I'll try to get through as fast as I can."

She nodded, closing the door silently behind her, then moved down the long corridor, trying not to make noise on the rickety floorboards. She peered into the occupied room, a large library, appointed with early-twentieth-century furnishings of heavy dark oak and blue velvet. Lace doilies adorned the overstuffed upholstery. Bookshelves filled with what looked to be rare, old volumes covered all four walls floor to ceiling.

Seated beneath a narrow beam of bright light, a stoop-shouldered man was engrossed in a book. Strands of thin white hair lay across a pink scalp, which shone in the light. He looked ninety if he was a day. A nearby wheelchair enhanced the aura of frailty about him. Leah could see the large, old-fashioned hearing appliance attached to his right ear. She stopped worrying about the creaking floorboards.

Just to be certain no other people were in the dilapidated old place, she made a thorough search of the second floor. One bedroom looked as if it was in use but the occupant was not at home. Probably a caregiver for the old man, whose sleeping quarters adjoined the library. She returned to Del, who was busily patching his way through to Gracie.

As soon as he paused to wait for a connection, she interrupted, saying, "I'm going to watch the front drive for any late arrivals." He nodded abstractedly as she turned and reached for the heavy brass doorknob and pulled it open. She froze. Del sensed something was wrong and swiveled his head around.

"Thought you'd put one over on a deaf old codger, didja?" The voice was high-pitched and uneven, as if rusty from lack of use. It belonged to a very old man whose thin, bent frame and wrinkled, pale face did not fit at all with his shrewd blue eyes—eyes that measured them with keen intelligence.

"We mean you no harm," Leah said quietly. "I thought you wouldn't hear us and we'd be gone without frightening you."

"Frightening me? My dear, when you've lived half as long as I have, not even Lucifer frightens you. Thought I needed that wheelchair, didja? Norton's silly wife insisted on buying it for me a couple of years ago. Boy finally got some sense and dumped her. Next step after I park my fanny in that contraption is some goddamned nursing home. I eat with my feet under my own table every night and sleep in my own bed. Plan to keep on that way till I'm gone."

"Norton? Is he your son?" Del asked.

"Grandson. His mother and the latest love of her life are living somewhere in the Hamptons."

"When do you expect him back?" Del asked.

"Who—my grandson or his mother's loverboy?"

"The one who lives here," Leah supplied helpfully.

"Oh, Norton's in Albany overnight. Working on some high-power deal for his insurance company."

"My friend just needs to use your computer," Leah said.

"Hah! Isn't mine. Computers are the ruination of Western civilization. That contraption of Lucifer's belongs to Norton."

"We're government agents working on a vital case. Your place was the closest and seemed unoccupied." They quickly produced badges, which he barely glanced at.

"A crime spree in Newburgh. Hah! Don't think so, girlie. FBI and BISC don't even know this place's on the map. You two on the lam?" He studied them critically, noting Del's unshaven face and the bulky bandage clearly visible beneath her ripped, bloodstained slacks. "I'd sooner trust a pair of horse thieves than FBI or BISC anyway."

Del was intrigued. "Why's that, sir?"

"I'll tell you, Special Agent Delgado—if you're really an FBI man, which I doubt."

The "old codger" had an amazingly sharp mind. Del and Leah exchanged meaningful glances as he scuttled into the room and took a seat on an office chair beside the computer station.

"Government's never been up to any damn good. Been up to a lot of the other stuff, though. Billions spent on drug wars and military weapons. Hah! You ask me, those politicians and generals are in the hip pockets of that Cartel. Wouldn't surprise me to see Benito Zuloaga running this country someday."

"You should meet a hacker friend of mine named Gracie. You two have a lot in common," Del said.

"Hah! Not if she works on those devil machines." He waved a gnarled hand toward Norton's equipment.

"It's a coincidence you should mention the Cartel's connections to Washington," Leah interjected. "That's what we're working on, and why we need to reach our superior." She didn't volunteer more, waiting to see if he'd go for it.

"Not much on details, are you, Agent Berglund?"

"It's top secret, sir."

"Hah! The old saw about if you told me, you'd have to shoot me." He did not seem worried about the possibility.

"Nothing like that, sir," she assured him. "But you do seem awfully calm considering you've just found two armed strangers inside your house."

"Like I said, when you get to be my age, you won't worry about much either. Besides, if you intended me harm, I wouldn't be talking to you now, would I?"

Del grinned. "You have a point, Mr.—?"

"Fenster, Abner Fenster. Call me Ab."

"Well, Ab, my associate and I would sure appreciate it if you'd let us use your grandson's computer link to reach our boss. It really is urgent."

Ab shrugged and waved his hand dismissively. "Help yourself, just don't ask me anything about how the goddamned contraptions work." He settled back in his chair, his shrewd blue eyes amused as he waited them out. Obviously he had no intention of leaving.

Del looked at Leah, who shrugged and said, "Go to work, Delgado."

He turned to the vid link and gave a voice command to resume. In moments Gracie Kell's spiky, chartreuse head filled the screen. "Where the hell you been, G-man? I have your spook boss hounding me for word from you. What gives?"

"We had to leave the last site in a bit of a hurry—a matter of life and death. Can you put Cal on now?"

"No problema." She grinned, peeling back black-glossed lips to reveal tiny, crooked teeth. "See, not in Havana a week and already I'm picking up the lingo." She turned to her keyboard and made a few strokes. Then Cal Putnam's face appeared on the vid.

"I was afraid the hogs'd eaten you, ole son. Damned if you both don't look like you've been sortin' wildcats," he said as Leah leaned over Del's shoulder.

"We're on a private link, Cal. Location Newburgh, New York." Del consulted the GPS for precise coordinates. They talked for a couple of minutes about the situation in Washington and how soon Cal could send a copter to get them.

That was when Leah heard the whir of helicopter blades. She dashed over to the window and peered into the side yard where the ship was landing. "We got company, Del!" She ran to the opposite wall and flicked off the lights.

"Gotta go!" He broke the connection as Leah instructed Ab, "Barricade yourself in the library. Turn off all the lights and wait, but first, do you have any weapons in the house?"

"An old double barrel. In my bedroom, just off the library." They followed him down the hallway.

He showed Del the case beneath his bed. It held an old Parker shotgun and some shells. As Del loaded the shotgun, Ab said, "There's a cellar exit they'll never find." The old man was already heading back into the library, fully expecting them to follow with their electric torches. They did. Ab chatted as if having his home under siege were an everyday occurrence. "My dad built it back in '56, a fancied-up fruit cellar turned into a fallout shelter. Outside entrance is all grown over with Virginia creeper now."

He showed them the hidden compartment behind a bookcase in his library. Steep, narrow stairs led down into utter blackness. "No electricity working down there anymore. You'll have to use your flashlights—er, torches, whatever they call the goddamned things."

"You'd be safest if you hid in the shelter below while we go outside, Ab," Del said, handing him the shotgun. "I don't mean to alarm you, but those fellows play for keeps and they don't leave witnesses."

"BISC, eh? They don't scare me. Hell, I faced Commies in Korea back in '50. You ever hear of Inchon?" he asked, following Del down the stairs.

Leah closed the hidden compartment behind them, wishing Mr. Fenster could move a bit faster on the steps. They didn't have much time until the men in the copter secured the perimeter. "I counted four men jumping out of the copter. We need to take out at least two of them without alerting the others."

Del snorted mirthlessly. "Anything else on your wish list?"

"That they won't have automatic weapons?"

"Christmas isn't coming early this year," he replied, then continued, "You're a better shot, but I have this." He patted the sheathed knife on his belt.

"How the hell did they find us?" she asked, not expecting an answer as their torches scanned the small, filthy room. On one wall enough food and water was stored to keep a family of four alive for a month. Cots, a primitive radio set, and a few other dust-covered necessities lined the opposite wall.

"There's the exit," Ab said, pointing to a steel door that resembled a bank vault.

"It's rusted shut," Del said, grunting as he tried to turn the wheel that would release the lock.

"Here, let me help," Leah said. They both wrapped their hands around the cobweb-covered metal and tugged until it suddenly made a tiny hissing sound and gave way. Chill night air rushed into the stale interior.

Del turned to Ab, who had taken a seat on one of the crates piled nearby. "Lock this after us and wait. We'll come back for you when it's safe."

"Safe. Hah! I could sit on these boxes until I was covered with cobwebs, too, by that time. I'll wait awhile, then go back upstairs and call the Newburgh sheriff. Man's a blithering idiot, but at least I know he's not involved with any crooks in Washington."

"Good plan," Leah said as she eased out the door, which they had only opened wide enough to squeeze through.

They pushed their way past the densely overgrown Virginia creeper. Working as quietly as they could, they crawled out from beneath the brush, all the while listening for sounds of the men searching the grounds.

"Shit, they're making as much noise as the D-day invasion," he whispered to Leah.

"Could be a decoy tactic."

He nodded, motioning for her to circle right while he went left. Ignoring the man who was thrashing around in the pyracantha bushes at the back of the house, they moved out into the darkness. Del paused every few feet to listen. By the time he'd moved halfway around the side where the copter had landed, he spotted the first one guarding it. *That nightscope will come in handy.* He liked the looks of the M17 the guy was carrying, too.

Unsheathing his knife, he began a slow crawl toward the copter, coming around it from the back. Sure enough, just as he suspected, a second man waited crouching in the shadows of a willow. *They figured we might try capturing the copter.* He moved behind the willow, glad a recent rain had moistened the ground cover enough to muffle any crunching noises as he drew close . . . closer. Then a soft pop sounded from the opposite side of the big old house.

Leah. She carried a silencer for the Ruger. At least he prayed it was her. His quarry stiffened, alert, ready to move out. It was now or never. He stood up and sprinted the last few feet, knife ready as the man struggled to level the M17 in such close quarters. Del knocked it up in the air with one hand and sliced his blade across the soldier's exposed throat with the other. A short burst of fire erupted into the night sky, bringing down a soft rain of willow leaves and twigs. The dying man crumpled to earth.

Delgado seized the man's weapon and flattened himself on the ground, rolling. The soldier guarding the copter ran toward him, firing rapidly, missing. No time to don the night-vision goggles. He was limned in moonlight. Del took him out with one clean burst from the M17.

He put on the goggles, then moved as carefully as he could toward the front of the house. *Come on, Leah. I want to hear that Ruger's silencer again.*

Leah let the second soldier's corpse fall silently to the ground, trying to catch her breath. Their struggle ended when her choke hold crushed her foe's windpipe. The woman had fought like a rabid wildcat after Leah had shot the man. As they fought, she'd heard a burst from an M17, then nothing. Delgado was in trouble. She grabbed the woman's rifle and goggles, then took off through the brush toward where the shots had originated, terrified he was dead.

Del saw her through the goggles, in deep shadows but moving much too fast and carelessly. Had she taken out the other two? He scanned the surrounding area, hearing nothing. "Leah, here, two down," he whispered.

She whirled swiftly, then made for him, sweeping the surroundings with her M17. "Two down," she whispered back, furious with herself for being so afraid for him that she'd blundered right into his sights. "I don't think there are any more," she said tightly. When he reached out for her, she brushed past him. "We'd better be sure before we go inside and get Mr. Fenster."

"How foolishly unprofessional of me, Agent Berglund," he said.

They circled the perimeter and found nothing.

"You'd think a couple of bursts of automatic weapons fire would rouse a few sleepers in a quiet little area like this, wouldn't you?" Del said as they slipped back into the house.

Leah shrugged. "This isn't far from Jersey. I expect if most people see a copter land in a deserted old place like this, then hear fireworks, they mind their own business. Still, I don't think we'd be smart to dawdle in case the cops do show. What I want to know is how the hell BISC has located us twice now. There's no way they could trace the cars we've stolen."

"*I've* stolen," he corrected. "I've been wondering about it myself. Globe Net couldn't make us. I'm sure we're not carrying a bug—"

"Shit! Yes, we are!" She held up her hands, palms out.

"The chips?" He thought a moment, recalling Gary's explanation about how they worked, but she had already figured it out.

"They're electroencephalographic, unique to me. That's how they meld agents with their needle guns. Our unique brain signatures are transmitted into our palms. When the agent dies, the chips die, too."

"But if the agent's still alive and on the run, they must have figured a way to use the signal from the chips as a tracer. How powerful could that sort of thing be, though?"

"My guess is not very," she replied. "Obviously they never told us anything about this possibility in training. But if they had a general idea about where I was and sent out sweeps—"

"Low-flying copters?"

"Yeah, that might be a way to pick up the chip's signal. But why didn't they use this technology to eliminate me before now?"

"My bet is they just figured this out. You have the tendency to make people work overtime, Agent Berglund," he said with a grin, opening the door to Ab's library.

His smile evaporated when she said, "You have to remove the chips from my hands, Del."

20.

Even though he'd never minded cleaning the game he and his cousins shot in Mexico, Del had always been queasy whenever Aunt Seri treated human cuts and scrapes, most particularly when they weren't his but those of his loved ones. Hell, he'd barely passed his CPR exam at the Bureau. Surgery was not a skill covered in the FBI training program, but he knew this had to be done quickly before another BISC team paid them a surprise visit. He wiped the look of consternation from his face.

"A better alternative than lopping off both your hands at the wrist, I suppose," he replied with coolness he didn't feel.

"I can do it myself, Delgado," she replied, noting the slightly greenish cast to his face as they walked through the library door.

He shook his head vehemently. "I don't doubt it for a minute, but even a whiz like you isn't ambidextrous. You'd hack the shit out of your gun hand, and frankly, my dear, since you're a better shot than I am, we can't afford that. I'll do the deed."

"You get 'em all?" Ab Fenster asked as he materialized from behind the sliding bookcase that hid the stairs to the cellar.

"We told you to stay put until the coast was clear," Leah snapped. The prospect of having Delgado slice into the palms of her hands was making her decidedly uncivil. Grudgingly, she was forced to admire the old man's sangfroid and added with a grim smile, "All's clear for now, but you'll have to get out of here before the next contingent arrives to check on their pals."

Ab made a snorting sound and waved a veiny hand as if brushing away a fly. "Nobody'll bother with an old coot like me. Now, what's that I heard about hacking the shit out of your hand?"

"Leah has electroencephalographic chips implanted in her hands. We just figured out that it's how BISC found us. I have to cut them out."

Ab fixed Delgado with a level gaze. "You don't look like much of a surgeon, sonny."

"The chips are only about three millimeters below the skin, two mils square." Del shrugged. "I'm the best she's got."

The old man cackled in that weird rusty voice of his. "I doubt it. When I told you I was at Inchon, I didn't mean I was dumb enough to be a jarhead. Hell, no. I was even dumber—I was a navy corpsman!"

"A medic?" Leah interjected, her voice a mixture of doubt and hope. She eyed his thin, age-spotted hands. They were rock steady.

"Yer a cool one, girlie. I like grit in a woman," Ab said with a sharp nod. "Just step this way into my operating room. I may be a little out of practice, but I'd bet I'll do a better job than your FBI boyfriend."

"I won't call you on that one," Del muttered grimly beneath his breath as he and Leah followed the old man down the hallway into the kitchen.

Ab turned on a bright overhead light, which shone on an oak table in the center of the big room. He gathered items from various drawers of the enameled cabinets built into the walls—a heavy magnifying glass, an old-fashioned razor blade, two pairs of tweezers, a roll of tape, and some sterile gauze pads. Placing them on the table, he extracted a bottle of disinfectant from beneath the sink and poured a cupful of it into a glass bowl, then dropped the razor and tweezers into the solution.

As he scrubbed his hands thoroughly, he asked, "You ever have any field cutting done on you before this?"

Del winced but Leah took the question in stride, replying, "Once. A couple of years ago. Hurt like hell."

"Well, this will, too. Sorry I don't happen to keep topical anesthesia around. The local drugstore won't sell me the stuff. Something about not having a medical license."

He dried his hands carefully on a clean towel, then examined her hands one at a time, probing with surprising dexterity for the location of the chips. After grunting to himself, apparently satisfied with what he'd learned, he used one of the gauze pads dipped in disinfectant to cleanse her right hand. "Now, take a seat here and lay your hand out flat on the table," he instructed gently.

Leah sat on one of the sturdy oak chairs and extended her arm, palm up beneath the bright light. Ab pointed to the big magnifying glass and said to Del, "You don't get off scot-free, sonny. Hold that over her hand—about so . . ." Delgado positioned the glass as he was instructed to do while Ab dried the razor and tweezers and laid them on another clean towel. "I got to see what the hell I'm doing. These old peepers aren't exactly calibrated the way they once were."

With that slightly disturbing pronouncement, he set to work, making a small, neat incision over the chip. Then, using one pair of tweezers to pry the flesh apart, he employed the other to extract the tiny piece of silicone. Leah never even flinched while he sliced and probed. "There . . . got that little sucker!" he said triumphantly, tossing it onto the table. He cleansed the incision once more, pressing a small gauze pad over it to stop the bleeding, and then expertly taped the wound.

Clamping his teeth into his lower lip, Del forced himself to watch without making a sound, although he had broken out into a sweat by the time Ab had duplicated the procedure on her left hand. Grit! Damn, the woman was tougher than a squirrel. "Jesus, I think I bled more biting my lip than you did while he cut into you," he murmured, massaging her shoulders.

"Hah! What'd you expect her to do? Jerk around so I sliced her whole palm open!" Ab said.

Leah experimented with flexing her hands. They hurt but not enough to keep her from firing a gun.

The old man patted her arm fondly. "You'll did good, girlie. Knew you would," he added with a wink. Then, all business once more, he said, "Now, stand up and drop those drawers."

Leah looked at him as if he'd just grown a second head. "Why the hell should I do that?"

Del was wondering the same thing. But he stood back, observing with amusement the exchange between the old man and his young "patient."

Ab pointed to the bandage on her leg. A fresh pink stain was soaking through the ripped, bloody cloth of her pant leg. "You're leaking. Better let me check the damage from whatever the hell some other BISC bastard's already done to you."

"Not much gets by you, does it, Ab?" she asked as she unfastened her slacks.

"Hah! I may not be the sharpest knife in the drawer but I damn well know how to recognize seepage from a stitched wound." He motioned for her to take a seat on the chair again, then began unwrapping the bandage the physician at the emergency clinic had placed on her thigh. He grunted crossly. "Too goddamn lazy to use sutures anymore. Gotta staple human beings like they were fence posts!"

Del and Leah exchanged an amused glance as the old man cleansed the bullet wound and applied clean bandaging to it. Without even looking up he said offhandedly, "You know, Agent Berglund, you have the best pair of gams I've seen since Cyd Charisse retired."

Leah sputtered, trying to think of a snappy retort. Who would imagine sexual harassment from a ninety-year-old man! With a man Ab's age, *is* it even harassment? Or a compliment? Or just simply a plain statement of fact? She was not sure.

Seeming to ignore her reaction, old man turned to Del and asked matter-of-factly, "You sleeping with her?"

Del replied with a broad grin, "Every chance I get, Ab."

"Good for you," Fenster said, giving Leah's knee a fatherly pat. He stood up slowly, using the table to support his creaky joints. "Be a waste of one fine-looking young woman if you weren't."

My face must be the color of a neon tomato. Leah struggled to close her mouth before a moth flew into it as she stood and quickly pulled her slacks up. "One fine-looking young woman?" she blurted out.

Ab chuckled, this time patting her shoulder as he said, "Didn't mean to insult you—or . . . er, what is it they call it now—harass you? But you sure have brightened up the life of one homely-looking old codger." Chuckling to himself, he gathered up the instruments and shuffled over to the sink to dump the bowl of disinfectant.

Del struggled to keep from laughing out loud. He stood with his hands in his pockets, staring down at the floor. Feeling her glare at him, he said, "Glad you don't have a needle gun handy."

"Since I don't have chips in my hands, it wouldn't do me any good, would it?" she replied. "But if I did, Delgado, you'd need more medical attention than Ab could provide."

"More than a team of Mayo Clinic surgeons could provide," Del said, grinning openly at her now.

"You two'd better save that sparring for another ring. If what you said's true, more of those black-helicopter bozos will be landing pretty quick." Ab's comment brought their attention to the business at hand.

"You're right," Del conceded.

"You could use some clean duds. Bloodstains are kinda conspicuous," Ab said to Leah. "Upstairs, second door to the right in the closet. My daughter's near enough your size. She left some of her old clothes behind."

"I'll get them," Del said before Leah could respond. She had been through enough already without climbing stairs with an injured leg.

Leah nodded and he quickly walked to the stairs. She picked up the two chips from the table and looked at them for a moment. They were a tangible symbol of her old life, the beliefs she'd sworn to die for—and kill for. "Now the whole damn world is turned upside down," she said, more to herself than to Ab.

Then she looked over at him. "I owe you big time, Corpsman Fenster. You're still one damn fine medic."

Now it was Ab's turn to be flustered. He made a dismissive gesture with his right hand, then offered it solemnly to her. Leah took it as he said, "It was my pleasure, Agent Berglund."

Del returned momentarily with a pair of navy silk slacks and a white blouse. She unself-consciously changed clothes as Ab spoke with Delgado.

"Go out and give that damn government hell! Same to you, Agent Berglund," Ab said with a wide grin.

"We'll deposit these chips a good distance from Newburgh, but you might still get another surprise visit before daylight. Call the police as soon as we're gone, then it might be safer if you went to stay with a neighbor or—"

Fenster shrugged off Del's well-meaning suggestion. "Hah! I can take care of myself . . . but I don't always let on that I can. Sometimes that's the best way to fool them that need fooling, if you get my drift. I'll phone that stupid idiot who calls himself a county sheriff and let him deal with a government helicopter and a yard full of dead bodies. That oughta give old Cy Wharton a coronary. Hah! Come to think of it, that's not so funny—I'd be the one who'd have to give him CPR and he's got breath that'd gag a buck maggot. You two just get along and ditch those chips as fast as you can."

When Del started to pull the black Taurus down the drive, Ab called after them in that high-pitched rusty voice, "Just don't forget to invite me to the wedding when this is all over!"

Neither of them said a word about old Ab's parting comment. Leah didn't intend to and hoped Delgado wouldn't either. She scanned the GPS on the console, which wasn't as fancy as the one on the Caddie. Maybe Del could boost a better model this time. "We need another car."

"Yeah, but first let's get rid of those damn chips," he replied as he turned back onto Interstate 84, heading west.

At the next exit they found a truck stop whose bright white lights proclaimed "Truckers Welcome!" Within five minutes Leah's microchips were southbound, taped onto the back of a big semi headed for Jersey. They parked the Taurus in a dark corner of the huge lot, beneath a big sycamore. While Leah stood watch, Delgado worked his magic on the ignition of a Bondo-colored Chevy junker.

"Climb in," he said as the engine rumbled to life. "It's not much, but we'll make it to someplace where I can get a better one that won't be reported stolen before we reach D.C."

They had agreed that trying to contact Cal Putnam again and have him send a copter had become a greater risk than was acceptable. The ADIC had already been informed of Waterman's assassination plans—at least as much of them as Del and Leah knew. If President Samson still intended to be on that podium at noon with his treacherous vice president in tow, they could do nothing to deter him that Putnam hadn't already tried.

Given Waterman's BISC resources, he could more easily track any aircraft sent to retrieve them than he could locate them on the ground now that Leah's "homing device" had been removed. They would make it into D.C. by late morning, carrying with them the damning evidence of the conspiracy contained in Adam Manchester's journal. Impeachment would be the least of Vice President Harmon Waterman's problems after that.

But only if President Samson was still alive.

When they reached the Pennsylvania border, Del remembered an old FBI buddy, now retired, who lived in Port Jervis. It was a risk contacting him and laying out why they needed his wheels, but stealing yet another vehicle was an even greater one. Al Hirshel took one look at Adam Manchester's journal and handed over the keys. His fancy new Grand Marquis TE with flash drive was equipped with every extra except a tail scanner, which was issued only to active agents.

Leah kept an eye on the GPS each time they neared a major interchange. They were making excellent time courtesy of Del's driving and Hirshel's expensive wheels. As they drew closer to D.C., she pored over her grandfather's journal, trying to figure out exactly how Waterman intended to kill Samson.

"All Mark Patrikas was able to learn about the assassination was that there would be fireworks on the Fourth—at least, that's all he told his father."

"It was enough to get them both killed."

"And almost Gramps, too."

"The senator is a remarkable man," Del said with genuine admiration.

"He and your uncle Mac are a lot alike. I think they'd like each other."

Del smiled at her. "I think you're right on both counts. Maybe they'll get the chance to meet one day now that my cousins' Special Forces unit aborted Sommerville's mission."

"That's the only good news Cal had for you. Why the hell won't Samson stand down from this stupid speech at noon?" Leah said, chewing her lip. "Fireworks on the Fourth has to mean Waterman intended to have Silva's men set off some sort of explosive charges, but how the hell did they figure to get close enough?"

Del shrugged. "With Samson onto Waterman's scheme, he'll have the 'Electric King' on the podium right next to him, according to Cal. The president won't have to worry about a bomb."

"Which only leaves an end run—some crazies of Silva's with their high-powered rifle sights trained directly between Samson's running lights," Leah said, disgusted.

"Still, you know, the more I think about the whole thing . . ."

"Yeah?" Leah looked over at Delgado's profile as he drove. Dawn was breaking to the east of them, the pale gold light limning his harsh features.

"Putnam's right about Abbie Rutledge. There's no way in hell Colombians of any political persuasion can get within two klics of Samson, much less come toting explosives or rifles."

Abbie Rutledge was the head of White House security, and the president never made a public appearance without her hovering like a mother hen, although, given her reputation in the Secret Service, "Shiva the Destroyer" was a more accurate description. She sent her agents over every square inch of any location where Samson was scheduled to appear with the ruthless thoroughness of army ants crossing a coffee plantation.

"So, how do you think they'll get by her? Obviously, Waterman must have a scheme . . ." Her words faded off as she once again began reading the journal.

"I never had a chance to go over your grandfather's stuff. Read me what Patrikas said about the assassination. Everything."

Leah skimmed back to where the entry started and began to read aloud.

"Wait a minute, back up," Del said as she paused for a breath. "Read that last bit again."

Leah frowned. "You mean the part about the fireworks? I've been turning that over and over. They can't do it, Del—not if Waterman's forced to appear on the same stage with Samson. . . . Unless the little bastard doesn't show at the last minute."

"With Cal Putnam at Samson's side, there's no chance in hell. Cal would drag Waterman by his short and curlies onto that stage if he had to. You can take that to the bank."

"Then it's gotta be a sniper."

"Just read it," Del reiterated.

"Okay. Old Stephan tells Gramps what Mark knew about the assassination. 'Waterman and his aides didn't trust Mark completely, but he overhead something about fireworks. We figure it has to be a bomb, but they became quiet when he entered the room. Mark said it was strange. They'd been laughing about Wade being a fighter pilot. Mark knew Harmon resented Wade getting the military glory, but he couldn't see how that connected with the way they planned to kill him.' "

"That's all. Gramps found out the assassination was scheduled for the president's speech at the Washington Monument on the Fourth and some of Silva's crazies were involved, but before he could learn anything more specific than that, both his sources were killed." Leah shuddered, thinking how close Adam Manchester had come to joining them. She looked over at Delgado, who was staring at the road with almost hypnotic concentration in spite of the hair-raising speed at which he drove.

Suddenly he punched the accelerator abruptly and they both flattened against the seats of the Marquis. "What the fuck! You're going to burn out the motor of Hirshel's car—or crash and get us killed before we reach Washington!" she yelled over the roar of the engine.

"I think I know how they're going to do it, Leah."

They made it as far as the I-495 outerbelt surrounding D.C. with no trouble. Leah cursed every time Del swerved in and out of the dense holiday-weekend traffic, especially when he made the switch to I-295 southbound into the capital, then switched again onto I-395 eastbound. They had less than an hour left by then.

As soon as Del explained to Leah what Waterman planned, they'd stopped at several Maryland cybercafes, but Gracie had informed them that Cal was no longer at the White House. He and the president were en route to the festivities. Cal's own link system was still not clear from whatever block had been placed on it. Gracie said she would keep on trying to reach Cal with their message. All they could do was get there before Samson climbed on that stage. Gaining admittance to the presidential entourage was going to be pretty dicey without Putnam's help.

They turned on the Ninth Street exit, speeding beneath L'Enfant Plaza only to emerge—in completely stalled traffic. "Pull over. We can hoof it from here quicker than sit in this damn gridlock," Leah said, almost swallowing her tongue as Del followed her advice, veering up onto a median where he hung his friend's beautiful Marquis tilted drunkenly on its left side.

Leah had the journal strapped to her back, concealed inside her shirt. She carried her Ruger and he his .50-caliber Smith & Wesson, also hidden by more clothing than either of them wanted to wear in the blistering heat, but they had little choice. Even the most corrupt D.C. cop on the El-Op pad would nail a civilian on the Mall packing heat when the president was making such a historic public appearance.

Every police officer on the D.C. force was on duty handling the crowds. Even several hundred retirees had been called back for the emergency, with officers from surrounding jurisdictions on loan for the special occasion. Both Del and Leah were keenly aware that the armed peacekeeping force included BISC operatives, any number of whom would be on the lookout for them.

The police were a grim-faced lot, armed with M17s and MP5s, sweating in full aerofoam body armor as they watched the crowd for any hints of El-Op activity. But having little to gain versus the risk of being taken down by armed police units on every street corner from the Capitol to the Lincoln Memorial, the El-Ops lay low. Business was good enough to suit them on the other side of Massachussets Avenue.

Delgado and Berglund jogged the short distance up to Independence Avenue and turned left. By the time they reached Twelfth Street, Del was favoring his injured knee. They were both drenched with sweat, but no one seemed to pay any attention as they blended in with dozens of Maryland and Virginia yuppie types taking advantage of a "safe" day in the city, jogging along the dirt paths of the Mall.

Leah slowed her pace so Del could keep up, but he waved her on, saying, "Cal trusts you—if you can find him first, go for it."

"Yeah, but if I can't find him, I won't get to first base with your pals in the Secret Service. That Rutledge dame would have me cuffed, flat on the asphalt in a nanosecond. Can't make it without you, Delgado."

"Touching sentiments. Save 'em for later," he grunted, gritting his teeth and picking up the pace. "We have fourteen minutes to cross the Mall and reach someone who'll let us talk to Cal or the president. I say we split up."

She looked over at him, uncertain.

He gasped for breath over the pain, willing it away. "Whoever said 'the zone' was a matter of mind over body lied like a used-car salesman. Go!"

Del watched her take off, vanishing into the assortment of tourists and ordinary locals braving the heat and danger of D.C. for a chance to celebrate. Doggedly, he kept on running, passing the long, gray monolith of the Agriculture Department, ignoring a cop's angry remonstrance when he jaywalked into Fourteenth Street traffic. Del was quickly swallowed up in the line of turgidly moving vehicles. He wended his way around cursing motorists sweating inside small EVs as their pitiful air-conditioning units wheezed and sighed in the sweltering heat.

The tall, white spire of the Washington Monument stood like a beacon at the center of the Mall. He focused on the destination, all the while running frantic ideas through his mind about how the hell either he or Leah could get past security to the presidential entourage. Putnam would have his key agents on the lookout for them, he was certain. But in this disorderly throng of revelers, the likelihood of spotting one man and one woman was lousy. *Jimmy the Greek would've loved the odds.*

He neared the security perimeter. No one got beyond the checkpoints without walking through the steel maw of one of the weapons detectors. The new ones were sophisticated enough to spot any sort of explosives and plastic as well as metal firearms. His .50-caliber cannon would light up that gate like a Canaveral launch pad. The only way to keep the gun was to convince security that he was working FBI on special assignment for Putnam. It could also seal his death warrant if he happened on a gate manned by Waterman's undercover stooges.

No help for it. He had eight minutes to get to Cal and the fastest way was to flash his badge and hope for the best. He scanned the crowd looking for Leah, then spotted her at a gate several hundred feet away. The military guard listening to her wasn't buying her plea to call the Secret Service. He shook his head as if she'd just announced that she was the Virgin Mary come to bless the presidential motorcade. At least he didn't pull a gun and try to ease her away from the gate—so far.

Might as well try my luck. Del pulled out his badge and discreetly handed it to one of the guardsmen as he reached the gate. "I'm Special Agent Elliott Delgado, on assignment for Assistant Director in Charge Putnam. I need to talk with him *now*—before the president reaches the grandstand under the monument!"

The guard, a kid with freckles and a serious marine buzz cut, gave him a squinting glance, then turned his attention to the badge as if he were an engraver examining a new hundred-dollar bill for counterfeit. "I dunno . . ."

"Look, Corporal, Abbie Rutledge will have your ass for lunch if anything happens to the president. He can't set foot on that stand!" That must've done the trick because the guard turned to his companion and the guy opened a channel on the squawking link at his belt. *In a moment I'll either be face-to-face with Cal . . . or dead as Nuñez and Crosby.*

Del waited outside the gate as a steady stream of American diversity passed through it onto the Mall grounds and milled around the tall, white obelisk. His eyes were fixed on the high wooden stage draped with red, white, and blue bunting. On a tiny vid beside the gate, he watched with heart pounding as the presidential entourage moved slowly down the wide pathway cleared from the parking deck off Constitution Avenue to the grandstand beneath the monument. Another couple of minutes and they'd be climbing the steps to the podium!

He looked frantically around and saw that Leah was no longer in line. She must have given up on the guards at that station. Then he heard the jangling wail of one of the security-gate Klaxons directly across from his station. The guards grabbed a hapless teenager with chartreuse hair that Gracie would envy and began frisking him. Del grinned when they pulled Leah's Ruger from the boy's baggy jeans and cuffed him. Agent Berglund was already through the gate, having slipped her weapon into the kid's pocket.

"Sir, Chief Rutledge says you're to be brought to her immediately," the young guard at Del's gate said.

Two Secret Service agents broke through the crowd, headed directly for him. From Ray·Bans to nubuck oxfords, they were dressed in black in spite of the heat. Rumor had it that their sweat glands were removed when they signed up. "Where's Putnam?" he asked.

"Don't know, one of the agents replied laconically. "We're taking you to the boss."

They cleared a path through the sweltering mass of humanity, heading for the left side of the grandstand, where he could see Abbie Rutledge's elaborately cornrowed head sticking above the sea of shorter mortals surrounding her. On the right side of the grandstand the presidential entourage was climbing the stairs. Several Secret Service agents led the way with the president and vice president just behind them. Various foreign dignitaries had already been seated at the right side of the enormous wooden structure. Samson stopped to shake hands with the Russian and Euro ambassadors as he made his way across the stage.

The band struck up "Hail to the Chief" and applause rippled across the milling crowd when Samson and Waterman came into view. Waving at the people, the two men walked toward the chairs on which they'd take their seats in a moment.

"No time for that. I have to get to Putnam now or Samson's a dead man!" Del hissed, but his words were drowned out as shrieks and catcalls erupted about fifty meters from the grandstands.

"What the fuck's going on?" the first agent asked, scanning the melee while his hand tightened on the 9mm in its shoulder sling under his coat.

"Naked women!" someone in the crowd yelled.

Leah spotted Putnam at the right side of the grandstand and fought her way closer. She saw the banners go up around a dozen or so statuesque females whose gaunt, angular bodies and striking faces proclaimed them fashion models. Only this time they were modeling nothing but skin—their own, after having dramatically flung off a substantial fortune in silver-fox fur coats. Everyone, including the president, stared at the spectacle as the models and their supporters chanted while trampling on the furs.

"Compassion is the fashion."

"Only cave people wear fur!"

"We'd rather go naked than wear fur!"

"Any president who'd end the import ban on Russian fox fur should have his hide tanned!" one striking female yelled at Samson, shaking her raised fist. She was a full head taller than any of the other models and easily the most striking. Her skin glowed amber bronze and the crowd could see every inch of it. Waist-length, espresso-black hair didn't do much to cover her nudity.

Leah studied the woman for an instant, then recognized her. Imelda Obregón, better known as the Inca, was one of the highest-paid supermodels in the world. She was also a rabid animal-rights activist—and a Colombian national! Police whistles shrilled over the chanting of the protesters, who condemned Wade Samson's recent decision to rescind the ban on the import of silver-fox pelts.

"They're decoys," she muttered, instinctively knowing that the seemingly harmless diversion had been orchestrated by Waterman's men. She spotted Putnam standing on the stairs, scanning the crowd, and began to yell at him, praying her white-blond hair and height would catch his eye before one of Waterman's BISC agents spotted her.

Putnam's head swiveled to the left and he caught sight of Leah Berglund. He grabbed the nearest Secret Service agent and pointed at her, then started down the stairs to meet her. "Where the hell's Delgado?" he yelled as she shoved past him, heading up the steps.

The protesters were removed as quickly as they'd appeared, the bare models most unwillingly swaddled in the furs they'd shed moments earlier. Sweating, swearing police shoved them to the rear of the grandstand as the signal was given from the podium for the band to strike up the national anthem.

Abbie Rutledge recognized Elliott Delgado the moment she caught sight of him, pushing his way toward her with two of her agents trying to keep up. She didn't like the grim expression on his face. Her gut tightened as she started down the stairs. "What the hell's going on?" she mouthed as he took the steps two at a time, headed toward her.

The last strains of "The Star-Spangled Banner" were fading. Representative Michael Monteal, majority whip in the House and longtime friend of Samson's, stepped up to the speaker's rostrum to introduce the president. Samson and Waterman stood to the left of the bunting-draped rostrum, their chairs positioned side by side behind them. Monteal raised his hand for the crowd to quiet down, and all those on the dais prepared to take their seats while he made his speech.

Leah took the last step onto the big platform with Cal wheezing behind her. She was too late! Samson and Waterman were at the opposite end, and she'd bet Bill Gates's net worth that the Secret Service agent standing nearest them was BISC.

Delgado knew this time he couldn't afford to be the second man in, bum knee or no bum knee. Leah was too far from Samson to make it. It was his show, no time to explain. As Waterman and Samson started to sit down, he cleared the last step and leaped across the stage. Elliott Delgado tackled the president of the United States.

They flew past Samson's chair, landing with the president sprawled facedown on the floorboards and Delgado on top of him. Then all hell broke loose.

21.

The crowd went wild as a phalanx of Secret Service agents thundered toward their downed president. The agent closest to the vice president drew his SIG-Sauer to shoot Del, but Waterman stood frozen between them like a jacklighted deer. Then the little man squeaked an obscenity and turned to bolt. Delgado grabbed him by one scrawny ankle, but Waterman kicked free. It was enough to make him loose his balance. He toppled backward onto the president's chair. His agent lunged to grab him but was too late. The tiny pressure-activated nitro-cordite shrapnel cannon beneath the chair exploded with an eerie whistle.

Jagged chunks of stainless steel burst straight through the chair seat in a tight pattern, ripping through soft tissue and bone. Shrieking in agony, Harmon Waterman shot two meters into the air. The shrapnel disintegrated his spinal column and viscera, ruptured his chest in midair, and tore his head from what was left of his body.

Filled with terror and revulsion, thousands watched as the vice president's blood and flesh drenched the stage like rainfall. What was left of his decapitated corpse dropped with a thud to the platform beside a dazed President Samson, who was by this time surrounded with a human wall of Secret Service agents.

Waterman's agent ran to the right side of the stage, but Leah stood directly in his path. She closed too quickly for him to get off a shot. He tried to sidestep but she grasped his extended gun arm, twisting it upward. Her foot hooked behind his knee, toppling him to the floorboards. She landed on top of him, then delivered a chop to his throat.

The pistol in his hand dropped uselessly at his side. She scooped it up and calmly trained it on him.

Harmon Waterman's head rolled across the grandstand to where Cal Putnam stood. The ADIC nudged it calmly with the toe of one shoe. He stared into the vice president's bloodshot eyes, then muttered to himself, "Well, ole son, when you roll snake eyes, you lose."

Abbie Rutledge issued curt orders over her link for reinforcements. She glared at Delgado as her men assisted the president to his feet. "Mr. President, I think it's best to get you back to the White House immediately." Without waiting for Samson to reply, the tall black woman turned to Don Trexler, her second-in-command. After conferring briefly with Rutledge, he motioned for the phalanx of agents to escort the ashen-faced leader from the stage.

Once satisfied that her presidential charge was safe, Rutledge turned hard brown eyes back to the former FBI agent. "You're supposed to be retired from active duty. Just what the hell is going on, Delgado?"

"That little ejection seat was intended for Samson, not Waterman," Del replied.

"That couldn't be more obvious. How are you involved?"

"Howdy, Abbie," Putnam interjected over the noise of the crowd below as police bellowed instructions over the sound system for everyone to remain calm. He looked over at what had been Harmon Waterman and shook his head. "Son of a bitch looks like a Hefty bag filled with vegetable soup dropped twenty stories."

Rutledge put one big hand with long crimson nails on a generously curved hip, cocked her head at Putnam, and began tapping the toe of her high-heeled Ferragamo shoe. She was legendary for how fast she could move in spike heels. The nails were said to be stained with the blood of anyone who crossed her. "Ah, the good ole boys' club's heard from. I might've known you be involved, Putnam."

"If you check what's left of that little bitty tin can planted under Wade's seat, I think you'll find some pretty interesting prints on it," he replied.

"And whose prints will we lift from that nitro surprise?"

"Don't know exactly, but you can bet that fine black ass it'll be one of Benito Zuloaga's players."

"I could nail you for a sexist, racist remark like that if I had time to fool with it," she snapped at Putnam. She obviously had more important things on her mind. "This was a setup to make it look like the Cartel assassinated the president."

"I think your man here may be able to shed some light on how that device was planted," Leah said, holding his own weapon on the Secret Service agent she'd captured. His bulldog features were impassive, but his glance darted from the horror that had been Harmon Waterman to the fierce predatory gleam in Chief Rutledge's eyes.

"Yeah, it had to be him," Del agreed. "He tried to keep Waterman from landing on the president's chair. He knew what was under it."

"The uproar with the animal rights activists was the decoy," Leah said. "Most of them were probably duped into staging what they believed would be a disruptive but innocent protest. I recognized the Inca and remembered that she's Colombian. While everyone's attention shifted to a bunch of naked supermodels, the big guy here slipped the device under the president's seat."

"But I bet Harmon was the one who brought it in, then handed it to him at the crucial moment. Even top-clearance personnel have to be wanded down before they come on the dais," Del said.

"But not the vice president," Leah added.

Putnam cursed. "I was watching Waterman closer'n a polecat stalkin' a pullet hen, but that must've got by me. Ole Harmon had to figger with me here, he couldn't bend over to attach the device. What he could do from the angle where I was standing was to pass it to the agent right next to him."

"You mean to tell me you knew Waterman was involved in a plot to assassinate Wade Samson and you didn't tell me!" Rutledge thundered. She towered over Putnam in her spike heels.

"Don't go gettin' your panties all in a twist, Abbie," Cal drawled. "Wade wanted to tell you, but I convinced him what we'd learned about Waterman's conspiracy was best kept strictly between the two of us. No one, not even his national security adviser, knew anything. We'd already learned Mark Patrikas was up to his ass in those gators. There's no way of knowing how many people—at all levels of government— will be flopping on the banks when we drain the swamp."

"And that skinny little white boy Electric King was behind all this?" Abbie asked incredulously.

Putnam nodded. "When his IQ reached fifty, he shoulda sold. Surprises me he'd have the balls to sit down beside Wade knowing what was going to happen, but he wanted all that power . . ." Glancing at the bloody pulp that had been the vice president's posterior, he added, "He wanted it bad enough to risk his 'skinny little white boy' ass."

"That device blasts a very narrow pattern," Leah said as a team of agents gathered up Waterman's remains and placed them in a body bag.

"That's how I figured it out," Del said. "The president's plane was shot down when he was a fighter pilot during the war—"

"And he used an ejection seat," Cal said, recalling the old news stories.

What Mark Patrikas had overheard made perfect sense when Del had explained it to Leah. "BISC uses pressure-activated shrapnel cannons when they have an undercover agent in proximity to a sentenced El-Op. The subject is propelled straight up, similar to the way an aircraft ejection seat works."

"Who in the hell are you?" Rutledge asked, bristling at the mention of BISC.

"This is one of my best people, Agent Leah Berglund."

"Former agent," Leah corrected.

Turning to Delgado, Abbie asked, "I assume you're back on the payroll, too?"

"Guilty as charged," Del replied with a grimace. "But don't feel too bad about being out of the loop. None of us working for Cal and the president had all the pieces of the puzzle. We were each given an assignment and told only what we needed to know. Even the director of the FBI was part of the conspiracy."

"What you're implying, Delgado, is that President Samson and his ace bird dog here think I might be in on this conspiracy," Rutledge said, narrowing her eyes on Putnam.

"Shitfire, woman, we weren't sure about the chairman of the Joint Chiefs when this whole mess started. General Sommerville was on the payroll. So was Brian Fuller."

Abbie blinked. "That nutcase Sommerville I'd believe, but Fuller was supposed to be a shoo-in for the Democratic nomination after the president's next term. Dammit, I would've voted for the son of a bitch!"

"No one will now. He's dead," Delgado said flatly.

"Let's fly this jailbird over to Bureau interrogation. I have me a real feelin' he's about to sing—ain't that right, ole son?" Putnam's genial tone did not match the hard light in his eyes.

"This might be a little extra help during the interrogation," Leah said, handing her grandfather's journal to Cal.

"Hot damn, I've been waiting for this!" He clutched the heavy volume and signaled the two men who'd served as lookouts when he'd met Leah and Del at Tysons Corner. They each took one of the duplicitous Secret Service agent's arms.

"Not so fast. This turkey is mine. Where he goes, I go." Abbie Rutledge's voice was lethal as she looked at "her" agent.

Delgado could see the man shiver. "He's probably glad to be in FBI custody."

"You trust her?" Leah asked as Rutledge followed Cal and his prisoner down the grandstand stairs.

"Abbie? Yeah. If she'd been in charge of killing Samson, the prez would be meat."

The crowds were dispersing slowly. They had come to see a gala celebration and had instead witnessed a literal bloodbath. Police swarmed over the vast expanse of the monument grounds, using the sound system to urge people to go home. The army band hastily packed up their instruments beneath the grandstand while Secret Service agents assisted shaken foreign dignitaries to safety.

As they decended the stairs, Leah said, "I'd like to be in on the interrogation of Waterman's agent."

Delgado shrugged. "Putnam'd probably let you since it was you and your grandfather who furnished the evidence that'll pull down the last of the conspirators."

"With Fuller, Sommerville, and Waterman all dead, who else is left?"

"For certain some fairly high-ranking brass in the Pentagon. I'd bet on a federal judge or two, and maybe a few more members of our esteemed Congress."

"Where will it all end, Del?"

"BISC will end—and along with it, the Martial Law Act. I'd bet the farm on that."

Leah swallowed hard, remembering how she'd been used by the agency to which she'd sworn such high-minded allegiance. "It can't be dismantled soon enough for me."

9 A.M., EDT, MONDAY, JULY 20
THE OVAL OFFICE

"I'm going to do it, Cal." Wade Samson sat behind the huge walnut desk with the presidential seal on it. He looked anything but presidential. His face was haggard and lined, his heavy hair shaggy and unstyled. Even his $4,000 suit looked as if he'd slept in it—a restless and poor sleep indeed.

Putnam watched his chief slump in the high-backed chair as he swiveled it toward the view outside his window, staring at the Washington Monument as if drawing moral support from it. "When?" was all the acting FBI director asked.

"My speechwriters are at work on it right now. I don't imagine it'll be ready for a few more days. But my press secretary's already alerted the media that I'll be making a major policy address next week. That really grabbed their attention"

"Polish up that speech till it shines like a new apple, Wade. This'll go hard on your presidency if you don't handle it right."

Samson sighed and combed his fingers through his hair. "I pushed through laws that took away the most basic due process rights in the Constitution. I'm responsible for the existence of BISC. Now I have to go in front of the American people and admit it was a colossal mistake that needs to be corrected at once."

"Don't go poundin' on yourself with too big a hammer," Putnam said, extracting a wooden match from a rumpled coat pocket and firing up his pipe. "The Slaughter made every man jack in the country ready to stampede that direction. You were only a trail drover. Now that Drescher's come to and is spilling his fat guts, we have the goods on two more congressmen, a senator, and a pack of midrange Pentagon types."

"Yes, but I caved in to congressional pressure and appointed Drescher director even though I knew he wasn't qualified. I even thought Cleve Mallory would make a solid addition to the Supreme Court!"

"That bites, I'll admit," Putnam conceded. "But we're cleaning house like a scrubby Dutchwoman now, Wade. Pentagon cryptographers are still working on Waterman's code. As soon as they break it, we'll nail every BISC agent who worked on Harmon's Sanitation Squads. Shitfire, already the fuckers're pounding on the Bureau's door to testify against each other for immunity." Putnam snorted and took a puff from his pipe. "Passel of vipers. No one involved in this will walk away, I promise you."

"You recall our conversations when you first came to me with this mess—what I said about this country needing someone absolutely incorruptible to deal with the Cartel?" Samson studied the older man who fussed with relighting his pipe. Cal always took his time thinking things over. The president liked that trait. There was no stampeding Cal Putnam. Samson waited him out, just to see what the cagey old man would say.

"As my grandpappy used to say, talk's cheap but it takes real money to buy whiskey. There a point to this, Wade?"

Samson chuckled and ran his fingers through his hair again. "Never could play the judicious statesman role with you, could I?"

"You're a politician born and bred to the bone. Nothin' wrong with that if you're doing what you're doing for the right reasons. Yup, I recollect you and me talking about the danger from BISC. The need to dismantle it and repeal the Martial Law legislation that put it in business."

"I also mentioned an expanded role for the Bureau."

"Some agency's got to take up the slack, that's for damn sure."

Samson smiled. "I have an offer for you, Cal. One I think you'll like . . ."

9:05 A.M., EDT, MONDAY, JULY 20
ALEXANDRIA, VIRGINIA

Delgado was still a slob. That would never change. Leah looked around the messy apartment's bedroom. The last time she'd been in his Pitt Street condo, she'd broken through his wretched security system and tossed the place as a BISC agent, looking for incriminating evidence that could have signed Elliott Delgado's death warrant. Now she was here as his lover.

She sat up in the middle of the large, rumpled bed. Sheets tangled around her legs, trailing off the mattress. The carpet was littered with clothes discarded during their swift, lustful undressing last night. Dirty briefs and T-shirts moldered on every surface. She wondered when Del had last done a batch of laundry . . . probably back when Bill Clinton was president.

Dust lay so thick that she couldn't tell if the armoire and night-stand were oak or pine. The closet door was ajar, the interior crammed with serviceable menswear, mostly jeans, sweaters, and polo shirts. A clotheshorse Delgado was not. He owned, by her quick visual tally, only two suits and three sport coats. Most of his ties were out of style, and the ones that weren't had fast-food stains on them like the blue-striped number dangling from the chair in the corner.

It says a lot about a man . . . what his priorities are in life, she mused. Being featured in *House Beautiful* or *GQ* was not among them. The only items in the room that were well cared for were an antique-gold-framed set of photos, mostly of Mike, along with various formal and informal shots of the Mulcahey clan taken in Mazatlán. He probably didn't need to dust them because he handled them so often.

Family was the most important thing in the world to her, too. She had just spent a week in Maine with her grandfather. Putnam and several presidential aides had exhaustively debriefed the senator, who thoroughly enjoyed using the publicity from the failed coup as a forum. She'd stood by his side at a news conference in Bangor yesterday morning as Adam Manchester had spoken eloquently about the abuses perpetrated by secret government agencies and the dangers of sacrificing constitutional rights for public safety.

Del had called her several times while she was in Maine. Cuff Bedford's heroism in unearthing the conspiracy had been made public. Wade Samson had attended the funeral of Del's old friend and presented Bedford's parents with a posthumous Presidential Medal of Freedom for their son.

Then Del had flown to California to help Diana and Mike get resettled after they'd returned home to La Jolla. Diana had insisted that Mike begin the school year with his old friends. Newly widowed, she needed to rebuild her life after the upheavals of the past months and wanted to provide as much normality for Mike as possible.

Leah slid off the bed and padded naked across the room to her suitcase, sitting unopened by the door. When she'd returned from Maine last night, Del had picked her up at the airport and driven to her old apartment in D.C. She'd quickly packed her personal belongings. That had not taken long at all. The bullet-scarred efficiency unit was a bitter reminder of how sterile her life had been during the years she'd worked for BISC.

She and Del had both needed the time they'd spent apart. But now she had to make some hard decisions about her life . . . and whether Elliott Delgado would be a part of it. She placed the suitcase on a chair and flicked the locks, reaching inside for a filmy aqua silk robe.

Del emerged from the shower as she was putting it on. He leaned against the doorframe and crossed his arms, wearing nothing but a towel draped casually around his hips. Moisture still glistened in his black, curly hair. He studied her with hooded eyes.

"You look good enough to eat, Berglund . . . and I'm a hungry man."

"I'm a hungry woman. You make breakfast while I shower," she replied, gliding past him in the narrow doorway to the steamy little bath.

"That's the trouble. No romance in your soul," he groused, removing the towel and scrubbing his wet hair with it. He rummaged through drawers until he located what was probably his last clean pair of briefs. Making a mental note to purchase more, he pulled on a polo shirt and jeans, then walked barefoot to the small alcove off the living room that served as an eating area. The wall fridge yielded a sack of oranges in various stages of decomposition, a carton of curdled milk, and half of a pepperoni pizza dried out enough to use as a Frisbee.

"Oh, well," he said with a shrug, closing the door. The freezer unit yielded a can of concentrated grapefruit juice, and there was coffee in the cabinet. By the time Leah emerged from the shower the fragrance of the fresh brew filled the stale apartment. He poured her a tall glass of grapefruit juice and a cup of black coffee and handed them to her, saying, "Sorry, but you'll have to drink it black. The milk went south while we were out saving the free world."

She accepted the coffee and juice, eyeing the small table in the corner. It was covered with unread newspapers, dirty dishes, and fast-food cartons. "Ugh, Delgado, how can you live like this?" she asked, setting down her glass and cup on one corner of the table. "Get those pizza boxes and the rest of the junk off the chairs so we can sit down."

"Yes, Sergeant," he said, clearing the two vinyl chairs and balancing the debris from them neatly atop an already overflowing trash can in the opposite corner.

She narrowed her eyes and concentrated on the pile as if she could will it to topple off, but it held. They each took a seat and sipped coffee and juice. The air was charged with a new kind of tension, unlike the frenzied lust that had characterized their earlier attraction while they were running for their lives. Last night had been different . . . sort of. That "sort of" made her uneasy.

She picked up the morning's *Post,* pulled off the wrapper, and started to read the headlines, passing him the rest of the fat paper. "It says here President Portillo-Ortiz is taking credit for stopping Sommerville's nuclear strike against Colombia. Claims he had spies inside who blew the whistle as soon as the joint forces headed down the coast. Oh, Raoul and Ernesto actually get a mention—at the bottom of the page."

"I imagine *el presidente* contritely sniveled to Samson so the Mexican government could come out of this smelling like a rose. If his administration was toppled, the Cartel would move in and take over Mexico," Del said cynically.

"What's going to happen with the Cartel now? Silva's on ice. No way he or his heir apparent will ever be restored to power in Colombia. We know the Cartel has nuclear capabilities and they're still really pissed."

"I couldn't say anything over the link, but Cal told me that Samson asked Uncle Mac to negotiate an understanding with Zuloaga and company. And, guess who else is working on the side of the angels with him?"

She looked over the top of her newspaper at his cocked eyebrow. "Not Inocensio Ramirez!"

"None other. Should be interesting to see what develops."

"Just so it's not World War Three. They still haven't uncovered anything about who the Cartel mole inside our government is, have they?"

"Nope. And that bothers me. Every scumbag around the Hill has crawled out from under a rock—or had his rock pulled off of him. They're all singing but no one knows about the mole."

"Someone in BISC? They haven't broken Waterman's link encryption yet, have they?"

Del rubbed his eyes. Something still niggled in the back of his mind. "Not yet. But I don't think the mole is BISC. They were either straight arrows like you or else Waterman's goons. I can't see either type selling out to the Cartel."

Leah shrugged. "Sooner or later the guy has to trip up. Maybe your uncle will figure it out. After all, he and Ramirez will be talking directly to Benito himself," she replied, returning to peruse the paper.

He did the same for a few moments, then laid the sports section down and looked over at her. She finally lowered the shield of newsprint and met his eyes.

Del studied her tight expression. When he'd called about picking her up at the airport last night, she'd insisted she could manage alone. Always alone. That was the Berglund way. He'd overridden her protests, saying if she didn't want him there, she'd just have to steal some security guard's gun and shoot him. No way was he letting her face that awful apartment by herself.

He'd insisted she gather up her things and spend the night at his place. By the time they'd reached his front door, they were tearing the clothes off each other. Sex always seemed to work for them. Talking the day after didn't. "So where are we going to go from here?"

Leah shrugged stiffly. "Damn if I know, Delgado. You mentioned something about applying for a transfer to your magazine's San Diego office."

He grinned. Of course she'd direct the topic to *his* plans. "Miss me already, huh? What about the job Putnam offered you? Interested in being a special agent with the 'new and improved' Bureau?"

"It's tempting . . ." She ran her fingertip over the sweat droplets on the juice glass, then moved it in a circular pattern on the tabletop.

"But you aren't going to take it." The quick euphoria he felt at her hesitation took him by surprise.

"No. I've had enough of law enforcement."

"Different laws pretty soon, Leah. Between them, Cal and your grandfather will see to it. What's the senator say about running again? If he threw his hat in the ring, he'd beat the tar out of Samson."

"Yeah, I think so, too." A wistful smile lingered at the corners of her mouth. "Even though he hasn't officially announced his candidacy yet, I watched a vid discussion he had with the chairman of the Republican National Committee. He'll come out swinging. Wade Samson better learn how to duck."

Del chuckled. "Wade'll cover his ass. Don't worry about a shrewd pol like him." He paused and waited a beat as Leah continued to stare into the bottom of her empty cup. "We've settled the fate of the free world, Berglund. Now all we have to do is figure out the rest of our own lives. I need to spend more time with my son, and frankly, getting out of the Capitol Hill rat race does appeal. In southern California I'll be closer to my family in Mexico. Mike and I can visit them more often."

"I know how important that is to you. It's a good decision," she said neutrally.

"Then what about Leah Berglund? What's she going to do if a high-power job with the Bureau's not what she wants, hmmm?" *It's like prying open a forty-kilo clam to get her to reveal anything personal.* When she didn't immediately reply, he went on, "I'll tell you what I want. I want you to come with me."

Leah looked up, unable to hide her startled expression, which quickly shifted to one of uncertainty. "I'm an East Coast girl, Delgado. What would I do out in LaLa land?"

Now it was his turn to shrug. "You told me about your brother. No matter what Uncle Mac can arrange with the Cartel, there'll always be a real need to work with young addicts. I happen to know a woman in San Pedro who runs a clinic for teenagers. You'd be good with them."

"My atonement? Counsel them instead of terminating them?"

"You're the one hung up with guilt. I know you and I know how badly you need to atone for what you think you did wrong—whether you actually did it or not. This would work . . . and it would also keep you close to me and Mike. No accounting for tastes but the kid really likes you."

His smile almost undid her. His next words finished the job.

"And so do I . . . in fact, well . . . if we were to keep seeing each other, get used to a more, er, conventional relationship—one where we weren't on the run with people trying to kill us—maybe we'd decide to make it a permanent deal. What do you think, Leah?"

She took a deep breath. This was like plunging off a high dive blindfolded, not even knowing if there was any water in the pool. He reached over and took her hand gently, just holding it, waiting . . . "Let me have a little time, Del. It's a big decision."

"Yeah, it is. Okay, I'm cool with waiting. In fact, I'm going down to Mexico next week to see Uncle Mac and Aunt Seri and the whole family. Stay here and think things over while I'm gone."

Then he grinned like the old Delgado she'd first met in the *U.S. News-Time* office and added, "Oh, while you're at it, you might even straighten up this joint a little. It could use a woman's touch."

22.

"If Inocensio knew I had this, he'd roast my balls over a slow fire," Francisco Mulcahey said to his nephew. They sat closeted in his study as the old man rummaged around in the big wall safe, searching for one small disc. The whole household had retired for the night except for them. Low calls from night birds and the distant hum of traffic on the *malecón* were the only sounds that broke the stillness.

Francisco extracted the audio disc carefully, holding it up to the light. "We'd been drinking to celebrate the end of the negotiations. That's why I think he made the mistake that enabled me to get this. Celebration was the excuse Inocensio used for getting drunk. The flight from Bogotá was pretty bumpy." Mulcahey grinned. "He'd never admit it, but he's terrified of flying and that old crate Benito sent us home in even gave me a few uncertain moments." Mac laughed, remembering the sweat-sheened face of the most feared drug lord on the Pacific coast when they'd hit that air pocket and dropped fifty meters over the Sierra Madre.

"I take it the Cartel didn't go for the idea of Raoul flying into their airspace," Del said drily. "They probably hoped you'd crash."

Mac grunted. "It was rough in Bogotá, let me tell you. Zuloaga and his boys were anything but happy about the Americans and Mexicans getting in bed with Silva's faction. They made it crystal clear they would've made a full nuclear retaliation."

"Mexico would glow in the dark, and fallout would hit the Southwest, not much question. Both countries owe you."

"All Ramirez and I did was oil the waters after the fact. Make a few promises on behalf of both presidents."

"But you didn't give them Silva or his Colombian 'freedom fighters.'"

"It was tempting, believe me," Mac replied. "Instead I gave them Samson's solemn pledge that Silva and his followers will face very serious charges in the American courts. Zuloaga knows Samson won't dare break his word. And Portillo-Ortiz will be retiring quietly to private life. Everyone who had any part in the plot will be forced out of office. Benito is no fool. He knows when to push and when not to. Rather like old Inocensio."

"Why has Ramirez let you alone all these years? You've run this city without interference. Even got him to help us against the conspirators." Del had always wanted to know the answer but had never before had the nerve to ask the question. He still was not sure his uncle would answer.

Francisco paused for a moment, a faraway expression in his eyes. Then he looked back at his great-nephew. "You are too young to remember Ursula."

"Ursula?" Del echoed, his mind sifting through the complex genealogy of their huge family, coming up empty.

"She was my baby sister, the youngest of the seven of us."

Del was stunned for he had believed his great-uncle had only two sisters. "No one's ever spoken of a third sister."

"That is because it was considered a great stain on the family honor. When she was only sixteen, she ran away with a boy the Mulcaheys considered unworthy. The son of a Sonoran border bandit, little more than a thug at the time . . ."

"Inocensio Ramirez."

"Yes. Inocensio loved her. She was the only person he has ever loved, I think."

"What happened?"

Mac shrugged stiffly, the pain still evident after all these years. "She fled with him up into the Sierra Madre when the *federales* came to arrest him. She was carrying his child. A son. The baby died and she followed him a few days later. Inocensio risked his life to come and tell me. I have never seen a man so grief-stricken. We had been friends as boys."

"He told me he worked on your father's shrimp boats with you when you were young," Del said, understanding now the peculiar bond between two men who had chosen such different courses in life. "I'd for damn sure rather have him for an ally than an enemy."

"He does not overreach like some others," Mulcahey said quietly.

"He wouldn't be fool enough to get involved in plots to overthrow the U.S. government. Or attack the Cartel directly. More his style to squeeze them out of business an inch at a time," Del speculated. "You have your work cut out for you, dealing with Ramirez—but you've been doing it for years."

"You and my grandsons have already performed a far more delicate task . . . with help from that beautiful American lady. Our whole family owes her a great debt of gratitude for saving Miguelito's life." Mac studied Del's face as he mentioned Leah. "Are you still seeing her? Your son is quite taken with her as I'm sure you know."

Del couldn't help but smile at his uncle's less than subtle hints. "Mike thinks she hung the moon. Diana's taking the idea of her son's crush on another potential maternal figure pretty well, all things considered . . . and, yes, I am still seeing Leah. But don't go getting your hopes up just yet. Leah's pretty uptight about relationships and really guilt-ridden about her BISC work."

"But that is foolishness. She and many other idealistic agents were being deceived and used by their own government. She has nothing to be guilty about, especially after what she risked to help you and to rescue Miguelito."

"True, but I think her BISC work and our relationship are sort of knit together in her mind. It'll take her a while to sort it all out."

"Ah," Mac said thoughtfully. Then he smiled at Del. "I have taught you to be a patient man, no?"

"Yes, Uncle, you have." Del replied with a grin before he shifted his attention back to the matter at hand. "Now, what's this disc about? If you pirated this copy from Ramirez, I see why you didn't mention it when I called."

Mulcahey nodded his head grimly. "Wait until you hear it."

"How'd you get your hands on it in the first place?"

"Ramirez monitors all communications going in and out of Cartel headquarters. He's had his own spy in their organization for a long time now."

Del whistled. "If he'd never go after Benny directly, why risk placing a mole in Colombia?"

"Self-protection." The old man shrugged. "For that, he must know their plans. His agent records every exchange Zuloaga and his key people have with foreign nationals. Inocensio and I had just landed in Culiacán when Cabril brought this disc to him right there on the tarmac.

"Cabril was really agitated. It seemed the disc held a transmission intercepted by some source in Cuba. Inocensio kept Cabril from saying more, then asked me to wait in his private car. I was curious, let me tell you, but there was nothing I could do. From his Lincoln I watched as the two of them climbed inside a small Ford TE.

"I was alone in the limo. His chauffeur was flirting with a pretty stewardess near the terminal entrance. So I took a big risk." The old man paused and a sly smile wreathed his face. "There is some pretty fancy equipment in that big car of Inocensio's. Raoul has been teaching me how to use homing recorders, among other things . . ."

"So you eavesdropped on Rameriz and Cabril as they played the disc."

"And recorded the whole thing," Mac replied proudly.

"I'll say it was a big risk. Ramirez will know you made a tape if this goes public."

"Since no one caught me while I was doing it, he'd have no idea that I was the one. Remember, this came from a source he doesn't usually employ—someone in Cuba. Most likely he'd blame a leak on whoever is at that end."

"But he knows you were there when he first received the disc." Del didn't like it. The idea of the Cuban connection bothered him, too.

The Samson administration had established close ties to Hector Ruiz's government in Havana.

Mac shrugged his big shoulders. "What's on this disc has no direct bearing on Inocensio's business dealings," he replied, dismissing his nephew's misgivings with a wave of his hand. "The sound quality is a little poor—some scratchy noise overlaying it. I fear I'm not the technical expert my grandson is. The disk was scrambled, so there is no way to identify voiceprints."

Ever since Del had landed in Mazatlán, a prickly feeling had been crawling up his back. "But you know who the speakers are," Del said, unable to shake his feeling of dread.

"Yes, I'm pretty certain. One is Benito Zuloaga. The other—"

"The mole in Washington!" Del's heart suddenly began slamming in his chest as if he'd run a hundred-meter sprint. "It's been bothering me ever since Inocensio first told me the Cartel knew all about the coup in the U.S. and the strike against them. Who high enough up in the government to know that information would have anything to gain from giving it to them?"

"Listen, and then you will have to figure out the reason."

Del was on the next flight back to Washington, a red-eye that touched down around five in the morning. The grim scene at Dulles Airport security matched his mood perfectly. He plodded through the mercifully shorter lines, grateful that things were relatively slow at this ungodly hour. The security forces monitored dispirited passengers closely. After the assassination attempt, the city was more paranoid than ever. If he was right about what was on that disc, how the hell would it affect public morale?

After clearing the airport, he rented a car and headed to his office at *News-Time*. Leah was probably still asleep back at the condo. He did not intend to wake her. He'd left his Buick for her to drive while he was out of the country. His first priority was to check in with Gracie Kell and see what she'd found for him. He'd contacted her from Mazatlán last night, a surprisingly simple task in view of how she usually moved around and took her own sweet time getting back to him. Helping to thwart a presidential coup seemed to have had a calming effect on the hacker.

When her voice came over the link in his office, he flicked on his visual. Recognizing him, she did the same and her image came into focus. She now had deep violet hair, which perfectly matched the dark purplish circles beneath her mascaraed eyes. "Christ, you look like shit, Gracie. Your hair matches your complexion and you apparently aren't getting any more sleep than me."

"Yeah," she said, mercilessly assaulting a cuticle. "Some guy calls me at three in the morning all the way from Mexico, wakes me up, and says I gotta save the world again. Funny how a girl can't get her beauty rest, Delgado."

"What do you have for me?"

"Plenty. It all checks out . . . once you know where to look," she said smugly. "But I ain't giving it to you over an open link," she added, peering suspiciously at the clutter in his office. "Shit, that place could have enough bugs hidden in it to stock an electronic warehouse and you'd never find a one."

He sighed. "All right, how about the same place as last time? Say, around ten?"

"Right. Bring me a jumbo Diet Coke. Better get one for yourself while you're at it, too. You look like you could use an upper," she snickered as she signed off.

"I shouldn't have made the crack about her hair," he muttered.

He had several hours to kill but the university cafeteria was not open this early. The magazine had extensive resource programs on their own link system. He decided to access what he could. *Anything to keep from thinking about what's happened.* All the while he worked, the copy of Mac's disc lay tucked in his shirt pocket. That hundred grams weighed him down as if it were a hundred kilos.

He thought about calling Leah, even dialed on the link, then broke the connection. No, she had enough baggage to deal with now. No way was he bringing her into this mess. He tried to think past it, to see the future out in California. A much more pleasant consideration. Screw the book offers. That would mean involving Leah and their relationship in the story, and that he was not prepared to do. He'd enjoy the new assignment in the magazine's San Diego office. Old Carolyn Etherington had offered him the managing editor's job and he'd jumped at the chance. At last he and Mike would have plenty of time to spend together.

But what about Leah?

A little after nine. Time to go. He banished thoughts of Leah Berglund and headed to the men's washroom to splash his face with cold water. He dried it off with paper towels and never once looked at his image in the mirror.

11:20 A.M., EDT, WEDNESDAY, JULY 22
ALEXANDRIA, VIRGINIA

The jangling link echoed over the noise of the shower. Leah turned off the water and fumbled for her robe as she raced to catch the connection. "Berglund," she said breathlessly, then added, "Delgado residence."

A deep chuckle rumbled on the opposite end of the link. "Ah, señorita, you may take the woman from the agency, but you do not so easily take the agency away from the woman, eh?"

"Mr. Mulcahey—Uncle Mac," Leah said, faintly embarrassed that he expected to find her in Del's place. *Don't be stupid,* she scolded herself. Francisco Mulcahey coexisted in a world with drug lords. He understood human relationships . . . a damn sight better than she did, she admitted, flicking her own vid switch so that he could see her.

"It is good to see your face again, Leah. I hoped to reach you there."

"Has something happened to Del?" Fear suddenly blossomed inside her.

"Do not worry. I just spoke to that rascal. He's back in Washington, but I am not surprised that he did not contact you. That is why I have called . . ."

His tone was all business as he gave her a carefully edited outline of what he and Del had learned without revealing names or incriminating details that might be monitored if Del's link was under surveillance. Given the nature of what he intimated, Leah could well believe that it was.

"I might've known that damn fool would play Lone Ranger on this!" she said, scrubbing her fingers through her hair in frustration.

"You better than anyone must understand why he has done this, but I do not want him taking such a risk."

"And I'm the best backup he could have this side of the Mulcahey clan?"

Mac smiled, watching her check her Ruger, then slide it into the holster. "We already consider you part of our family. Perhaps one day you and El Tigre will make it official, eh?"

His gentle suggestion resonated beneath her frantically churning thoughts as she raced from the condo and jumped into Del's Buick. If traffic wasn't too bad coming up through Rosslyn, she'd make it in twenty-five minutes.

11:30 A.M., EDT, WEDNESDAY, JULY 22
WASHINGTON, D.C.

Gracie was always thorough. She had a hell of a lot more than he'd been able to piece together at his office that morning. Everything checked out. Travel dates, link conversations, enough circumstantial evidence to warrant a full-scale FBI investigation when considered in conjunction with the incriminating conversation on the disc.

As he retraced his steps across the campus, he observed students strolling in the warm summer sunlight, laughing and chattering without a care. Odd how resilient the young were. Of course, they'd grown up with police guards and security gates surrounding their schools. They were accustomed to the siege mentality. It was truly amazing how quickly the buzz had died down after the July Fourth pandemonium on the Mall. A president almost assassinated, a military coup and a nuclear catastrophe averted by inches, yet here life went on as usual.

He tried to remember when he'd felt as if there was really hope for the future. Back when he was gung ho FBI, he supposed, Cal Putnam's star pupil. That was a long time ago. God help the nation now. After all the political upheavals that had already transpired, how many more shocks could the structure of government stand before it came tumbling down?

Damn good thing those kids are resilient, he thought as he climbed back into the wretchedly cramped little Chevy EV and punched in a code on his link to make the necessary appointment.

"Yeah, I'll be there in twenty," he said, signing off after a brief conversation. Well, the die was cast. Nothing left to do but play out the rest of the game. He leaned back against the seat of the rental, rubbing his burning eyes with his fingertips, then shook his head to clear it. He was jet-lagged out after the trip from Mazatlán, "flying on fumes," as his cousin would say. The Diet Coke Gracie had suggested hadn't helped.

He reached into the glove compartment and took out his .50-caliber Smith & Wesson. Hell, in his condition, was his hand even steady enough to fire the damn thing? "Please, God, don't let me have to find out," he murmured to himself as he turned the ignition and drove toward Georgetown.

The street looked deserted, brick and frame houses baking in the hot afternoon sun. Here and there a maple or birch tree offered a bit of shade but no consolation to him. Delgado searched nervously for the glint of gun barrels in the shadows. Had he been followed? Was his link being monitored?

He pulled directly into the driveway and stopped under a big old-fashioned cochere. Cal Putnam stood waiting, holding the side door ajar for him as he slipped quickly from the car and entered the director's house.

"Ain't nobody here but us chickens, so no need to jump every time the pendulum on my granddaddy's clock swings," Putnam said, closing the door behind him.

"You have any agents posted to watch the house?" Del asked as they walked down the long hallway to the library. He noted that Cal did not move directly in front of the French doors but detoured around the far wall to take his seat at his desk.

"My security's good enough" was the noncommittal reply as he motioned for Delgado to pull up a chair beside the desk. "It's a little early in the day to strike a blow for liberty, but you sounded like you might need a little fortifying when you called," Cal said, holding up a bottle of George Dickel bourbon. When Del shook his head, Putnam grunted and replaced it in the drawer, then took out his pipe and began the ritual of lighting it. "Now, what's put the hornet in your outhouse, ole son?"

Del tossed the disc on Cal's desk. "This. It's a conversation between Benito Zuloaga and our mole."

Putnam set his pipe in the ashtray and picked up the small black chip. "Where'd you get this?" he asked, turning it over in his hand. "It the original?"

"A copy. Came to me via a source in Cuba."

When Del paused, gathering his thoughts, Cal leaned back in his chair and drew on the pipe. "That so. Go on."

"You know, it's been eating at me ever since Ramirez first told me the Cartel had a man inside our government . . . someone who had the highest security clearance, someone who knew about the collusion between BISC and the military. Then when Sommerville's little legion took off down the coast, Benito and his boys were ready for them. But who the hell in Washington had anything to gain from playing ball with the Cartel? Not a superpatriot psychopath like Sommerville. He was the man heading for glory—or death. Not Harmon Waterman or Brian Fuller. Hell, they expected to ride into the White house using Zuloaga as their whipping boy.

"For certain not that scared little rabbit Mark Patrikas, or the president he tried to protect by exposing the plot. I considered Drescher. Hell, Cal, I really wanted it to be that son of a bitch. With BISC dismantled, the situation could've played right into his hands if he'd kept his mouth shut. But we both know Samson would never have trusted him to be the director of a new super law enforcement agency."

"And so, by process of elimination, that leaves me standing out like a polecat at a prayer meeting," Cal said.

"I knew you were the mole the moment I heard the disc."

"Had to be voice-scrambled, didn't it? How could you recognize who Benny was talking to?"

"You can disguise the voice, but there's no way to cover up the diction . . . ole son," Del drawled. "Allow me?" He motioned to the link on Cal's desk. When Putnam nodded, he fed it the disc and gave the command for it to play. As the conversation between the Cartel leader and the American began, Del said, "My source thought that scratching was the result of some copying error when the disc was made."

Putnam looked down at the old-fashioned wooden match he'd just struck to relight his pipe. The rasping sound was duplicated over Zuloaga's voice as he complained about how his American informant was taking advantage of him. Then the American replied, "The way I see it, some days you're the dog, some days you're the hydrant, ole son."

The disc played out the rest of their deal in which Zuloaga promised to divert a convoy of ships loaded with pure cocaine destined for the Texas coast and sell it in the Azores in exchange for further information about Pentagon plans to invade Colombia.

"You told them enough so they could strike first."

Putnam leaned forward in his chair, eyes narrowed intently on Del. "And why do you think I would do that, ole son?"

"To bring down BISC. That was first on your agenda. As soon as Patrikas told you about Waterman's conspiracy, you knew it was your golden opportunity—you could expose a Tribunal member in league with high-ranking Pentagon brass who were using BISC agents as their private assassins. But you needed more evidence than Mark could provide so you enlisted people you knew you could rely on, like me and Leah, then took what we dug up to Samson. Once the coup started to unravel, it was more and more apparent to the president that you were the only man in Washington he could trust.

"Who better to take charge of the whole drug enforcement program than the man responsible for exposing the corruption of BISC—in spite of the fact he himself had been a Tribunal member?"

"Pretty good fishing expedition, but nothin's biting," Putnam said with a mirthless chuckle. His eyes were watchful, his face expressionless now. "If I wanted to head up the new Bureau, why get in bed with ole Benito?"

"You needed to make damn certain Sommerville's invasion failed. What if he'd succeeded in taking out the Cartel's key cities in a lightning sweep? Caught Zuloaga with his pants down? It wouldn't have mattered that it was unauthorized or insanely dangerous. He'd have been the hero of the day. Samson might have gone along with a fait accompli. Then the general would've been sitting in the catbird seat instead of you.

"But I'd like to think that you still possessed some small modicum of decency, Cal. I know you didn't sell out for the money."

Putnam leaned back again, lacing his fingers behind his head, regarding Del somberly. "You know, ole son, the only difference between a rut and a grave is the depth. I spent my whole life working to put the bad guys in jail. Lost my wife. Never made much money. Never even took a damn fool vacation. And what for? Due process and all that shit Wade's been spouting off about since he got religion? The plain truth is, it purely doesn't work worth a tinker's damn—not the way you and I tried it, not the way BISC tried it. So, if you can't beat 'em, I figure you gotta try an end run around 'em."

Sighing, Putnam sat forward in the chair and placed his elbows on the desk. "You have any faint idea how much fucking money the Colombians have? How much power?"

"That's what it's really about, isn't it, Cal? Power."

"Don't go sniffing at power, ole son. It's the grease rotating this tired old planet, make no mistake about it. The Cartel's always focused on peddling their death here . . . until recently. We're the closest market. But the Euros are sitting over there, getting more fat and sassy every year. The Russian Mafia and the Iranians want their action, but Zuloaga can give ole Boris and the ragheads a run for their money . . . if someone here is smart enough and tough enough to act as a broker."

"You mean divert the Cartel to the Old World? A pretty nifty juggling act, Cal."

"It can be done. The right man can provide the Cartel with some real incentive to look for new markets, make this one a damn hard sell. Oh, it won't go away overnight. Shitfire, it won't ever go away completely. You'll never stop drugs, not here, not anywhere. Never. But you can *control* 'em."

Del shook his head. "Power, again, Cal. Power. When Samson first announced his new agenda for a superagency, I was bothered by it. Not the same way BISC bothered me. After all, the judicial system will be employed to prosecute drug offenders, no more death squads.

But the idea that one agency—or one man—can safely exercise absolute control over any situation is wrong."

Cal sighed. "I was afraid you'd be mulish as a jarhead drill sergeant. Where are you planning to go with this? I admit I got a mite careless palavering with my pal Benny, but this one little bitty disc ain't worth squat, ole son."

"Gracie Kell just dug up a bushel-basketful of evidence for me, Cal. She found out who your go-between is in Cuba, the interior secretary in Ruiz's cabinet, Salvador Piedras. And that's just for starters. Once I was able to tell her what to look for, it was easy . . . if you're Gracie Kell."

"That woman could take ole Benny's job if she put her mind to it." Cal's eyes were hooded as he focused on his young protégé. "You'd disappoint me if you came here without a backup plan."

"Gracie's already accessed Samson's private link in the Oval Office and downloaded everything."

"And just in case that's not enough to convince you to give up, he has me," Leah said, stepping inside the French door. "I heard everything, Putnam. You used us, you motherfucker." Her voice was icecold. Inside she seethed with rage.

Cal's smile was beatific as he slowly stood up. "Sticks and stones, Agent Berglund," he tsked. "I don't intend to stand trial as a drug trafficker. The way I figure it, I'd rather go out clean and quick . . . the BISC way." Never taking his eyes off Delgado, he slowly drew the old .38 Chief's Special from inside his jacket.

Automatically, Del pulled the Smith & Wesson from its holster. His hand was shaking. "Don't make me do it, Cal."

Raising his weapon inexorably and leveling it directly on Del, Cal said, "I don't think you *can* do it, ole son—"

A single shot broke the silence.

Putnam's body rocked back, collapsing on his swivel chair. "But she could," he murmured, "that's why I handpicked her, after all."

EPILOGUE

A cool wind with a hint of autumn in it scudded the first few brown leaves across the gently rolling hillsides lined with small, white marble markers. A slow drizzle had begun about a half hour earlier, soaking the already soft earth. His shoes sank in the grass as he stood over the gravestone. Delgado read the inscription one last time.

CALVIN ALBERT PUTNAM
June 15, 1954-July 22, 2017
The last full measure of his devotion
given in service to a grateful nation

Del remembered the media frenzy during the funeral. The hero who had foiled a military coup and exposed BISC had died tragically. Wade Samson and the nation mourned the loss of "this invaluable public servant," as the president had eulogized him. Del still tasted the bitterness of ashes when he looked down at the gravestone.

"Well, old man, you finally went to the funeral and you were the corpse. The star, that's damn straight," he murmured, wondering if he'd ever be able to put his mentor's betrayal behind him. It didn't really matter. He had a new life now in California. It was time to go home to Mike.

Rather than hear it, he sensed her approach. The familiar essence of her. She still did not wear fragrances—they gave away position. But he would be able to recognize her scent blindfolded.

"I didn't take the head shot because I wanted him alive," Leah said quietly.

"I know." They'd never talked about it, her ability to act when he froze . . . just the way Cal knew it would happen . . . if it ever had to happen.

"When I aimed for his shoulder, how the hell could I know the son of a bitch would have a heart attack?"

Delgado laughed softly at the irony of it. He turned away from the grave, facing her without touching her, just enjoying the view. "You know, Agent Berglund, you're not half as tough as you think you are." His eyes swept up her tall, strong body, noting the slight curl in her hair. "You're letting it grow."

She touched the white-gold feathering at her nape self-consciously. "Yeah, no more BISC regs. I haven't had long hair since I was in high school . . . I kinda thought it might be interesting to see what it feels like."

"I know you wanted to see justice meted out to Cal."

She shrugged. "Presidential politics. I understood why Samson covered up Putnam's connection to the Cartel. After all, how would it have looked if the man the president had put all his faith in to clean up the mess from BISC turned out to be as dirty as the rest?"

"Cal's motives were different, Leah. I'm not defending the man," Del said, looking down at the marker again. "He was wrong. Dead wrong. But by his own twisted lights, I suppose he thought he was doing the best thing. At least, that's the spin Wade Samson put on the cover-up."

"He had the power to make Cal's death appear to be from natural causes. Just a peaceful coronary." She no longer sounded bitter.

"That's the damning lure in this town—power. Too much power."

"The president used those words. 'Absolute power corrupts absolutely.' Gramps used them, too. Lord Acton, he said."

Del nodded. "What are you doing in town? I thought you were going to stay in Maine and help your grandfather prepare his campaign strategy."

She smiled. "Gramps is surrounded with advisers who've forgotten a lot more about politics than I'll ever remember. He's in his glory."

"Glad to hear it. . . . You know, it hurt when you fled Washington after the whitewash of Cal's death. I sort of thought you blamed me for not speaking out."

"I was the one who'd shot him, Del. He planned it that way. He knew I was a natural born killer—"

"That's not fair, Leah."

"All reports are in, Del. Life is officially unfair."

"Damn it, cut the self-flagellation. You are not a 'natural born killer,' for chrissake!" He reached out and took her hand, heartened when she didn't flinch away as she'd done during the days after the shooting. "Progress, hmmm," he murmured, drawing her to walk with him down the hill toward his car. "How'd you find me?"

"Gramps has been keeping tabs on you. And Uncle Mac calls at least once a week to let us know what you and Mike are doing. He says the job is going good for you."

"Yeah, I work regular hours, can relax and enjoy my son for the first time in his life. It's pretty great." He put her hand in the crook of his arm, careful on the slippery, wet grass. "The sun always shines in southern California, haven't you heard?"

"As a matter of fact, I have," she replied, looking into his eyes as they approached his Buick TE. "I took a cab. You'll have to give me a ride back to the city." She waited a beat. "Oh, did I tell you I took that job with the drug rehab clinic in San Pedro?" she asked as she slid onto the passenger seat.

He closed the door, then leaned through the open window and asked, "Do you want to call Ab Fenster or shall I?"